LT FIC SAVARIN JULIAN
Savarin, Julian Jay.
Romeo summer /
VISA●

ROMEO SUMMER

Romeo Summer

Julian Jay Savarin

Severn House Large Print
London & New York

This first large print edition published in Great Britain 2007 by
SEVERN HOUSE LARGE PRINT BOOKS LTD of
9-15 High Street, Sutton, Surrey, SM1 1DF.
First world regular print edition published 2003 by
Severn House Publishers, London and New York.
This first large print edition published in the USA 2007 by
SEVERN HOUSE PUBLISHERS INC., of
595 Madison Avenue, New York, NY 10022.

British Library Cataloguing in Publication Data

Savarin, Julian Jay
    Romeo summer. - Large print ed.
    1. Germany (East). Ministerium fur Staatssicherheit -
    History - Fiction 2. Police - Germany - Berlin - Fiction
    3. Suspense fiction 4. Large type books
    I. Title
    823.9'14[F]

    ISBN-13: 978-0-7278-7590-7

Printed and bound in Great Britain by
MPG Books Ltd, Bodmin, Cornwall.

For PB, who brings the light.

One

Berlin. Monday, 08.00 hours.

Pappenheim looked up at the morning sky, and sniffed.

'Smells like rain,' he said with a certainty born of long experience. 'And I hate Mondays.'

A thin tendril of smoke from the cigarette clamped between his solid index and middle fingers, and held slightly away as if to protect his clothes, hung about him like a static wraith. The air was so still, it appeared to be waiting for something to happen.

'That was a song,' Müller said.

'That was what a sixteen-year-old young woman said in explanation,' Pappenheim corrected, 'after she had opened up with a rifle on her schoolmates. Her exact words were ... "I don't like Mondays". *Then* someone wrote a song about that little piece of human history.'

'You never cease to amaze me, Pappi.' Müller glanced upwards. What he saw was a bright, cloudless bowl of blue. 'Your nose tells you about the rain, does it?'

7

'Never failed me yet.' Pappenheim drew gratefully on the cigarette, and blew out two neat smoke rings that hovered about the ghostly wisp. Some ash speckled his jacket. 'Even though this is supposed to be high summer, don't forget I was born on a farm. I know more about the weather than those little doxies they have on TV. Forget that nice, dry time they said we're going to have today.'

Müller looked at him tolerantly. *'Doxies?'*

'Chicago cop I know,' Pappenheim began in explanation. 'He calls the Ami weather girls doxies.'

'Pappi, you know so many people from so many places, it's a wonder you still speak German.'

'I can speak Greek too,' Pappenheim said helpfully.

'I wouldn't be surprised.' Müller glanced down at the Friedrichstrasse, four storeys below. 'Now, why the hell did Kaltendorf go into this pantomime of calling us up here to the bloody open roof? I've got work to do.'

All about him was an urban landscape in constant rejuvenation.

'You, lowly *Hauptkommissar*,' Pappenheim remarked drily. 'Me, even lowlier *Oberkommissar*; he, brand new, probationary Director of Police. Three *golden* stars to your silver three. Even if those gold stars may be temporary ... he calls, we still jump ... Well, I do ... sometimes. You ... almost never.'

'So why did we come?'

'To admire the view? Or perhaps it has

8

something to do with the fact that the Great White Shark was himself ordered from higher up to summon us?'

'Something like that,' Müller confirmed sourly. 'I'd rather be somewhere else.'

Müller and Pappenheim could not have been more unalike. Yet they worked exceptionally well together. They were a team that got more results than any other. Müller's unconventional approach to policing – a bane to Kaltendorf – and Pappenheim's almost supernatural ability to obtain information where no one else was apparently able to, made the two men seemingly unbeatable. That, too, grated upon Heinz Kaltendorf; and Pappenheim's almost suicidal loyalty to the younger Müller was the stuff of Kaltendorf's nightmares.

Müller seemed far too young for the rank; but his hair, thick and dark but so long that he wore it in a ponytail, had barely perceptible thin streaks of grey. Despite his blond eyebrows, the hair was not dyed. A tall man – over six feet – his outwardly delicate frame effectively hid its true strength. He found this camouflage extremely useful in his profession. It gave him an unseen advantage which led others to underestimate him; Kaltendorf included. Among the many things about Müller which drove Kaltendorf to distraction was that hairstyle, and the single earring that the *Hauptkommissar* wore. Kaltendorf hated the earring with a passion, and never ceased to search for ways – official and not so official

9

– to deprive Müller of it. It was a never-ending contest of wills.

Müller's taste in clothes and cars was an added bone of contention. Müller had sufficient private money to enable him to buy designer clothes – mainly Armani – and to acquire a new Porsche Turbo which he also used for police work. This rankled with the probationary police director like acid in an ulcerated stomach.

Pappenheim was an altogether different animal. Most certainly not rich, Pappenheim was the kind of policeman who was so smart, he gave those who didn't know the impression that he was stupid. Pappenheim could ferret information from the unlikeliest of places, and had contacts in areas where bold angels would seriously fear to tread.

A solidly round man whose immaculate fingers belied his chain-smoking habit and indifferent choice of clothing, he prided himself, however, on his taste in ties. They were always well chosen. Pappenheim's girth belied the speed with which he could move, when the situation demanded it.

'As long as my fingers are clean, and my ties good,' he was once heard to say, 'then my world is a happy one.'

But there was much, much more to Pappenheim.

The modern glass palace with polychromatic windows, upon whose roof they now waited, housed the police unit to which they belonged, and was part of the city's rejuvena-

10

tion. Its square rooftop was a wide flat area in the middle of which a cluster of antennae sprouted. Next to the antennae was the access point. Mint new, the building stood in what was once part of East Berlin.

'Me too,' Pappenheim said. 'Me too. And I only brought one smoke.' He made it sound as if he had missed breakfast. 'And speaking of rain...'

Müller turned to see Kaltendorf approaching.

At about the same time in the exclusive *Villenviertel* in Bonn, Heino Emmerlin, fifty-ish and successful financial guru, was slowly driving his brand-new BMW 750 out of the garage of his villa-like home.

He never made it.

Two perfectly round holes, close together, appeared in the windscreen and mirrored themselves where his eyes had been. The smooth leather behind him was suddenly full of the detritus from the disintegrating back of his head.

He had died very quietly.

The sound of the glass being penetrated had barely made it above the low, powerful noise of the car's engine. Gear still engaged, it continued to nose slowly into the street. An approaching van saw it in time and braked hard, the driver shouting an obscenity.

Then he saw what was left of the man's head, and vomited over himself.

★ ★ ★

11

On the rooftop in Berlin, Müller and Pappenheim studied Kaltendorf warily as their superior approached.

Kaltendorf – a clumsy dresser who was certain Müller looked down upon him because of it – was carrying a substantial blue folder tucked beneath his arm. He came up with slow, measured steps, and halted before them. He looked at each in turn, almost like a schoolmaster about to ask them to hold out their hands for inspection.

'You're probably wondering why I called you up here...'

'No, sir,' Pappenheim said cheerfully.

'Yes, sir.' Müller's voice was firm.

Kaltendorf looked as if he wasn't certain which of the two was being insubordinate, and decided to choose Pappenheim.

'Put out that damned cigarette!'

'Yes, sir,' Pappenheim agreed too easily. He decapitated the glowing end surreptitiously and flicked the dead cigarette off the roof.

'*Oberkommissar!*' Kaltendorf barked, staring in outrage at the path of the cigarette's exit. He snapped his head round to Pappenheim. 'You are a senior policeman! What kind of behaviour is this? What if your cigarette starts a fire?'

'It would burn us out. Many people would probably like that. And besides, it wasn't lit.' Pappenheim dropped the glowing end, and ground it out with a heel.

Kaltendorf was not mollified. He stared with distaste at the spot where Pappenheim's

12

shoe had extinguished the stub as if it had been on the polished floor of his living room. No less outraged, he glared at his subordinate.

'One day, Pappenheim. One day.'

'Yes, sir,' Pappenheim said, horribly polite.

Kaltendorf gave him a cold stare, then turned to Müller. 'You're his superior, Müller. Can't you—'

'With respect, Herr *Direktor*,' Müller interrupted. 'We've been up here for some time and I have some work to catch up on...'

It was not exactly the smartest thing to do, but Müller was not in the mood for one of Kaltendorf's rants.

Twin spots of red appeared in Kaltendorf's cheeks. 'You too, Müller! That attitude of yours will sink you one day! Belonging to the faded aristocracy, and friends in high places will not save you—'

'I don't have friends in high places...'

'Stop interrupting me!'

Pappenheim was meanwhile finding great interest in the toe of his left shoe.

Kaltendorf's eyes switched to him. 'Are your shoes dirty, Pappenheim?'

Pappenheim looked up. 'Clean as—'

But Kaltendorf was thrusting the folder at Müller. 'Forget any work you have. I've been ordered to give this to you.' He sounded as if he had first been tied to a chair and his teeth pulled. 'Who gave the order is unimportant at this time ... although why you, escapes me. You two will study these documents up here.

13

I will be back for them. You have fifteen minutes.'

Kaltendorf turned and left them without waiting for a reaction.

They stared after him, waiting until he had disappeared through the roof access before speaking.

Pappenheim was first. 'He really likes making these exits. Must be the freshness of the rank, plus the fact that he has to fight to keep it, plus the fact that he must wait for old Hagen to be kicked upstairs before having it fully confirmed ... It's all gone to his head. And as for you, Jens Müller, Herr Graf von Röhnen, *Polizeihauptkommissar* ... you like playing with fire. Kaltendorf wants to roast you. He'll blame you if he feels his promotion is in jeopardy. All he needs is an excuse.'

Müller was still staring at the access. 'And what about you? You're not exactly the model of restraint when it comes to the Great White.'

'Must be the company I keep.' Pappenheim grinned shamelessly. 'Hah! Faded aristocracy. That's a new one. Those little phrases of his make one feel so warm inside. So ... what little present has he brought us?' He looked at the folder in Müller's hands. 'Dark-blue, with a black border. I know that kind of file. Definitely not one of ours, and definitely not police.'

Müller looked at him. 'You've *seen* this type of folder before?'

'Umm ... I know someone...'

14

'I don't think I want to know from where, do I?'

'No.'

Müller studied Pappenheim for a few moments. 'I see. Well ... wherever this comes from, I suppose we'd better check it before the man returns.'

'Fourteen minutes.'

'What?'

'We've got fourteen minutes now...'

'Thank you, Pappi. I'd worked that one out.'

Müller opened the folder gingerly, as if expecting it to bite him. They studied the contents in complete silence for several minutes. There were five scene-of-crime photographs accompanied by single-page reports. All the photographs were of dead men.

Pappenheim sensed movement and looked round. 'Our fifteen minutes are up.'

Müller closed the folder just as Kaltendorf reached them. He handed it over silently.

'Well?' Kaltendorf began as he took it. 'Can you handle it?'

'Is that a real question, sir?'

'Or?' Kaltendorf waited.

'Or do we have a choice?'

'No.'

'As I thought,' Müller said.

Kaltendorf favoured Müller with one of the coldest stares in his armoury. 'You will report directly to me...'

'Can I use my own people? Or does whoever this folder belongs to have other ideas?'

'You can pick your team...'

'But?'

'Did I say there was a *but*?'

'There always is.'

Kaltendorf thought about that, as if checking to see whether he could make a case for insubordination, then decided to let it pass. As far as he was concerned, Müller was a bad policeman who had been promoted far too quickly, and who did not play by the rules.

'The rules on this one are simple,' Kaltendorf said, looking at Müller as if he expected the *Hauptkommissar* to break them as soon as possible. 'As I've just told you, you report directly to me. This is without exception. Apart from Pappenheim,' he went on, not even glancing at the *Oberkommissar*, 'you will discuss the case with *no* one ... except with me. Whoever you pick for your team must operate on a need-to-know basis, which they do not. Very simple, really. Oh ... yes ... you may well have a helper ... a sort of liaison...'

Kaltendorf paused, but not because he expected objections.

Müller said nothing. Pappenheim said nothing. Both men looked at Kaltendorf neutrally which, in a way, was far worse than if they had been overtly critical of him.

'Nothing to say?' Kaltendorf demanded curtly into their silence.

'What should we say ... sir?' Pappenheim asked mildly.

16

Kaltendorf looked from one to the other. 'See to it,' he snapped. Then he was striding away without a backward glance.

'Exits,' Pappenheim said as Kaltendorf returned to the access. 'He really loves making them.' He stared thoughtfully out at the Berlin skyline. 'I need my Gauloise.'

'You just finished one,' Müller reminded him.

'Just? That was nearly half an hour ago. You know me. One after another.'

'I know you indeed, Pappi. You'll be back in your ashtray of an office soon enough,' Müller went on. 'So tell me ... who would want us on something like this? Five dead men ... from all walks of life, from different parts of the country, with no obvious connection to each other ... all apparently professionally hit.'

They began walking towards the access.

'But there must be a connection ... somehow...' Pappenheim offered.

'Which the file does not tell us...'

'But somebody gives it to Kaltendorf...'

'Orders—'

'*Orders* Kaltendorf to dump this on us, who then insists we report directly to him. "Oh ... yes ... you may well have a helper",' Pappenheim went on, accurately mimicking Kaltendorf. ' "A sort of liaison". I take it you want me to do some digging into those places you don't want to know about.'

'Something like that. There's a nice reek coming out of this one.'

17

'Oh how we love the reeky ones.'

'I can live without them, and especially without "helpers".'

They had reached the access.

'Me too,' Pappenheim said. 'And I need my cigarette. Can't live without that.'

'You'll die with it.'

'Such nice things, the man says.'

The Rhine barge, *Isabella Lütz*, was a cargo vessel with a difference. Though at first glance she seemed indistinguishable from her sister ships – the many types of container barges of varying sizes that plied the river route – her double deck marked her out.

The familiar long, protruding hull with its aft-based superstructure and telescopic bridge, was bigger than average. Twin-decked and painted black with white edgings, it hid spacious quarters of exceptional, and un-expected luxury. Apart from the size and unusual paint scheme of the structure, and the small conformal sundeck that sprouted from the lower section of the bridge, there were no other real signs to betray the differ-ence. Her paintwork also seemed to be permanently fresh.

The owner and master of the *Lütz*, Udo Hellmann, made an extremely good living with a unique idea: combining the barge's normal cargo-carrying duties with luxury river cruises along the working route, for the more adventurous who liked their comfort in such an unusual setting. Fitted out very

18

expensively, even the most fastidious of the *Isabella Lütz*'s customers found little to complain about. Silent ship technology ensured a far quieter existence for both passengers and crew than was the norm for such a vessel. There was a dining lounge that would not have been out of place on a large motor yacht, and three fully equipped suites to accommodate a maximum of six paying guests. Two extra crew and a chef, specially hired to attend to their needs, ensured a pampered exclusivity. The concept was highly popular and very rarely did the barge sail without passengers. On occasion, a family with children would book all the suites.

Hellmann was himself married with two daughters in their late teens, both of whom had recently gone up to university. One had remained in Germany, the other choosing to go to the States to study in California. Hellmann's wife, who had always loved the river, now took every opportunity to sail with him.

Two days into her journey from Holland on her way to Budapest the *Lütz* was approaching the Wesseling bend, just south of Cologne, when Hellmann's mobile phone rang. His wife – herself a skilled river sailor who could handle the barge – was on the bridge chatting with the duty crewman. He was therefore alone in his relatively spartan but spacious cabin on the top deck at the time, reading, and feeling that all was very right with the world.

Frowning slightly, he sighed in mild

annoyance, put the book down and picked up the phone. 'Hellmann...'

'Your time is up, Romeo,' the voice said coldly in his ear. The transmission ended abruptly.

Hellmann paled. The world was suddenly very dark indeed. With a shaking hand, he took the mobile away from his ear to stare at the display, hoping to see the caller's number. There was nothing.

He put the phone down seconds before his wife entered.

She stared at his face. 'Udo? Are you alright? Is something wrong?'

'No,' he said as calmly as he could. 'It's nothing. I just feel a little queasy. Must be something I ate.'

'Will you be able to have dinner with the guests tonight? They're expecting it.'

'I'll be fine, Isa. Really nothing to worry about.' He stood up. 'I think I'll go up to the bridge. Get some river air into my lungs.'

He went out, leaving her to stare anxiously after him.

In Berlin, Müller followed Pappenheim along a corridor which, by Kaltendorf's decree, had been plastered with no-smoking signs. A door off it led into the *Oberkommissar*'s own smoke-scented office.

Pappenheim's desk was a mess. Pride of place among the carelessly strewn files, sheets of notepaper full of scribbles, and desk paraphernalia, was taken by an over-full ashtray.

20

Next to it was an open packet of Gauloise *blondes*. Pappenheim hurried to the desk, sat down, grabbed at the pack like a drowning man, tapped one out and lit it. He took a long, satisfying pull.

'Aah!' he sighed with pleasure. 'That's more like it.'

Müller, who had watched his antics with the benign air of one who'd seen it all before, took the only chair that had no papers on it.

'And now that you've had your nicotine hit...' Müller said, and waited.

Pappenheim took another drag before saying, 'Well ... we have an insurance salesman, a well-known offshore speedboat racer, the owner of a car-hire firm, a flying school instructor, and a night club singer ... all dead ... and, by the look of things, certainly all professionally shot. The insurance man came from Hamburg; the racer – though German – lived in the south of France, but was shot on home ground; the car-hire stiff lived in Ulm; the flyboy operated near Saarbrucken, and the night club singer was a doughnut...'

Müller stared at him.

'From here in Berlin,' Pappenheim explained. 'Berliner ... the doughnut ... you know ... the round things with the hole in the middle...'

Müller still stared at him.

'Oh, alright,' Pappenheim said, giving in. 'My little joke ... we need some laughs around here. I'll try my sources,' he went on quickly. 'See what connection these people

21

had, if any.'

'Can you do that without Kaltendorf finding out?'

Pappenheim squinted at Müller through a smoke ring. 'Who is Kaltendorf?'

Aboard the *Isabella Lütz*, the bridge was raised because the river level was low enough to allow it to pass safely beneath the many road and rail bridges that spanned the Rhine, and to afford a clear view above the containers. Like a water-borne air-traffic-control tower, it dominated the barge. Its radar – surrounded by a comprehensive suite of communications antennae – rotated soporifically, probing the stretch of water ahead as the barge rumbled upstream.

Hellmann paused by the sloping companionway that led up to the bridge, and briefly touched the fence of a caged area. A smaller version of that seen at tennis practice courts, it had been built on to the starboard deck as a secure children's playpen. Even the top was sealed off, with a solidly welded grid. Within the play area was a swing. On the port deck, there was enough room for two cars parked side-by-side, but only one was secured there: a newish Audi S6 in black. Next to it was a davit, stowed lengthways, arm pointing towards the bows. Among its uses was the loading and off-loading of the car.

Hellmann went to the entrance of the cage, unlocked it, and ambled over to the swing.

He pushed at the seat gently, then stood away as it swung back and forth. His daughters, when much younger, had played there, flanked by the magnificent views on either side as the ship had made its way up and down the river. They had used the swing often. That had been well before the entire vessel had been refitted, and the quarters converted to their present standard. Now it was for the use of the passengers' children, whenever any were aboard.

He stood there remembering, and seeing in his mind's eye his daughters at play. After a while he went out of the cage, locked it, then slowly made his way up the companionway to the bridge.

'Rudi,' he said to the crewman as he entered.

'Captain,' Rüdiger Honneff acknowledged. He did not glance round from his regular scanning of the high-tech console with its various display screens, the long cargo deck, and the river before him.

'All OK?'

'All OK, Captain.'

Hellmann nodded slightly, then went over to the starboard side to stare without really seeing as Wesseling went by at a steady eighteen kilometres an hour.

Ahead of the bridge on the first deck of the superstructure, the sundeck was framed by a high railing. Two of the guests were on canvas loungers, taking in the view. Another, a young woman, was working her camera overtime, as if the passing scenery went by too fast for her to get in all her shots.

Honneff glanced down at her. 'Look at that, Captain,' he said with a chuckle. 'The young American woman will use enough film to fill a warehouse. She's been at it since we crossed into Germany.'

But Hellmann was preoccupied with his own thoughts.

'What? What was that, Rudi?'

Honneff frowned. The captain didn't sound his usual cheerful self.

'You OK, Captain?'

'I'm fine, Rudi. Something I ate.'

Honneff sniffed. 'It's that chef and his fancy cooking. You should stick to normal barge stuff. It's OK for those tourists ... but for us river rats...'

'Basic German food, eh?'

'Nothing wrong with basic German food. I'll eat *Schweine braten* till pigs grow wings.'

Despite himself, Hellmann smiled briefly. 'The good old pork roast ... with potatoes, of course.'

'Of course.'

'Don't ever change, Rudi.'

'Don't you worry. I won't.'

But Honneff frowned again. Something was definitely troubling the captain.

Pappenheim blew three smoke rings in echelon formation into the tendrilled air of his office. He watched for some moments as they floated towards the ceiling, still holding

24

formation.

'If you can take time off from admiring your handiwork, Pappi...' Müller said.

'Ah ... yes ... my contacts.' Pappenheim returned his attention to Müller. 'There are one or two who belong to the ... er ... crowd who use those blue folders. They owe me some favours. I'll do a little squeezing. Might even find out who leaned on the GW to lean on us. Would be interesting.'

'Just make sure whoever it is does not realize you're digging.'

Pappenheim's expression was eloquent. 'When I dig, I'm invisible. I'll have the beginnings of something well before the end of the day. Now go away and enjoy life and the pleasures of high rank, while I get to work.'

Müller got to his feet. 'You need an oxygen tent in here.'

'Don't be ridiculous. That would kill me.'

Anyone seeing Udo Hellmann off his barge for the first time would believe he was someone they had seen in a television film. He had the look of a leading man: not too brutal, not too effete. A handsome man dressed in naval white shirt and trousers, his longish, dark-blond hair completed the picture, giving him the look of a daring corsair in a film; or at least, someone who spent his days on a wildly expensive motor yacht in the Mediterranean. Burnished by the river air, he was tall and fit, but without the overt machismo one would have expected. His

25

charm was undoubted, and female passengers of all ages tended to find any excuse to engage him in conversation. His very dark eyes, which could sparkle for his guests, friends, and family, at times seemed fleetingly opaque, indicating to the perceptive that many secrets could be hidden in there.

He stared out at the passing landscape, thoughts very far from where he stood.

Honneff shot him a speculative, anxious glance, but made no comment.

Back at his desk, Müller stared at the Mondrian on his office wall. Long ago, he had discovered that the geometrical structure and colours of the painting actually had a calming effect upon him, especially when Kaltendorf sought to make life difficult; which was often.

Not unexpectedly, Müller's office was a complete contrast to Pappenheim's. It was almost as geometrically neat as the painting. Almost. The polished surface of the large desk gleamed, and there was not an ashtray in sight. No papers were haphazardly strewn upon it. No badges from various police forces – both national and international – adorned the walls. In fact, if the office were itself not within a police building, nothing about it gave the impression that the occupier was a policeman.

The two telephones on the desk – one black, one steel-grey – looked as if they had been recently cleaned and sanitized. The document trays were full of tidily stacked reports and notes. An antique reading lamp – clearly not police issue – stood at a left corner, and placed centrally at the back was a totally unexpected item: a perfect model of a Hammond B3 drawbar organ, about the size of a telephone base unit.

Müller looked from the Mondrian to the Hammond, and touched the model reflectively.

The steel-grey phone rang.

Müller picked it up. 'Results already, Pappi?'

'Remember our history lesson about Mondays? You'll be liking this one less and less. Hot news from Bonn...'

'Official?'

'My grapevine. You-know-who won't be in the loop for hours ... officially.'

'And the news?'

'Some guy in the financial industry managed to acquire two neat holes where his eyes used to be,' Pappenheim replied. 'Through the windscreen of his nice new BMW.'

'Where?'

'Right on his doorstep.'

'Any witnesses?'

'A van driver. But the only thing he really saw was what was left of the head of the BMW driver. The car rolled out in front of him and he had to stamp on his brakes.'

'What did he have to say?'

'Not a lot. Puked a lot, though.'

'Thanks for the flowers, Pappi,' Müller said. 'And you feel this is part of the case the GW dropped on us?'

'This news comes from one of those invisibles who use the kind of folder we saw.'

'Ah. And I suppose the *official* reports will come via the GW.'

'You suppose correctly.' A sucking noise punctuated Pappenheim's speech. 'So show surprise when he delivers his version of the news ... which I am certain he will do personally.'

'He just loves making my day.'

'You know he hates everything about you ... your car, your earring, your hair, your title, your Mondrian original, your Armani suits, the fact that, unlike his, there is not a single police badge on your wall ... The list is so long, I won't continue. Enjoy,' Pappenheim ended with a chuckle as he hung up.

'And thank you too, Pappi,' Müller commented drily as he replaced the receiver.

A knock sounded.

'Come in!'

He looked up enquiringly as a young woman in leather-jacketed police uniform entered and looked about the office wonderingly.

'I have never seen a police office like this!'

There was a winged badge on her jacket.

Müller glanced at it, fascinated, then got to his feet. '*You* are my liaison?'

She was startled by the question. 'No, sir! Not as far as I know. I am Engels.'

Müller frowned. 'Engels?'

'Yes, sir.' She now looked confused. 'I was

28

told to report to you today. *Oberkommissar* Pappenheim told me on the phone last week...' The words faded uncertainly.

'*Oberkomm* ... Ah! Engels! Of course. The helicopter unit.'

'Yes, sir,' she confirmed, relieved. 'I am an observer...'

'And soon to train as a pilot.' Müller held out a hand. 'Welcome to the madhouse. So Pappi was as good as his word. He poached you from your old unit. You did very good work for us on our last case.'

'Thank you, sir,' she said, pleased by the compliment as they shook hands.

'Now that we've met,' Müller continued, 'I'll take you to the person who will be responsible for your training ... *Oberkommissar* Wolfgang Speyer. What he does not know about flying helicopters would be hard to find on a—'

The black phone interrupted him.

'Excuse me,' he said to her, picking up the receiver. 'Müller.'

'*Hauptkommissar* Müller,' an unknown voice began. 'Are you enjoying your Monday so far?'

Müller frowned. 'Who is this?' he demanded sharply. 'And how did you get this number?'

The person at the other end laughed, then hung up.

Müller stared at the receiver for brief moments before replacing it. 'Comedian.' He turned to Engels. 'Sorry, Engels. Change of

plan. I'll have someone take you to Speyer.'
He picked up the grey phone. 'Pappi, I've got
Engels with me. Send someone to take her to
Wolfgang Speyer, will you, please?'

'There's something in your voice. The GW
is also with you?'

'No. But there's been a development. I'm
on my way.'

'Alright. I'll send Berger to shepherd Engels.'

'Thanks.' Müller hung up, then turned once
more to Engels with a brief, rueful smile.
'Never a quiet moment, as you'll soon
discover. Berger will take you to Speyer. One
of our best, is Berger. You'll like her.'

'Yes, sir,' Engels said, looking as if she felt
she had arrived at the wrong time.

'Can't keep away, eh?' Pappenheim greeted
as Müller entered. 'You should worry about
passive smoking.'

'*I* should worry?'

'Kaltendorf does. He'll come in here in a
space suit, one of these days. So what made
you cut your meeting short with the angelic
Engels?'

'Such embarrassment, Pappi,' Müller said
as he took his seat on the uncluttered chair. 'I
had no idea who she was.'

'She'll forgive you. So ... what was it?'

'I got a phone call.'

'Hope you asked for a date.'

'I don't think he was interested in dates.'

'A *he*. Then you should have asked if he had

a sister...'

'Pappi!'

'No, no. This is not as crazy as you think. When I was a lot younger, and before we met and came here to Kaltendorf's Kingdom, I was assigned to catch an obscene caller. I was at the victim's home when he next called. I took the call and asked him if I could date his sister. He lost it completely. He raved for so long on the phone, the tracers had plenty of time to catch the bastard. He was still bawling into the public phone when the boys grabbed him. Works every time. The perpetrator never likes a dose of his own medicine.'

'Well, this one will be a little more difficult. He asked me how I was enjoying my Monday so far. He knew my name and rank, *and* he came through on the black phone.'

Pappenheim's hand froze in the act of putting a cigarette between his lips. 'This,' he said, 'is not good.'

'This is worse than not good. Somebody out there apparently knows more about this case than we, Kaltendorf, and perhaps even the blue-folder people do.'

The cigarette continued its journey.

Pappenheim lit it, and spoke through a cloud. '*They* certainly know more than we do.'

The door opened suddenly.

Both Müller and Pappenheim looked sharply towards it. Pappenheim was about to yell something at the intruder, when he paused to stare at what had entered.

31

A man with severely cropped blond hair, and wearing a suit so new it shone, closed the door with a heel. His mouth turned down, and he gave a hacking cough.

'God!' he wheezed. 'It stinks in here!'

'I didn't hear your knock,' Pappenheim said coldly. 'Would you like to go out and try again? And you seem to have forgotten your sunglasses too.'

The man peered at him through the smoke. 'Sunglasses?'

'Never mind,' Pappenheim said, dangerously friendly.

'You are Pappenheim?'

'*Oberkommissar* Pappenheim to you!'

The man's thin mouth twitched. It could have been a smile of contempt. 'I stand corrected. *Oberkommissar* Pappenheim.'

'And who the hell are you?'

For reply, the man reached into his jacket. Both Pappenheim and Müller tensed, almost reaching under their arms for their own weapons.

The man paused, lips now drawn back in a rictus of a grin. 'Tut, tut ... we are twitchy...' He slowly drew out a folder and approached Pappenheim's desk. 'I've been instructed to give this to you.'

Pappenheim glanced at Müller, then took the blue folder with the black border. 'That was quick work.'

'We are quick,' the man said. It was not a boast, but a statement of fact.

'Do you have a name?'

'Call me Enteling.'

'Duckling.'

The man's eyes squinted at Pappenheim. 'What?'

'Oh ... don't mind me. I make bad jokes from time to time. And your rank?'

'Not important at this time.'

'I see.' Pappenheim appeared not to mind. 'So? Do I keep this folder?'

'No.' Enteling glanced exaggeratedly around the office with a grimace of distaste. 'I'll wait in the corridor while you study it.'

Having ignored Müller completely, he went out without waiting for comment.

Pappenheim looked at Müller. 'You were quiet.'

'I thought as you were doing so well...'

Pappenheim shook his head slowly. 'Where do they get them? His suit is so shiny, it makes yours look rough.'

'Shiny, but cheaper.'

'Definitely cheaper,' Pappenheim agreed.

'We'd better see what the duckling brought from your contacts,' Müller prompted.

Pappenheim extinguished the cigarette he'd barely started when Enteling had appeared, immediately lit another, and drew deeply upon it. Almost reverently, he opened the folder. He briefly studied some photographs, then read a single line.

'Oh shit,' he murmured, and looked up. He pushed the folder towards Müller. 'You'd better continue. The photos in here are nothing like the ones the GW showed to us. As the

33

senior officer, I think you should have this.'

Müller gave his deputy a sideways, questioning glance before picking it up. He didn't have to read very far.

'Jesus!'

'Er ... I don't think he's going to help us, somehow.'

Müller studied the photgraphs disbelievingly. He read everything in the folder, while Pappenheim leaned back in his chair and blew smoke rings at the ceiling.

When he had finished, Müller closed the folder slowly, then put it back on the desk.

'Can I look down now?' Pappenheim asked.

'You better read this,' Müller said in a dead voice.

'That bad, eh?'

'That bad.'

'Oh well ... since you're giving me an order.'

Pappenheim began to study the contents of Enteling's present.

Kaltendorf turned a corner into the corridor where Enteling was waiting. He made a beeline for the man.

'Who are you?' Kaltendorf demanded as he drew up.

Enteling studied him superciliously. 'And who are *you*?'

Kaltendorf's eyes grew round and his mouth opened in readiness to bark something appropriately commanding at the visitor.

But the door to Pappenheim's office opened suddenly and the *Oberkommissar*, complete with lighted cigarette, unceremoniously grabbed Enteling by an arm.

'Aah! There you are!' he greeted, as if seeing Enteling for the first time. 'Sorry to keep you waiting.'

He half-hauled, half-pushed Enteling back into the smoke-filled room. Enteling tried to resist, but was astonished to find he made no headway whatsoever against Pappenheim, whom he had mistakenly judged to be soft.

Pappenheim shut the door to face Kaltendorf.

'Who was that man in the cheap suit?' Kaltendorf barked, loud enough for those in the office to hear.

'Helping us with our enquiries,' Pappenheim replied smoothly.

'Must you always deal with these criminal types, *Oberkommissar*?'

'Good intelligence, sir, can come from the unlikeliest of places. Would you like to question him, sir?' Pappenheim looked at Kaltendorf, baby-blue eyes at their most guileless.

Kaltendorf stared pointedly at the cigarette between Pappenheim's fingers. 'I never enter your office unless I need to. And right now, I don't need to. And stop smoking in the corridor!'

'Yes, sir. As you wish, sir.' Pappenheim backed into his office, and shut the door on Kaltendorf.

He stared at Enteling. 'Our boss thinks you wear a cheap suit and look like a criminal.

Don't glare at me, sonny. You heard him. Likes to form quick opinions about people ... but I'm certain *you're* not like that.'

Enteling's lips tightened. 'Are you finished?'

Pappenheim nodded. 'We are.' He handed back the folder.

Enteling glanced at Müller as he took it.

'That,' Pappenheim began pointedly, 'is *Hauptkommissar* Müller.'

Enteling's eyes widened. 'Graf von Röhnen?'

'Aah!' Pappenheim said to Müller. 'Fame at last.'

'You know of me?' Müller asked.

'Yes, sir!'

'He calls you sir!' Pappenheim exclaimed, as if overwhelmed. 'Rank does matter, after all.'

'And how do you know of me?' Müller enquired.

'Sir, in our department, you are well known.'

'How come?'

For the first time since his arrival, Enteling seemed unsure of himself. 'Er ... I think I'm speaking out of turn. I should leave now, and take this folder back.'

Müller stared at Enteling curiously, but Pappenheim was moving towards the door.

'Better let me check the corridor ... unless you want to talk to our boss.'

'No. No,' Enteling said hurriedly.

Pappenheim opened the door and looked out. 'All clear.'

Enteling went out quickly.

'And give my thanks to...' Pappenheim began to add.

But Enteling was hurrying away as fast as he could.

Pappenheim slowly closed the door. 'A strange man,' he said to Müller. 'He seemed at once respectful, and afraid of you.'

'I was thinking the same thing,' Müller said thoughtfully.

Two

Leonberg, near Stuttgart.

Helmut Ries and Jörg Pinic were eighteen, and close friends. They were also petty criminals and, if they made it to their twenties, would be well on their way to becoming hardened thugs. Both had seen the inside of corrective youth institutions. Neither had learned anything from their experiences, except perhaps to be even more set upon their chosen course. Both were also very good hackers, Ries the better of the two. While Ries came from a well-off family – his father chairman of an electronics firm – Pinic had humbler beginnings. Both, however, had come from good homes; but that had made little difference to their particular outlook on life.

They were thin individuals of average height, Ries being slightly the taller of the two. Ries had a mean and narrow face topped by short, dark hair that had been spiked with gel. With his small eyes, this gave him the look of a petulant hedgehog. With Pinic, despite his thinness, there was an impression of plumpness. Perhaps it was because of the roundish face and the hair cut so short it grew in a nap upon his skull. Both wore loose jeans low upon their hips, baggy T-shirts, and trainers.

Ries's parents had bought him a brand-new, yellow Golf – his choice of colour – for his birthday. A desperate attempt to buy his good behaviour, it had been a dismal failure; but it was a measure of the friendship that Ries and Pinic shared the upkeep of the car equally, and that Ries frequently allowed Pinic to drive it.

Among their many activities was the theft of mobile phones, from which they had found many lucrative ways of profiting. The more expensive ones were passed on to taciturn individuals who found ready customers in various eastern European countries and further afield. Pinic and Ries also made personal use of those they did not pass on. Contract phones would be used until vast bills were run up before the owner discovered the loss; or the phone was disconnected. Card-operated phones were used until the card ran out, then chucked away. But before these stages were reached they had other, nastier games in their repertoire.

Nuisance calls were made to the saved numbers on the phone. Private messages were read and used for blackmail, if the contents allowed. A teenaged girl, whose messages to and from her boyfriend they had read, had been pressured into meeting them, and then systematically raped by both. Threatened with revenge if she spoke about it, their victim had been too afraid and too ashamed to report the crime. They were therefore still walking around free.

On that Monday morning, they were planning something similar.

Pinic had been prowling the multi-level car park of a shopping mall, while Ries had gone on a scouting mission. Pinic was sufficiently familiar with the place to know the location and blind spot of every one of the security cameras. Unobtrusively working his way from blind spot to blind spot, he had checked cars at random, to see if any had been left unlocked. He knew from experience that, despite all the warnings, many people still continued to do so.

It was not long before he had come upon one: a silver Lexus Cabrio. He marvelled that anyone able to afford such a car could be so careless with it. Inside, still in its bracket, was an expensive-looking mobile phone.

Within fleeting seconds, the phone was in Pinic's possession, and he was walking unhurriedly away. Once well clear of the car park, he had called Ries on his own stolen, card-operated mobile and arranged to be picked up. He did not show Ries the mobile until they were in the car park of a service station on the A8 Autobahn. They remained in the car.

Grinning hugely, Pinic took out the phone. It was a solid unit in gleaming black, with a

40

host of functions that far exceeded those of an average mobile.

'Is this a beauty, or what?' Pinic said. 'It looks like something out of a science-fiction movie.' He offered it to Ries, laughing. 'Perhaps it's a mini transporter.'

Ries was staring hard at the phone. He did not take it. 'Where did you get that?'

The way he spoke made Pinic frown. 'What do you mean, where? From a car in the car park in Leonberg. What do you think?'

'That's my father's phone.'

'Oh yeah. Sure. Since when did he change his Jaguar for a Lexus? And what would he be doing in the shopping mall in Leonberg? Knowing your father, would he leave a mobile like this in the car, anyway?'

Ries's small eyes stared at the phone, trying to make sense out of the situation.

'It's definitely my father's mobile and this morning he left for work in his Jaguar. And you're right. As long as I can remember, his car's always been a Jag.' Ries continued to stare at the phone, but still did not touch it. 'But it is his mobile. I should know. I've cracked his code...'

Pinic stared at him in disbelief. 'You hacked into your father's phone?'

'Yeah. Why not? He's good with electronics, but I'm better.'

'You did this to challenge him, or what?'

'Why not?' Ries said again. 'And he didn't even find out.' He reached for the mobile. 'Let's prove this once and for all. Here. Give

41

it to me. If I can't get into it, it's not my father's...'

'I don't think it is,' Pinic insisted, handing it over. 'But just supposing ... what if he *knows* you hacked into it and changed the code to trap you?'

'Not a chance.'

'Perhaps it's even registering where it is right now,' Pinic added with some anxiety.

'Don't be dumb.' Ries studied the phone closely. 'I can get in, even if he's locked the keypad.'

Ries began to work at the phone. In less than a minute, he had broken through. 'I'm in.'

'Ooh, shit!' Pinic remarked softly, staring uncertainly at Ries. 'It really is ... But ... but how did your father's phone get in that car?'

'That's what I'd like to know,' Ries said tightly. 'If that's not his car, then whose?'

He began to search the mobile's phone book.

'*What are you doing?*' Pinic tried to restrain Ries, but his hand was roughly brushed away. 'You can't...'

'I can, and I will!'

Ries was already reading the saved messages, and studying the numbers in the phone book. Then he stopped abruptly as one particular message came up. He read it through twice.

'What the fuck?' he said slowly. '*What the fuck? The bastard is seeing another woman!*' His mean eyes were suddenly blazing. '*The*

42

bastard is seeing some whore! Can you believe it? *How can he do this to my mother?'* Considering his normal contempt for both parents, it was a bizarre sense of outrage.

Knowing his violent moods, Pinic studied him warily. 'What are you going to do?'

'Teach her a lesson!' Ries snarled. 'Watch.' He dialled the number he had found. A woman answered. 'Hello, my little rabbit,' he said, using the pet name he had seen in the message.

There was a shocked silence. Then a tentative, 'Who ... who is this?'

'Wouldn't you like to know, my little rabbit? What would your boyfriend's wife say if she knew what her Frido got up to?'

'Or where,' Pinic, deciding to join in, added coarsely.

They both laughed, but Ries's mean little eyes were not smiling. *Frido is her pet name for him, as you should know, bitch!*

'Who ... Who are you?' the woman asked again fearfully.

'You can pay for our silence...'

'You can't blackmail me...' It was bluff, and Ries knew it.

'Alright,' Ries told her airily. 'We'll just call his wife and by the time she's finished with him in the divorce courts, he'll have nothing left to buy those fancy little things you like so much ... and you'll lose the car you got for your birthday, because he won't be able to pay for that either. Bye...'

'Wait! *Wait!'*

They grinned at each other, knowing she was hooked.

'Where ... When can I meet you? And how much?'

'We want thirty thousand euros...' Ries began.

'*What?* I can't...'

'Fine. We'll talk to the wife.'

'No! Wait! I'll ... I'll see what I can do...'

'Listen, you toilet of a whore!' Ries snarled. 'You won't *see* what you can do. You will *do* it! You can afford it. And don't forget, we know where you live. Perhaps we'll pay you a visit. Then you can give us some of what you give your rich bastard Frido. And if you even think of calling the police, we still know where you live!'

Short, agitated gasps of breath now came from the woman. 'Look ... Look ... just tell me where to meet...' She sounded very frightened, and as if the tears were not far away.

'*No police!*'

'No police. I ... I swear...'

'You'll be doing more than that if you're lying to me.'

'I'm not! I'm not...'

'Alright. We'll call you again with your instructions. Get the money!' Ries ended the call abruptly and grinned at Pinic, who jerked a fist in approval. 'After she gives us the money,' he continued, 'I think we should have some fun with her, just as we did with that stupid girl.'

'It will be as if she's paying us to do it to

44

her,' Pinic said with a smirk of anticipation.

'Oh, we'll do it to her,' Ries confirmed harshly. 'She'll never forget it. Tonight, we'll see what my father's piece of meat tastes like. She sounds young, so we should have some hot fun.' His expression was thunderous. 'They tried to buy me off with this car on my birthday, and *he* buys her with a sports car on *her* birthday. He should be more careful about where he leaves his phone,' he went on viciously. 'And he should have erased his messages too. Now I've got him, the bastard!'

Unknown to them, someone had piggy-backed on to their conversation, had heard everything, and had lifted the data from the mobile.

A loud banging sounded on Pappenheim's door.

He tunelessly sang, 'Someone's knocking on my do-or. Shall I let them in? Oh no...'

The intensity of the noise increased.

Pappenheim sang louder, then gave in with a sigh. 'Suppose I'd better,' he muttered.

Half-burnt cigarette between his lips, he reluctantly left his desk to go to the door ... and opened it to an irate Kaltendorf whose raised fist seemed to freeze in mid-bang, scant millimetres from Pappenheim's nose.

Pappenheim stared at the fist, smoke trickling from the cigarette and into the corridor, and said nothing.

Kaltendorf stared mesmerized at his own fist. 'I...' He lowered it abruptly. 'Where is

45

Müller?' he demanded sharply.

Pappenheim stood back slightly so that Kaltendorf could enter if he wished. 'Not here, sir.'

'Have you seen him?'

'No, sir. You can come in to check if...'

'I will,' Kaltendorf snapped and despite himself, clearly not believing Pappenheim this time, brushed past his subordinate to enter the room. He coughed exaggeratedly. 'And where's that criminal type you had in here?'

'Long gone, sir,' Pappenheim replied mildly. 'I think you scared him off.'

'I did?' Kaltendorf almost sounded happy.

'I think he didn't want to mess with you, sir,' Pappenheim added, pushing his luck.

That seemed to please Kaltendorf. 'A lesson that could be learned elsewhere.' He waved uselessly at the wreaths of smoke. 'What progress are you making on the case?'

'We're getting somewhere, sir,' Pappenheim answered smoothly 'But it's much too soon to say precisely where. With your permission, *Hauptkommissar* Müller suggests we keep at it until we have something solid to give you.'

'Can't he speak for himself?' Kaltendorf said irritably. 'I'm always chasing around to find that man.'

'He's a busy person, sir.'

'And so am I! Don't either of you forget it!'

Kaltendorf whirled out of the room as if he could not get out of there soon enough.

Pappenheim shut the door quietly.

46

'Yes, sir,' he said to it. 'And he has political ambitions too, God help us...'

The phone rang just as Pappenheim returned to his desk.

'Buy you a coffee?' Müller's voice said in his ear.

'Your place, or mine?'

'Neither. Outside.'

'I know a place ... Not where good policemen should go.'

'Thought you might. Meet me in the garage.'

'Now?'

'Your jacket not on yet?'

'Got the message,' Pappenheim said. 'On my way.'

In the undergound garage, Müller was already waiting in the seal-grey Porsche. He started the engine just as Pappenheim climbed in.

'Whenever I see this car,' Pappenheim began as he settled in, 'I always get the feeling I should genuflect. He's looking for you, by the way.'

'He's always looking for me.' Müller put the car into gear and moved off. 'Where are we going?'

'To a little Italian bistro,' Pappenheim answered. 'Go towards Checkpoint Charlie. I'll direct you from there. The Great White doesn't know of it.' He gave Müller a sideways glance as they emerged into the street. It was raining. 'What did I tell you?' He peered up at the cloud-laden sky and briefly turned down his mouth. 'Weather girls ... We can talk there,' he continued. 'It's secure. That's what you want, isn't it?'

Müller nodded.

Pappenheim was not smoking, and did not light up. He never smoked in Müller's car. Whenever they travelled together in the Porsche, he was somehow able to beat his addiction for a while. On long journeys, he would even hold on for about two hundred kilometres or so, then, almost gasping for breath, would ask Müller to stop so that he could get out for a puff. The drive to the Italian bistro was therefore child's play by comparison.

They headed south in the increasingly heavy rain from Berlin-Mitte, towards Kreuzberg. After they had passed the tourist attraction of the reconstructed US-Army checkpoint post, they continued southwards, heading for Neukölln. Many side streets later, they pulled up before a small restaurant that looked as if it belonged in the former DDR.

The rain was still falling strongly.

Müller peered out at the sign as he switched off the engine. 'An *Italian* bistro that looks retro-DDR, with a sign in *English* that says *Death Strip*?'

'Don't let the façade fool you. Inside, it's very Italian, and very clean ... if a little smoky.'

'What a surprise. And that name?'

'He used to call it *Casa Luigi*,' Pappenheim

said. 'Very boring, he thought. Every other Italian place is always Casa something, Villa something, Trattoria something, and so on. Luigi was born in Bremen but came here to the East in the mid-nineties, and has never been to Italy. Ignore his Italian-accented German. He speaks better German than I do. My very limited Italian is probably better than his, despite his grandmother who's been here since the fifties, and who still only speaks Italian. Then he had the bright idea to rename it – in English – after the infamous strip during the days of the Wall. Ghoulish humour, but it worked. He gets great business.'

'From whom?' Müller asked, once more peering at the sign doubtfully.

'Usually from people who don't like policemen very much.'

'What a surprise.'

'But good for us. No snoopers.'

'Does he know you're a policeman?'

'Of course. I know some people he has a lot of respect for.'

'What another surpise,' Müller commented drily.

'He is also a very good source of information. Kaltendorf would probably have a seizure if he knew I used this place ... Which gives me all the more reason to like it. His name is Luigi Bocca.'

Müller stared at Pappenheim. 'Luigi the *Mouth*?'

'I didn't make that up. It is his real name.

49

He once said to me it could have been worse. It could have been Boccanegra. And he doesn't like Verdi. Grandma is a sweet little lady … and a die-hard fascist of the old school. Got it all from her father, who was an actual Blackshirt. Had Luigi's father when she was seventeen. Luigi, however, is soft hard left. Interesting family. Come on. Let's go in. Your car will be safe. No one would dare touch it in front of Luigi's.'

They scrambled out of the car and hurried in the rain to the bistro.

Luigi Bocca, a small, quick man in his thirties with lively dark eyes and smoothly shaven head, came to greet them as they entered. The interior of the place was indeed at great odds with its exterior. It had been tastefully decorated in Tuscan style and was bright and cheerful, despite the rain. There were many customers, mainly dark silent men with sharp eyes.

'Ah, *commissario*!' he greeted Pappenheim. 'Nice to see you again. And your friend?' he added, looking at Müller. 'Also a *commissario*?'

'My boss, Luigi. His name does not matter.'

'Ah!' Luigi exclaimed, as if that explained everything. He glanced outside. The shape of the Porsche could just be seen. *'Fantastico auto,'* he went on to Müller. 'They must pay Berlin *commissarios* well.' He held out a hand. 'Welcome to my humble establishment.'

Slightly bemused, Müller shook it. 'Thank you…'

'Call me Luigi. The *commissario*'s friend is my friend.'

'Thank you, Luigi,' Müller said. He took a swift glance around. 'Very quiet customers.'

'Very discreet,' Luigi corrected. 'Secrets are safe here.'

'That's good to know.'

Luigi gave a slow little sideways nod in acceptance. 'The usual room?' he asked Pappenheim.

'The usual, Luigi, thanks.'

'It is free right now. Shall I...?'

'We can find our way.'

'Of course. And the usual coffee? A pot, perhaps?'

'Please.'

'I will bring it. *commissario*s.' Luigi gave them a short nod and went to prepare the coffee.

They made their way past the silent men and into the room Luigi had mentioned, Pappenheim leading. Again decorated in Tuscan style, the place looked more like someone's living room than part of the restaurant. There were two sofas, a low table between them, and a floor-to-ceiling shelf unit filled with Tuscan artefacts.

'This doesn't seem to be in the restaurant at all,' Müller said as they entered.

'It isn't. We're now in his home. They live above the shop, so to speak. Luigi and his wife do the cooking, while grandma looks after their small child of about three. He'll probably grow up to be a fascist ... just like

51

his great-grandma and her father. Luigi also does the serving. The food here is excellent. You should try it.'

'Perhaps I will,' Müller said dubiously.

'Don't worry. It's all very clean.'

They sat down opposite each other, Pappenheim lighting up and taking a long drag with relief, as they waited for Luigi to return. He arrived almost immediately carrying a tray with a tall pot of hot coffee, two Tuscan cups, milk, and sugar. He placed the tray on the table.

He was about to serve when Pappenheim said, 'We can do that, Luigi. Go see to your customers. And thank you.'

'Gentlemen.'

Luigi was about to leave, when Pappenheim said, 'Oh, Luigi...'

Luigi paused.

'We are secure?' Pappenheim asked mildly.

'That is understood, *commissario*.'

'Good.'

As soon as Luigi left them to it, Müller got up and began to search the room.

Pappenheim stared at him. 'What are you doing?'

'I know you trust Luigi...'

'Not that much,' Pappenheim said with a tiny smile. He too got to his feet. 'I go through this routine every time I come here. Wanted to see whether you would.'

'You've taught me a lot, Pappi ... but I'm not a student any more.'

'One can never stop learning.'

'That's certainly true, Teacher.'

Pappenheim grinned as he joined Müller in the search. They did it swiftly, but minutely. They even checked the tray, and everything on it. The room was clean.

Pappenheim poured the coffee as they sat down again, before saying to Müller, 'Now it's your turn.'

'I am certain you have contacts in North Rhine-Westphalia,' Müller began.

'I do. An *Oberkommissar* in Köln.'

'How discreet?'

'Very. I trust him. Completely.'

Müller knew that if Pappenheim said he trusted someone completely, then that person was totally dependable.

'I'm going over to Bonn,' Müller continued. 'Arrange cooperation, but no one, except your contact, is to know I'm there ... unless I decide to make it known. I will not make contact with them until it becomes absolutely necessary.'

'In other words, if the brown stuff hits the fan, you don't want the locals popping off at you.'

'Police shooting police is not fun.'

'Segelmann can handle everything. He's also a very good weapons man, if you need back-up.'

'I hope I won't, but it's good to know.'

'He's also almost as good as I am, when keeping the high brass off your back.' Pappenheim looked his most guileless.

'Praise indeed. Do you have any contacts

who aren't?'

Pappenheim gave another quick grin between sipping from his cup. 'No. Like minds. Great network. May I ask where exactly you're going? And should the Great White know?'

'I'm first going to where that financial guru was shot. The guys over there don't know what we know ... which is little enough. They might have missed something. As for Kaltendorf ... not even if he pulls out your fingernails.'

Pappenheim did his squinting-through-the-smoke act. 'Sounds painful ... But I haven't even seen you, if he asks. Will you be going back to the office?'

'No. I'll drop you off, go home to pack some things, then I'm gone.' Müller smiled. 'It also means I'll be absent when that liaison turns up.'

'No need to take me back,' Pappenheim said. 'Besides, you don't want to risk Kaltendorf spotting your car. No point saying I haven't seen you if he spots me getting out of the seal-grey machine. Even I could not lie my way out of that one.' He took a final drag on the cigarette, killed it, then lit another. 'I'll hang on here for a while to chat with Luigi. Those silent men back there come from all over Europe, many from the East too ... like Poland, Bulgaria, Ukraine, Russia ... They know things even the blue-folder boys would sell their own grandmas for. Never know what I might find out.'

'What about that secret-keeping Luigi made so much fuss about?'

'There is secret-keeping, and then there is secret-keeping.'

'Of course,' Müller said drily, knowing that Pappenheim could ferret information out of a stone. 'According to the file that Enteling brought us,' he went on, 'all the victims are DDR Romeos ... the connection – perhaps – that we've been waiting for. This means many of them have got second families somewhere ... Here in the East, or over in the West.'

'When the DDR boys started that little gag,' Pappenheim said grimly, 'they had no idea of the time bomb they were priming.'

'Or perhaps they did. Now someone's defusing it by systematically killing them off. The question is ... why? And why now? The Wall's been down for over ten years. Why wait? What has become important enough for them to start knocking these people off? Revenge?'

'Like the betrayed wives ... not to mention offspring ... getting together and having some pro take out the bastards who wrecked their lives? Sounds attractive, but I doubt it. Too easy.'

'I agree,' Müller said. 'Some of the photographs we saw in Enteling's folder ... Unbelievable stuff. All of the dead men in the one Kaltendorf showed us, all married in the DDR, then married again in the West without first getting divorced. Taking up with a new woman—'

'Who had first been thoroughly researched as a potential source of intelligence by his masters before being picked—'

'And compromised ... all under orders.'

'Think of the kids from those ... liaisons ... if I may use the word,' Pappenheim said grimly. 'Imagine how they'll feel when they find out.'

'Many have not, if we are to believe Enteling's folder.'

'It's a bitch. I take it you will be checking out those in the photos who are still alive?'

Müller nodded. 'Interesting how they gave us addresses, or pointed us to where we might otherwise find them.'

Pappenheim stared at Luigi's ceiling, and blew a perfect doughnut of smoke at it. 'And if they get hit after we have known ... Is there a slight feeling of manipulation running up and down your spine? Mine's almost dancing by itself.'

'Then it has a partner.'

Pappenheim ended his contemplation of the ceiling, and looked at Müller. 'You didn't mention the big one.'

'Thought I'd keep that for last...'

'Alright,' Pappenheim began. 'I'll dare speak the words that would rather remain unspoken. Star billing in the snapshot show goes to an aspiring politico, who's set himself up for election ... right here in Berlin. The blue-folder boys clearly believe he will soon join the list of victims. So ... are all these leading up to the real one? Almost as if whoever's behind this is ... are ... deliberately sending a warning? If so ... why? Why not just pop him off? And why can't the blue-folder boys protect him?'

'Because they don't want to.'

Pappenheim nodded slowly. 'Because they don't want to. Some of that information comes from embargoed Stasi files ... and we get the poisoned chalice. Someone out there really hates us.'

'Perhaps they don't like his politics.'

'*I* don't like his politics.'

'I don't either,' Müller said, 'but perhaps whoever sent the folder to Kaltendorf – with specific instructions to assign the case to us – doesn't trust their own people with it...'

'Meaning there could be a Romeo among them?'

'Anything is possible in this business.'

'That would be a stinker. And you think my contact might know?'

'Would he—'

'Or she...'

'Or she ... know?'

'I can but try to find out,' Pappenheim said. 'But I guarantee nothing. And what about our friend Udo Hellmann?' he continued. 'Still alive, river-faring, luxury barge owner. His case is a little different. He seems to have been the decent one of this bunch. I say "decent" advisedly. If we can believe Enteling's folder, he was very reluctant, and had to be pressurized into going through with his mission. But he did it. Now he has a very comfortable living indeed with his wife Isabella – formerly Lütz – and their two daughters. But I keep thinking of the other woman, husband gone, also with two kids, not having a very comfortable life at all, and who knew him by another name. And ... someone gave him a lot of money to sink into that boat.'

'What about him?'

'Is he on your list of visits?'

'Not sure about the visit ... but check on the boat. Find out its current itinerary.'

'Already being done. Thought you might want that.'

'One of these days, Pappi, you will see into my head.'

'What do you mean "one of these days"?' Pappenheim asked, smiling through the smoke.

Müller lived in Berlin-Wilmersdorf, not far from the Kurfürstendamm.

The house was a classic, elegant three-storey building that had been reduced to a shell during the Second World War. Rebuilt to its former glory during the fifties, its thick, solid walls and its high ceilings had been faithfully recreated. Müller had inherited it from his father, who had in turn inherited it from *his*. It had been modernized and converted into vast, three-bedroom, two-bath luxury apartments during his father's tenure, and Müller now lived alone in the penthouse. His access was totally separate from the shared entry of the lower floors, which had been rented out ever since his father had first lived there as a single man.

On taking over, Müller had redecorated the apartment in a close blend of classic and modern styles bordering on the minimalist, giving it a brightly uncluttered, airy feel. The polished floors of the wide colonnaded hall, the living room, dining room, and the sitting room, were sparingly laid with large Persian rugs. The kitchen was a reverent homage to stainless steel. The walls of the entire apartment were adorned with carefully chosen paintings and prints, and a few family portraits.

Among the portraits were two of people he had last seen at the age of twelve: his mother and father. Both had died in a plane crash.

Two of the bedrooms had been fully furnished and carpeted wall-to-wall; but the third was very different. Here, a single Mondrian and the two separate portraits of his mother and father were all that had been hung upon the walls. There was no furniture as such. In the middle was a single rug, an island marooned upon a gleaming wooden sea. Placed in L-formation along adjacent walls were a quartet of unexpected items. Highly polished and in perfect condition, were two mighty Hammond organs: a B3 and its modern, digitally enhanced clone the XB3, each complete with twenty-five-note, detachable pedal boards. The lids were folded back, revealing the twin, sixty-one-note manuals, and the thirty-six drawbars in four groups of nine on both instruments. Each instrument had a Leslie cabinet connected.

Another wall was completely taken up by a floor-to-ceiling bookcase of polished cherry wood, filled with books and music scores. Next to the bookshelf was a large inlaid desk, with a high-backed leather swivel chair and a document cabinet close by. These were the sole contents of the vast room.

Müller paused on his way to his bedroom to look in, then decided to enter. He went towards the XB3, studied it for a moment, then turned it on. He switched on its Leslie, but left the rotation of the speaker horns off.

He sat down on the stool. None of his police colleagues except Pappenheim knew of his secret passion for organ-playing, Hammonds in particular. The music he played on them followed his widely varied taste; from classic to rock to jazz, and anything in between that appealed to him at a given moment.

The digital capabilities of the XB3 enabled him to program the organ so that he could create an eerie emulation of a harpsichord. He began to play a haunting interpretation of the andante to Bach's *Italian Concerto in F Major*, then followed that with the presto. Scarlatti's measured *Sonata in F Minor* was next, both movements. He loved the two compositions and played them with great skill and emotion, without once having recourse to the scores. Müller allowed the music to transport him, temporarily driving thoughts of Kaltendorf and the Romeo killings out of his mind. When he had finished, he sat unmoving at the instrument for long moments. He patted it, switched it off, then stood up and went over to the B3.

He turned on the older instrument, and waited for it to warm up. He turned on its Leslie and selected slow rotation of the speaker horns. When the B3 was ready, he made his drawbar choices, selected a hard percussive effect for the notes, and began to play 'Green Onions', Booker T. Jones's phenomenal instrumental hit.

As with Bach and Scarlatti, Müller played this piece with great skill. He put fire into his playing, extemporizing like a veteran. Though the XB3 very closely emulated the unique tonewheel sound of the original, the B3 sounded as only a B3 could. The valve-amplified Leslie spewed out the screaming, wailing, roaring sound throughout the apartment as if both in pain and exhilaration. Müller was not worried about disturbing the neighbours, for the thick walls offered a secure privacy.

He let the organ do its stuff and played until beads of sweat appeared on his forehead and cheeks. At last, he stopped, switched off and, as with the XB3, waited quietly for some moments. He also gave the B3 an affectionate pat.

'Time to go,' he said.

Pappenheim was on his way back to his

office, scrupulously observing the no-smoking rule in the corridor. He had garnered some useful strands of information from a couple of Luigi's customers and was feeling rather pleased with the world in general. He knew that, as things went, this feeling of benevolence would not last long. It didn't.

'*Pappenheim!*'

Pappenheim toyed with the idea of pretending he hadn't heard and continuing on his way. But the idea died on its feet. Kaltendorf's bellow could not by any stretch of the imagination have gone unheard.

Pappenheim glanced wearily upwards. 'Why, Lord, isn't my guardian angel ever on duty when I need him?' he muttered grumpily.

He stopped, and turned round to wait for Kaltendorf's pock-pocking steps to reach him.

'Pappenheim,' Kaltendorf repeated, barely short of his previous yell as he drew up. He glanced at the *Oberkommissar*'s hands to check if a hastily extinguished cigarette lurked there.

'Sir?' Pappenheim said mildly.

'Müller! Where is Müller?'

Knowing that Müller would safely be well on the way to Bonn by now, Pappenheim replied easily, 'I've no idea, sir. He said he was following a lead, and that was it. You know how he works, sir.'

'Work? That man is never here when he's wanted. The tax-payer is funding an office that is seldom used! Then there's that expensive, fuel-drinking car of his...'

Pappenheim danced on the edge of insubordination. 'The tax-payer would be less than pleased if he did not solve cases, sir. And his car uses less fuel than some of our own fast cars. He covers more kilometres in it on police business than private, and claims less than his fuel entitlement...' He did not say unlike some people, but the inference seemed to hover moodily.

Kaltendorf was glaring dangerously at Pappenheim. 'Is there something else hiding in those remarks?'

Pappenheim was innocence itself. 'No, sir. I...'

'*Sir!*'

Both Kaltendorf and Pappenheim turned to look. Berger was approaching them, a thin file in her hand.

Kaltendorf immediately assumed he was the one addressed. 'What is it, *Obermeisterin* Berger?'

Berger looked at Kaltendorf respectfully. 'Sorry, Herr *Direktor*. I brought this for *Oberkommissar* Pappenheim.'

'Is it to do with the case?' Kaltendorf demanded, holding out a hand for the file.

But Berger was on the ball. 'What case, sir?' She looked from Kaltendorf to Pappenheim, eyes wide.

Pappenheim took his cue. 'Thank you, Berger,' he said. 'Wait in my office, will you, please?'

'Yes, sir.' Berger was on her way before Kaltendorf could do anything.

Kaltendorf watched helplessly as she disappeared into Pappenheim's office. Thus thwarted, he rounded upon his subordinate.

'I know your methods, Pappenheim! And Müller's too! Why you two were assigned this case at all continues to defeat me. But I am in command here, and I expect reports of progress from both of you. And you will do this *through* the chain of command. This means Müller comes to *me* with these progress reports, unless I say differently.'

'And if he is busy elsewhere, sir?'

'He still reports to me!'

'Yes, sir. I'll tell him.'

Kaltendorf glared balefully at Pappenheim. 'Don't try to humour me, Pappenheim. It won't work.'

He glanced towards the closed door of Pappenheim's office, but said nothing more. He turned abruptly and walked away, stamping his heels as he went.

Pappenheim waited until he had turned a corner before continuing on to his office.

'Guardian angels can come in all shapes and sizes,' he said to himself as he reached the door. He opened it and went inside, lighting up as he did so, inhaling deeply. 'Thank you, Berger,' he said as he blew the smoke away from her. 'There's nothing in that file, is there?'

She smiled. 'No. I thought you might need some help.'

'So you heard his yell?'

'I think everyone on this floor heard it.'

'God ... that man ... and you didn't hear me say that.'

'Say what, sir?'

Pappenheim smiled. 'My thanks again. And you had no thoughts of pulling a fast one on the Director, did you?'

'None at all, sir.'

'Good. Then I have no reason to discipline a police sergeant for possible insubordination to a police director.'

'No reason at all,' Berger said, beaming at him as she went out.

He stared at the door for some moments. 'And I'm still far too old for you,' he said softly.

Berger had left the door open a crack, and so heard Pappenheim's softly spoken words.

'No, you're not,' she said to herself, and teased the door fully shut.

It made no sound but Pappenheim spotted the movement. A reflective smile touched his lips as he reached for one of his phones.

'Pappenheim,' he said when the person at the other end answered. 'Got the *Lütz* itinerary for me yet?' He paused for a quick drag while the other spoke. 'Excellent,' he continued. 'Could you fax it right away? No. To my direct fax. Good. Good. Thanks. I owe you one. What? You still owe me? Even better.' Pappenheim chuckled as he hung up. 'Sometimes, even Mondays go well.'

★　★　★

Müller was on the A2 Autobahn, well out of the state of Brandenburg and into Saxony-Anhalt. He was just approaching the Magdeburg exit when the Porsche's communication system pinged, interrupting a singing guitar solo from Santana on the CD.

He glanced at the display on the central console. The message from Pappenheim read: CALL ME WHEN YOU CAN.

It blinked out, and Santana's interrupted guitar continued its singing.

Müller put on some speed and the car seemed to gather itself to launch along the road. There was no rain, but the surface was still damp from an earlier downpour. A fine mist billowed in a high plume behind the fat wheels. He waited until he had passed Magdeburg and was heading for the next service station at Börde-Nord. He filtered off the Autobahn, making for the car park, where he remained in the car to call Pappenheim.

'Tell me,' he said when Pappenheim had answered.

'Ah! There you are. Where?'

'I've passed Magdeburg.'

'Oh good. I can't find you then.'

'Looking for me, is he?'

'Like you're his favourite, lost puppy.' The fluting wheeze of Pappenheim's drag on his cigarette came through clearly. 'His blood pressure readings must be heading for space. But to better things ... I have our friend's itinerary...'

'That was quick.'

66

'Quick. That's me. His next stop...' Pappenheim paused, then began to quote: ' "*Consortem cleri consignat confore calvum* ..." "They gnaw'd the flesh from every limb..." '

'The bald bishop, Hatto. So our friend's going to Mainz.'

'Oh what it is to have an education!' Pappenheim said. 'No wonder you-know-who hates you...'

'Today, Pappi ... today!'

'Yep,' Pappenheim continued, unabashed. 'Mainz it is ... Tomorrow, twelve o'clock. He usually stops there when he's carrying passengers to give them a chance to do the usual touristy things in the city. So ... any change of plans?'

'I'll still go on to Bonn,' Müller replied. 'Plenty of time. Then I'll head down to Mainz. I take it you have one of your contacts with the Rhineland-Pfalz people?'

'Do flies take off backwards?'

'I should have known,' Müller commented drily.

'Do the usual, shall I?'

'Do the usual.'

'If you need to make contact, her name is Wittental, *Kommissarin*. Like Segelmann, pretty good with weapons. Don't let the rank fool you. She has been known to make directors of police quake. Tough, tough cookie ... but heart of gold if she likes you. With your charm ... who knows?'

'Thanks, Pappi. I think I've got the picture.'

'Just so you know.' Pappenheim sounded as

if he were grinning. 'Back to our friend. This trip, he's carrying a load of antique furniture ... the real stuff, not repro ... in a single tier of containers. Must be worth several fortunes, so his cut will be very tasty. The *Isabella Lütz* is a thousand-tonner, with one thousand two hundred cubic metres of cargohold capacity. She is eighty metres long and nine wide. Draught is two point five metres. Top speed is nearly twenty knots but, as it's the river, they like to give it in kph so that's about thirty-six kph to you and me. But he clearly does not take it to that speed.'

'You are well informed. Where's he headed?'

'Budapest. Although, given what might happen with the weather, he'll be lucky if the Danube doesn't go apeshit. My guess is the stuff's going further east ... but it all seems legal. Paperwork clean. Oh ... and Segelmann will smooth any path to the river police, if you need them.'

'Service indeed, Pappi. Thanks.'

'That's me,' Pappenheim repeated. 'And there's some opaque info from two of the Strip's customers. Seems there's a loose cannon running around who may be linked to our little problem. They refused to give me a name, no matter how uncomfortable I told them life could be if they were not more helpful...'

'I know what your idea of uncomfortable is, Pappi. Those hardened characters must have been more scared of someone else than of you.'

'Chastening experience, but I finally had to accept it. This person must be something else. He could be the creature who called you this morning. Watch your back. He could be anywhere.'

'Advice taken.'

'There's still the aspiring politico. He's got a couple of private bodyguards ... but we both know it wouldn't be the first time in history the bodyguards did it. I could always pull them in...'

'No. If the loose cannon is our man, he would simply switch targets till our attention is elsewhere ... or is *made* to switch elsewhere ... We should cover the politico invisibly...'

'Reimer and Berger. They can handle that perfectly.'

'Fine. Anything else?'

'Oh ... only that the GW seems to think you spend your time racing along the roads of Germany in your seal-grey machine. You're out of your office so often it's a waste of the tax-payer's money ... etcetera, etcetera...'

'So what else is new?'

They laughed, and terminated the call together.

Three

In Berlin, Pappenheim called Berger and Reimer into his office.

'A little job for you two,' he told them. 'Discreet cover.'

'We can be very discreet,' Reimer said.

'You won't be so eager when I tell you the target,' Pappenheim remarked sourly.

'Should we worry?' Berger asked.

'It could be dangerous. Very. Worse, you've got to ensure he stays alive ... without his knowing you're around. That goes for just about everybody else.'

'So who's the opposition?' Reimer asked.

Pappenheim blew a triple set of smoke rings in Reimer's general direction. 'We don't know.'

'Oh,' Berger said. 'An easy one. And who's this so-important target ... sir?'

Pappenheim grinned at her without humour. 'You know that nasty little man on the edge of decent politics who thinks he's got all the answers for Germany and hopes to be Chancellor one day?'

Reimer groaned. 'Not Heinrich Gauer! Don't do this to us, Boss. In our guts ... we would prefer to stand and watch, instead of interfering.'

'I don't like his politics any more than you do ... and if it's any consolation, neither does the *Hauptkommissar* . But ... we are the police. I shouldn't have to tell you what that means.'

'No, sir.'

'Good. I hate barking at my own people ... you two most of all. So get out there and do the job I know you can.'

They nodded, and turned to go.

'And Berger ... Reimer...'

They paused.

'Don't get any more holes in you than the ones nature gave you ... or I'll be so upset, I'll add a few of my own.'

They grinned at him and went out.

'I mean it,' he said to the smoke ring he blew at the ceiling.

Bonn. 17.30 hours.

The rain had not come to Bonn, making it a proper summer's day. Müller had used the stop at Börde-Nord to fill up with petrol and to book a room for the night at a Bonn-Hardtberg hotel. He had then made a non-stop, high-speed run to the former capital. There was plenty of light left in the day as he now cruised in the villa district, towards where the Romeo in the BMW had been shot.

When he turned into the street, the first thing he saw was the police tape barring further access. It was still some distance away

71

but the broadside-on, green and white patrol car and the two officers in front of the house emphasized the point. Not keen to introduce himself at this stage, it was the last thing Müller wanted. He had hoped that the crime scene would have been cleared by now, and any family members in the house moved to safety.

He slowed to a stop.

The policemen were now looking with casual curiosity in his direction, but they seemed more interested in the car itself.

In front of the house, one of the two officers said, 'Look at that thing. It looks ready to fly.'

'Wonder how many speeding tickets *he*'s got,' the other remarked with a knowing smirk.

'He can afford this, he can afford the tickets.'

'Berlin number plate. From the big new capital to the small, old and forgotten one. Even Beethoven being born here couldn't save us.'

'Perhaps he lost his way,' the first one suggested. He too hated the fact that Bonn had lost out to brash, rejuvenated Berlin.

They both laughed.

A clean-shaven, stocky man in civilian clothes and a bristle haircut came out of the house, and walked down the drive towards the two officers.

'Share the joke?' he said to them.

The first policeman jerked his head in the

72

direction of Müller's car. 'Rich Berlin boy took a wrong turning. Perhaps he got the Bs mixed up.' He grinned.

The man in civilian clothes frowned briefly. 'Perhaps. Let's check, shall we? You two wait here.'

He lifted a section of the loosely hung tape, stooped his way through, and began walking towards the Porsche while the others looked on expectantly.

Müller watched as the stocky man approached, then slowly climbed out just before he reached the car.

The man studied him with a sideways look, head slightly lowered. *'Hauptkommissar* Müller?'

Müller showed no surprise, though he was taken aback. And though he had guessed, he still asked, 'And you are?'

'Stefan Segelmann, sir. Pappi said you'd be coming here.'

'And he got you to come all the way to Bonn just to welcome me?'

'I can understand your being suspicious ... but I am Segelmann. Pappi described your car. Hard to miss.' Segelmann gave a brief smile. 'If you want my ID...'

'Not necessary,' Müller said. 'I won't shake hands, though. No need for the officers to realize I'm anything but a tourist.'

'They're already making jokes about rich Berliners mistaking Bonn for Berlin.'

'I'll bet they are,' Müller said, glancing in

the direction of the curious policemen.

'So ... how can I help?'

'I'd been hoping the scene would have been cleared by now...' Müller began.

Segelmann gave a tiny, quick smile. 'Oh it is. This is my little charade. The officers believe I'm doing an additional check. In fact, I was waiting for you to turn up.'

It was Müller's turn to smile briefly. 'Pappi was right about you. And how do we get rid of the watchers?'

'Easily. I'll tell them I'm finished. They'll be very happy to leave. They've been here all afternoon.'

'Alright. Since they think I'm lost, we might as well prove them right. Make a show of giving me directions. I'll leave the area, then return in about thirty minutes.'

'Do you want me to wait? I've got my own car. I don't have to leave with them.'

As Segelmann had been so accommodating, Müller decided it would be unkind of him to refuse. 'As long as I'm not messing up your plans...'

'Not at all. I'll be here.'

Müller nodded. 'Thank you. See you in half an hour.' He re-entered the car as Segelmann returned to the waiting policemen.

'You were right,' Segelmann told them as he came up. 'He was lost. I gave him directions.'

'We saw,' one said. 'Perhaps he'll end up in Berlin this time.'

The two patrolmen laughed again.

74

Segelmann kept a straight face. 'All finished here, in any case, so you two can push off.'

'Thank God for that,' the other said with relief. 'The place is empty now, anyway...' He stopped, looking at Segelmann warily. 'What I mean—'

'It's OK, Walter. I appreciate you've both been here most of the afternoon ... so off you go. Leave the tape for now.'

Both policemen nodded at him thankfully, and got into their car. Within seconds, they were driving away from there.

When Müller returned, there was no sign of Segelmann; but the police tape was still in place.

He did not go into the house, choosing instead to remain by the car. After five minutes of waiting, he began to feel the hairs on his back rising. He looked about him warily, and decided to call Pappenheim. He got out his mobile.

Pappenheim was still there.

'Pappi ... how well do you know Segelmann?'

'Very well indeed. Years and years...'

'Is he stocky, with a brushy haircut?'

'That would be difficult. He's thin, and bald...' Pappenheim's voice faded abruptly.

'Stupid! *Stupid!*' Müller said tightly of himself.

'What happened?' Pappenheim enquired sharply.

Müller told him.

'I'll try his office,' Pappenheim said briskly.

As he waited, Müller continued to look about him, wondering if he were under surreptitious scrutiny. The tiny hairs along his spine still felt as if they wanted to push through his shirt. The big Beretta 92R in the shoulder holster beneath his lightweight jacket was suddenly a pressure that needed to be relieved. He resisted the urge to draw the weapon.

Pappenheim was back. 'Any sign?'

'Nothing,' Müller said.

'Well ... he's not in his office...'

'If I haven't been talking to Segelmann ... who the hell was it?'

'I hate to say it,' Pappenheim remarked grimly. 'And I hope Stefan is alright.'

'If that was the bastard we're dealing with,' Müller said, 'then he is as bold as he is dangerous. Warped sense of humour too. "My little charade"...'

'What?'

'Something he said. He also said he was waiting for me to turn up ... and even offered to show me his ID.'

'Hard nerves. But how could he know where you would be?'

'That, Pappi, is the big question. We both know my car cannot be bugged, because of its sensors...'

'Don't forget he has your direct line ... if he is the one...'

'Even in the unlikely event of his being able

76

to burn through our office systems to piggy-back, you and I have said nothing on it to...' Müller paused.

'We're having the same thoughts,' Pappen-heim said.

Müller said nothing. Instead, he took the mobile away from his ear to stare at it, then briefly spoke. 'I'll be in touch.'

He ended the transmission, tight-lipped, and looked slowly about him once more.

'Hitching a ride on my mobile, are you?' he muttered to his unknown adversary. 'Let's see how you enjoy it from now on.'

He was about to re-enter the car when movement at the corner of his eye made him crouch behind it as he searched out the direction. A thinnish man with a bald head was staggering out of the villa. This had to be the real Segelmann. Even so, Müller waited, just in case.

Segelmann walked unsteadily down the drive, rubbing the back of his neck tenderly. Müller checked about him, but could neither sense nor see anything that was immediately dangerous. He had to move.

Quickly, he rose from cover and hurried towards the unsteady figure. 'Segelmann?'

The man paused, weaving slightly as if drunk, and gazed uncertainly at Müller. *'Haupt ... Hauptkommissar* Müller...?'

Müller nodded, reaching out a hand to steady Segelmann. 'Yes.'

'Stef ... Stefan Segelmann. Sorry. He took me like I was a rookie...'

77

'Don't worry about it,' Müller said grimly. 'You were not the only one. Come on. We'd better get you to a hospital. What happened?'

'He got past the boys outside,' Segelmann replied haltingly as they made for Müller's car. 'While I was in the house. He showed me a proper ID ... an *Oberkommissar* Renner. There was absolutely nothing wrong with that ID. Next thing I know, something very sharp stings me in the neck ... and that was it ... until you saw me back there. My turn to ask what happened.'

Müller helped him into the car as he explained what had occurred with the fake Segelmann.

'The bastard!' Segelmann uttered with some feeling as Müller got in behind the wheel. He continued to rub the back of his neck. 'Using my damned name. What the hell ... did he put in me?'

Müller started the car. 'Hopefully, nothing more than a basic knockout drug. The doctors will be able to tell ... Where's the nearest hospital?'

'Not far. I'll show you. My car...'

'Can be picked up later.'

Müller drove away.

The man who had impersonated Segelmann was talking to a couple in their garden. Screened by bushes, neither he nor the couple could be seen from the road.

He smiled to himself as he heard the Porsche go by.

'Well thank you very much for your kind help,' he said to the couple. 'I'll be on my way.'

'But we haven't been much help at all,' the husband protested regretfully. 'We didn't see or hear anything, *Oberkommissar*. Wish we could have been more helpful.'

'Oh you have. Believe me. Thank you again. We will not be troubling you any further.'

He smiled at them, and walked away, leaving them looking as if they really wished they could have been much more helpful.

'What a nice policeman,' the woman commented wistfully. 'If only they were all like that.'

'They're only human,' the man said philosophically. 'Some good, some bad ... like the rest of us.'

As he stopped the Porsche near the hospital's emergency entrance, Müller said to Segelmann, 'Just follow my lead.'

Still groggy, Segelmann nodded.

Müller helped him out, then half-carried him the short distance to the building.

As they entered, a staff member said, 'You can't—'

'This is a police officer!' Müller interrupted sharply. '*Oberkommissar* Segelmann. I found him wandering around. There's something wrong with his neck. Better get someone to check him out right away ... unless you want to be responsible if it's something serious.'

The man's attitude underwent a rapid

79

transformation. 'I'll take him. Are you—'

'Do you want to waste time with petty bureaucracy while this man could be dying?' Müller barked sharply.

'No! No ... I'll take him to a doctor right away.'

'Thank you. You can always check his ID while he is being examined.'

'Yes. Yes.'

The man hurried away as fast as he could with Segelmann.

'Everyone wants to cover his back,' Müller said to himself.

He looked for and found a public telephone, then called Pappenheim.

'I found Segelmann,' he began when Pappenheim had answered.

'Thank God,' Pappenheim said with relief. 'What the hell happened?'

Müller explained.

'But Stefan's an old pro,' Pappenheim said. 'How could he fall for something like that?'

'Don't be too hard on him. I fell for it too. I made the fundamental mistake of allowing my expectations to cloud my reason.'

'I'm not going to make it easy for you...'

'Didn't think you would.'

'It was stupid...'

'Thank you, Pappi. I've been there.' Müller could sense Pappenheim's grin. 'And you can wipe that grin off your face.'

'You've got powers that even allow you to see down telephones? My, my ... So what did that lowlife put into Stefan?'

'Perhaps no more than something to put him out for a while. I'll remain here just long enough to find out.'

'I see by my display you're on a public phone. Is this how we communicate from now on?'

'As we both agree he's been piggy-backing, we should ... for now. We shouldn't even use the scrambler. Talk to our resident electronics genius Herman Spyros. Renner – or whoever he is – may also be able to break through it; but Spyros may be able to tell us whether that's possible ... or not. The unit on my mobile is supposed to be hardened against this sort of thing ... but we both know there isn't a defensive system yet invented that can't be penetrated, given enough time.'

'OK. I'll have a word with old Herman. Should I—'

'Just a moment. Someone's coming ... a doctor. Perhaps he'll have news of Segelmann. I'll call you.'

Müller hung up just as a tall man in a doctor's smock came up to him.

'I'm Dr Lindtke,' he said to Müller. 'You brought in Herr Segelmann, I believe?'

Müller nodded. 'How is he?'

'Perfectly OK. He was given a common anaesthetic ... but whoever did it knew how to administer the drug. The point of entry was professionally done. Although a potent dose was given, your colleague is a healthy man. His recovery will be fairly rapid and he'll be quite fit for duty within a few hours. But keep a lookout for any signs of tinnitus, light-head-edness, confusion or numbness However, nothing we have seen points to any side effects. There are two other possible stages, both with symptoms of increasing serious-ness. Don't wait for those.' Then the doctor gave a knowing smile. 'No names.'

Müller gave a slight frown. 'No names?'

'I asked Herr Segelmann whether he knew you, his Samaritan ... so to speak. He said he'd appreciate it if I did not ask.'

'I ... see.'

'You government people have your rea-sons...'

'Er ... yes.'

'You can see him if you wish. He is fit to leave.'

'Thank you, Doctor. If you'll show me...'

'Of course. Please come with me.'

A bemused Müller followed, wondering what Segelmann had actually said to the doctor.

'He wanted your details for his report,' Segelmann began as they reached the area where the phones were. 'I imagined at least ten copies of it floating around, so I said you were on government business – which is true – and that the paperwork was unnecessary...'

'Well, you've got him thinking I'm some sort of spy.'

Segelmann, looking better by the minute, gave a lopsided smile. 'He's been watching all the wrong movies.'

Müller pointed to the phones. 'Perhaps you should give Pappi a call. He's been worried about you.'

'He can be an old hen sometimes.'

'I won't tell him you said that.'

'I feel like an idiot.'

'He can tell you that. He's already told me off for getting conned.'

'*He* told *you* off? You're his senior officer.'

'Have you ever known Pappi to be bothered by senior officers?'

Segelmann grinned. 'Never.'

'Well then. You're of equal rank, so call the man and take your medicine.'

Segelmann did so and winced when Pappenheim answered.

A couple of minutes later, Segelmann ruefully handed the phone over to Müller. 'Thank God I'm not one of his subordinates.'

'I heard that!' Pappenheim said in Müller's ear.

'It's me, Pappi,' Müller said.

'Ah! Well...'

'We're going back to the house.' Müller glanced at Segelmann to see if he wanted to accompany him.

Segelmann nodded.

'I'll get back to you later,' Müller continued.

'I've talked to Herman.'

'And?'

'He's working on something. But he thinks your unit's sufficiently hardened. So it's up to you.'

'I'll play safe for the time being. There's too much we don't know.'

'Wise decision.'

'Alright, Pappi. We'll talk later.'

'All things considered, I won't say watch your back. You've had your warning.'

'You're all heart, Pappi.'

'My heart is pure ... therefore I must be a good man.'

The Porsche rumbled slowly along a narrow street in the villa district. Müller pulled into a roadside parking slot and stopped.

'We walk from here,' he said to Segelmann. 'Whatever Renner was looking for, he can't have found it. He could be back in there.'

'He may not have been looking for anything.'

'True. He claims to have been waiting for me. Flattering, but I always look for the extra reasons.'

'Pappi did not tell me what's behind all this. I suppose you won't either.'

'I can't.'

Segelmann nodded to himself. 'Understood. Can we stop by my car first? It's just round the corner from the villa. I need to get something from it.'

'Alright. Are you sure you're fit enough for this? The doctor said a few hours...'

'I'm fit.'

They got out of the Porsche.

Segelmann studied it critically. 'Can I get one like that?'

'No.'

'Worth a try.'

They went to where Segelmann had left his car, out of sight of anyone within the dead man's house. He unlocked the boot and took out a pump-action shotgun with a folding stock.

Müller stared at it. 'Where did you get that?'

'From a cop in—'

'Don't tell me. Chicago.'

Segelmann was busy getting spare rounds from the boot. 'How did you know?' He paused briefly to look at Müller before continuing to ferret.

'I know these things. Pappi was right about you,' Müller went on, then added drily, 'At least this time I'm saying it to the right person.'

Finally satisfied, Segelmann shut and locked the boot. He stuffed the spare rounds into every available pocket.

'Got this as a present when the cop came to visit,' he said.

'Is it approved for use?' Müller took out his Beretta, and checked it.

'Is that?' Segelmann countered, looking at the massive automatic.

'Don't be rude to your superior officer. Now let's see if anything's infesting that house.'

They worked their way to the villa, coming at it from two sides. The door was still as Segelmann had left it. Covering each other with Müller leading, they cautiously entered. They saw no one.

They split up, working their way into every room on the ground floor. Still no one.

They made their way up the stairs. Nothing on the second floor. On the top floor, Müller entered the main bedroom. Clothes were strewn all over the place, and over a massive four-poster bed. The bedclothes had also been roughly hauled off and the mattress upturned. Someone had been searching without bothering to be patient, or respectful. Had he and Segelmann interrupted the search?

Müller carefully checked out the room. No one. He was just about to leave when someone said, 'Bad move.' The German was vaguely accented. Müller froze.

'This thing against your spine is a very nasty pump-action shotgun. If you force me to use it, there won't be much of your back left.' Segelmann, talking to the person behind Müller.

Müller turned, and saw that the shotgun was indeed against the man's back. It wasn't the man who called himself Renner.

Müller took away the automatic the man had been pointing at him. He looked at it closely. 'Makarov. Long way from home. But these days, perhaps not. Anyone seems able to buy them.' He made the weapon safe, then put it in a jacket pocket. 'You are?'

The man, thickset with dark cropped hair and a Stalin moustache, did not respond.

'I hate repeating myself,' Müller said. He glanced at Segelmann. 'Have you got handcuffs?'

'Always.'

'You have a customer.' Müller pointed the Beretta at the man. 'Any move *you* make, *will* be a bad one.'

The silent man did not resist as Segelmann put the handcuffs on. He smirked at Müller.

'Cuff him to the bed,' Müller told Segelmann. 'Check him for an ID, then let's see what other rats are in here.'

'Will you please move over to the bed, sir?' Segelmann said to the man politely.

The man obeyed, still smirking, while Selgelmann secured him to the heavy iron bed and then searched him.

'Not a single piece of paper,' Segelmann said when he had finished. 'Not even a wallet, or money. No credit cards. This is Herr Nobody.'

'I really don't like this,' Müller said, watching the door.

The smirking man said nothing.

'He might shout a warning,' Segelmann cautioned.

'That won't help anyone coming to look. Besides, he would have shouted before now.'

The man decided to end his silence. 'You're in above your head.'

Müller turned back to him. 'So ... it speaks. Are there more of you in this house?'

'No.'

'Where is Renner?'

87

'Who is Renner?'

'We can play this game till the next ice age,' Müller said, 'but I have neither the time, nor the inclination. I almost wish you had tried to shoot me. Then you would have had your back shattered by a shotgun blast, and we would be one problem short.'

'But you'd be dead too.'

'I doubt it. My colleague is very fast, and short on patience.'

For reply, the man went back to his smirking.

'Don't go away,' Müller said as he and Segelmann left.

They combed the house thoroughly, Segelmann acting as rearguard for Müller, pump gun seemingly hungry for action.

But no one came to disturb them. By this time, darkness was approaching.

'Whatever they were looking for,' Müller said, 'they've either already found it ... or it never was here.'

'We could always ask our friend upstairs ... a little harder.'

'If you're thinking of frightening him, forget it. Earlier today I saw some characters who come from the same mould. *He* has probably done things that would make you or I vomit. People like that are frightened of just one thing ... their own mortality ... perhaps in some cases, not even that. And since we can't shoot him in cold blood ... which he is well aware of, we're stuck...' Müller paused. Segelmann was rubbing at his neck. 'Are you alright?'

'I'm fine. I would just like to meet up with that bastard again.'

'You might just get your chance ... but this time, treat him as you would a striking cobra: with your survival instincts on red alert. Come on. Let's leave this place.'

'What about the smiler upstairs?'

'Leave him. His friends will be back for him.'

'I don't understand,' Segelmann mildly protested as they left the villa.

'Let's get to your car,' Müller said, putting his gun back into its holster.

When they got there, he stood to one side thoughtfully, while Segelmann reluctantly put the unused shotgun back into the boot. The spare rounds followed, then Segelmann shut and locked it.

'Can you find two officers who would pass as a student couple?' Müller asked.

'I know a local *Kommissar* who should be on duty right now. He could get us a pair like that.'

'Good. Sure you're OK to drive?'

'I am OK. Honestly.'

'Alright,' Müller said. 'Go find your *Kommissar* ... *Don't* call him on your radio. Meet him in person. Tell him to find them quickly. If they're not on duty, he should drag them back on.'

'The two I'm thinking of don't live far from here, and really are students ... part-time at the university. Both are studying for degrees. They're ambitious...'

'Good for them. Have your *Kommissar* get them out here fast. They are to unobtrusively observe who returns to the villa ... *but make no move whatsoever to interfere.* They are no match for these people. When they've reported what they've seen, call Pappi.'

'Got it,' Segelmann said. 'I won't ask where you're off to.'

'I would not answer.'

Segelmann gave a rueful smile. 'I might have guessed.' He held out a hand. 'Nice working with you. Let me know if and when.'

Müller shook the hand. 'I will. And watch that neck. If you feel any dizziness...'

'Call the doc,' Segelmann said, getting into his car. 'I know. He told me.'

He started the engine.

Müller was still thoughtful. Then, suddenly, he put a hand on the door. 'Of course! The damned car!'

Segelmann cut the engine. 'What?'

'The BMW. Where is it?'

'In the unit garage of the *Kommissar* I just told you about.' Segelmann was looking up at Müller with a slight frown.

Müller went round to open the passenger door and climbed in. 'Back to my car. I'll follow you to your *Kommissar*. I want to see that BMW. Let us hope Renner, or whoever he is, hasn't had the same thought as yet.'

The BMW was in a quarantine area, well

away from other vehicles.

The *Kommissar* on duty was called Lessinger. Segelmann had obtained access without having to disclose Müller's presence. He had also got Lessinger to assign the two officers – who had indeed been off duty – to carry out the unobtrusive surveillance of the villa. Two phone calls and they were on station within ten minutes of Segelmann's talk with Lessinger.

Lessinger was now with Segelmann, near the BMW.

'Do you know what you're looking for?' Lessinger asked.

'Not really.'

Lessinger handed over the bunch of keys that had been in the BMW at the time of the shooting. 'You'll have to make it quick ... and don't leave any marks. Some bigwigs want to inspect it.'

'Really?' Segelmann remarked casually. 'Any idea?'

Lessinger shook his head. 'No one's told us. I've got an instruction that tells me he or they could come over tonight, or tomorrow morning. With luck, they'll turn up after I've gone off duty, and Wertz can have the headache. I'm off back upstairs. Be as quick as you can, will you?'

'I will. And thanks again, Hansi.'

'No problem,' Hans Lessinger said.

Segelmann waited until Lessinger had been gone for at least five minutes before opening a door to let Müller in to the garage.

'All set?' Müller asked.

'I've got the keys.' Segelmann held them up.

'Excellent. We must do this quickly.'

'Lessinger said the same thing, almost ... but his reasons are very different. Some "bigwig" – according to him – is coming to look at the BMW ... tonight, or tomorrow morning.'

'Renner?'

'He couldn't say. No one's informed him. All he has is the instruction.'

'If it *is* Renner, we must be out of here long before he arrives. He's not likely to use the same name, either. Did you tell Lessinger about what happened?'

'No.'

'Good. It will save his life if he doesn't react. Renner isn't likely to be so stupid as to try anything inside a police building, unless provoked into doing so. He'll want to come in here, search the car, then leave without any fuss. So we'd better find whatever it is first.'

'Hell of a business,' Segelmann said. 'With the diplomats and spies long gone...'

'You thought all this sort of thing had migrated to Berlin.'

'Well ... yes.'

'It has ... but as you know, the whole of Europe is a new battleground for all our nightmares ... which come in many guises these days.'

'Who would be a policeman, eh?'

'Who indeed.'

★ ★ ★

The couple, arms about each other, walked down the street towards the villa until they came to the police tape. They turned left into a corner and after a few metres sat on a low wall that bordered someone's garden. Their position gave them a perfect view of the villa. It was now dark enough for the street lights to be on, but none showed within the house itself.

At infrequent intervals, a vehicle would rumble by. As the evening was a fine one, there was also a trickle of walkers taking in the night air; and even an occasional jogger would pound wearily past. The couple's presence was therefore quite normal. They seemed totally occupied with each other.

About half an hour after their arrival, the bristle-haired man strode past them without interest. He crossed the road to walk up the drive and into the villa.

In the villa, the man with the many IDs had a weapon out as he slowly made his way on silent feet, checking every floor, before moving to the next. He did not call out.

When he eventually reached the master bedroom, he paused outside to listen. The barest sound of metal on metal came through. He waited.

'Bastards!' came a harsh grumble.

He put a hand through to switch on the light in the bedroom. The man with the moustache, still secured to the bed, blinked back at him.

'You took your bloody time!' the shackled

man snapped in a language that was not German. 'Have you any idea how many hours I've been shackled to this thing?'

The other put his automatic away and actually smiled. 'I had things to do.' Though he clearly understood the language, he spoke German. 'So he didn't even arrest you,' he continued. 'He left you here like a Judas goat. This means he's got people outside to check who came to get you. Any one of those I just passed could be police. I wonder which ... the jogger who nearly bumped into me? One or two of the strollers? The couple eating each other's faces? I like the way his mind works.'

'Well you can admire him all you like,' the tethered man snarled, reverting to German. 'Just get me out of these things!'

'What did you tell him?'

'Nothing. What do you think I am? Come on! Get these damned things off me!'

'And did you find it?'

'No. Nothing here. I took the place apart.'

'I can see that.'

'You didn't find anything ... I didn't find anything. So what now?' The man rattled the handcuffs against the bed. 'And get these bastard things off!'

'What now?' came the soft response. The weapon was out again and a silencer was swiftly screwed on to it.

The man barely had time to register what was happening before the gun was pointed at him, and fired twice. His mouth stretched open, but only a strange gargling sound came out. His eyes, wide, scared and enraged at the same time, stared at his killer.

'That's what now,' the other said, and turned away.

The man's dying breaths wheezed out of him faintly, like an engine slowly running out of steam; and his staring eyes, swivelling almost of their own volition, followed the departing shape, who very calmly switched off the lights.

'Sleep well,' was the last thing he heard.

In the police garage Müller stood by the open boot of the BMW, staring at the car.

'I've missed something,' he said.

'But what?' Segelmann looked slightly frustrated. 'Short of taking the car apart piece by piece, we've looked everywhere ... inside, outside, underneath, in the boot, under the bonnet ... around the engine...'

'We don't need to take it apart. It has to be something that is accessible somehow, without having to go to such an extreme.'

Müller continued to stare at the BMW, while Segelmann looked at him enquiringly.

'Yes, I know,' Müller said. 'We're running out of time.'

'I didn't say...' Segelmann began awkwardly.

'No need to. I'm thinking the same thing myself. Where's the first-aid box?'

'Back in the boot ... but I've already checked it out. It's just a normal first-aid box...'

'I know. Let's have another look anyway.'

95

Segelmann got it out again and handed it to Müller.

'Thanks,' Müller said as he took it. 'I know, Stefan. I know. But sometimes ... just sometimes...'

Müller studied the box closely. There was no discernible seam running round the outside.

'No false bottom,' he said thoughtfully.

He opened it and began to take everything out, just as Segelmann had done before. He stared at the black lining on the bottom.

'And certainly nothing in here.'

Müller continued to stare at the lining. Suddenly, he lifted the box to eye level, then lowered it again.

'That lining is too high for the thickness of the casing,' he said, and began to probe at it with an index finger. He stopped. 'Bingo.'

He began to pull at the lining. It came away with a soft tearing sound as the adhesive released it. Underneath was a small catch that had been effectively masked by the thickness of the lining.

Müller slid the catch back, and a panel lifted slightly. 'A false bottom, after all.' He lifted the panel fully out.

Beneath was a thin folder with almost the same dimensions as the hidden compartment. He took out the folder, placed it carefully on the roof of the car, then began to put everything back the way it had been. With the panel and lining back in place, there was again no overt sign of the hidden section.

Segelmann was staring from the folder to the box, and back again. 'I'll be damned,' he said. He stared at the folder as if it were alive.

Müller was already replacing all the contents of the first-aid box. 'He was clever, our corpse. Right there before our very eyes, but not there at all.' He put the box back into the boot. 'Now Renner – or whoever – can look to his heart's content.' He picked up the folder. 'Can't let you see this, Stefan.'

Segelmann raised a hand in surrender. 'I don't want to know what's in there. You were never here, and I never brought you here.'

'Pappi, as usual, chose well,' Müller said.

'I have a lot of time for Pappi.'

'When those two by the villa report in, send the results, as I've said, to Pappi.'

'Will do.'

Müller held out a hand. 'Thanks, Stefan.'

Segelmann shook it. 'Any time. If you should need me again...'

'Don't call you?'

Segelmann grinned. 'Call me. I want to pay that bastard back.'

'I'll see what I can do.'

The killer walked unhurriedly away from the villa. The couple, he noticed, were gone; but the jogger was not. He saw the man coming towards him, and braced himself for whatever action would be necessary.

But the man ran past without a glance, and continued running.

★ ★ ★

The hired Mercedes saloon came to a stop a short distance from Lessinger's police building. The driver got out, and unhurriedly walked the rest of the way. He entered, and approached the officer on duty at the reception desk.

He held out an ID. '*Hauptkommissar* Lörrandt, BKA,' he introduced himself. 'Your senior officer on duty, please. I am expected.'

This time, the bristle-haired man wore thick-rimmed glasses, and a dark wig that was so good, the officer had no reason to believe it was not real hair. The ID was itself perfect in every way.

'Yes, sir,' the officer said. 'Please come with me.' He turned to a colleague. 'Watch the desk will you?'

The other policeman nodded as the officer went out, followed by their visitor.

When they came to Lessinger's office, the uniformed man knocked and poked his head through. 'Chief, I have a *Hauptkommissar* Lörrandt from the *Bundeskriminalamt* to see you...'

'Ah yes. I'm expecting him. Thank you, Kristof.' Lessinger's voice did not betray the chagrin he felt at having to deal with this.

'Chief.' Kristof stood back to allow the newcomer to enter, then closed the door and returned to his desk.

Lessinger was on his feet, hand extended.

It was ignored. 'I don't have much time. So if we can dispense with the niceties, I'd like to see the car right away.'

Lessinger, stung by the rebuff, frowned. 'Of course,' he said tightly. 'I'll take you to it.' He took the keys to the BMW out of a drawer.

They went to the garage in total silence.

When they got to the BMW, the man who now called himself Lörrandt said, 'If you don't mind, I'd like to do this alone.'

'Naturally,' Lessinger said curtly. He handed the keys over, and left.

When he was once more on his own the man walked around the car slowly, a predator surveying its prey. He did so twice, studying it closely. It looked clean. There was no sign that it had been touched recently.

He immediately went to the boot and opened it. There was a purpose in his movements that said he knew precisely where to look. He took out the first-aid box and unceremoniously emptied it all over the floor of the boot. He lifted the lining and slipped the catch. He took out the panel.

For long seconds, he stared at the empty space; then, in a sudden fit of rage, he threw the box with great force against a wall. It hit with a resounding slam, bounced off the wall and crashed with loud echoes to the floor of the garage. He slammed the boot lid shut, its own echoes chasing the others.

Then he stood there, perfectly still in the lights of the garage, neck muscles corded as he fought to regain control.

'Müller!' he said at last through gritted teeth. 'Your destiny is coming.'

He went back up to Lessinger's office, and

barged in.

'Has that car been searched?'

Startled, Lessinger rose to his feet slowly and stared at him. 'Of course. A crime was committed in it...'

'I don't mean at the scene of the crime, or when it was first brought here. I mean more recently.'

Lessinger realized that his patience with the BKA *Hauptkommissar* was evaporating by the second; but rank protocol forced him to respond politely.

'*Oberkommissar* Segelmann...'

'*Segelmann?* Not Müller?'

Lessinger was genuinely puzzled. 'Who is Müller? Only Segelmann was here.'

'Only Segelmann,' came the muttered comment. 'Müller would not have allowed himself to be seen...'

'I tell you there was no Müller!'

The fake BKA man suddenly reached across the desk with both hands, grabbed Lessinger by the shirt and hauled him closer. *'Listen, you stupid provincial dwarf of a policeman...!'*

'Everything alright, Chief?' Kristof had again poked his head through.

The man let go abruptly. He threw the BMW keys on to Lessinger's desk. 'Morons!'

Without another word he brushed roughly past Kristof, slamming doors on his way out.

'Bit rude for a *Hauptkommissar* wasn't he?' Kristof said.

'Much more than rude,' Lessinger said,

adjusting his shirt.

'You OK, Chief?'

'I'm fine.'

'What an asshole,' Kristof said, looking at the slammed doors.

Four

Leonberg, near Stuttgart. 23.00 hours.

Ries and Pinic, in the yellow Golf with its pumped-up arches and wheels and loud music, cruised towards the parkland area and their rendezvous with the woman they were blackmailing.

Ries cut the music as they got closer.

'What if she lied and did not come, but the police are waiting instead?' Pinic asked worriedly. 'She's not going to come all the way out here on her own at this time of night.'

'Don't be stupid. Of course she'll come. She wouldn't want to lose her nice car, her apartment, which my father probably paid for, and all the other goodies she gets from him. If she involves the police, she'll lose it all because it will become public, and my mother will clean my father out for this. She'll be there. OK. We'll stop here and walk on. She might know the car. He might have told her about it.'

Ries slowly pulled off the road and into a small clearing, then cut the lights as he turned off the engine.

'Masks,' he said.

They pulled on black, full-head balaclava type masks with holes for the eyes and mouth.

'OK. Let's go!'

They got out, and began to make their way to where they had told the woman to meet them.

Soon they saw the Lexus Cabriolet with dipped headlights and roof down, parked by a tree. The backglow from the lights showed a solitary woman sitting in the driver's seat, looking anxiously about her.

'See?' Ries said triumphantly. 'Right by the tree as I told her. Wouldn't come, eh? Self-interest over common sense.'

'We've got to get her out of the car,' Pinic said as they drew closer. 'She can just throw the money at us, then drive off. How can we...?'

'You let me worry about that.'

They were soon close enough to see her properly. They paused by a big tree. She had still not realized they were there.

'She looks a bit Asian to me,' Pinic said. 'And older than I thought. When you said she sounded young...'

'She's not old,' Reis corrected. 'Perhaps thirty ... great age for women, they say, and perfect for guys our age. And as for being Asian ... she's only got a bit of the blood in there somewhere, but it looks good on her. So my father likes it a little exotic. Well ... so does his son. Anyway, why should *you* worry? Half of you is German. The rest comes from what used to be Yugoslavia. Just think of the fun we're going to have. You move round so that you come up from behind, but stay out of the lights. Alright. Let's do it.'

'Good evening!'

The woman gasped in fright when she saw the mask. She said nothing but kept staring at it, mesmerized.

'I'm glad you came,' Ries said. 'That was very smart. Got the money?'

She nodded urgently.

'Good. Now get out of the car!'

'No!' She was very frightened now. 'Please! Here...' She lifted a paper bag with handles. 'It's all in there. Please take it and let me go home. I've done what you asked.'

'Not everything.'

'What ... what else is there?'

'Did you tell your boyfriend?'

'No! I told no one...'

'Good girl.' Ries moved closer. 'Alright. I'll take the bag.'

This made her so happy, she looked as if she would faint with relief.

Ries, however, had other ideas. With her guard so completely down, he swiftly reached across, took the keys out of the ignition, and stepped back.

'Now ... will you get out?'

As her predicament dawned upon her, the terror returned with a vengeance.

'Oh God ... please! Don't do anything to

me. I won't tell anyone...'

'Get out of the fucking car, whore!'

She literally jumped at the suddenness of his shout. But now, she seemed stuck to the seat, so terrified had she become.

Impatiently, he reached for the handle and yanked the door open. In her desperation she tried to hang on to it, but was not strong enough.

He looked down. 'Well, well ... will you look at that ... A short skirt with a split. Very ... very nice. Get out! I'm losing my patience...' Ries made a beckoning motion, but not to her.

Her head swivelled round, and she saw Pinic's figure emerge from the darkness.

'Oh God ... no! Please don't do this...'

'Did you think of your boyfriend's wife when you were fucking him?' Ries yelled at her. 'Did you say please don't do it? Did you? *Did you?* Of course you didn't. You were too busy enjoying the ride. *Whore! Whore! Whore!* Let's see what you can do for us. *Out!'*

She began to cry.

'And now she cries,' Ries said contemptuously. 'Now she...'

He never finished. A great bloom erupted from his chest to shower her with a dark glistening that spattered her face, the car, and her clothes. He fell across the door and on to her.

She screamed and continued screaming in an increasingly demented, high-pitched keening that pierced the night and the ear.

Pinic, not understanding what had occurred and not wanting to believe what he had just witnessed, halted in mid-stride, staring in horror and instinctively placing his hands against his ears in an attempt to mute the terrible screaming. He waited too long. His head suddenly disintegrated, shards hurtling in all directions to vanish into the darkness.

The woman kept on screaming. She was still screaming when the police arrived.

In his hotel bedroom in Bonn, Müller lay propped up in bed and opened the folder he had taken from the first-aid box.

He began to read:

If you are reading this, it means they have got me.

My name is Karl Esske. It is not the name by which I am known to my wife and children here in Bonn. I was born in a small village in the former DDR state of Sachsen. I am a Romeo; but a member of a very special team of Romeos called Romeo Six. This is not because of the number of individuals in the team – there are more. The name comes from one of the most successful Romeos who ever operated. His codename was Romeo Six. We were never told who he was, only that we were named to honour a very illustrious operative. My rank at the time was captain.

In the beginning, none of us knew the identities of the other members of the team. We were meant to remain active even after the Wall came down. The team was commanded by a colonel of police, but we never knew his real name. He was introduced to us as Romeo Alpha, but I do not believe he was ever a Romeo at all. This was just his command name.

After the Wall came down, we tentatively tried to discover the whereabouts and identities of each other. The first I knew of this was an unstamped letter addressed to me at my home as Karl Esske. My wife was out that day – a Saturday – and I had the impression that this was known by the person who had left it. In the letter was a telephone number. That was all. I called it, and discovered for the first time that the Romeos were trying to find each other.

There was the belief that something had gone wrong with the operation. I heard nothing more for some time. Then another letter arrived. I was warned that whatever had gone wrong was now seriously awry. A loose cannon was about, planning to terminate Romeo Six. No reasons were given for this.

I have therefore decided to put down all that I know, in case the worst happens. One name I do know from the days before we were made fully operational was a major of police called Heurath.

However, I have no idea what his real status was. I believe he was promoted to lieutenant-colonel just before I left on my mission. I have never seen him since.

Some of the Romeo Six: Myself. Udo Hellmann, Heinrich Gauer, Martin Ries, Paul Eisenberg, Franz Gracht (these are the names by which they are now known).

Later in this statement, I shall set down dates and events in chronological order, as well as more names.

The writing ended. It was clear that Esske had much more to put down, but had begun to unburden himself far too late. Someone had prematurely terminated his narrative.

Müller slowly closed the folder. Esske had cleared a little of the fog but had also created some of his own, because of his sudden demise. Whoever had turned the house upside down looking for this incomplete document had obviously believed – *feared* – there was much more. Even so, it contained information that even the blue-folder boys knew nothing of; perhaps.

Müller looked at the folder. 'Incomplete as you are, you are dangerous to somebody ... and to me too, for that matter, because that somebody may well suspect that I've got you.'

He was just about to put out the light when his mobile buzzed. He picked it up, knowing it could only be Pappenheim.

'Should you be calling me on this?'

'Hit the scrambler.'

Müller did so. Pappenheim would not have called without very good reason.

'Can you hear me?' Pappenheim asked.

'Very clearly, if a little spacey.'

'Then it's working. Anyone trying to piggyback will hear nothing but emptiness – but worse for him, Herman has added a little gizmo to my phone that automatically locks on to any attempt to piggy, and zaps to the source, where two things will happen: the source will be logged, and then any machine being used will crash. End of system, end of piggy. Neat, wouldn't you say?'

'Very. Thank our genius.'

'Already done so. He just cost you six bottles of the finest from your wine cellar ... and I mean finest ... not supermarket stuff.'

'I like it when you give people presents from me.'

'Smile when you say that.'

'I'm smiling so much it hurts.'

'Oh good. Smiling keeps you young. So ... did I wake you?'

'No. I was reading.'

'Like smiling, reading's good for you.'

'That depends on the material.'

'Ah-ha! Something interesting happen during the communications blackout?'

'I found something.'

'Ah-ha!' Pappenheim repeated. 'But, of course, you don't want to talk about it at the moment.'

'Not even though Herman Spyros has built us a safe cocoon.'

'Then I'll have to wait.'

'You will ... but not too long. I'll be on my way back after I've been to Mainz.'

'Well, I have two hot pieces of info for you. Segelmann called. It seems Lessinger had a visitor.'

'The man with the needle.'

'You're so quick sometimes,' Pappenheim said cheerfully. 'By all accounts, he was not a happy man at all. Seems he lost it and actually manhandled poor old Lessinger in his own office. Called him a stupid, provincial dwarf of a policeman. Nice turn of phrase, that. What *did* you do to him?'

'Spoiled his fun.'

'You must have. He took it out on a first-aid box. Do you know why he would do that? Seems deviant to me.'

'I know exactly why.'

'Uh-oh. I should wait to hear about that too, I think.'

'You should.'

'Alright, next item. Again from Segelmann. The same needle-man returned to the villa before he tried to lift Lessinger out of his chair. Segelmann took a team in to check ... and found that Herr Nobody – as Stefan calls him – whom you two had left nicely cuffed to the bed, had two neat holes in him. No points for guessing who did the drilling. Going by Stefan's description, I'll do some checking. Should have something on the nobody by the time you're back. Lessinger's visitor by the way had dark hair, wore glasses and

110

called himself Lörrandt, promoted himself to *Hauptkommissar*, no less, and said he was from the BKA. Again, the ID was perfect. Sure it's the same person?'

'Definitely. This is a man who can hide in plain sight. He's a chameleon.'

'Item three...'

'There's a three? You said two.'

'So who's counting? It's been a busy night. Baden-Württemberg this time. A park near Stuttgart had some excitement. Two young criminals were sniped to death. Pro hit. Why? Well may you ask ... Seems they were blackmailing a woman, and were planning some nasty fun with her too, as dessert. Then things got red as one lost his chest over her and her car, and the other lost his head. Do you see a connection?'

'Not really ... no.'

'Neither do I,' Pappenheim said after a pause. 'But there's something very strange about the incident. The woman, who was ... not surprisingly ... extremely hysterical, kept babbling on about a phone which belonged to her lover, a married man. Seems the little ticks hacked into its phone book, got her number and sought to blackmail her. She decided to meet them, foolish woman. I have the nagging feeling the entire thing was set up.'

'Not by the woman, surely.'

'Not by her at all ... but perhaps by the shooter.'

'To what end?'

'I'm not sure as yet, but I'm working on it. Seems the ticks were well known as mobile phone thieves, and tended to make nuisance calls or worse. There is a suspicion – but no real proof ... victim refused to talk – that these sickos used a similar ploy to gang-rape a young girl ... so I can't feel sorry for them. They deserved what they got.'

'Perhaps the shooter was out for revenge and suckered them...'

'Perhaps. On the other hand ... given the way this whole business is shaping, it could be something far more complex. A member of the girl's family, or a boyfriend, would not have been so clinical. This was a well-laid trap which ended in an execution, given the details. The woman talked so much the investigators wished she would shut up.'

'Do you have their names?'

'I do. One is a Jörg Pinic ... mother German, father from what used to be Yugoslavia ... and the other a Helmut Ries, son of Martin Ries, very rich businessman and side-stepper. It gets better ... The woman's boyfriend is none other than Ries senior. Seems the son wanted to share daddy's little nightcap. A psychologist would have fun with this. Hello? You've gone very quiet...'

'Follow this one up, Pappi. Find out all you can.'

'You're telling me that this...'

'I'm telling you. Believe it.'

'Alright. I'll follow through. I won't ask why you think I should.'

'You'll know soon enough.'

'Good enough for me.'

'And get some sleep,' Müller said.

'I can doze right here in the office. Work to do. And don't you get your back into any crosshairs.'

'Not if I can help it.'

'Alright then.'

They ended the call together.

In a room in Berlin, a man ripped the headphones off his head.

'*Shiiit!*' he yelled in pain.

His companion looked at him. 'What was that all about?'

'He knows.'

'What do you mean "he knows"?'

'I just got the full blast from a jammer. My ears will be ringing for a week.'

'They will have sent a tracer too.'

'Don't worry. I shut down in time. Anyway, I think our machine also just crashed out.'

'We'll have to try something else.'

'It will have to be quick. This way's dead for good. Müller's no fool.'

'No one's said he is.'

In his hotel room, Müller got out of bed, removed the two sheets of Esske's unfinished statement from the protecting cover, and folded them together neatly, so that they would fit into the pouch of one of the two spare magazines attached to his holster. He then tore the plain folder into very tiny pieces, and flushed them down the toilet.

He checked that the lock on the door to his room was fully home, and left the key half-turned in it to prevent even key entry. He returned to bed, put out the bedside lamp and settled down for the night, keeping the Beretta very close to hand. The Makarov he had taken from the unknown man was locked away in the glove box of the Porsche.

He did not fall asleep immediately.

Who, he wondered, was the original Romeo Six of whom Esske had written so admiringly?

The *Isabella Lütz* cruised in the darkness towards Mainz.

By virtue of the silent technology incorporated into her refurbishment, her engines were remarkably quiet; and her guest suites, well insulated from the noises and vibrations normally associated with vessels of her type, ensured an undisturbed night's sleep. As a result, she appeared to glide up the river, a sibilant ghost on her night-time journey.

Udo Hellmann stood on the upper starboard deck and watched as the lights of the western bank of the river drifted past. It was always beautiful to see, he thought. He loved the Rhine, and the job he did. But for how much longer would he be able to enjoy it?

Unlike so many other nights when – sometimes accompanied by his wife, sometimes by his daughters – he had stood at this very spot and had enjoyed every passing second, this

114

night was full of foreboding. He no longer saw the beauty of it. Instead, the night served to hide unseen, and unknown, enemies. The past was harnessing its legions to hurl against him.

He was about to turn away, when he spotted movement on the lower deck. He leaned slightly over to look down. In the soft glow of the deck lighting, he could see it was the American woman. She had come out of her suite to look at the passing nightscape.

Sensing she was being watched, she turned round and looked up. 'Captain Hellmann.' She spoke softly, but her voice carried clearly to him on the night air. 'May I come up?'

'Be my guest, Miss Harris,' he replied in perfect English. He waited as she made her way to the upper deck. 'Can't sleep?' he continued as she joined him.

'I've no problem sleeping. I just came out for some night air. I find it incredibly beautiful to watch the lights float by.'

Hellmann returned his attention to the land. 'It is beautiful.'

'I could almost hear a sigh in there,' she said. 'You sound as if you're saying goodbye to it.'

'I certainly didn't mean to, Miss Harris. But sometimes...' He stopped, retreating into his thoughts.

'Look,' she said. 'I'm obviously disturbing you. I'm sorry. I'll go back down...'

'No, no. You're not disturbing me at all. May I ask you what may seem like an impertinent question, Miss Harris?'

'I'd be interested to hear.'

'I find it intriguing that someone like you ... is doing this trip on her own.'

'You mean without a man.'

'Now it is I who should apologize,' Hellmann said. 'I have caused offence...'

'You haven't. And your question is easy to answer. I am trying to forget someone.'

'Ah.' Hellmann nodded slowly, understanding.

'I felt a trip like this would be a good way to do it. It gives me time to gather my thoughts.'

'A wise decision. Too many people seem to want to do everything in a hurry. They miss so much by doing so. They are never aware of the many things that pass them by. Even though I have sailed this river for many years ... the Rhine is always new to me. Its history, sometimes very bloody, is still a treasure house.'

'I have a connection to its bloody side.'

'Oh?'

'My great-uncle. He was at Remagen during the Second World War.'

'I saw you photographing the old bridge as we passed. You took many pictures. Many old soldiers of that time come from America to see it again.'

She shook her head slowly. 'Not my uncle. He swore he would never return. Several of his old buddies have gotten in touch with him over the years and tried to persuade him. Never, he would say. He hated that battle with a vengeance. Wasted lives, he says ... on both sides. The whole war was a waste ... and should never have been allowed to happen.'

'He hated being a soldier?'

'He was a very green second lieutenant at the time. He didn't like it one bit; but despite himself, he was a good one.'

'Always the case,' Hellmann said. 'The reluctant ones frequently turn out to be heroes. Was your great-uncle a hero, Miss Harris?'

'He wouldn't think so.'

'Which means he was. I know the type.'

'Were you ever in the military, Captain?'

He nodded. 'Conscription.'

'My great-uncle was drafted too. He hated going.'

'But he still went ... and that says many good things about him. Where is he from?'

'California.'

'Ah! One of my daughters has just gone to college there.'

'Really? She'll like it.'

'I hope so.' Hellmann again sounded thoughtful. 'On many, many nights when they were younger, she and her sister would stand up here with me. They love the river too.' He paused, seeming to go deep into thought. 'Have you ever sometimes wished you had not taken a certain turning in life, Miss Harris?'

'Too many times,' she answered.

He nodded slowly. 'They used to so love the river,' he remarked quietly.

'Then I'll leave you to your river, Captain. The night air has done its job. I'm feeling kind of sleepy.'

'Then have a good night's sleep. By noon tomorrow, we shall be in Mainz. Because we are not a dedicated passenger ship, our berth will be in the container harbour, instead of the ones along the riverside by the city centre. However, the *Isabella Lütz* has a special berth which allows the easy disembarkation of passengers. Will you be going ashore?'

'I certainly shall.'

'Then enjoy it. You will find much to interest you.'

'Thank you. I will. Goodnight, Captain Hellmann.'

'Goodnight, Miss Harris. But don't miss the boat. We sail at four p.m.'

'I won't.'

He touched his cap at her as she left.

Halfway down, she turned briefly to observe him. He was again staring across the river to the lights on the bank, as if seeing them for the last time.

Isabella Hellmann went up the deck just as she returned to her suite. They did not see each other.

Hellmann turned his head briefly as his wife joined him. 'Miss Amy Harris was just here,' he said.

'Oh? What did she want?'

'Nothing. She was taking the night air and came up to say hello. I asked her why she was travelling alone.'

She smacked him playfully on the shoulder. 'Udo! You should never ask a woman such a thing!'

'She didn't seem to mind. She's trying to forget somebody.'

'I thought it might be something like that. She's young, good-looking, and is very intelligent. Smart men would not leave such a woman alone unless she was determined to be so.'

'I suppose not.' Hellmann put his arm about his wife and breathed in deeply of the river air. 'Remember how the children used to stand up here with us?'

'I remember.' She glanced up at him. 'You sound as if you're missing them.'

'I always miss them when they're not here.'

'We both do, but we've been accustomed to it. Tonight … you seem more…' She paused. 'You were alright at dinner. The stomach upset…'

'No. No. I'm fine. Tell me, Isa. I've given you a good life, haven't I?'

Now she looked at him for long moments. 'What is it, Udo? Are you ill and you're keeping it from me?'

'No, no. Not at all.'

'Of course you've given us a good life. We had some hard times in the beginning … but look at us … smart, lovely daughters, our own boat, good business, and the river. What more could a wife ask for?'

His arm tightened briefly about her.

'We are lucky,' he said, staring out at the darkness and the lights.

In Berlin, Berger and Reimer parked their car in the shadows of a tree-lined street and waited. Berger was at the wheel.

Ahead of them, a dark Mercedes saloon pulled up before a late-night café. The rain of the day had been followed by a night that was dry and warm. Though reasonably crowded, there were still some empty tables on the café's wide terrace. The doors of the Mercedes opened and Heinrich Gauer, accompanied by his two bodyguards, got out. The doors shut with synchronized thuds, and the three men took a table close to where the car was parked. Around them, the mainly young people looked on with barely-concealed disapproval.

'His prospective constituents certainly don't seem to like him,' Berger observed.

'Shows they've got some brains,' Reimer said. 'I can't believe we're actually protecting that piece of shit,' he added disgustedly.

'Pappi says we do it...' Berger said, '...we do it.' She would never have called Pappenheim 'Pappi' to his face as things currently stood between them, no matter how informal the given situation.

'And talking of Pappi,' Reimer said. 'Still carrying that torch for him?'

'I like you a lot, Reimer ... Don't make me begin to think I'm making a mistake.'

'Take it easy ... I'm not attacking you here.

120

It's just that the man's still in love with his wife, and she's been dead for...'

Berger rounded on him. *'Hey!* Leave it!'

'OK ... OK! I'm not coming on to you, for God's sake. I've got a girlfriend.'

'I know you've got a girlfriend. I introduced you to her...' Berger paused. 'Look!'

'What? Where?'

'Motorcycle ... *Motorcycle!*'

'Got him...'

As Reimer watched, the slow-moving motorcyclist in full leathers was coming towards them, and just about to reach the café. A hand was rising ... and there was something in it, pointing...

Reimer was out of the car and drawing his weapon. Berger was not far behind.

The motorcyclist was quick. He spotted swiftly-moving Reimer and the drawn weapon. He brought his hand back down, did a wheel-smoking reversal and accelerated back the way he had come.

Reimer had taken cover behind a tree, keeping out of the diners' line of sight. Berger joined him.

'Strange, don't you think?' she began. 'The bodyguards never spotted him. Look at them. They're just staring up the road as if nothing had happened. Probably thinking it was some idiot doing a wheelie. And Gauer didn't even look up from his papers. He'd have died still trying to work out how to make his nasty slogan sound more acceptable.'

'That would have been a benefit for the

country,' Reimer said, putting his gun away.

'Or maybe the bodyguards were not all that stupid,' she said as they made their way unobtrusively back to their car.

He gave her a searching glance. 'What do you mean?'

'Even for slow bodyguards, they were very slow. What if it's a set-up?'

'You mean they brought him here to be shot?'

'Why not? It wouldn't be the first time something like that has happened.'

They had reached the car and got back in, Berger again behind the wheel. 'You can forget your Gina for this evening, Reimer,' she continued, perilously close to glee. 'It's going to be a long night.'

'Thanks for reminding me,' Reimer remarked sourly.

'Any time. Wait a minute...'

'What now?'

'That shooter spotted you. He couldn't see you well enough to recognize you again, but his people will realize that Gauer has back-up. And that means ... get out of the car!'

'*What?*'

'*Get out!*'

Berger was already doing so, not waiting to see if Reimer did likewise. She moved swiftly away from the car to take cover behind a tree, five parked cars away. Some moments later, a puzzled Reimer joined her.

'Would you mind telling me—'

'Wait.'

'But—'

'Just wait, Reimer.'

They waited in silence. They could still see Gauer's table. Gauer and his bodyguards were now drinking coffee. Minutes passed. Reimer began to get impatient.

'Just wait,' Berger repeated before he could say anything. 'You're supposed to be a good undercover man. How did you survive out there if you're so impatient?'

'I'm not...'

'Now look at what's coming. Not that direction. Behind us.' As she spoke, Berger crouched lower, so that she was hidden from anyone looking from the street.

Reimer spotted what she meant and he too ducked lower. 'Well, I'll be ... How did you know?'

'I didn't. It was just a feeling.'

The motorcycle came slowly up the street from the opposite direction. The rider seemed to be checking all the cars as he passed. They heard the cadence of the motorcycle change as it passed where they were hidden. The sound continued, then slowed to idle.

'He's stopped by our car,' Reimer said in a whisper. He moved carefully until he could see their car.

The motorcyclist had stopped, one foot on the ground, to peer into the car. The street-lights perfectly silhouetted the outline of the person.

'Shit!' Reimer whispered.

'What's happening?'

123

'It's a *woman* on the bike!'

'You're joking...'

'See for yourself.'

Berger was able to look just as the motorcyclist turned and went slowly back.

'Well?' Reimer asked.

'You're right.'

Though they waited for several more minutes, the motorcyclist never returned. Then they saw Gauer and his bodyguards rising to their feet. They hurried back to their car and got in just as Gauer and his minders entered the Mercedes. The big car drove off, followed at a discreet distance by Berger and Reimer.

Though they checked frequently, they never saw the motorcycle again.

Berlin-Kreuzberg. 03.00 hours.

Berger called Pappenheim. 'He's home now.' She told him about the incident with the motorcyclist.

'Change of back-up,' Pappenheim said. 'Just in case. New car, new people. So you two had better come in. You'll be relieved in less than thirty minutes. Good work, Berger. Reimer too.'

'Thanks, Chief,' she said, very pleased.

In the surveillance room, the man who had suffered the ear blast was on the phone. When he ended the conversation, he turned to his colleague.

'The hit failed. They're covering Gauer.'

124

'Who's "they"?'

'Müller's people, of course.'

'You don't know that. There are many others in this little game. Was there a positive identification?'

'No ... but I still think it's Müller and his people. If they know about Gauer, they may know about the rest.'

'We don't know that, either.'

His partner was not ready to give in. 'I know there are others in the game ... but Müller is the most important ... and the most dangerous to us.'

'Probably why he was given the case in the first place. But neither you nor I are in a position to make tactical decisions. That's for those who tell us what to do. We just listen, and report. Our line to Müller may be dead for now ... but it was not the only one we've got access to. Anyway, if he hadn't worked that one out, I'd have been very disappointed in him. He is, after all, supposed to be good.'

'Better than the colonel?'

'We'll just have to wait ... and see.'

Müller woke early, having had an undisturbed sleep.

No one had tried to enter his room. He checked that Esske's statement was still secure in the magazine pouch. It was. He showered without haste, got dressed and was just about to leave for breakfast when the doorknob turned, very slightly.

Müller paused to watch. It did not happen

again. He heard no departing footsteps. Even through the thick door, he felt certain he would have heard something.

He waited for a full five minutes. The doorknob still did not turn. He had the strongest impression that someone was directly outside, listening. He waited another five minutes. No movement outside the door. Then the distant sounds of the cleaners working in one of the rooms came through.

Müller drew the Beretta quietly and held it, muzzle down, behind his back. With his other hand, he unlocked the door swiftly and waited, flattened against the wall. He listened for the sound of footsteps hurrying away. Nothing.

He turned the knob and yanked the door wide open in a flowing movement. He stood back, waiting. He could see through the doorway clearly. No one was there. Cautiously, he moved until he could check out the entire corridor. No one.

He put the gun back into its holster. Turning to memorize the position of the suiter he had brought with him, he went out, pulling the door firmly shut.

The sounds of the distant cleaners continued unabated.

No one joined him in the lift as he went down to breakfast. He took a table that gave him a full view of the entire dining room, and ate unhurriedly. He was certain that whoever had earlier piggy-backed his mobile would have known of the hotel he had booked for the night. Segelmann's impersonator, using one of his apparently easy supply of police IDs, would simply have gone to the hotel reception to check on a guest named Müller.

As Müller had long made it a habit of never booking into any hotel as a police officer, the receptionist, assuming it to be a normal police enquiry, would have readily given the information. Even so, Müller gave the outward appearance of being totally unconcerned. Whoever he really was, the man with the bristle cut could be anywhere.

Breakfast over, Müller went back up to his room. Again, no one followed him. The suiter had not been disturbed. He hung around for a few minutes, freshened up in the bathroom and made a production of it, tempting whoever had turned the doorknob to try again. But nothing happened.

He picked up the suiter and went back down to reception to check out. The day receptionist said nothing about anyone making enquiries about him. He would not have expected her to. The man from the villa would have ensured that she or her colleagues said nothing.

As he paid his bill, Müller studied her surreptitiously, but she gave no indication that she was hiding anything from him. He went out to the hotel car park to his car, put the suiter behind the seats and got in. No one followed as he drove away from the hotel.

★　★　★

127

Autobahn A61, Brohltal service area, halfway between Bonn and Koblenz. 09.00 hours.

Müller called Pappenheim from the car park of his hotel, using his mobile. He stood near the car, looking about him casually as he spoke.

'Morning, Pappi. Had a good night's sleep?'

'My clothes are rumpled, but my brain is sharply pressed. You first? Or me first?'

'You.'

'Then here goes,' Pappenheim began. 'There was an incident with Gauer.'

'Dead?'

'No. Berger and Reimer were on the ball.' Pappenheim related the incident with the motorcycle.

'Close one,' Müller said.

'Very. I've replaced them with new faces, just in case.'

'Good idea. It looks like we're dealing with a network of killers.'

'Definitely looks like it. Anything happen your end?'

'My night was not as exciting, but someone tried my room this morning ... the doorknob ... just once. Then nothing, and no one. And no tail so far.'

'They don't need to. When they could still piggy-back, they got enough to know your next destination...'

'And could have gone on ahead, perhaps immediately after trying my door ... if that was Renner.'

'Mmm-hmm,' Pappenheim said. 'Which also explains how he got to Bonn before you.'

'The nearest plane from Berlin ... assuming, that is, he came in from Berlin.'

'Precisely.'

'Anything in yet on Ries senior?'

'I've done a trawl of the duckling's people. My contact has no indication that he could be a possible target.'

'They're wrong.'

'The way you've said that tells me enough. I'll keep at it. Incidentally, shall I alert the *Kommissarin*?'

'Leave her out of it for now. I'll let you know when I get there.'

'You're the boss. Don't let the bad boys frighten you.'

'Too early in the morning, Pappi,' Müller said, shaking his head slowly.

'Ah, those terrible jokes of mine. Is it morning already?'

The door to Pappenheim's office was flung open just as he hung up. Kaltendorf stood there.

'My God, it stinks in here!' was Kaltendorf's opening gambit. He went into his exaggerated coughing routine. 'You look as if you've slept in those clothes.'

'I have,' Pappenheim said mildly, squinting at Kaltendorf through a smoke ring. 'But my jacket's OK. How can I help, sir?'

Slightly taken aback, Kaltendorf said, 'Where's Müller? I've checked his office. He's not there.'

'He's not here, sir.'

'I can see that!'

'Following leads, sir. He—'

'Following leads, following leads! We should give his office to a homeless person. He'd make better use of it!'

'If he sat in his office all day, sir,' Pappenheim began patiently, 'he would never solve all those cases he has. And this unit would not have such a good record ... sir.'

Kaltendorf stood in the open doorway glaring at Pappenheim, slightly lost for words. 'On your feet, *Oberkommissar*!' he barked.

With surprising accommodation, Pappenheim rose. Specks of ash drifted off him.

'You are disgusting!' Kaltendorf said, following the drifting ash with his eyes; then he turned and went out, closing the door firmly.

'Disgusting ... yes, sir...' Pappenheim said to the closed door as he sat down again. 'But smarter.'

On the *Isabella Lütz*, Amy Harris was well into a breakfast of hot rolls and croissants.

She was the sole diner. She had taken a chair that faced towards the bows, so that she could see out of the large nearby porthole, which was square, with rounded corners. Her camera, a brand new Minolta Dynax 9, was on the bench seat directly beneath the porthole, ready for use. The only other person in the dining lounge was the crew member on breakfast duty. He came to her table with a pot of fresh coffee.

'Another cup, Miss Harris?' he asked in English.

'Yes, please. Mmm! That smells good.'

The crewman smiled, filled her cup with fresh coffee and went back to stand by the buffet counter with its very generous spread.

She got up, and went over to the buffet. 'Such great food every day,' she said to him. 'As always, my compliments to the chef. I'll miss this boat.'

'Then you must sail with us again.'

'You bet. We passed through a beautiful stretch of the Rhine during the night, didn't we?'

'The best is still to come, Miss Harris. We're not yet at the St Goar bend. You will get some great pictures of the castles on the high cliffs all along the stretch from there to Mainz ... and of the Lorelei too.'

'Then I'd better eat and get up on deck.'

She returned to her table with a well-laden plate, and continued breakfast heartily.

Five

The world had crashed about Martin Ries's ears.

From the moment that the two police officers had appeared on the doorstep of his large house in one of the best residential areas of Stuttgart, his current life had been changed for ever.

'Herr Martin Ries?' the senior officer had commenced when Ries had appeared in his black silken dressing gown in answer to their forceful ringing of the doorbell. 'We have some bad news...'

Then the nightmare had begun.

Now sitting alone in his vast kitchen, Ries looked a wreck. His normally sleek greying hair, which he wore fashionably on the edge of neck-length, looked like straw. His usually tanned skin – a product of the sunshine of southern climes to which he had often travelled on 'business' trips with someone who was not his wife – was now a greyish pallor. The shock of the disaster that had befallen him was hard to take in. There was plenty of horror too.

The police had not been sparing with the details. Given what they had heard from the

132

hysterically frightened woman, their faces had barely hidden the contempt they had felt. Ries's wife, staring into the far distance during the police disclosures, had retreated into a hard and cold isolation in a combination of sorrow for her dead son, shock for the manner of his passing, disgust for the now unvarnished truth about his activities and sexual proclivities, and an unquantifiable rage at her husband's long-term betrayal. She had not spoken a word to him since that time.

But these were not all that preyed upon his mind. They all paled into insignificance when compared to what, he now realized, was truly behind the entire disaster. The clincher had been what the police had said about the mobile they had found; *his* mobile. Apart from the fact that it had been wiped clean, he knew that the mobile had somehow been stolen from him with a singular purpose, and deliberately planted in a car that had been an exact copy of the one he had given to his lover.

Though ostensibly set for his son and Jörg Pinic, the trap had really been for him. *He* was the true target. He knew this with a clarity born of a secret knowledge. The trap had been closed with a mercilessness that was implacable. He could not understand why this had been done to him; why all the certainties and promises of the past had been reneged upon. His destruction was complete. His life, he knew, was finished.

He stood up. 'I was serving my country,' he

133

said in the voice of a man suddenly much older than he actually was.

Ries left the kitchen and went into his study. He found someone he had not expected, waiting there, standing by his desk. His wife.

A painfully thin, dyed blonde, she had the pinched face of her son. At that moment, her eyes were meaner than her son's could ever have been. She was holding something behind her back.

'*Looking for this?*' she screeched at him.

She brought it out, and pointed it at him: a Makarov pistol.

'Is this what you want?' she continued in her unnerving screech. 'You *coward*! Taking the easy way out? Eh? *Eh?* Afraid of the publicity? *Well, no*! You won't deny me my revenge! Revenge for my son ... and revenge for your betrayal ... *fucking* that *whore*!'

For a man facing a gun in the hands of an enraged wife, he was remarkably calm. Perhaps it was the calm of the already doomed.

'Your son,' he said quietly. 'Yes. He was more yours than mine. From the day he was born, you spoilt him. Everything little Helmut wanted, Helmut had to have. Mother's little toy boy. You focused every emotion you had on him. It was obscene. You ruined him! You turned him into a deviant little *shit*!'

'*Shut your dirty mouth! Shut it*!' The gun shook in her hands, such was her fury. '*I'm going to clean you out*! I'll take it all! And I'll

134

make certain that everything that whore got from you is taken away! *Every* damned thing! She'll be lucky if she has any clothes left by the time I'm finished with her! If she wants the lifestyle to which you made her accustomed, she'll have to work for it! On the *street* ... where she belongs...'

'And where do *you* belong, you selfish bitch?' he suddenly yelled at her. 'For years, I've put up with your self-obsession, your moods, your tantrums, your bitchiness. I've watched you spend money like water on anything you thought would make you look like a skeleton! You've got more money than you can spend. You've got *three* cars. You've got a large house. You've got a daily cleaner. You've got a personal hairdresser, a personal manicurist, a personal dietician and all those other people who come here just to make you face yourself every day. I've put up with your frigidity, your stupid society hostess act and, worst of all, with your overprotective attitude to a son who should have been taught some harsh lessons early in his life before it became too late to do so. And what did you produce? A sociopath ... a rapist!'

'Shut up, shut up, *shut up*! Don't talk about him like that!'

'Why not? It's the truth! When I married you, you were warm and kind. Then he was born and, like a switch being turned on, you became a monster. For nineteen years I watched you spoil that boy. God help me ... I even went along with your stupid idea to give him a car...'

'And then you gave your whore one! Was it worth it?'

'Yes, yes, *yes*! It was worth it! You should ask yourself why...'

'You bastard! *You bastard*!' She screamed the words in a rising cadence that echoed through the house.

In the final moments of their life together, each was spewing out long years of resentment upon the other.

'So what are you going to do?' he goaded. 'Shoot me? First learn how to use a gun before you point it at someone.'

He walked towards her. She pulled the trigger. Nothing happened. She pulled it again and again. Still nothing happened.

'It won't fire! *It won't fire!*' she raged.

In her frenzy, she kept pulling at the trigger. She was still trying to shoot him when he reached her and wrenched the gun away.

'This is how you use a gun,' he said, cocking it.

He fired twice. The force of the bullets at such close range threw her scrawny body hard against the desk. She made a bizarre squeaking sound as she slid down to the floor. There was no pain in her eyes as she glared at him. There was only room for hate, and rage, before the light faded out of them.

Ries stared at the body for some moments then, very calmly, he put the pistol to his head, and blew his brains out.

★   ★   ★

The phone rang in Pappenheim's office.

He picked it up. 'Pappenheim.'

'Ah, Pappenheim,' Kaltendorf's voice reverberated in his ear. 'Any news as yet from Müller?'

'No, sir,' Pappenheim answered, and braced himself for another tirade.

But it did not come. 'Very well. I shall be out for the day. Perhaps you can bring me up to speed tomorrow morning?'

Pappenheim stared at his ceiling wonderingly. 'Of course, sir.'

'Thank you, Pappenheim.'

The connection clicked off. Pappenheim replaced his phone gingerly, as if it had suddenly become fragile.

' "Thank you, Pappenheim"? What's wrong with him? He sounded almost human.' He took out the cigarette he had been smoking and looked at it. 'What do you think?' He quickly put it back between his lips. 'Strange man.'

The phone rang again.

'That's more like it,' he said. 'What I just heard must have been a dream.'

But it was not Kaltendorf. 'I have some news,' the voice said.

Pappenheim recognized it immediately. 'Shoot...'

'...is the right word. Ries is dead. Wife too.'

'A hit?'

'Not from outside. Shot wife, then himself. Thought you'd like to know. More details later.' The line went dead.

137

Pappenheim replaced the phone, then puffed furiously at the ceiling.

'Hmm,' he said.

Kaltendorf was driving himself to Berlin-Tegel airport. There was a softness to his face that Pappenheim would have been astonished to see. He was even smiling. As he drew closer to the airport, the smile widened in anticipation.

When he got there, he parked quickly and hurried to the arrivals lounge to wait for the 11.10 from Paris. Again, Pappenheim would have been surprised to see him. Kaltendorf was as jittery as a schoolboy on a first date as he kept staring at the arrivals board, shifted his gaze to the gate, then back to the board again. The flight had landed safely, but Kaltendorf was as nervous as if waiting for an interview.

Then at last, a young girl of about seventeen appeared among a group of arriving passengers. She wore jeans and T-shirt, carried a small backpack and a travel bag, and was exceptionally beautiful. Her eyes searched the waiting people anxiously, then lit up when she saw Kaltendorf. Kaltendorf himself appeared to melt.

The girl broke away from the group and rushed over to him, dropped the travel bag, then flung her arms uninhibitedly about him.

'Papa!' she cried softly.

Kaltendorf held on to her tightly. 'Solange! Solange!' he said. 'It is good to see you,' he continued in perfect French.

'Good to see you too, Papa,' she said in the same language.

They released each other, looking happy.

'Good flight?'

She nodded. 'Very smooth. I think I will marry the pilot.'

'You'll marry whom I tell you to,' he said with mock severity.

'And I will, of course, resist.'

'Of course. What else?'

They grinned at each other.

'You can marry anyone you want,' he said to her benevolently. Then added grimly, 'Except perhaps Müller.'

'Who's Müller?' she asked, immediately interested.

'Someone you're never likely to meet, thank God.'

'Hmm,' she said teasingly.

Kaltendorf picked up her bag. 'Let's go. I'm in a short-term car park.'

'You're a senior policeman,' she said as they began to walk. 'They can't give you a ticket.'

'Oh yes they can. You don't know these ticket people. Worse than Genghis Khan.'

Solange Jeanne-Marie du Bois carried a goodly portion of her mother's South Seas genes, though they were diluted by those of her maternal, French grandfather. Her mother's name had been Jeanne-Marie, and she bore this with pride. With her gleaming dark hair and pale grey eyes, the result was an outstanding natural beauty that halted many in their tracks. There was also a calmness about her, combined with an aura of self-confidence that belied her years.

People turned to stare at her and Kaltendorf, who wore his own proud look upon his normally strung-out, harrassed face.

'They probably think you're my sugar daddy,' she said to him with a bold smile at the starers.

'Let them,' he said with a rare light-heartedness.

In the car park, the car windscreen was free of the tell-tale slip of paper.

'Do you see?' she said. 'No ticket.'

'That's because I've still got a few minutes left,' he said as he put the bag in the boot.

They got in, and he drove away from the airport at a leisurely pace.

'I'll be with you all day today...'

'Oh good!'

'But tomorrow you'll be with some friends of mine ... Only while I'm at work,' Kaltendorf added quickly. 'You ... don't mind, do you?'

'No. As long as we can have time together.'

'Yes,' he said, much relieved. 'We'll have plenty of time together. My friends have a daughter about your age ... Noni...'

'My German is terrible...'

'Don't worry. Noni speaks excellent English, so the two of you will have no problem in that language.'

'What kind of things does she like?'

'No need for worry there, either. She is not

one of those teenagers who likes going to discos...'

'Then we will get on.'

'I am certain you will.'

'We can't see your family?'

Kaltendorf's lips tightened briefly. 'No.'

'They still won't speak to you because of Maman?'

'*I* won't speak to them. I should have been stronger before you were born, and stood up to them. I have regretted it ever since. If it hadn't been for that...' Kaltendorf swallowed. His voice shook slightly as he continued, 'If it hadn't been for that—'

'It's not your fault...'

'Yes it is. I should have had the guts to marry her, despite my family. She wouldn't ... wouldn't have gone back to the island, and wouldn't have drowned out there ... all alone ... She died because of me.' He cleared his throat loudly.

Solange reached up with a finger and wiped some moisture from the corner of his eye.

'I ... I still love her, you know,' he said, voice cracking a little.

'I know,' she said.

Kaltendorf was so preoccupied, he did not see the motorcyclist coming up rapidly behind. The bike roared past, then pulled into the inside lane. It slowed down so that Kaltendorf, in the outside lane, would drive past.

As the car overtook, the motorcyclist's helmeted head, with visor down, turned slowly to look at Solange.

Neither Kaltendorf nor Solange noticed.

The motorcyclist waited until the car was well past, pulled once more into the overtaking lane, then roared off again at high speed.

The head did not turn to look as the bike flashed past and receded into the distance.

Müller had chosen to make the journey at an easy pace as he had plenty of time before the *Isabella Lütz* made her stop, and had decided to forsake the Autobahn at Koblenz, in favour of the *Bundesstrasse* 9.

The B9 was one of his favourite roads, which in his opinion skirted the most beautiful stretch of the Rhine: between Koblenz and Mainz. It also had the practical benefit of enabling him to look out for the *Isabella Lütz* on her journey to the container port.

As he drove, he saw in his mind's eye more than the surface beauty that continued to captivate the unending line of landscape pilgrims who visited this section of the river. He saw more than the many castles of legend, perched atop precipitous heights; more than the eternal bronze Lorelei upon her high rock; more than the glistening surface of the water far beneath her, which in certain light appeared to belong to another world; felt more than the strange, fairy-tale atmosphere of the valley, bordered by its darkling green ramparts. He saw the centuries of blood upon which those castles had been built, and which had streamed into that river; and felt a sense of awe.

Just after passing the bend in the river near St Goar, he was relieved to see that a café he had not visited in years was still in business. It had a prime position almost on the river itself, its terrace virtually built upon the water, but high enough to avoid being flooded when the river rose.

He pulled off the road and into the small car park, finding a spot at the far end, with a clear view of the river. He got out, locked the car, and went through the building and out on to the terrace. At this time of day, there were not many customers as yet so he was able to take a table with an almost panoramic view.

A slim man in his fifties with short hair that was still black, came to the table.

'Can I...?' He stopped and peered at Müller. 'I know you, don't I? Yes ... yes ... it's Herr Müller, isn't it? The student on the bicycle. My God! How many years since?'

Müller grinned at him. 'Too many, Herr Rünau.' He stood up and held out a hand which Rünau shook vigorously.

'You used to come here every year. Then nothing. What happened? You are obviously no longer a student.'

'Work, Herr Rünau. That's what happened.'

Rünau looked him up and down. 'And very successful by the looks of it. You still have the long hair, and the earring ... and you look young while I ... Age catches up with me. I saw the car with the Berlin plates and thought

143

... why do I know this person? Business must be very good.'

Müller smiled, but did not elaborate as he sat down once more.

'So,' Rünau went on, 'the usual coffee, as I remember it?'

'The usual, and the cake too ... if you have it.'

Rünau's face suddenly clouded over. 'I am sorry. The cake ... I know how you loved it but you see ... my wife ... she used to make it and ... well ... she is no longer with us. We have never sold that cake since. Four years now since she...'

'I am so sorry,' Müller began apologetically, feeling guilty. 'I—'

But Rünau had brightened once more. 'How could you know? My daughter and her husband now practically run the place. She makes her own special cake.' He glanced back and said in a low voice, 'Not as good as her mother's, of course, but still quite good. Would you like to try a piece?'

'I would indeed.'

Rünau beamed. 'She will be pleased. She remembers you.'

He went away, leaving Müller to ponder upon the transience of life. Only the river and its surroundings, he mused, continued in permanence.

He glanced towards his left at the river's bend, the direction from which the *Isabella Lütz* would appear. He was sufficiently ahead of it, giving him enough time to quietly enjoy

144

his coffee and cake before it came round the bend in the river.

'You used to sit there, too.'

Müller turned from the river. Rünau had returned with the coffee and cake.

'Not at this same table, of course,' the older man continued as he put them down. 'But in the same spot. My wife used to watch you sit there, just looking at the river.'

'I love this part of the Rhine,' Müller said.

Rünau straightened to stare out across the water. 'Things and people pass on. But the river is always there.' He lowered his voice. 'Now try your cake. My daughter is watching.'

Müller picked up the fork. 'This looks good.' He speared off a piece and put it into his mouth, nodding as he ate. 'And this ... is excellent.'

Rünau beamed as if he himself had made it. 'I'll tell her.'

The sound of marine engines made them both look up. A police boat was racing downstream.

'Water police,' Rünau said drily. 'Probably hunting for another fake crocodile, like the one some jokers put into the river last year.'

'You don't like the police?'

'Oh, they're OK, I suppose ... never there when you want them, but always there if you go a bit over the speed limit, or park for a short while in the wrong place. With your car, you must have a lot of trouble with them.'

'I sometimes do have trouble with the

police,' Müller said with a straight face, thinking of Kaltendorf.

'There you go,' Rünau remarked sympathetically. 'I'll leave you to your cake. Enjoy.'

'Thank you. I will.'

Müller did enjoy his coffee and cake as he sat there, watching the river. It was a hardworking river too. No less than six cargo barges, of varied dimensions and carrying a wide variety of freight were within view, going in both directions. He watched their choreography interestedly, as they set themselves up to take the double bend. As yet, there was no sign of the *Isabella Lütz*.

The *Isabella Lütz* was just approaching the first bend that would lead into the St Goar waters.

Amy Harris was on deck, taking pictures of everything in sight it seemed.

'We'll soon be coming up on the Lorelei,' a male voice said. 'We're going to video that.'

She took the camera away from her eye to turn round. Jack and Betty Grogan, an American couple, were smiling at her like fond parents.

'I'd like to get a picture too,' she said.

'Mark Twain wrote a poem about it,' Grogan informed her. 'He came along here during his travels.'

'Wow!' she said.

Müller was enjoying the tranquillity the river had brought to him.

Even though he knew this would be a temporary state of affairs, he was determined to make the most of it. The cake had proved to be so excellent, he was sorely tempted to order another chunk, accompanied by a fresh cup of coffee. He had just come to that decision, when the *Isabella Lütz* hove into view.

For a freight-carrying barge, he thought, she was an impressive-looking ship. The twin-decked superstructure, with its unusual paint scheme, gleamed in the morning sun. A cloud formation caused the rays to spear down like a giant spotlight to bounce off the surface of the river, bathing the vessel in a luminous curtain that seemed to sparkle as the boat went through it.

'Beautiful, isn't it?' Rünau's voice said behind him.

Müller glanced round. 'It is quite remarkable what the light can do at this section of the bend.'

'I don't always catch it, but when I do...' Rünau allowed his words to fade. Then he went on, 'Was the cake good?'

'It certainly was. In fact, I was just about to order another piece, and more coffee.'

'My daughter will be pleased. I shall see to it.'

Müller kept his eyes on the *Isabella Lütz* as she began to turn, entering the St Goar stretch of the river. People were on the sundeck, no doubt working their cameras overtime. They were still made indistinct by distance. He continued to watch, as the ship slowly drew closer.

Amy Harris had fitted a zoom lens with a max focal length of 300mm to her camera. She had it pointed at the St Goar bank of the river, while the Grogans were occupied with videoing the Lorelei rock.

The second couple, middle-aged German nationals from the north, were simply content to watch the passing scenery.

Amy Harris was panning her camera, when she suddenly stopped.

'No!' she whispered to herself. 'I know that car ... but it can't be!'

The image in her lens was of the Porsche. It was broadside on to her line of sight, making the front number plate impossible to read. The rear plate was not visible. From the current angle of the ship and given her own position, her view of the terrace of the café was temporarily blocked by the containers at the bows.

'Same seal-grey colour,' she continued. 'Same yellow brake calipers ... No, no, *no* ! It isn't...'

Though reluctant to believe she was looking at the same car, she decided to get off the sundeck. The colour of the car, the yellow calipers for the ceramic brakes, and the very car itself, all spoke of the one she knew; though reason told her there must be others which looked similar.

Even so.

'Hey, Amy!' Grogan called as she started to leave. 'You'll miss the Lorelei!'

She glanced back at him, looking embarrassed. 'Must go, Jack. The bathroom.'

'Ah!' he said, understanding. 'But hurry. You don't want to miss it in this light. Chance of a lifetime.'

'I'll do my best.'

She hurried to her suite and sat down, keeping away from the windows.

'Jesus,' Carey Bloomfield, who called herself Amy Harris, said. *'Müller?'* She did not want to believe it. 'What the hell would *he* be doing out here?'

Müller was drinking fresh coffee and doing serious damage to Hilde Rünau's cake, watching as the *Isabella Lütz* set herself up for the St Goar stretch. He saw the four people on the sundeck as the ship drew ever closer. He had the impression there had been five, the fifth being female.

Something nagged at him, but not sufficiently strongly to make him pay much attention to it.

The boat came so close, he could see the people very clearly. The man with the video camera waved. Müller smiled and waved in return. The man videoed him.

He studied the others. One woman, clearly the video man's companion, remained close to him. The other couple seemed less close. From time to time, they viewed the landscape from opposite sides of the boat.

149

The *Isabella Lütz* was herself even more impressive close up, and seemed to glide almost silently upstream.

'A beautiful boat,' Müller commented to himself.

'It is.' Rünau was back, wanting to talk. 'I've seen it go up and down river many times. There isn't another like it.'

They watched in silence as the *Isabella Lütz* moved powerfully past. Müller saw a tall man on the bridge, looking straight ahead. A woman was sitting in the helmsman's chair. Was she the woman he'd seen?

'That's the captain standing,' Rünau said. 'How do you know?'

'You get to know who's who over the years. People stop by. You get to learn things. The woman is his wife. She's good with the boat. It's named after her.'

Another silence fell as the *Isabella Lütz* showed them her stern as she continued towards Mainz, her next port of call.

Mainz. 11.50 hours.
Having continued his journey at a relatively easy pace, Müller had arrived at the Mainz container port in plenty of time before the *Isabella Lütz* was due in. He had found the berth where the vessel was expected, and had left the car in a secluded spot behind a building. He had checked to ensure no one had trailed him by deliberately taking a haphazard route to the port, sometimes going over particular sections more than once. So

150

far, he appeared to be clear of surveillance.

He was standing well away from immediate earshot near the expected berthing point and was just about to make a call to Pappenheim, when someone shouted, '*You!*'

Müller put his mobile away and turned. A man was striding towards him.

'Security,' the man began truculently. 'That your car behind that building?'

'Yes. It's not causing an obstruction, is it?'

'No, but you're not allowed to park there.'

'If it's not causing an obstruction,' Müller began reasonably, 'can't I just leave it there for a few minutes? I'm waiting for a boat. It will be here soon.'

'You can wait, but your car goes ... and don't give me any trouble.'

'I promise you I want no trouble,' Müller said.

'Good. Now move the car, or I call the police!'

'Ah yes. The police.' Müller stared at the man coolly. 'What if I were to tell you that I am the police?'

The man looked Müller up and down disparagingly. '*You?* With your Porsche? Don't piss about with me. *Move it! Sir!*' The 'sir' was even more disparaging.

Müller sighed. 'Alright.' His eyes became very hard. He took out his ID. 'Müller, *Hauptkommissar.* Why I am here is none of your business. You will go back to wherever you've come from, and you will tell no one you've spoken to me, or that I am here.' He put the ID away. 'I will know if you do otherwise, and you will not like what will happen next. Clear?'

The security man's eyes first widened, then squinted uncertainly. 'Er ... er, yes. Sorry. I thought...'

'Forget it,' Müller said, and began to turn away.

'Excuse me...'

Müller paused.

'What do I say to the other policeman?'

Müller stood very still. 'What other policeman?'

'An *Oberkommissar* Renner...'

'Stocky, with very short hair ... like a brush?'

'That's the one.'

'That's OK. I know about him ... but you do not talk to any of us again.'

'Understood ... but ... but *he* talked to me. Wanted to know where the *Isabella Lütz* was coming in.'

'And you told him, of course.'

'Well yes...'

'I see. Where is he now?'

'He left.'

'I see,' Müller repeated. 'Thank you. He won't be returning.'

The security man nodded uncertainly, then went away. Müller was quite sure that despite his cautioning, the security guard would blab just as easily if the man with the bristles came calling a second time.

He forced his sense of disquiet to the back

of his mind, and remained where he was. He doubted that the impersonator would risk shooting him so publicly, especially as he needed to know what was in the Esske document. It was the only way the man with the many names could assure himself of the extent of Müller's knowledge.

He would also be smart enough to realize that Müller would not leave it in the car. Müller was certain the man would need to make an exchange of some kind, using a bargaining chip that Müller would be powerless to resist; and might also have it in mind that Udo Hellmann could have important information that Müller would be after.

Müller looked out towards the water and saw the double decked superstructure. The *Isabella Lütz* was right on time.

Could Hellmann be the bargaining chip?

The day, which had started brightly, appeared to have become a mixture of sun, cloud, and rain. The clouds had clustered themselves to the east. The sun held its own in the west, while the rain sent speculative droplets that ceased almost before they hit the ground.

In her suite, Carey Bloomfield – in tight jeans, trainers and a sleeveless, loosely-fitting shirt – was getting ready for the spell ashore. Satisfied with her preparations, she picked up her camera to take some shots through the window, prior to going out on deck. She continued to wonder whether she had been completely mistaken, and that the car had not been Müller's at all.

She still had the 300mm zoom lens fitted to the camera. She brought the camera to her eye and zoomed out to 300mm. She then began panning across the port, looking for a good shot to compose as the boat moved closer towards its berth. Then she froze in mid-pan.

She had not been mistaken about the car.

'*Müller!*' she exclaimed in a shocked, low voice. '*Shit!* What the hell is *he* doing *here*, of all places?'

She moved quickly away from the window and sat down where she could not be seen from the outside. As the boat turned broadside-on to its mooring points, she saw Müller standing so close to the edge of the dock, she felt she could almost touch him. Then the boat's manoeuvring shifted him out of sight.

'Now what?' she muttered to herself. 'Your move, Bloomfield.'

She heard the boat being made fast. Someone knocked on her door.

'Miss Harris! If you're going into the city, the car is waiting.'

'I'll be right there,' she responded.

The person moved on, knocking on the doors of the other suites.

Then she heard a new sound. The davit was being operated. Was something being loaded? Or offloaded? She had to find out. Taking a chance on being spotted she opened her door slowly and peered out. Müller was nowhere to be seen.

Her suite was starboard aft, so she was quite close to the point at the stern where the davit was mounted. She cautiously worked her way along the deck to a position where she could see it offloading Hellmann's car.

She went quickly back to her suite to get her things, including the camera. As she made her way out again, the crewman who had knocked was coming back to remind her.

'Miss Harris,' he said. 'You're going the wrong way. Passengers disembark over there.' He pointed.

'I know. But I just saw them offloading Captain Hellmann's car. I don't really want to do a group thing today. I'd sort of prefer to do a few things on my own ... I ... wondered if the captain would mind giving me a ride into town?'

He looked uncertain. 'I'll ask.'

'Thank you.'

He nodded, and as he hurried away, she went back into the suite.

He was soon back, knocking urgently. 'Miss Harris. Miss Harris!'

'I'm here,' she said, opening the door.

'The captain said he isn't going into Mainz...'

'Oh...'

'But he will drop you off at the nearest bus stop, if that will help...'

'That will be fine. I'll get my things.'

Müller had been about to board the *Isabella*

155

Lütz, when he saw the car being offloaded. He decided to wait, and moved some distance away to unobtrusively note what would happen next.

He saw Hellmann get into the Audi, then wait for someone to join him. The person who hurried to the car was a startling surprise.

'Carey *Bloomfield*? *Carey* Bloomfield?'

As he made his way urgently back to where he had left the car, he understood what had been nagging at him. The shape he had briefly seen – and subconsciously recognised despite the distance – had not been the captain's wife; but his mind could not have imagined this wholly unexpected development.

Carey Bloomfield. Müller well remembered the inauspicious beginnings of their association. Posing as a journalist doing historical research on the Berlin police, she had been saddled upon him by a smugly gleeful Kaltendorf. She had been no journalist. Instead, working for an American military intelligence department, she had been on the trail of a killer he himself had been hunting; a killer who had later turned out to be his own, very distant and distaff relative. Her quest had been at once personal, as well as official.

He was ready to move when the Audi passed the building.

Müller shadowed the S6 by driving slowly along a corridor made by the tall stacks of containers, parallel to the car. In this manner, he worked his way towards the exit that Hellmann and Carey Bloomfield were headed for.

In the Audi, Carey Bloomfield's thoughts were racing. As surreptitiously as possible, she would glance behind at infrequent intervals, to check if Müller were following. She did not see the familiar Porsche. Müller's presence, first at St Goar, then at the waterside, had wrecked all the carefully laid plans to keep Hellmann under covert observation. Müller had been waiting for the *Isabella Lütz*, and had clearly been trailing the boat for some time. That meant he knew all about Hellmann. But why did he have an interest? The possibility had not been foreseen.

She would have to call Toby Adams.

She glanced round. Still no Porsche. Where had Müller got to? No Müller was in a way worse than seeing him around. She was convinced he had not suddenly decided to leave.

'Are you expecting someone, Miss Harris?' Hellmann enquired. 'I've noticed you looking behind...'

Hellmann was good to have spotted that, she thought drily; but then, he would be, given his history.

'I'm just checking my bearings,' she replied smoothly. 'As I'll be coming back on my own, I thought I'd better. Don't want to miss the boat.'

Hellmann gave a brief smile. 'I can quite

understand. I am sorry I can't take you into town, but I have an appointment some way from here and I want to get to it in plenty of time, then get back to continue our journey. The *Isabella Lütz* has a tight schedule.'

'I appreciate that, Captain. Thanks for giving me the ride.'

'That is no problem. There is a bus stop at Feldberg Platz on Rheinallee, not far from here. You can get into town in minutes. This is a Roman city. The streets are mainly laid out in grid form – like your American cities...'

'We copied the system,' she said, smiling.

'Then you will find your way around easily. Or would you like a taxi...?'

'No. The bus is OK. More time to see things.'

He nodded. 'More relaxing.'

'Yes.'

But she was not as sanguine as she sounded. This meant he would be out of her surveillance for several hours. It was not what she wanted, but there was not much she could do about it. Such a turn of events had most definitely not been foreseen. No one had pre-warned her that he might do this. By the time she could find a taxi in which to follow, he would be long gone; a seriously unwelcome development.

The Audi came to a halt.

'And here we are,' Hellmann said. 'Feldberg Platz. You won't have to wait long.'

'Thanks again, Captain, for going out of your way,' she said, as she got out.

'My pleasure, Miss Harris ... but please, be on time for the boat.'

'I will.'

He gave her a brief wave, and the Audi moved off with a deep roar.

'You're in a hurry,' she said as the car turned right and went out of sight.

She took out her mobile, and made a call.

Within nanoseconds the call was switched by secure connection to a terminal in Washington, then re-routed to a commercial building in Berlin. Toby Adams saw the number on the display as he picked up his phone.

'Carey!' he said expansively. 'So nice to hear from you. Where are you?'

'Cut the bonhomie, Toby. Why the hell didn't anyone tell me Müller was in this?'

'*What?*'

Adams sounded genuinely astonished.

'So you didn't know?' she asked in a thoughtful voice.

'Of course not! Are you sure it's him?'

'I was almost close enough to pull his earring if I wanted to ... or stroke his Armani suit...'

'Carey ... I appreciate you're upset...'

'Upset? Me? I like unpleasant surprises.'

'OK, OK ... I've got the message. What the hell is going on?'

'You'd better find out, Toby ... because I saw his car earlier where it should not have been and I saw *him*, just a short while ago. He's right here.'

'Which is ... where...?'

'Where I'm supposed to be.' She ended the call.

'Taxi?' a voice said behind her.

She jumped. *'Jesus!'* she exclaimed in English, recognizing the voice and turning round. *'Müller!* Do you have to sneak up on people?' A little way beyond him she saw the Porsche at the side of the road, with indicators flashing.

'What a nice surprise, Miss Bloomfield,' he greeted in the same language, glancing down as she quickly put the mobile away. 'I didn't even know you had returned to Germany. What are you doing here?'

'Don't I have the right?'

'You have the right to be anywhere you wish ... within reason. This is still a free country.'

'And you, Müller? You're a long way from Berlin. On holiday?'

'Alas ... no. Those with criminal intentions won't let me be. Do we stand here passing the time of day while I cause a traffic obstruction with my car? Or do we try to catch up with Hellmann?'

'Who?'

Müller looked pained. 'Spare me the act, Miss Bloomfield...'

'Carey...'

'Miss Bloomfield ... I saw you get off the *Isabella Lütz.* I even spotted you at St Goar, but I didn't realize it at first. It was so unexpected. Somehow, I don't think you're on that boat for a Rhine cruise ... and while we stand here, Hellmann is getting further away. I'm going back to my car. You can follow if you wish.'

He turned, and began walking back to the Porsche.

'Damn you, Müller!' she muttered to herself. But she hurried after him. 'Wait up!'

He did not slacken his pace, forcing her to almost break into a run to catch up. 'Damn that man,' she hissed to herself. She stared at the car when she eventually caught up with Müller.

'Looks as neat as ever,' she commented as she climbed in. 'Hello, again,' she said to the Porsche, looking around. 'Nice to see you. It still smells new, Müller,' she continued as he got in behind the wheel. 'What do you do? Polish it every day?'

'This is cosy,' Müller said, smiling tolerantly. 'Here we are, back together ... working as a team. Oh. Of course not. We're not a team. This meeting was a surprise ... to both of us.'

'Have your fun, Müller.' Carey Bloomfield glanced at the speedometer. 'Aren't we driving a little slow in this rocket ship of yours? I thought we were chasing Hellmann.'

'Are we? I thought you didn't know of him...'

'OK, *OK*. You've made the point, Müller. Yes, I am keeping Hellmann under surveillance...'

'Doing your CIA thing...'

'I am *not* CIA!'

'So you're not my liaison...'

She stared at him. *'What?'*

'Obviously not,' Müller said calmly.

'Can we have some more speed here?'

'Why? Hellmann isn't getting away.'

She gave him another stare. 'Excuse me?'

He kept his attention on the traffic and for reply turned on the navigation system, then called up a page. On an area map of Mainz, a red dot was moving.

'See that dot?' he began. 'That's Hellmann. While you were having your short ride with him ... I called Pappi, who called the local police, who put up a helicopter. They have him in sight, and data-linked his position to my system.'

'The red dot.'

'The red dot. Notice anything about it?'

She looked at the screen for some moments. 'What the hell? He's coming back into town! He told me he had to go *out* of town.' She studied the movements of the dot. 'Now he's doing a roundabout tour of the city...'

'Mr Hellmann is afraid. He knows there are people out there who mean to do him harm. He's laying a false trail. He's hoping that anyone who may have followed him is looking for him out on the Autobahn.'

She looked up from the screen. 'Do him harm?'

'I do hope you are not playing the innocent, Miss Bloomfield.'

'I really don't know what you're talking

about.'

'How long have you been on the boat?'

'Since she sailed from Holland.'

'Mr Hellmann is a member of an acutely endangered species.'

'And that's why he went into that production of offloading the car ... and the rest of it?'

'Yes.'

'I still don't know the real reasons behind it. Are you going to tell me more?'

'No.'

'That figures. You...'

'I think our quarry has stopped. The Altstadt.'

She turned back to the screen. The red dot was stationary in the old centre of the city.

'Luckily,' Müller went on, 'we're not far. We'll stop here and walk. Have you still got that cannon of yours?'

She seemed to hesitate.

'Have you got your Beretta?' he asked again, patiently.

'Have you got yours?' she countered.

'Yes.'

'Then I've got mine.'

He shook his head slowly.

'What?' she said. 'What?'

'You ... are something else, Miss Bloomfield. However, as fate has decided to throw us together, we might as well make the best of the situation. I have no desire to start throwing bullets around in the town ... but we may need to, if Hellmann's pursuers manage to catch up with him.'

'I want him alive too.'

'I thought you might. I just thought I'd let you say it.'

'Aaah...!'

'Don't tell me to shut up. We've only just met since we last saw each other. It wouldn't be seemly.'

'*Seemly?*'

'Are you a civilian now? Or still in the military?'

'Sort of.'

'What does that mean exactly? Sort of military ... or sort of civilian?'

'Sort of.'

'Very clear. Come on, Miss Bloomfield.'

Hellmann entered the small café in the Altstadt. It was the kind of place that catered for both the local and the tourist trade. He was pleased to note it was a quiet period despite the time of day, with few customers.

As he went in, the small, round man behind the counter stared at him in surprise. A young woman was serving the customers.

'Anne,' the café owner called. 'Watch things for a while for me, will you?'

'Yes, Herr Diefenhausen.'

Diefenhausen nodded to Hellmann to follow him into a back room, where Diefenhausen then turned and said, 'Are you mad? Why did you come here? We were never supposed to meet here.'

'Situations change. I got a phone call.'

'What phone call?'

'Someone called me on the boat ... on my mobile. "Your time is up, Romeo", he said. The exact words. And that was it. He cut the call right there.'

Diefenhausen's eyes had widened. 'Shit.' He looked worried.

'You told me a long time ago,' Hellmann said, 'that this would never happen. I trusted you, Sepp.'

'This is not my doing, Udo. I swear it. I was hoping that what I heard was wrong...'

Hellmann frowned. 'What? You heard something was going wrong and—'

'Wait, wait! Don't jump to conclusions. I only got bits and pieces. All I heard was that some people wanted to end the active Romeo Six programme. Others didn't like the idea, wanting it to continue. Then the group who wanted it to continue decided that it was too dangerous to leave members of Romeo Six running around...'

Now Hellmann's eyes were wide. 'What are you saying? At first I thought that call meant I was going to be unmasked ... I saw my business being ruined ... my marriage, my family. I've got two daughters...'

'It's a lot worse, Udo.'

'You mean ... they're out there ... *killing* us off?'

Diefenhausen just looked at him.

Hellmann went pale. 'I had a feeling there was more to it. That voice was so ... cold...' He walked agitatedly around the room for a few moments.

'There's no easy way to tell you,' Diefenhausen said, turning around to keep Hellmann in view. 'It's already begun. Stop moving, for God's sake. You're making me dizzy. The authorities,' he went on, when Hellmann had stopped, 'are keeping a tight lid on it for now, so there are no headlines ... but sooner or later...'

Hellmann clamped his jaws tightly as he fought to control himself. 'Who ... Who's gone?' he finally asked.

'Gracht, Ries, Esske ... those are the ones I know of. There may well be more. Martin Ries was suicide. But, given the situation, it was a killing. They killed his son...'

'Oh God!' Hellmann said, thinking of his own daughters.

'Nasty story about the son,' Diefenhausen went on. 'He was a little crook with a sideline in rape. He tried to rape his father's mistress, but he and a friend got shot at the scene. They had planned to make a night of it with her. The woman blabbed to the police, who of course went to Martin. He should have kept his libido under more control. He shot his wife, then killed himself. He obviously knew he was finished.'

'Who told you all this?'

'Do you really want to know?' Diefenhausen's eyes were suddenly very hard.

Hellmann shook his head.

'As I said, there may already be more killings,' Diefenhausen went on, 'but I have no

166

information. At least Heinrich Gauer seems to be very much alive. I saw him on TV recently, peddling his stupid politics. Perhaps someone's protecting him.'

'But not us,' Hellmann commented bitterly. 'Gauer,' he continued with distaste. 'I could never understand why he was put into Romeo Six.'

'Because he's a piece of shit. They needed someone like that in the group ... if the mission succeeded. He would be the razor's edge. Looking back ... it seems crazy that something like that was ever started; but in those days, we didn't think so ... except perhaps ... you.'

'I still did it. I can't escape that. The thing is ... what do we do now? I can't go to the authorities and say ... hello, I'm Josef Warneck, although I am known as Udo Hellmann. I am a member of Romeo Six, a group whose operational goal is to destabilize the new, united Germany. I have a wife and two daughters as Udo Hellmann, and another wife and daughter ... as Josef Warneck. They now believe I am dead. My first wife divorced me in my absence because our controller told her to. They would throw away the key by the time they were finished with me.'

Diefenhausen looked at him steadily. 'I can't give you any advice. I was coordinator to the group in the field. I knew your identities. You all knew me individually, but not each other. Then I had an early warning that the whole thing was going dirty. I began

167

to make contact with each of you, to get you to know each other. Then it went quiet for a while. I didn't get hold of everyone. I still haven't. In case you're wondering, I'm no safer than you are. I know too much. So do you.'

'So you're going to sit around till they come?'

'I have insurance.'

'What kind of insurance?'

'I have things written down, and the whole lot is in a very safe place. Perhaps you should do the same. It might stop the wolves.'

'That won't help if they don't know it's been done.'

'I've made certain the news has got through,' Diefenhausen said. 'They'll leave me alone ... for now. Perhaps for good, if I'm very lucky.'

'Talking of wolves,' Hellmann began. 'Can you remember a psycho bastard called Heurath? He was in his twenties at the time and already a major. He was like a shadow ... there, but not really there. He sometimes accompanied our controller. Have you ever heard of him again?'

Diefenhausen shook his head. 'I think I may have seen him just once ... back then ... but I haven't heard of him since. Why?'

'No reason in particular. When you mentioned wolves, it reminded me of him. A true wolf if ever there was one...'

'And how is dear Pappi?' Carey Bloomfield

asked as they walked towards the Altstadt. 'Still his old self and smoking like a chimney?'

'Very much his old self.'

'And giving Kaltendorf hell?'

'That too.'

'Kaltendorf still hate you?'

'He was not likely to change in a year. He's been promoted too ... probationary Director of Police.'

She paused to stare disbelievingly at him, then continued walking. 'You've got to be kidding.'

'No.'

'What did he do to deserve a promotion like this? Ah...' she went on. 'He took the credit for your last case.'

'I didn't say that.'

'You didn't have to. I was there, remember?'

'I well remember.'

'Jesus, Müller. Why did you let him get away with it?'

'He needs it more than I do.'

'Must be all that money you've got. It does things to a person. Makes you indifferent.'

'I am certainly not indifferent. I'm just not bothered about accumulating ... "brownie points" ... as you would call it.'

'No wonder he hates you. You make him feel small.'

Müller glanced up at the sky. 'Strange isn't it? Big chunks of Europe under water, and not a drop of rain here.'

'Changing the subject. OK. We saw it all on TV on the boat,' she said. 'Large areas of at least five of your eastern states, plus parts of Bavaria; then Austria ... Hungary ... the Czech Republic ... Russia ... unbelievable. Some August. The last time we met, Müller, it was raining like the last day on earth. Should we keep meeting like this?'

He turned a palm briefly upwards. 'As you can see, it isn't raining here.'

'Give it time,' she said. 'We ... the passengers,' she went on, 'wondered whether what happened with the Danube and the other rivers would happen with the Rhine. The boat is going to Budapest ... but with the Danube in high flood, I don't see how it can continue ... even if the water level starts to drop and...'

'Forgive my interruption,' Müller said, stopping, 'but look over there ... just ahead. That parking place in front of the Café Diefenhausen. Hellmann's car.'

'I see it. Do you think he's in there?'

'One way to find out. He knows you, so I'll go.' He glanced behind. 'Go to that café we just passed ... but inside, in case Hellmann makes a sudden appearance. And keep a lookout for stocky men with bristle haircuts. They can be dangerous.'

He walked on without waiting for her to respond.

'Sir, yessir!' she acknowledged sarcastically, but not loud enough for him to hear.

Müller entered the café and took a table near the entrance. From that position he could see a good stretch of the cobbled street, without

170

being immediately seen from outside.

The young woman called Anne approached with a warm smile. 'Can I get you something, sir?'

'A milk coffee, please.'

'Yes, sir.'

As she went off to attend to his order Müller looked casually around, wondering where Hellmann had got to. Had he simply parked the car and then gone on somewhere else?

Then his questions were answered. A small man had appeared behind the counter, from somewhere in the back.

'Anne,' the newcomer said. 'Bring us two coffees, will you, when you're done with that. One black with sugar, and the usual for me.'

'Yes, Herr Diefenhausen.'

'Thanks, Anne. I won't be much longer.'

'It's OK,' she said. 'We're not too busy right now.'

Diefenhausen glanced around, eyes pausing briefly on Müller without recognition, before returning to where he had come from.

But Müller had recognized Diefenhausen. He remembered the face from the file Enteling had brought. Diefenhausen had asked for two coffees. Hellmann, Müller decided, had to be the second person.

'Your coffee, sir.' The warm smile was back.

'Thank you ... Anne, is it?'

She beamed at him. 'Yes, sir.'

'Well, thank you, Anne.'

She almost curtseyed. 'My pleasure.' She gave him another smile as she turned away.

Müller relaxed with his coffee, and waited.

In the back room, Diefenhausen said to Hellmann, 'There's a customer in there. He doesn't look like your average tourist.'

Hellmann looked at him anxiously. 'One of them?'

'No one I recognize. He doesn't look the type. And besides, I can smell them upwind and downwind. The man in there, if he's just a tourist, has money. He looks it. None of the people I know would look like that. There's something about them ... a feeling they give off. He doesn't have it.'

Anne knocked on the door. 'Your coffees, Herr Diefenhausen.'

He went to the door and opened it. He took the coffees from her, so that she did not have to enter.

'Thank you, Anne. That man in there ... has he been asking any questions?'

She smiled when he mentioned Müller. 'No, Herr Diefenhausen. He's just quietly drinking his coffee.'

'Alright. And Anne...'

She paused, waiting.

'Don't fall for the customers.'

She blushed a bright pink, pushed the door shut, then hurried away.

Diefenhausen shook his head slowly as he went towards Hellmann. 'Young women. But we know just how easily they can fall, eh?'

Six

Carey Bloomfield had found herself a window seat in the café across the street.

She had been toying with her coffee, wondering how long Müller was going to be. From where she sat, she had a clear view of the Café Diefenhausen, and some distance beyond; which was why she was able to see the person approaching it.

A stocky man, bristle-haired.

She quickly paid for her unfinished coffee and hurried out.

Müller was startled to see Carey Bloomfield hurry past without glancing in.

He frowned in annoyance. What was she playing at?

Then he heard her speaking loudly enough for him to hear, in English, her American accent exaggerated.

'Excuse me, sir? Can you help me? I'm kinda lost. Can you tell me how to get to the Gutenberg?' She sounded very close.

Intrigued, Müller waited for the reply.

'Which one?' came the response. 'The museum? The memorial? His house...?'

Renner.

173

Then Müller was no longer listening. 'Smart work, Miss Bloomfield,' he said to himself as he got to his feet and approached the counter.

Anne blushed, and beamed at him.

'Anne,' he began crisply. 'Herr Diefenhausen. Where is he?'

Confused, she instinctively glanced towards the back. 'I ... I...'

'Hurry, Anne! This is very important! I am a policeman.'

'Yes ... yes.' Uncertain and anxious at the same time, she went to where Diefenhausen had gone, followed by Müller.

She knocked on the door. 'Herr Diefenhausen...'

Müller reached for the door and opened it. The two men inside flinched in astonishment.

'What...' Diefenhausen began, outrage and fear in his eyes.

Hellmann looked resigned, as if all the years of his double life had finally caught up with him.

Müller cut Diefenhausen short. 'Müller, *Hauptkommissar*. If you two wish to continue living, show me the back way out.'

They hesitated.

'I can walk out of here perfectly safely,' he told them harshly. 'But you two will have to get past a stocky man with a bristle haircut...'

Their eyes were filled with a sudden horror.

'*Heurath!*' they said together.

'He's still alive,' Diefenhausen added in

heartfelt disappointment. It was very clear that he had been hoping that the man they both so obviously feared had died during the intervening years.

'We can discuss his identity later. *Where's that way out?*'

'You go with him,' Diefenhausen said quickly to Hellmann. 'I'll show you,' he added to Müller.

'What about you?' Hellmann asked of Diefenhausen.

'I can handle it. I've got insurance, remember?'

' "Insurance"?' Müller asked.

'Udo can tell you. Are you really a *Hauptkommissar*? You don't look it.'

Müller swiftly showed his ID.

'You still don't look it,' Diefenhausen said, but he hurried out to show them the way, saying to Anne, 'Take the rest of the day off, Anne...'

'But ... the customers...'

'It's a quiet time, you said. Do it. Please. See you tomorrow ... usual time.'

'Yes ... Yes, Herr Diefenhausen.'

She removed her small apron, hung it on a rack, got her bag, and quickly left.

Diefenhausen took them along a narrow passage which came to a dead end. He pressed a light switch, but no lights came on. Instead, he placed his hand against the painted wall and gave a sideways pressure. The entire partition slid open for about half a metre.

'Go left,' he said. 'There's a door at the end. Slide the spring bolt. When you're outside, just push it shut. It will lock automatically. The door leads to a narrow passage behind a high wall. Go along the passage until you come to an iron gate that's just as high. Slide the bolt back, and open the gate. It will also lock automatically when you close it again. You will find yourselves in a short alleyway. Turn left at the end and you will soon find out where you are. There is nothing outside to show there is a back way out of here. Now get in. Hurry, please.'

Müller, followed by Hellmann, entered a second narrow passage that was blocked off to their right. The partition was already sliding into place as they made their way towards the door Diefenhausen had spoken of.

The rest of the short distance was made in darkness.

'He's certainly well prepared,' Müller said drily.

Hellmann said nothing.

Müller reached the solid door, fumbled and found the bolt, and slid it back and pushed the door open. He briefly squinted his eyes as light flooded in brightly. They went out, and he pushed the door shut behind them, hearing the bolt again slide into the lock.

'My car...' Hellmann began.

'Smarter to leave it where it is,' Müller advised. 'I'm assuming the parking space is Diefenhausen's. He will look after your car ... if he survives the encounter with ... whom did

176

you say...?'

'Heurath.'

'Heurath. Ah yes. I know him by several other names ... and he probably has many more. You can tell me all about him while I take you back to your boat. And about Diefenhausen's insurance too.'

As Diefenhausen returned to the counter in the café with the two cups from the back room, he heard a female American voice discussing directions with someone. He put the two cups among the other used crockery.

Then an impatient voice on the edge of civility said, 'That is it, Miss...'

'Harris.'

'That's it, Miss Harris ... you cannot now be unable to find your way to the Gutenberg Museum. Goodbye.'

'Er ... bye. And thanks again.'

There was no response. Then came the sound of firm footsteps and Heurath, who called himself Renner among many other names, entered the café. He glanced unsmilingly at the few customers, then went directly up to the counter.

'Tourists!' he said contemptuously.

Diefenhausen stared at him as he would a cobra. 'Christ! *You?*'

Heurath smiled tightly. It was a grimace, the eyes dead spheres of obsidian in his face. 'Yes, me. Not Christ. How are you, Diefenhausen? Or should I say ... Föhnach?'

'That person is long gone.' Diefenhausen

177

glanced at the customers.

Heurath followed the look. 'Ah. Yes. I agree with you. We should be private. Just give me a moment.'

He went to the middle of the room and took out an ID which he held slightly raised, and forward.

'Sorry to disturb you, ladies and gentlemen. *Oberkommissar* Renner. I am carrying out an investigation, and this establishment must be temporarily closed. Don't worry if you haven't paid as yet. It will all be taken care of. Thank you.'

People were leaving even as he returned to the counter.

'See?' he said to Diefenhausen. 'No one refuses a free meal. Easy.'

'And who's going to pay for the coffees, the other drinks, and the food?'

'You've had plenty of money from us to put into this tourist trap. Don't push your luck.' Heurath glanced back. The place was empty. 'They didn't waste time. So ... *Diefenhausen* ... time to begin. Where is Hellmann, or should I say ... Warneck?'

'I don't know.'

'You don't know. I see. His car – magic thing that it is – drove here all by itself. I know these are good cars, but that good? Somehow, I doubt it. *Where* ... is he?'

'I've just told you ... I don't ... know!'

'Don't try my patience. His car ... *is out there*!'

'I haven't seen it. He's not supposed to

come here. Perhaps he was coming, but saw you.'

'Recognized me, did he? After all these years?'

Diefenhausen looked pointedly at the haircut. 'Perhaps you should change the way you cut your hair.'

Heurath breathed deeply. 'Bold. Very bold. This is either the bravery of a rabbit which knows it has no chance ... or ... ah yes ... of course. It has come to my attention that you have written a sort of ... let us say ... memoir. And naturally, you have put it somewhere safe. Should anything happen to you, etcetera ... Am I on the right track?' He gave his chilling smile once more.

Diefenhausen continued to stare at him, but said nothing.

'You know I could make you tell...'

'Not before you killed me. Then where would you be? There must be someone – or something – that even you are afraid of. My information, in the wrong hands, can kill you.'

The cold eyes stared back at Diefenhausen. 'The boldness of a rabbit. You shouldn't believe in talismans. They don't always work. Things are frequently never what they seem. Do you mind if I search this place?'

'You will do it, anyway, with or without my permission.'

Heurath did not smile. Without another word, he went through to the back. Diefenhausen remained where he was.

Heurath made a thorough search, eventually ending up in the corridor with the dead end. He stood there for long moments studying the sides, the ceiling and the blanking partition.

He went up to it and knocked hard. It gave off a solid sound, and did not budge, even slightly. He stood back and looked around him, then peered closely again at each wall, pressing at their surfaces at random. Nothing gave.

He went back to join Diefenhausen. 'I did not really expect to find him. You would not have been so accommodating. Is there a back way out of here?'

'You looked. Did you find one? And why should I need one, anyway?'

'A way out in case of fire?'

Diefenhausen pointed to a door to the left, near the counter. 'That leads out to the street.'

Heurath did not even look at it. 'Your staff. Don't you have staff in this tourist-milking place?'

'I gave them the day off.'

'All the answers, eh, Diefenhausen?' Heurath poked a hard finger at Diefenhausen's chest, punctuating each word with a jab. 'Remember ... things ... are ... never ... what ... they ... seem.' The jabbing stopped. 'Remember too, it's a dangerous world out there. You, of all people, should know that.'

Then Heurath suddenly turned, and went out.

He paused in front of the café and looked slowly about him. Satisfied, he walked on, turned the first corner and worked his way round the back. He came to the tall iron gate and shook it. It barely moved, and remained firmly locked.

He peered through, but could see nothing that remotely appeared to be part of Diefenhausen's building.

He smiled thinly, and continued walking.

The Porsche was on its way to the container harbour. Müller drove at an easy pace, while Hellmann stared straight ahead. They had been travelling in silence for some time.

'Well, Herr Hellmann,' Müller began. 'It seems as if you're out in the cold.'

'How do you know of me?'

'Wrong remark. What you should have said was, "Thank you, *Hauptkommissar* Müller, for saving my life back there".'

'Out of the goodness of your heart?'

'No.'

'Your job.'

'Among other things ... yes. I also don't like people going around murdering other people. It makes life ... difficult for me.'

Hellmann glanced at him. 'You don't look like a *Hauptkommissar*.'

'That's what your friend's already said. My cross. People never seem to think I am. Must be my hair. And talking of hair ... you will not have seen the last of Heurath. He's a kind of exterminating angel ... although, angelic he certainly is not.'

Hellmann said nothing, having retreated deep into his own thoughts.

'We can help you,' Müller pressed on after a minute or so. 'And keep your family safe.'

'If I talk.'

'Every little helps. For example ... who is Heurath really? And what is Diefenhausen's insurance? That sort of thing...'

'I have plenty of thinking to do.'

'I am certain you do. But don't take too long about it. In addition to your own, you have other lives to think about. I am thinking of your family.'

Another silence fell within the car. It lasted until they had reached the port.

Müller stopped the car in the same place as before. 'Here we are, Herr Hellmann. Your boat awaits. It would be good for you to be able to keep it, and all that it represents.' Müller reached into a pocket and took out a plain white business card with nothing but a number on it. He held it out. 'Here. When you've done your thinking, call this number. You'll get my deputy, Pappenheim. Just say Mondrian, and he'll take it from there.'

'Mondrian,' Hellmann said absently. 'So you're an art lover too. Strange choice, Mondrian. He always reminds me of restriction ... like being trapped.'

Müller looked at Hellmann steadily. 'Must be the kind of life you've been living.'

Hellmann took the card as he opened the door. 'Thank you, *Hauptkommissar.*' He climbed out, and began making his way to the *Isabella Lütz*.

He did not look back.

Müller watched until Hellmann had gone out sight, then made a quick call to Pappenheim.

'Ask the locals to switch the helicopter to a patrol over the port, centred on the *Isabella Lütz*,' he said as soon as Pappenheim had answered 'Until she leaves.'

'Will do.' There was a short pause. 'Are we watching the *Lütz*, or something else?'

'Both. Particularly for Renner, or Heurath. So give his description, but no explanation. My belief is that when he sees the chopper, he'll keep well away.'

'Heurath ... Heurath...' Pappenheim was saying thoughtfully.

'You've heard the name? I was about to ask you to check it out.'

'Not heard. I've read it somewhere ... quite some time ago.'

'It's another of Renner's names ... but this could be the real one.' Müller quickly explained about Hellmann and Diefenhausen. 'Both are clearly terrified of him ... and, from what we know so far, with very good reason.'

'I'll look up Diefenhausen too.'

'Thought you would.'

'I'll start with the picture we got from the duckling's pals. And how's our American friend? I'm just getting back on to the chair I fell off when you told me.'

'She was very helpful a short while ago.'

183

'Well, well, well. At this rate, you two will soon be getting married.'

'Still too early for the jokes, Pappi.'

'A touch of levity now and then does wonders for the—'

'Later, Pappi...'

'If you insist. Back to the *Lütz*,' Pappenheim went on, unchastened. 'She won't make it to Budapest. At least, not to schedule. The floods in the east make the Danube a no-go area until things get back to normal...'

'I agree. According to Bloomfield, the passengers are already worrying about it. Shipping on the Danube is stopped, and that's that. He'll have to remain on the Rhine for the time being.'

'Which makes life a little easier for us.'

'Any news on our Makarov man?'

'Nothing yet. What does that tell you?'

'The information is being sat on.'

'Give the man ten out of ten. But that won't help them. I'll burn through the jamming.'

'If anyone can, Pappi ... it's you.'

'Such nice things the man says. And speaking of Gauer – even if you didn't – he's still breathing, worse luck, and gave an interview on television a short while ago. Usual stuff. Not quite *ein Reich, ein Volk*, but you get the drift. From extreme left communist, to extreme right fascist. Once an asshole, always an asshole. These kind of people will plague us for centuries ... But we've got to protect him ... for now.'

'Pappi...'

'OK, OK. We continue to protect him. Berger and Reimer would be shocked to hear me say this. A while ago I gave them a speech about being honourable police officers when they expressed the same feelings.'

'Take your own advice.'

'I'll have to,' Pappenheim said, again un-repentant. 'One piece of good news, though. The GW is out for the day. For once, his blood vessels remained intact when he mentioned your name. Hope that doesn't mean he's getting to like you. I would be seriously worried.'

'So would I.'

A sound made Müller look up. A helicopter was describing wide, slow circles above the harbour.

'That was fast,' Müller went on. 'The chopper's here.'

'I have eight hands.'

Müller smiled, and ended the call.

Carey Bloomfield had seen the bristle-haired man enter the café, and had waited in a secluded position to see what would happen next. Very soon, the customers had hurried out; but no Müller.

When no sudden burst of gunfire had disturbed the day, she had waited longer until she saw the man come back out, then turn into another street. She had still waited, to see if Müller would also come out. Müller could take care of himself, so she had not been particularly worried and had assumed

185

that he had found another exit.

She had continued to keep watch on the café and when neither Müller nor the bristle-haired man had returned, called Toby Adams.

'Have you something for me?' she said as soon as he answered.

'You are in a hurry.'

'Things are happening. What's the news on Müller's involvement?'

'Nada. So far, nothing's come up on the radar. They're keeping a very tight lid on this one.'

'Well something's come up here.'

'I'm waiting...'

'The brush-haired man. Using Hellmann as Judas goat worked.'

'Ah...!'

'Müller knows about him.'

'Damn it!' Adams said fiercely.

'What are you keeping from me, Toby?'

'Nothing ... I swear...'

'Don't swear, Toby. That would make me nervous.'

Adams thought about that. 'Carey ... you know I worry about you...'

'If I get those crocodile tears I'll really know I'm in trouble.'

'Trust me...'

'Another bad choice of words.'

'Damn it, Carey! Don't make it so hard for me. I'm standing between you and a hell of a lot of hardasses...'

'Then find out about Müller. We had a co-operative effort when the brush-hair came

186

visiting—'

'You *worked* with Müller?'

'Yep. I carried out ... let's call it a diversion...'

'And?'

'No gunfight. Müller had gone into this café place after Hellmann. Then the hairbrush turned up.'

'Are you sure it's the guy we're after?'

'No ... I'm not. The haircut's the same like that one in the old picture I was shown, as is the stockiness of the build ... but that picture's nearly twenty years old...'

'You saw the computer aging analysis.'

'That doesn't mean it was correct.'

'Did Müller say it was Heurath?'

'Müller's telling me zilch. He's not dumb, Toby.'

'Look ... as you've now met ... use the situation to your advantage. And Carey ... we want Heurath *alive*.'

'If he'll let me...'

'Carey ... and Hellmann too!'

'Know anyone who wants a boatload of antique furniture, Toby?'

'Heurath and Hellmann alive, Carey!'

'Bye, Toby.'

'*Carey*—!'

She cut transmission.

'Guess I'd better go back to that café and see if Müller turns up,' she said to herself.

Hellmann was greeted by his wife as he boarded the boat.

187

'Where's the car?' she asked, eyes searching the immediate area.

'Some idiot of a tourist hit it,' he replied without hesitation, putting the correct amount of annoyance into his voice.

'Oh no! Our nice new car! What happened?'

'He jumped some traffic lights. But don't worry. His car has more damage. We only lost a headlight. The local dealer will sort it out and we can pick it up on the way back, good as new. They couldn't fix it in time for our departure.'

'I was looking forward to Budapest and a drive out into the countryside, but perhaps it's just as well. We'll be late for Budapest, anyway. The news is full of the floods in the east ... and we have a shipping message that the Danube is closed. What do you want to do?'

'We can wait it out at Ludwigshafen. I'll explain to the passengers. There will be plenty for them to do and see; but those who want to leave can do so. We'll refund the money for that section of the trip. As for the cargo, the owners can't expect us to sail the Danube when it's closed.'

Hellmann glanced up at the circling helicopter. Were they keeping watch up there? And was it Müller's doing? He hoped so. It would keep Heurath away till it was time to sail.

Isabella Hellmann followed her husband's gaze, watching as the helicopter briefly hovered above a huge red container bridge crane, before resuming its circular tracking.

'Probably hoping to find smugglers,' she said.

'I suppose,' he said, keeping the relief out of his voice.

At least she hadn't spotted the anxiety in his eyes.

'If we've got to stay in Ludwigshafen,' she said, glancing up at the helicopter once more, 'I could always pick up the car...'

'I can do that, Isa. Don't worry. I'm going up to the bridge,' he added. 'Coming?'

She followed him.

'We'll take it, Johann,' he said to the crew-man on watch.

'Right, Captain.'

Hellmann sat down at the console as the man left, and called up the Bamberg/Main-Danube Canal water level message screen on a monitor. The graphic display showed blue columns delineated by dates, their spiked tops showing the peaks and troughs of the rise and fall of the water level, with each date notched in quarters. The historical levels were for seven days to current time.

'It's still below the two hundred and eighty centimetre mark,' Hellmann said. 'Not much variation over the past few days. First warning usually comes at three hundred.' He paused. 'We could still go up the Main and wait nearer the canal ... but there'll be other boats held up too. It will be a traffic jam. We stay with Ludwigshafen. The passengers can use the time, as I said, to do some extra sightseeing. Plenty to interest them between there and Speyer. We'll put an off-roader at their disposal, and they'll have a longer trip, all at no additional cost. That should please them, shouldn't it?'

She nodded. 'I would think so.'

Müller was walking back to the café where Carey Bloomfield waited.

She looked up from the tourist guide she had been pretending to read and saw him approaching. A tiny smile touched the corners of her mouth.

'He didn't get you, after all,' she greeted in English when he had entered and reached her table.

'He didn't get me, after all. May I join you?'

She stared at him, and sighed. 'Müller ... stop being so damned formal and sit down!'

He sat down opposite.

She studied his expression closely. 'What's funny?'

'That was an excellent diversion. You were quick out of here, and you gave me all the warning I needed. Thank you.'

'Good thing I was here to do it.'

'Yes. My good fortune.'

She gave him a probing, sideways look. 'That's a compliment, isn't it?'

'An expression of gratitude.'

'I suppose I'll have to...'

A waitress had come to their table, and was looking enquiringly at Müller.

'A milk coffee, please,' he said to her in

German, then looked at Carey Bloomfield.

'Same for me,' Carey Bloomfield said, also in German. When the waitress had gone, she switched back to English. 'Why do these young women always smile at you? It was the same the last time I was here in Germany. I remember two policewomen at your head-quarters in Berlin.'

'She was not smiling. She was just being polite. I'm a customer. That is all. As for Berlin ... I'm their boss. They're always polite to the boss.'

'Oh sure.'

'So ... *are* you my liaison?'

'Repeating the question does not make it fact. As you saw earlier, this really is news to me.'

'Kaltendorf must have got it wrong.'

'Riddles, Müller?'

'Life's a riddle.'

'Philosophy with the coffee, too. And how's your Aunt Isolde, Müller?' Carey Bloomfield continued, watching him speculatively. 'Still running that beautiful Schlosshotel down there by the Saale?'

'Still running it and wondering why you never got in touch.'

'Ouch. I felt that needle. The job, Müller. You, of all people, should understand.'

'Ah, yes. The job. I still find time to call her now and then. Talking of which ... I must check to see whether she is in danger of being flooded out. There's no indication that the Saale is about to burst its banks, but you

191

never know...'

'Alright ... don't rub it in. But she's *your* aunt ... and that place is another home to you. Me ... I was there for—'

'She would have liked to have heard from you. That's all.'

'Well. Now that you've made me feel bad...'

'And now that the pleasantries are over,' he added, 'aren't you going to ask what happened?'

'I'm sure you'll tell me ... the parts you want to.'

His eyes focused steadily upon hers. 'That makes two of us. But no matter. Your presence is opportune...'

'Opportune...?'

'Your presence is opportune because it is good to know someone is covering Hellmann...'

'Wait a minute ... wait a *minute* ... You want *me* to cover Hellmann for *you*?'

'Why not?' he asked mildly. 'You're already doing so...'

'Hold on. Rewind the tape. Until you saw me, you had no idea I was here...'

'And *you* had none that I was here. However, I am carrying out a very sensitve investigation.'

'And I am—'

Müller shook his head slowly. 'No ... no ... no. Me ... policeman. You ... tourist.' He paused, waiting.

The waitress came with their coffees. Carey Bloomfield studied her pointedly. She smiled at Müller.

'See?' Carey Bloomfield hissed as soon as the waitress had left. 'She didn't even look at me.'

'All in your imagination.'

'Like the threat you just made?'

'I made no threat.'

'If I don't do as you say, you'll take me off that boat...'

'I have no wish to do that.'

'But?'

'No but. I'm asking you for assistance. Hellmann has no idea who you really are. Let that state of affairs continue.'

'Are you giving me orders, Müller?'

'Heaven forbid. But I seem to remember that when we first met in Berlin last year, you were posing as a journalist. Your pose this time is as a tourist ... a very special tourist of course; a tourist who carries a big gun on her person...'

'And that isn't a threat? You're not saying to me ... hey, if you don't do as I say, I'll pull you in for carrying that gun?'

'I am certain you would claim diplomatic immunity and your people would step in, and you'd be gone in the blink of an eye...'

'But before that could happen I'd be off the boat and my mission screwed.'

'I didn't say that.'

'You didn't have to.'

They drank their coffees in silence.

The waitress looked at them and thought they were having a lovers' tiff.

'Ah! There you are, Amy!'

Carey Bloomfield's head swivelled round. She stared at the Grogans, who were both beaming at her. They looked at Müller, then back to her.

'Er ... Hi!' she said, smiling quickly.

'We saw you from outside,' Grogan continued, 'and thought we'd perhaps come in and say hi. But we won't disturb you.' They glanced at Müller once more.

'Er ... Jack and Betty Grogan,' she began to Müller. 'They're on the boat with me. Jack ... Betty, my friend Jens.'

'Hi, Jens.' Grogan, a burly man with a bushy grey moustache, and a tuft of white-grey hair and kind-looking eyes behind spectacles, held out a large hand.

Müller got to his feet and shook the hand, then did likewise with Betty Grogan. 'A pleasure,' he said.

Betty Grogan, roundish and about the same height as her husband, kept smiling benignly.

'You from around here, Jens?' Grogan asked.

'No,' Müller replied. 'Berlin.'

'Berlin! Some city, huh?'

'That it is.'

'And what a history!'

'You are a student of history, Mr Grogan?'

'Jack, please.'

'Jack...'

'Not so much a student, Jens, as having lived it. I spent some time at Checkpoint Charlie.'

194

'Interesting...'

'And now look at it ... a tourist attraction.'

'The world turns, Jack.'

'It sure does.' Grogan was looking at him as if trying to remember something. 'Well ... we'll leave you youngsters alone. See you on the boat, Amy.'

'Later, Jack.'

When they had gone Müller said, as he sat down again, 'Are they really tourists?'

'They really, really are,' Carey Bloomfield replied. 'What do you think? The entire passenger list is made up of—'

'Intelligence agents? Why not?'

'A boatload of spooks? That would be over-kill.'

'Would it?'

'Come on, Müller. You don't even believe that.'

'I always keep an open mind.'

'Oh sure. Umm ... and thanks for not telling the Grogans.'

'Why should I?'

'Thanks, anyway. So who is this man I nearly drove to distraction with my dumb, touristy questions?'

'Someone very dangerous who will remember your face, should you have the misfortune to meet him again.'

'If he's so dangerous, why haven't you arrested him?'

'Don't fish, Miss Bloomfield,' Müller said mildly. 'You won't catch anything.'

★ ★ ★

195

Heurath sat in his car enjoying an ice cream. He was well away from where the *Isabella Lütz* was berthed, but could see the circling helicopter.

He smiled tightly. 'Your doing, Müller? You don't know what you're getting into.'

He bit savagely into the cone, filling his mouth with a mixture of cone and ice cream. A trickle of white leaked down the edge of a lip.

He did not wipe it away.

Carey Bloomfield glanced at her watch. 'The boat leaves in half an hour. I'd better get going.'

Müller looked towards the waitress, who arrived at the table with alacrity. He paid, and she rewarded him with a smile as warm as Anne's had been in the Café Diefenhausen.

'I thought her face would crack,' Carey Bloomfield commented as the waitress went away. She got to her feet.

Müller stood up. 'I didn't notice.'

'Sure you did.'

As they went out, the waitress smiled again.

'She included you this time,' Müller said.

'Like hell she did. So tell me, Müller,' Carey Bloomfield continued as they walked to where he had left the car. 'What will you be doing while I'm enjoying my Rhine travels?'

'Keeping you, and Hellmann, out of the reach of the bristle-haired man.'

'For now.'

'Permanently, if possible.'

'You're going to take him?'

'Not yet,' Müller said.

'Playing your cards close to your chest, Müller.'

'So are you.' They had reached the car. 'Please get in,' Müller said as he unlocked the Porsche with the remote. 'I'll take you close to the *Isabella Lütz*, but not so close that Hellmann might spot you with me.'

She climbed in without another word as Müller took his seat behind the wheel. He started the engine and drove off, turning into the Rheinallee a few minutes later. The short distance to the port was covered in continued silence; then he slowed down, filtered right, pulled to the side of the road and stopped.

'If you turn right just over there,' he told her, 'you'll see the boat.'

She heard a sound and leaned sideways to look up. 'There's a helicopter up there. It's in police green. Was that your idea, Müller?'

'Yes. It should keep the bristle-haired man away till the boat leaves.' He got out to open the door for her. 'Be prepared for anything,' he went on. 'And watch yourself.'

She looked at him for long moments. 'Don't talk to any strange men, Müller.'

She walked away and did not look back as she turned the corner.

'You too, Miss Bloomfield.'

He got back into the car, turned it round to rejoin the Rheinallee, and headed out of the city.

★ ★ ★

197

She waited until the sound of the car had faded, peered round the corner to make certain Müller had indeed gone, then took out her mobile and called Toby Adams.

'Anything yet, Toby?'

'About Müller … nothing. All lines to him are blocked.'

'Damn!'

'What about your end?'

'Let's put it this way. I'm cooperating. He didn't actually say he'd arrest me for carrying a weapon…'

'But the veiled threat was there.'

'From where I'm standing, not so veiled.'

'And Heurath?'

'No sighting since my little charade. Müller's got a helicopter over the port. Heurath should keep away from there … if it *is* Heurath. I'm certain they'll have high-scan cameras up there, and Heurath will know it.'

'But Müller's still given no indication that he knows anything about Heurath?'

'Müller is giving nothing away.'

'You sound annoyed in a way that makes me think you've got a soft spot for the guy…'

'Don't be ridiculous, Toby.'

'Do not protest too much.'

She ignored the remark. 'He knows much, much more than he is admitting … and he's letting Heurath run, when he could have pulled him in. Just find out Müller's interest in this for me, Toby. That's all I ask. I don't want to discover that I've played the river tourist all the way from Holland, just to have the job screwed. There's something else going on that either you don't know about ... or you're not telling me. He even asked if I were his liaison. I thought he was joking ... Toby? You there?'

'I'm right here. It seems to me you'll have to stick with him...'

'And how do I do that on the boat?'

'From what you've told me, he won't be far away. He wants Hellmann to stay alive, and sooner or later, he will take Heurath. It's just a matter of time...'

'*We* want Heurath.'

'Yes ... we do, and remember, Hellmann too ... both alive.'

'You're repeating yourself. Do you see the problem here, Toby?'

'I'm sure you'll find a way. Neither is of any use to us dead. People have memories of the last time you went out to bring someone in alive. He didn't make it.'

' "People", Toby?'

'I'm always on your side, Carey.'

'Don't want to miss the boat. I'll be in touch.'

'Carey—'

As before, she cut transmission on him.

'Always on my side?' she muttered as she put the mobile away. 'We'll see.'

Her hand was still in the bag when a car pulled up next to her. 'We meet again!' she heard in English.

She turned to look. *The bristle-haired man.* She kept her nerve and went into her

199

vacuous tourist mode. Her hand remained in her bag, as if she had been interrupted in her search for something. She wrapped her fingers about the gun.

She beamed at him, walking away from the port. 'Oh! Hi!'

Had he seen her leave Müller's car?

The car reversed then stopped a little ahead of her, forcing her to come to a halt.

His eyes did not join the smile he gave her. 'Not lost again, are you? This is a bit of a way from the city centre.'

'Oh no. I was taking some pictures up by the Theodor Heuss bridge and was walking along the river when I spotted this big red crane in the distance. I wanted a closer look.' She pointed to the huge container bridge crane, and babbled on like an overenthusiastic tourist, 'I find these things fascinating structures. But I'm done now. My friends are waiting just up the road, by the river.'

'*Oberkommissar* Renner,' he said, introducing himself. 'I am sorry I was a little brusque earlier. I am investigating a case.'

'I see. Well ... I didn't mean to get in your way,' she said in her best oh-gee manner. 'I'm Amy Harris. Hope you have success with your case.'

'I will,' he said. 'Enjoy Mainz, Miss Harris.' He gave a brief wave and began turning the car round.

She waited until he had completed the turn and had merged into fast-moving traffic, going in the opposite direction to the one

200

Müller had taken. Only then did she slowly remove her hand from the bag.

She glanced up at the helicopter. 'He didn't keep away, Müller.' She knew that Heurath would not venture into the port on foot. In a car, however, he was anonymous. He could position himself anywhere, to survey the harbour through binoculars; or in secure cover a further distance away, through the scope of a high-powered rifle. The huge container crane was a good vantage point for a sniper. There was a direct line of sight from it to the *Isabella Lütz*.

But he had to get there first ... and undetected. With the helicopter on constant watch, he had no real chance; certainly, not before the boat left.

Despite this, she took no risks. Choosing a route back that kept her within the cover of the tall stacks of containers and screened her from the dock where the *Isabella Lütz* waited, she hurried on.

She was well aware that Heurath could easily have stopped anywhere along the road, to double back. She wanted to be well gone by then.

She made it to the boat with scant minutes to spare.

The Grogans were on deck, adding to their video record of their trip. Grogan was using the camera. He lowered it when he saw her.

'We were getting worried about you, Amy. We sure thought you would not make it in time.'

Betty Grogan beamed at her. 'That was a nice young man in the café.'

'He's ... OK.'

Betty winked at her husband. 'What do you think, Jack?'

'I think she thinks he's more than OK.' He chuckled hugely, then frowned. 'Seems kind of familiar, but damned if I know where I've seen him before. Oh, Amy,' he went on. 'The captain wants to speak to all passengers once we're under way. In the main lounge.'

'I'll be there,' she said.

They returned to their recording as she hurried on to her suite. Above their heads, the helicopter continued its wide circling.

In her suite, Carey Bloomfield got out her camera, zoomed the lens to 300mm and went to the porthole. She took a series of shots of the harbour, covering a wide area, including several of the crane ... just in case Heurath had somehow managed to make it. But though she held the crane within the lens for long moments, there was no sign of anyone attempting to sneak up one of its ladders.

At precisely 16.00, the *Isabella Lütz* slipped her moorings.

Heurath had indeed done precisely what Carey Bloomfield had suspected.

As soon as he could, he turned off the Rheinallee and into a side street that would enable him to double back on to the main road. By the time he was again heading back towards the container port, she was nowhere

202

to be seen.

'You're a fast walker, Miss Amy Harris,' he muttered, turning his head from side to side as he tried to locate her.

He turned off the road again, to reverse his direction once more.

He headed towards the spot where she had told him her friends were waiting. He took a left turn which led him towards a riverside car park where he stopped and got out of the car. From this position he had a wide expanse of the river in view. The Theodor Heuss bridge was reasonably close by, over to his right.

There was no sign of Amy Harris, or of her friends.

'Very fast walker indeed,' Heurath remarked softly.

He looked to his left, and spotted a vessel just nosing into view, going upstream. The *Isabella Lütz*.

He smiled tightly.

'And you shouldn't believe in talismans either, Udo Hellmann. Or should I say ... Josef Warneck? You won't escape me. I have many strings to my bow, and you've got a surprise coming.'

With the smile still fixed, he got back into his car.

Carey Bloomfield was a little late. Hellmann was already in the lounge, as were the other passengers.

'Sorry,' she said.

203

He smiled at her. 'Quite alright, Miss Harris. You are the passenger, and this is not a naval ship. You will all have watched the news on the televisions in your suites,' he went on. 'The scenes of the flooding in the east are very shocking. As a result of what has happened, it will not be possible to continue to Budapest until the situation has stabilized. We could go up the Main to wait at the head of the Main-Danube canal, in the port of Bamberg.

'However, there is a shipping jam up there as boats wait for the waterways to be cleared again for traffic. I think it is best to go on to Ludwigshafen to wait this out. There is plenty to see and do between Ludwigshafen and Speyer ... especially Speyer cathedral, for the historians among you. An Audi Allroader will also be at your disposal. There will of course be no extra charges for this emergency extension of your journey ... but if any of you would prefer not to continue, either because you can't spare the time, or for any other reason ... then the correct percentage of your fare will be returned.'

'We've already discussed the situation amongst ourselves, Captain,' Grogan said. 'So I think I'm speaking for all of us. We're not jumping ship.'

Hellmann smiled, pleased by the response. 'Then the *Isabella Lütz* is entirely at your service. We shall celebrate with a special dinner this evening. Thank you.'

Seven

In Berlin, Kaltendorf and Solange had greatly enjoyed their day, father and daughter proudly accompanying each other about the city. Wide-eyed, she had taken in the sights of the ever-rejuvenating Berlin, a child in a land of wonder.

They were now at the Brandenburg Gate. She stared up at the Quadriga.

'On New Year's night in 1990,' he said to her, 'some people managed to climb up there to place flags. One, unbelievably, was Canadian.'

She giggled. 'A *Canadian* flag? Why Canadian?'

He smiled at her. 'Ask the mysterious person who put it there. I have often wondered myself. Perhaps it was someone who had escaped from the East during the time of the Wall, and had made it to Canada. Perhaps a soldier – or the son of a soldier – who had once served near the Wall. Perhaps none of these.' He checked his watch. 'We should be getting back to the car,' he continued. 'I'll introduce you to Noni and her family, then we'll go home.'

'Home,' she repeated, savouring the word softly.

'Your home is here too,' he said. 'Not just in Cap Ferrat.'

She gave his hand a light squeeze. 'I know.'

Such was their happiness, neither of them realized that throughout the afternoon they had been kept under observation by the same motorcyclist who had overtaken them on the way from the airport.

When they got to the car and drove off, they were still oblivious. Perhaps Kaltendorf's unaccustomed sense of euphoria had dulled his normal police instincts. Whatever the reasons, he remained quite unaware that he was being followed as he drove to Noni Erlenhausen's family home.

In Mainz, Heurath returned to the Café Diefenhausen.

There was just the one customer paying for a coffee and, by the time Heurath had entered, the man was on his way out.

Diefenhausen paused halfway between the counter and the table he had just served.

'What do you want?' he demanded of Heurath coldly.

Heurath gave one of his dead smiles. 'The bravery of the doomed rabbit is still with you, I see. You clearly believe in the powers of your talisman.'

'I'll repeat what I told you before. I'll be dead before you get anything out of me, so you might as well go and frighten someone else. My insurance is safe.'

Heurath took a deep breath, stared up at the ceiling for some moments, then back at Diefenhausen. 'You say that as if you believe it.'

'I believe it.'

Heurath seemed to pause to think. 'I do have a question.'

'You know what you can do with it.'

Diefenhausen continued walking back to the counter and went behind it. He busied himself with stacking crockery.

Heurath was remarkably undisturbed by Diefenhausen's attitude. 'I'll ask it, anyway. Hellmann's car is still out there ... and his boat has just left. I stopped to have a look, and it was already approaching the Theodor Heuss bridge, heading upstream. I find it very strange that he leaves his car – which seems very new – outside your café, then simply goes on his way. And you haven't even seen him. Doesn't all that seem very mysterious to you?'

'How should I know?'

But Heurath was persistent. 'Does Hellmann also have ... let's call it ... a talisman ... in a safe place?'

'How should I know?' Diefenhausen repeated, not looking up and continuing to stack his crockery as if Heurath were not there. 'I'm sure you'll tell me.'

Heurath still remained undisturbed, a warning in itself which Diefenhausen chose to ignore.

'I won't tell you at all.' Heurath had taken out his silenced automatic, and was pointing it at Diefenhausen. 'Except that you shouldn't believe in talismans ... and neither should Hellmann.'

He shot the astonished Diefenhausen twice.

Eyes reproachful, Diefenhausen fell heavily against his crockery, which crashed to the floor with him in a cascade. Diefenhausen died beneath a shroud of broken cups, saucers, and tea plates, without uttering the slightest sound.

'You got your wish,' Heurath said, putting the gun away.

Without even looking to see where Diefenhausen had fallen, he walked unhurriedly out of the café. As he passed Hellmann's car, he gave the driver's door a vicious kick. It made a slamming sound, and a dent appeared in the gleaming bodywork.

A middle-aged tourist couple walking by paused to stare at him, scandalized.

He stared back at them. '*Yes?*' he snarled at them in English.

They looked quickly away, and hurried on.

The *Isabella Lütz* made her way upstream, pushing against the force of the river's flow, her powerful engines thrusting her forward with ease. Her passage was relatively quiet when measured against the normal engine throb of the other boats.

Beneath her keel were conformal blisters that housed various sensors. One was a recent addition.

It was very different, because it was not a sensor at all; but there was nothing about it to betray this overtly. It looked just like any other blister.

Its purpose, however, had little to do with navigation.

Within its electronic brain a silent, invisible countdown had started; a countdown to detonation.

Rüdiger Honneff was again on watch when Hellmann went up to the bridge.

'All OK, Rudi?'

Honneff did not glance round, keeping his eyes on constant surveillance of the ship's monitoring displays, the river and the cargo deck.

'All OK, Captain. Oh ... I've got something for you. Been waiting to get you alone.'

Intrigued, Hellmann went closer.

Honneff reached into a compartment in the console near his right leg, and took out a mid-sized brown envelope.

'This came with the mail from Mainz,' Honneff continued, handing over the envelope. 'I thought it best to give it to you personally.'

'Thank you,' Hellmann said as he took the envelope.

Puzzled, he studied it closely, even feeling it gingerly to check for the slight undulations that would betray the presence of thin wires. But it felt just like an ordinary document, not a letter bomb. It was unmistakably addressed to him, was marked private, and had been posted in Mainz days before. There was no return address.

'Has my wife seen this?'

'No, Captain.' Honneff still did not look round.

Hellmann nodded, and went over to the port side of the bridge where he carefully began to open the envelope.

What came out of it made him stare in shock.

He slowly placed the seven pages of a closely handwritten statement down on the bridge console, in free space between two monitor screens. A note had been clipped to them.

'*Some insurance*,' he read silently. '*Keep it safe.*'

The note was from Diefenhausen.

A quick scan of the writing was all that was needed for him to realize that Diefenhausen had sent him a hot potato. As much as could have been comprehensively put down in seven pages about the Romeo Six operation, was there. Names, details, planned phases. This, he realized, would be a goldmine for Müller. He also realized that Heurath would kill anyone to get at it.

Diefenhausen had intended to keep his 'insurance' as safe as was possible under the circumstances. Where better than on a boat that was in a different place every day? Anyone looking for such a document would expect to find it in the usual places: somewhere hidden in a house; in a bank safe deposit, and so on; not on a boat on the Rhine.

With slightly trembling hands, Hellmann put the pages back into the envelope and sealed it with adhesive tape from a roll he took from a small drawer.

'I'll be back in a minute, Rudi,' he said to Honneff.

'Right, Captain.' Honneff did not interrupt his periodic scanning as Hellmann went out.

Hellmann quickly went to his cabin and was relieved to find his wife was not there. That spared him having to explain the envelope. There were two safes, fixed behind panels which were themselves hidden by family photographs. One was his wife's safe, in which she kept her personal documentation, as well as cash, jewelry, and anything else she wanted to put in there. The other was his own. Neither had ever gone into the other's safe without permission. It was an arrangement between them of many years' standing.

He put the envelope into his safe, and prayed Heurath would never suspect what Diefenhausen had done.

As he made his way back to the bridge he paused, and felt in a pocket for the card Müller had handed to him in Mainz.

He went back to his cabin.

Pappenheim, a cigarette firmly between his

lips, was looking slowly through a file that Enteling had just brought. Enteling was himself standing awkwardly, as far as possible as he could from Pappenheim.

Pappenheim drew loudly on his cigarette as he leafed through the file. There were some photographs in transparent, protective sleeves. He paused to study one, took the cigarette out of his mouth and gave a low whistle.

'This ... is serious, serious stuff.'

Enteling gave a slight cough.

Pappenheim looked up. 'My smoking troubling you?'

Enteling gave another cough and cleared his throat. 'I shouldn't be here at all.'

'You shouldn't be here in my smoke? Or you shouldn't be here with this file?'

'Both.'

'Very decisive. None of us should be here.'

'What I mean—' Enteling began tightly.

One of Pappenheim's phones interrupted him with a sudden ring.

Pappenheim picked it up. 'Pappenheim.'

'Mondrian,' the voice said.

'Call me in exactly one hour,' Pappenheim said crisply, and hung up. He looked at Enteling. 'We'll have to cut this short. I need to keep this file for a while.'

Enteling looked ready to object.

'We can do this the easy way,' Pappenheim began, cutting into whatever Enteling had been about to say. 'Or the hard way. I borrow the file for a short while and nobody ever finds out it's been here ... or...' He paused, baby-blue eyes fixed upon Enteling. '*Or* ... I make a phone call and ask for it officially, quoting its full index number...'

Enteling looked furious. 'We're trying to help and you want to drop us in the shit?' he accused venomously.

Pappenheim leaned back in his chair and blew a smoke ring at Enteling. 'Ah yes ... help. As the Americans would say ... the jury's still out on that one. Goodbye, Enteling.'

Enteling glared at Pappenheim, stood there indecisively for some moments, then stalked out of the office without another word. He slammed the door.

'You should get together with Kaltendorf sometime,' Pappenheim said with a smile at the door. 'You both have a way with exits.'

In the eavesdropping room, one of the listeners touched his left headphone and turned to his colleague.

'I just got a clear call to Pappenheim.'

'Let's hear it.'

The man played the short recording through speakers.

'*Mondrian*,' they heard.

'*Call me in exactly one hour*,' came Pappenheim's voice.

The recording ended.

'That's it?'

'That's it.'

'Not a lot to go on.'

'But we know the Mondrian voice, don't

we?' the one with the headphones said.

'We certainly do.' The other picked up a phone.

Aboard the *Isabella Lütz*, Hellmann looked at his mobile satphone and wondered whether he had made the right decision.

He returned to the bridge and waited for the longest hour of his life to pass.

Müller was still using the *Bundesstrasse* 9, going in the same direction as the *Isabella Lütz*. He was just passing Ginsheim when the console screen pinged and a message from Pappenheim came on: WHEN YOU'RE READY.

Müller pulled off the road as soon as he was able to and made the call.

'I'm ready,' he said, as soon as Pappenheim answered.

'I got a Mondrian call.'

'That will be Hellmann,' Müller said with relief. 'He wants to talk. A breakthrough for us.'

'I told him to call back in one hour.'

'Tell him he will be met.'

'As his phone will certainly not be secure, I'll make it very brief.'

'Good. Anything else?'

'You'll need to sit down for this one.'

'I am sitting down.'

'You'll need to hang on to something...'

'Pappi...'

'The duckling was here when the call

came,' Pappenheim said quickly.

'He brought news?'

'He brought very hot news. Something called *Romeo Six*. Sketchy ... but enough to chill the brain.'

Müller was quiet for long moments.

'Hello?'

'I'm here,' Müller said. 'I have a piece of the puzzle. I'll explain more when I get back.'

'Understood. What the duckling brought ties in with something I picked up from ... less conventional sources. We have a bite on the man with the hairbrush.'

Müller felt a rush of excitement. 'I always enjoy good news.'

'Wait till you hear it all. You might change your mind then.'

'Try me.'

'Manfred Heurath – if even *that* is his real name – is a man of multiple guises. To the names we know he has used, you can add Enrico Bonnaci...'

'Enrico *Bonnaci*?'

'Perhaps he worked in Italy for a while,' Pappenheim said drily. 'According to my information, he operated in and out of Germany both during *and* after the DDR. He is a killer of psychotic dimensions. He loves his job, and is adept at inventive means of carrying it out. He was so well regarded by the then Soviets that they gave him training with the Spetsnaz, from which he emerged with flying colours. He is reported to have been on operational missions with them, but this has not yet been positively substantiated. Are you still holding on?'

'I'm holding on,' Müller said grimly.

'His primary job with Romeo Six was the elimination of anyone who began to seem shaky, and the liquidation of the entire team ... if the operation turned sour.'

'Nice. The planners covering their back-sides.'

'Exactly. Even in his early twenties, he was already a major of police and had long made it to lieutenant-colonel by the time the DDR imploded.'

'The Romeo Six operation had a control-ler...'

'I'm coming to that. The controller was known as Romeo Alpha. I don't have the real name as yet ... but give me some time. Our hairbrush has other qualities too,' Pappen-heim continued. 'A comprehensive know-ledge of electronics ... not just the theoretical side. One of his special talents in that field is the manufacture of clever little bombs, with an explosive force out of all proportion to their respective sizes ... particularly under-water...'

'*What?*'

'I repeat ... particularly underwater. He is a fully trained combat diver. Your hair standing on end yet?'

'It's getting ready to walk off my scalp.'

'I think we are both thinking the same thing. A water-police intercept?'

'With bomb-disposal divers. The *Isabella*

Lütz is not far from where I am. They are to guide her to the nearest possible mooring that will take her draught so that she can be safely evacuated, and a search commenced. They are to pick me up first, so arrange a pick-up point, then let me know...'

'Will do.'

'I'll get one of the water uniforms to quietly tell Hellman to board the police boat, while I wait out of sight. Tell them they are also to make the intercept as low-key as possible. We don't want gawkers, and we don't want to alarm the passengers. They should make it look like a snap inspection ... the divers doing a safety check of the hull for integrity ... so forth. If they can also take her to one of those isolated gravel-loading channels, so much the better.'

'Will do,' Pappenheim repeated. 'There's more on Heurath, but that can wait till you're back. I should also have some more details by then. Your American friend would have a fit if she knew she may be sailing with a bomb.'

'We could be seeing this the wrong way and there isn't one at all...'

'On the other hand...'

'Precisely.'

'I'll get on to it,' Pappenheim said.

Both Hellmann and his wife were on the bridge of the *Isabella Lütz*.

'The passengers are looking forward to the dinner,' she said.

'Yes. They are. I like the way they went
217

along with the change in the schedule. They're a good bunch. Not at all like some we've had.'

'God,' she said. 'Can you remember that family who booked all the suites on the last trip?'

Hellmann gave an expressive shudder. 'I'll never forget! What ghastly brats they had. Bad-mannered little savages. Meddling in everything while those horrible people looked on as if their darlings were angels. I kept hoping they would fall into the river.'

'Then their parents would have sued the boat from under us.'

'That they would have. At such times, you feel no amount of money...'

'Hello,' she interrupted. 'What's this about?' She was pointing upriver.

He looked and saw the flashing lights of a twin-funnelled police boat approaching.

The 'Rhein 2000' police boat was new. Nearly 18 metres long, it was a high-tech machine which, powered by twin 500hp marine engines, could hit a speed of 46 kph. Computerized, it was steered by a joystick instead of the expected spoked wheel, and was equipped with an anti-explosion protection system.

At the controls was a policewoman with the twin narrow golden ribbons of a *Meisterin* on her shoulders. The remainder of the crew was the narrow three-striper of a hardened *Obermeister*, and the broad two-striper of the

Oberkommissar, who was the boat commander.

Out of sight within the boat were Müller
and three police divers. The divers already
had most of their gear on.

The policewoman swept the boat past the
Isabella Lütz, then, using the river's flow,
performed a sweeping U-turn that brought
the police boat on to a parallel course with
her quarry. She increased speed to catch up,
then matched velocity with the *Isabella Lütz*
to come alongside. It was very stylishly done.

The barge was already slowing down and
within minutes both vessels were keeping a
pace that made it easy for the boat commander to jump aboard. He went up to the
bridge.

'Well, Max?' Hellmann began, without
looking round. 'What's the trouble? I haven't
broken the river regulations, have I?'

Oberkommissar Max Alsterhoven and
Hellmann knew each other from before
Alsterhoven had even attained the first of the
Kommissar ranks, and there was no tenseness
in the meeting.

Alsterhoven removed his cap, wiped his
brow with the back of his hand and put the
cap back on.

'Isa,' he greeted Isabella Hellmann.

'Max.'

'No trouble, Udo,' he went on to Hellmann.
'Just the usual spot check. You know how it is.
Got to keep my bosses happy. Can Isa take
the helm while you and I go down to your
219

cabin for the usual with the documents?'

Hellmann glanced at his wife.

She nodded and he handed over control of the boat.

'This is not the usual check,' Alsterhoven said as soon as they were in the cabin. 'I didn't want to alarm Isa. There's someone on my boat waiting to see you.'

Hellmann did not seem surprised. 'Müller?'

The surprise was Alsterhoven's. 'How did you know?'

'I expected something ... I just wasn't sure what it would be.'

'It's more than you think, Udo. I've got divers too. To Isa and your crew and passengers, we're carrying out a routine hull check. But you should know that what we plan to do is see if someone has left a nasty present on your boat.'

Hellmann stared at him. 'What do you mean?'

'I have bomb disposal men aboard.'

Hellmann whitened. 'Bomb...' He instinctively glanced upwards at the cabin ceiling, above which the bridge towered. 'Isa...'

'Must know nothing. Müller's instructions. We want to do this as low-key as possible.'

'But how...? Who...?'

'Müller thinks you may know. And that's all I know, or want to know. You'd better go see him.'

Hellmann nodded.

'OK.' Alsterhoven said. 'We're going to lead

you to a gravel-loading berth just under two kilometres upriver from here...'

'I know the one.'

'It's isolated, away from prying eyes. We'll disembark the passengers, Isa, and the crew, while we check that everything is fine...'

'Or not,' Hellmann finished with grim foreboding. 'Alright. I'll be with you in a minute. Let me talk to Isa.'

Alsterhoven nodded. 'See you on the boat. And bring a diagram of all your underwater sensor positions.'

Hellmann waited until the river policeman had left, then went to his safe and took out Diefenhausen's envelope. He then returned to the bridge.

'I'm going over to Max's boat for a short while, Isa,' he said as he took the diagram out of a chart drawer. 'He's going to lead us to the gravel dock to do the hull check. Can you inform the passengers, please, before they start to worry? I won't be long. I'll talk to them when I get back.'

She nodded. 'Let's hope Max and his people will be quick about it.'

Hellmann gave a quick kiss on the cheek. 'Thanks.'

Alsterhoven led Hellmann to where Müller was waiting. The divers and Alsterhoven then left them to their privacy.

'Thank you for calling the number,' Müller said as soon as they had gone, glancing at the envelope Hellmann had brought. 'It was a wise decision.'

Hellmann handed the envelope over. 'I feel safer getting rid of it.'

'A hot potato?' Müller suggested, taking it.

'Very. It will answer many of your questions.'

'Thank you. Alsterhoven has told you what we suspect?'

Hellmann nodded and passed over the sensor diagram. 'Max asked for this...'

'He told me you've known each other for years.'

'Even before he made it to *Kommissar*. This diagram shows all the sensor positions. Anything more than those marked doesn't belong. If there is a bomb under my boat,' Hellmann continued, 'when ... when could it have been put there?'

'Quite possibly before you started this trip. If one definitely is there, it will be on a timer, programmed for a specific moment. As whoever did the job couldn't have known you would still be on the Rhine, it may have been timed to go off when and where it would do maximum damage to the river traffic system, as well as getting rid of you...'

'And my wife, my passengers, and my crew.'

'I think we both know that would cause no grief whatsoever to the person or persons responsible for placing it...'

'Heurath,' Hellmann said tightly.

'Perhaps ... perhaps not. Now you'd better get back to look after your boat and its people. Meanwhile, I'll have a quick read of this.'

'It's from Diefenhausen. He was even more worried than he appeared. He posted it to me before I saw him in Mainz. There's ... some stuff in there about me too. And ... thank you for keeping this whole business from my wife.'

'That state of affairs may not last for much longer,' Müller said. 'Sooner or later, she is going to start asking you some awkward questions as this thing develops.'

Hellmann nodded once more. 'I know. It's been on my mind for years. Deep down, I knew the day would come eventually. One way or another, I've got to face her reaction, and those of my daughters ... But thanks, anyway.'

Müller watched expressionlessly as Hellman made his way back up to the deck of the police boat.

Then he opened the envelope and began to read.

In her suite, Carey Bloomfield had been wondering about the sudden appearance of the police launch. When she'd heard Isabella Hellmann's explanation over the boat's address system, her curiosity increased.

Was this also Müller's doing, as with the helicopter in Mainz? But why set up a hull inspection now?

There was a knock on her door. 'Amy?'

Grogan.

'Just a minute, Jack,' she called. She went to the door and opened it.

Grogan, carrying his inevitable video camera, said, 'It's all kind of strange. When I saw the police boat, I took my vidcam on deck to record it, but one of the police guys on the damned boat made a chopping motion. Pretty damned clear we're not allowed to film.' He sounded outraged. 'We're all going to the lounge for coffee, and to talk about this. Coming?'

'Be with you in a minute.'

'OK.'

She closed the door slowly as Grogan went off. She picked up her bag, but left the camera. In the bag was her Beretta.

In Berlin, Kaltendorf was driving home with Solange, north eastwards from the Erlenhausens, who lived in Gatow, Spandau. He lived in Reinickendorf, just on the other side of the district border with Spandau.

'You seemed to enjoy that,' he said to her.

'I did. They have a lovely big house...'

'With a swimming pool...' he said, smiling.

'With a swimming pool, *and* a winter garden, *and* a big garden...'

'I have none of that, I'm afraid. Just an ordinary house.'

'I wouldn't care if it were just a study, Papa.'

Kaltendorf's smile widened, much pleased by her remark. 'And how did you like Noni?'

'I liked her a lot.'

'I could see you two were getting on. I'm glad.'

'She's going to take me to Prenzlberg

tomorrow, on a round of the Kollwitzplatz cafés.'

'You'll enjoy that. It's quite a lively scene, I'm told.'

'She's a bit crazy, though ... but who isn't?'

'Who isn't, indeed.'

Both Müller and Pappenheim would have been astonished to see Kaltendorf behaving so light-heartedly; a glimpse, perhaps, of what he must have been like before his life went sour on him.

Behind them, the motorcyclist followed at a discreet distance.

Kaltendorf remained unaware.

The loading station that Alsterhoven had spoken about was to starboard of the *Isabella Lütz*.

A deep basin had been dredged, forming a large U-shape that was bordered by high earthen banks. Its entire perimeter was edged by a wide, flat landing stage. Stone steps led up from it at several points, to the top of the banks, each a good eight metres high. Unpaved roads for the lorries that served the station criss-crossed the area with a secondary, *Landstrasse*-class paved road leading from them to join with the B9.

One arm of the U protruded finger-like, forming a mole to the entrance of the basin. On top of it a wide stone path had been laid. Beyond the basin to riverwards, a small elongated island formed a barrier between the basin and the main river route.

225

The station was isolated. No houses were nearby and the B9 was some distance away from that stretch of the river. At that time of day the basin was empty and loading work had long been stopped. No one was there.

On the *Isabella Lütz*, Grogan was holding forth.

'Why won't they let me film?'

'They are police, dear,' Betty Grogan said reasonably. 'You know how police are. They don't always like cameras.'

'With good reason,' he grumbled. 'Look at some of the stuff people get on the cops back home.'

'I'm sure it's nothing that will disrupt us too much,' Carey Bloomfield said. 'And I think it's a good suggestion of Mrs Hellmann's that we have an open-air dinner on land while the police are doing their inspection. Look at it this way, Jack, it's a nice break in the trip, as we can't go down the Danube anyway.'

Grogan thought about it. 'Guess you're right. 'Sides ... should be interesting to watch those frogmen work. OK, what the hell. You've done it again, Amy ... pacified my raging soul.'

'You're a pussycat, Jack.'

Grogan grinned at her, then turned to his wife. 'See, Betty? A lion tamer.'

'A pussycat, she said, Jack.' Betty Grogan smiled fondly at her husband.

The other couple smiled at everyone.

Aboard the police boat, Müller slowly put

Diefenhausen's seven-page testament back into the envelope. He had already passed the sensor position diagram to the leader of the dive team.

The seven pages that Diefenhausen had sent to Hellmann were whistle-blowing of monumental proportions, making Esske's barely finished document child's play by comparison. Diefenhausen, formerly Erwin Föhnach, had been the unknown centre which had invisibly coordinated the Romeo Six operatives in the field. Diefenhausen had not been allowed to create his own fake family. That had not been his job. But what he knew made him a prime target; and he had been fully aware of it. Despite his own position within the Romeo Six team, his knowledge of Romeo Alpha, Heurath himself, and the mysterious Romeo Six from whom the team had derived its name, was sketchy.

Diefenhausen did not know Romeo Alpha's real name, nor even his rank. He had no idea who Romeo Six had been. Only Heurath seemed etched upon his mind; but only because the man with many names scared him so much. He knew little else about the psychotic killer.

Pappenheim had gleaned more from his own sources. Even so, the document made grim and frightening reading.

He had to return to Berlin, Müller decided, and as quickly as possible.

A change in the cadence of the police boat

engines told him that the gravel-loading basin had been reached. He peered through a porthole and saw that the *Isabella Lütz* was already being moored.

Descending footsteps made him look round. Daniel Stein, the dive-team leader and a *Kommissar*, approached him.

'We've studied that diagram till our eyes hurt,' he began with a grin. 'We now know what should and shouldn't be on that hull.'

'Watch yourselves under there.'

'I was a *Bundesmarine* combat diver before I changed to the river navy. I guess that's why they gave this one to me. I have a little toy that tracks electronically controlled explosives. If one is there, we'll find it.' Stein paused. 'Do we remove it?'

'Only if you can do so without blowing yourselves up with it.'

Stein grinned once more. 'Don't worry. I want to see my wife and kids again. Well...' He peered through another porthole. 'Although we'll be using lights down there, I'd better get going before we lose too much of the daylight. The *Isabella Lütz* is secured.'

Müller held out a hand. 'Thanks.'

Stein shook it. 'Thank me if I don't find anything.'

Müller watched as he went back up on deck; then Alsterhoven was descending.

'The passengers are having dinner in the open air,' he said to Müller. 'I've asked that each comes aboard for a document check first, as you wanted.'

Müller nodded. 'Miss Amy Harris is to be the last.'

Alsterhoven looked questioningly at Müller. 'I'm sure you know what you're doing.'

'I do. Leave the diagram just where I said.'

Alsterhoven nodded, then went back up.

Grogan did not like the idea at all.

'A *document* check?' he said, massively annoyed. 'Where the hell's this? The good old *DDR*?'

The policewoman looked at him patiently. 'I am sorry, sir,' she said to him in perfect English. 'But it won't take long.'

'Go on, Jack,' Betty Grogan encouraged gently. 'The longer you take, the longer before we get to dinner.'

'Oh, alright. But I don't like it one bit, young lady,' he added to the policewoman.

'I wouldn't either, sir, in your place,' she said pacifyingly.

'Hmmpf!' Grogan said, but he went along with it.

On the police boat, Müller watched from seclusion as each passenger was deliberately left alone for brief moments with the diagram in full view. Grogan didn't look. His wife did. The couple from the north both glanced at it. As did Carey Bloomfield.

Then she stood waiting slightly impatiently, bag slung from her shoulder, for the policewoman to return from speaking with Alsterhoven.

Müller knocked softly on the companion-way.

Carey Bloomfield frowned, then came forward to peer down. Her eyes widened. '*You!* Jesus, Müller ... you're everywhere!'

'I'll take that as a compliment. Come on down, Miss Bloomfield...'

'*Carey*, damn it!' But she made her way down. 'Is this charade just a way of getting me on this boat?'

'It is.'

'You intercept the *Isabella* with police divers—'

'Ah. That, is a different matter altogether. Not just to see you. For a reason far more serious. There may be a bomb under that boat.'

She stared at him. 'You've got to be kidding me.'

'Bringing the police crew out here costs, and I never kid about spending the tax-payer's money ... Or mine, for that matter,' he added, almost to himself.

She peered briefly through the porthole that Stein had used. The divers were in the water, and the first one was submerging.

'How long has it been there?' she asked, turning back to Müller.

'If there is indeed one, since you left the Netherlands is my guess.'

'I've been sleeping on a goddamned bomb?'

'You and the others ... *If* there is one.'

Unconsciously, she hugged herself. 'Jesus,' she said quietly.

He glanced at the bag. 'The gun in there?'
She nodded.

'Good thing this was not a real document check,' he said, straight-faced. 'The river police might have been startled by your cannon.'

'Quit joking, Müller. The idea of that bomb gives me the shivers.'

'I never joke about guns. And, for your information, the idea of a bomb gives me the shivers too. There are three policemen in the water looking for it. I am not comfortable with the thought that, if something is down there and it becomes unstable, I might be in-directly responsible for lowering the river police complement by three.'

It was Stein who found it.

He signalled to his men to leave the water. They hesitated, and he emphasized his order with forceful motions. They were still reluctant, but they obeyed.

As they climbed, grim-faced, back aboard the police launch, Alsterhoven looked from one to the other.

'Where's Daniel?' he demanded.

'Under the boat,' one answered. 'It's there.'

'What? And you left him?'

'He ordered us to leave,' the other said reproachfully.

'OK, OK. Sorry. Editha...' he said to the policewoman.

'Sir?'

'Get on the controls. When I say move it,

231

you move it.'

'But sir ... *Kommissar* Stein...'

'You *move* it, I said!'

'Yes, sir.'

'Where's that passenger?'

'Still below with *Hauptkommissar* Müller.'

'She might as well stay there. If that thing blows ... Christian,' he went on to the other uniformed police officer. 'Board the *Isabella Lütz* and get everyone off. *Everyone*. Take no excuses. Just get them off. Tell them to tell the others to move as far away as possible from the basin. Then you get back here quickly. I don't want you going up with it.'

'On my way.'

As the *Obermeister* left, Alsterhoven hurried down to Müller.

'Your expression tells me,' Müller said to him.

Alsterhoven glanced at Carey Bloomfield.

'It's alright,' Müller told him. 'I take full responsibility.'

Alsterhoven gave her another uncertain glance, then continued, 'Thank God there are no houses nearby, and the loading station is empty. The road is far enough away, so there's no danger to what traffic there is. The island between us and the other river traffic, and the buttresses around the basin, will be good blast shields if that thing—'

Suddenly, there was shouting.

All three ran up on deck. Several things were happening at once. The policeman on the *Isabella Lütz* was in mid-spring, leaping

232

back to the police boat. He made it. Stein had risen out of the water like a breeching creature of the deep and was yelling. Everyone heard all too clearly.

'Go, go, go! Booby-trapped, booby-trapped!'

Alsterhoven was barking at the police-woman, *'Move it!'*

Tears welling in her eyes, Editha Ellerhof obeyed her commander and sent the launch surging out of danger.

There was a moment of eerie stillness, as if the launch were charging away, but not moving at all. Everyone could see Stein, suspended half out of the water, as if somebody had pressed the freeze button on a video player.

Then the *Isabella Lütz* was rising out of the water on a giant waterspout. The first explosion broke her back while she was still in the air. The second ripped both sections apart. One of her propellers whirled like the blades of a helicopter and skimmed across the basin to scythe into one of the earthen banks. It went all the way in, until only a tip showed. Glass from the bridge shattered into lethal spears that rainbowed in the fading light, a swarm of monstrous, glinting insects that darted in every direction, seemingly hunting out prey to impale. Shards of antique furniture and ripped containers flew upwards in a widening corona.

The *Isabella Lütz* catapulted her pieces into the air, an expanding ball that raced to apogee before falling back into the still-rising

233

waterspout. Then all collapsed into the boiling channel which quickly returned to its previous calm, now carpeted by the detritus of what had once been a proud boat.

Something clanged against the fleeing police launch, then hummed on its way. Then all was silent. Even the sound of the river had a subdued air about it. Remarkably, there was no fire, but a dark smoke spiralled upwards. A glistening on the surface of the basin betrayed the presence of fuel from the *Isabella Lütz*'s ripped tanks.

Stein had vanished.

Editha Ellerhof had slowed the police boat down, had turned it round and was cautiously heading back towards the basin. The tears were flowing unheeded down her cheeks.

Alsterhoven, eyes full of shock, cleared his throat. 'That was good work, Editha,' he said gruffly. He gave her a brief pat on her shoulder.

Everyone on the boat, and on land, was staring in disbelief at the scene of destruction.

'Dannie,' Alsterhoven said softly.

No one else on the boat spoke, then, as if activated by a switch, everyone except Ellerhof at the controls began hurrying along the deck, searching for Stein.

Something bobbed up from under the water, near the entrance to the basin.

Carey Bloomfield spotted it. 'There!' she called, and pointed.

'It's the boss!' one of the divers crowed.

234

'And he's moving! He's swimming! How the hell...?'

Smiles had returned to their faces.

'Editha,' Alsterhoven said. 'You know what to do.'

'Yes, sir!' she said happily, finally wiping away her tears.

The boat cruised to where Stein was bobbing. He climbed aboard without difficulty. They all crowded round, staring at him in wonder. His divers smacked his shoulders in huge relief.

'Tell us, you old fart,' Alsterhoven began. 'How did you get out of that?'

Stein grinned as he removed his carbon-fibre tank with the help of eager hands. 'I'd spotted a depression just past the entrance,' he answered. 'I knew I would have no chance to make it if I tried to swim away. I got into the depression and prayed the explosion wouldn't bring the whole thing down on top of me. I was worried about the concussion too. But luckily, the force of the blast was upwards. I caught a bit of it, but not enough to rip me out of there. My equipment was not damaged, so I was able to wait until everything had quietened down again.'

'My God,' Alsterhoven said in awe. 'You gave us a bad time. Editha was in tears.'

'No, I wasn't!' she protested.

They all smiled at her.

'I'll have a few bruises,' Stein said to Müller. 'But I get to see my wife and kids.'

'That you do,' Müller said.

'A debrief?' Stein said after a few moments.

Müller nodded. He looked at Carey Bloomfield. 'You. Come with me.' He glanced at Alsterhoven. 'You too, Max.'

When they were all back below deck, Stein unclipped something that looked like a big mobile phone from his diver's harness. It was protected by a yellow waterproof casing.

He glanced at Carey Bloomfield before speaking.

'It's OK,' Müller said to him.

Stein held the unit so that they could all see it clearly. It had a display window at the top, just as with a mobile, but only two large buttons, one red and one green.

'This is not police issue,' he began. 'Once we had located the bomb and I sent the guys back up, I pressed the green button. When you do that, it lights up, and this clever thing begins to scan for the bomb's setting code. Once it finds it, it breaks it, stops the programming, then kills the bomb itself ... all electronically, and all done very, very quickly. The green light then blinks three times to give you the all clear. But it also, thank God, has a bug-out capability. That's the red button. Both lights are necessarily bright, given some underwater environments, but the red one's like a searchlight. No mistaking it's purpose. When *that* starts to blink, you have a specific amount of time to give warning and get the hell out. If not for that thumbnail-sized red button, I'd be floating with all those other pieces out there.'

Stein took a deep breath and looked at Müller.

'Whoever set that thing,' he continued, 'is a clever, calculating, murderous bastard with a nasty sense of humour. He created a triple-booby-trap system, each more complex. A rapid countdown begins so that each time you break through, you're running out of time at an increasing rate. If you persist in trying, you never make it. Attempting to disarm the bomb, or even to move it, was meant to have the same result ... detonation. The *Isabella Lütz* was doomed the moment he attached it to her hull. The owner may have kept his life, but someone's just sunk his business.'

'And a lot more,' Müller said, but did not elaborate. 'Better get the land uniforms to see to those people out there, Max,' he went on to Alsterhoven.

Alsterhoven nodded. 'Editha will have already passed on the message, but I'll go ashore with Christian and start things moving.'

They could feel the police boat nosing towards a mooring point outside the basin, on the river side of the mole.

'Fine. Oh ... and send Hellmann over when you meet him.'

'Why would anyone want to bomb Udo's boat?'

'Sorry. I can't tell you.'

Alsterhoven stared at him, then glanced at Carey Bloomfield. Then he went back up on deck without saying anything further.

'I take it you want me to leave too,' Stein said drily.

'If you wouldn't mind, Dannie.' Müller held out his hand. 'Once again, thank you.'

'I wish it hadn't been there for me to find,' Stein said as they shook hands briefly.

'So do I.'

Eight

On land, they had gathered loosely on top of the banks to stare down in shock at the debris of the *Isabella Lütz*.

The mole had a narrow landing, with steps leading up to the top. They watched as the police boat inched its way to the mooring point and stopped, the water boiling at its stern. They watched as two of the river police jumped off and climbed the steps. They watched, mesmerized, as what was left of the *Isabella Lütz*'s bridge spookily popped up from beneath the surface, pushing light debris aside, rolled over, then submerged once more. It was as if the Rhine ship was still fighting to survive.

Isabella Hellmann stared down at the wreckage of her dreams and cried silently. Hellmann stood next to her, face impassive, eyes fixed upon a point that was far beyond the basin where his ship had died.

'Who would want to do this to us, Udo?' she asked him softly. 'Who?'

At that moment, Alsterhoven and his crewman arrived, saving Hellman for the time being, as all attention focused upon the river policemen.

'Miss Harris!' the woman from northern Germany said. 'She isn't with us!'

'Miss Harris is quite safe,' Alsterhoven told them in English for the benefit of the Grogans. 'She was still on our boat when it happened...'

'Thank God!' Betty Grogan said with relief.

'Understandably, she is very shaken ... but I am certain she will join you soon. Has anyone been hurt?'

All shook their heads.

'What happens now?' Grogan asked, looking down at the water, then back to Alsterhoven. 'When we booked this trip we didn't reckon on being bombed off the boat.'

'You will be fully reimbursed, Mr Grogan,' Isabella Hellmann said. 'Our insurance—'

'No one's talking about reimbursement, Mrs Hellmann,' Grogan said quickly. 'We lost some things, sure ... but we realize you've lost your beautiful boat, and your business. What I meant to say to the commander was, what happened here? How come a boat like this gets bombed?'

'We don't have naval ranks in the water police, Mr Grogan,' Alsterhoven continued in English with a thin smile. 'I am an *Oberkommissar*...'

'Kind of like ... a police lieutenant?'

'That is a reasonable approximation.'

'OK.'

'All I can say at this time,' Alsterhoven continued, 'is that we have no ... er ... idea how this came to be. But of course, an investigation is already under way. However, our immediate purpose is to get you all accommodation for the night, which will be done without delay. The land police are on their way here. Did you take your personal documents with you when you left the boat?'

'We always do,' Grogan replied. 'Our cash and credit cards too. Even our plane tickets and my vidcam,' he added. 'I filmed the explosion. After the last time, when I was prevented from filming, are you going to take the camera off me?'

'Not the camera, Mr Grogan ... but I am afraid I must ask for the film.'

Grogan sighed. 'Figured you might.' He snapped open a small panel in the video camera, took out a minidisc that was still within its casing. 'As you can see, it isn't a film. It just slots in as it is. Your people got something that can play that?'

Alsterhoven gave another thin smile. 'I am sure we will find a way. Thank you for your cooperation, Mr Grogan.'

Grogan glanced at the basin. 'Least I can do.'

Alsterhoven nodded, then turned to the German couple and asked them in German about their documents. They too had brought theirs.

'The land police will soon be here,' Alsterhoven said, reverting to English. 'Now, if you'll excuse me, I must talk privately with Captain Hellmann. My colleague will remain with you until the police arrive.' He turned to

Isabella Hellmann, again going back to German. 'Isa, I cannot tell you how sorry I am about this. I must talk with Udo about the whole thing. Usual police procedures. I can talk with you later but first, busy yourself with the passengers and crew. You're the second in command, so your place is here with them.'

She nodded slowly, eyes red as she looked down into the basin at what was left of her beloved boat.

'We've been ruined,' she said distantly.

'You're a strong person, Isa. You can rebuild. Your insurance will cover you.' Alster-hoven touched her gently on the shoulder. 'Now I must take Udo to the boat. He won't be long. Come on, Udo.'

Hellmann gave his wife a brief hug, then followed Alsterhoven.

On the police boat, Müller said to Carey Bloomfield, 'You look rather pale, Miss Bloomfield.'

Above them, the muted chatter of police transmissions was a constant background to all the other sounds.

'Carey,' she said. 'Ah, what the hell ... call me what you want.'

'As you wish.'

'And of course I'm pale. It's not every day I find out that I'm sailing with a bomb. Do you realize, Müller, if you hadn't been mixed up in this, somewhere along the route ... I'd be among those pieces out there?'

'The probability is high.'

' "The probability is high",' she quoted. 'I'm saying thank you, Müller. Don't be so ... correct all the time.'

'Kaltendorf thinks the very opposite.'

'To hell with Kaltendorf! So what now?'

'What now is that you return to the group. You continue your watch on Hellmann...'

'He's got no boat...'

'True, but he's still a target. When the hairbrush and his friends discover that the bomb went off too early, they'll check to see whether Hellmann is dead. It won't take them long to find out he isn't...'

'So I'm the shield?'

'You were, the moment you took this assignment.'

They heard the sound of something being dragged along the deck.

'What's that?' she asked, glancing up.

'I would think it's the divers about to lay a boom across the entrance to the basin. This will prevent the spread of oil from getting into the river. It was fortunate this happened here. It will make the job of the clean-up and recovery teams much easier.' Müller glanced at her bag. 'You've got all your personal documents in there with that cannon?'

She nodded. 'My brand-new camera's gone for a swim, though. But it's small beer compared to what happened to the boat.'

'Talking of cameras. Keep an eye on the Grogans.'

She stared at him. 'The *Grogans*? Are we thinking about the same people? Oh come *on*,

Müller. Those two are—'

'Humour me.'

She still looked at him disbelievingly. 'You're serious.'

'I am.'

Footsteps on the deck made them pause.

'That will be Alsterhoven returning with Hellmann. Time for you to leave. Watch yourself out there.'

Briefly, her eyes searched his. 'You too, Müller.'

She went up to the deck just as Hellmann entered the wheelhouse.

'Miss Harris,' he began. 'I am glad you are safe. We were very worried.'

'I was perhaps in the safest place,' she said. 'I am so sorry, Captain. The *Isabella Lütz* was so beautiful. I wish I could do something...'

He smiled wearily. 'Thank you for the thought, Miss Harris. My wife and I will find a way.'

'Then I wish you all the luck.'

He gave a tight smile and nodded, then went below.

Alsterhoven was just behind Hellmann. 'Miss Harris, the others are waiting for you. They know you're safe. The land police are on their way and will take you all to your hotel for the night. Can you make your way over?'

'Yes, yes. I'll be fine.'

'Very well.'

He touched his cap at her, and followed Hellmann.

244

'You have saved our lives, *Hauptkommissar* Müller,' Hellmann said. 'I thank you.'

'I wish we could have saved your boat,' Müller told him. 'But the moment that limpet was stuck to the hull, the *Isabella Lütz*'s fate was sealed. It was booby-trapped against any kind of tampering. Our diver leader, as you saw, barely escaped with his own life. I am truly sorry about the boat.'

Müller was surprised to find that, despite what he already knew about Hellmann, he really meant it.

Hellmann glanced at Alsterhoven, who was holding up Grogan's minidisc.

'Mr Grogan took a video of the whole thing,' the river policeman said to Müller as he handed it over. 'He was very cooperative.' Alsterhoven spoke with some astonishment, as if he had expected more resistance from Grogan.

Müller took the disc and looked it over. 'Very high-tech.'

'He asked if we had equipment that could play this,' Alsterhoven went on. 'He sounded very doubtful. I said we could but, of course, my unit hasn't anything that can handle this.'

'We have someone who can make anything electronic work,' Müller said. 'May I keep it?'

'Be my guest.' Alsterhoven glanced from one to the other. 'I know you two will have plenty to discuss, so I'll leave you to it. Got to see how the guys are getting on with containing the pollution. Talk with you later,

Udo,' he added to Hellmann as he turned to
go.

Hellman nodded.

'Max,' Müller began.

Alsterhoven paused.

'Do you know Pappenheim?'

Alsterhoven shook his head.

'You're one of the few,' Müller said drily.

'But I've heard of him.'

'That does not surprise me.'

'I think Dannie Stein knows him, though,'
Alsterhoven said.

'That doesn't surprise me either,' Müller
said. 'He's my deputy. Here...' He handed
Alsterhoven a card like the one he'd previ-
ously given to Hellmann. 'Call this number.
When he answers, say Mondrian.'

'Just that?'

'Just that. He'll hang up and call you back
on a secure transmission. Tell him what has
happened here.'

Alsterhoven nodded. 'OK.'

He went back up to the deck.

'I have read Diefenhausen's document,'
Müller said to Hellmann when Alsterhoven
had gone. 'It makes very grim reading. If you
had any doubts about the danger you're in,
the remains of your boat should convince
you. And if Heurath has any idea that you
may have received Diefenhausen's testi-
mony...'

'I don't see how he can...'

'Captain Hellmann, as far as Heurath is
concerned, expect *anything*. Whatever you

may believe is not possible, put it out of your mind. *Assume* he will try very hard to get you once he finds out his bomb has missed all its targets. The destruction of your vessel was merely a means to an end. The means failed. He will not be very happy about that at all. I believe the *Isabella Lütz* was programmed to blow up where she would do the greatest damage to the Rhine shipping industry, taking you – and all aboard – with it. He intended to combine his liquidation of one of the Romeo Six with an attack upon the state. He came close to succeeding.'

'Then he'll also realize you were responsible for spoiling his plans,' Hellmann said. 'He will come after you too.'

'He is already after me. But I am better equipped to deal with him than you are. We can take you into protective custody. Your wife too. The passengers and crew will not find this unusual. They won't know the true reasons, but they would expect the both of you to be temporarily held by the police for questioning after what has just happened.'

Hellmann shook his head. 'Unless you are arresting me, my place is with my wife, my passengers and my crew. There's plenty to take care of ... personal, and business. Are you arresting me?'

Müller shook his head. 'No, Captain. I am not. I understand your concerns about your affairs, but I must warn you that you are taking your life into your own hands...'

'After what just happened, there's not much

of a life left. I only want enough time to put things right with my wife and to make sure that the passengers, my crew, my family ... are taken care of.'

'You could be committing suicide...'

'Not suicide, *Hauptkommissar*. Just doing something I should have done years ago...'

'Going up against Heurath by yourself is either very brave, or very foolish.'

Hellmann smiled tiredly. 'A truly brave man would not have agreed to become a Romeo. And as for being foolish ... perhaps.'

'I will still do my best to have you protected. It is my job to prevent people from getting murdered, if I can do something about it.'

'This murder, Mr Müller, if it does happen, began years ago. You were certainly not with the police then.'

'I was too young. Even so, I have my responsibility. What can you tell me about Romeo Six?' Müller continued, studying Hellmann closely. 'Diefenhausen mentions him, but says nothing about what he might have been like.'

'I'm sorry. I know even less about Romeo Six than Diefenhausen does ... and he had more knowledge of the entire operation than any of us.'

'No matter. What about Romeo Alpha, your commander? You never knew his name ... but can you describe what he looked like? Anything will help, no matter how sketchy.'

'Even after all these years, there are certain things I do remember about *him* .'

Hellmann began to describe Romeo Alpha. As he did so, Müller felt a chill grip his spine. He said nothing when Hellmann had finished.

Hellmann stared at him. 'Mr Müller? Are you alright?'

After a while, Müller said, 'I am fine. Thank you, Captain Hellmann. You had better go and see to your people.'

Confused, Hellmann said, 'Yes ... Yes. Of course.'

He looked at Müller for some moments longer, but Müller seemed deep in thought.

Hellmann went back up the companionway to the deck.

Some minutes later, Alsterhoven returned. He looked at Müller questioningly. 'Problem?'

'No. No. I was just ... thinking about something. Did you get Pappenheim?'

'Yes. I told him what happened. He said Dannie Stein has nine lives.'

'That he has ... although one was certainly used up today. Anything else?'

'He wanted to know when you'd be back in Berlin...'

'I'm going back tonight. If you wouldn't mind, could you take me back to my car?'

Going by road would mean being spotted by the people from the *Isabella Lütz*, particularly the Grogans, who had already seen him with Carey Bloomfield in the café in Mainz.

'No problem,' Alsterhoven said. 'Another

boat is on its way and should be here soon. I'll be remaining here, but Editha and Christian can take you back, then return. They'll set off as soon as the other boat arrives.'

'That will be fine. Make sure the land boys keep an eye on the Hellmanns, just in case. They should also watch out for anyone taking a particular interest in what has happened here.'

'You believe the bomber will try again?'

'The people responsible for this are not going to stop until they have achieved what they set out to do. And that's my headache.'

'The B9 goes inland before it gets here, then comes close again to the river later on, which was lucky for any traffic passing at the time; but the rail tracks are not so far. Christian took a quick look. Nothing seems to have landed on them ... but I'll get the clean-up people to make a detailed inspection, just to be safe.'

Müller nodded. 'We don't want the media on to this as yet. The explosion was relatively subdued, given its destructiveness. A derailed train would bring them here in droves; but your land colleagues should be here before any start showing up. And when the press do arrive on the scene ... I was never here.'

Alsterhoven was silent for some moments. 'Pappenheim has already said as much.'

'Pappenheim is worth his weight in gold to me.'

'I think I'm beginning to understand,' Alsterhoven said. 'I feel truly sorry for Udo and Isa,' he went on. 'Isa's a strong woman ... but they've lost their life's work...'

'A can of worms was opened up today, Max,' Müller said obliquely. 'Hellmann is going to need friends like never before.'

Alsterhoven looked at him, not understanding.

Kaltendorf also lived in one of the many classic buildings of Berlin that had been superbly renovated. The two-storey house had four bedrooms and a fair-sized garden; but though spacious, neatly decorated and furnished, it was almost utilitarian by comparison with Müller's apartment.

Kaltendorf's taste in furniture, while not quite as bad as his ties, was inevitably dull. The items were not cheaply bought, but their dark wood solidity gave the house the atmosphere of a little-visited museum. His study was a sanctum whose walls were adorned with all things to do with his profession. Anyone entering it would be left in no doubt that this was the home of a policeman. But it was a lonely house, existing in a solitude where lightness of spirit had long since fled.

Kaltendorf had another home, a large apartment in Berlin-Mitte, reasonably close to his office. This was a very different place with two very spacious bedrooms; but it was much smaller by comparison. However, it had been decorated and furnished with great taste. This was not Kaltendorf's doing. The top floor property had been constructed by the builders as a showcase apartment, and he had acquired it lock, stock and barrel. Though he at times gave dinners and lunches at the house, it was mainly the Erlenhausens who went there. It was at the apartment that he frequently entertained those who could foster his political and professional ambitions. In each case, the dining arrangements were handled by caterers. When not entertaining he invariably ate away from either home; even breakfast, apart from a morning coffee before leaving. As a result, Kaltendorf had two of the most unused kitchens around.

He seldom drove himself. A police driver picked him up daily, from whichever dwelling he had decided to spend the night in.

In the interests of keeping her existence secret from his colleagues and from those whose patronage he courted, he did not tell Solange of the apartment. She already knew that only the Erlenhausens had been entrusted with knowledge of the true nature of their relationship, Kaltendorf having long since told her that keeping this fact secret was for her own protection. If it were openly known that she was his daughter, this could put her at risk from those against whom he worked.

Kaltendorf drew up before the house and the outside lights automatically came on. One of the doors of the two garages began to lift. The day had prematurely darkened and had been threatening rain for some time.

Solange peered through the windscreen at the building. 'This is not a small house, Papa.

It's huge!'

He smiled as he drove into the garage. 'It's your home. Come on,' he added when he'd stopped the car. 'Let's show you to your room. It's got its own bathroom too, so you can spend as much time in there as you like.'

She smiled at him. 'I'm very quick in the bathroom. I had to be. Grandpa used to bang on the door to get me out.'

'Well that won't happen here.'

Outside, a fine rain had started to fall.

In the shadows, the motorcyclist waited until the exterior lights went out, then turned round and rode unhurriedly away.

Müller had returned to his car and was on the B9 heading for the nearest Autobahn, for a fast run to Berlin. He had decided not to call Pappenheim, preferring instead to go directly to his office. He was certain that Pappenheim would still not have gone home.

As he sped along the B9, his route took him back towards where the *Isabella Lütz* had been destroyed. He saw the flashing police lights and slowed down. Two patrol cars and a patrol motorcycle were on station at the junction of the access road. Two of the men from the patrol cars were on one side of the B9. Each of the car drivers was behind the wheel of his vehicle, one in conversation with the motorcycle policeman. When the Porsche appeared, they all looked in its direction.

Müller could see the distant glow of floodlights over to his right.

The motorcyle patrolman came up to him when he had stopped, and leaned over to peer in.

'*Hauptkommissar* Müller?'

Müller nodded.

'We were told you would be passing through,' the man went on.

'Are the people from the *Isabella Lütz* away?'

'Yes, sir. Off to their hotel some time ago. Nasty business.'

'Very.'

'A special armed team is deployed between here and the river, and the clean-up people are down by the water. It's going to take some time.'

'I'm afraid it will. Any press people show up as yet?'

The motorcycle policeman shook his head. 'Still quiet.'

'That won't last for much longer.'

Müller was certain that as soon as one of the passengers, or crew, talked in the hotel and said the magic word 'bomb', the news would spread like a plague.

'Are we dealing with terrorists, sir?'

'A word of advice ... don't let any journalist hear you say that. With the first anniversary of 9/11 coming next month, everyone's twitchy. Keep a firm perspective on things.'

'No, sir. Er ... right, sir.'

'And do a careful check on all the people arriving here as members of the press ... But if you are suspicious of someone, don't take

254

action by yourself. Stay calm and alert the special team.' Müller didn't expect Heurath to be so obvious. 'And check out any policeman you don't know or expect.'

'I don't know you, sir,' the motorcycle cop said with a straight face.

'But you were expecting me,' Müller countered.

The man smiled. 'Yes, sir.'

Müller gave him a slight wave and drove on, watching in his mirror as the officer and his colleagues turned to look. None of them stood a chance against Heurath.

Müller hoped they would not have to find out.

Some kilometres ahead, Heurath was on the B9, approaching from the direction of Mainz. By the time he was a kilometre away from the police roadblock, Müller had already turned off to head for the Autobahn.

Heurath slowed down as he approached the roadblock, then stopped the car.

As with Müller, the motorcycle policeman walked towards the newcomer. This time, however, there was a change of attitude in all five policemen. While the police motorcyclist continued towards Heurath's car, the others stood at readiness, hands on their sidearms.

The motorcycle policeman stopped short of the car and assumed an alert stance.

Heurath looked at him and smiled. 'Who's in charge here?'

'What's it to you?'

'I am *Oberkommissar* Fieseler, BKA.'

The motorcycle policeman did not relax. 'Please step carefully out of the car and show me an ID ... sir.'

Heurath was politeness itself. 'Of course.' He climbed out slowly and mimed a move towards an inner jacket pocket. 'May I?'

The other nodded. 'But very carefully.'

'Of course.' Heurath got out the ID and handed it over.

The motorcycle policeman studied it. It was as genuine as could be.

He handed the ID back. 'Sorry, sir ... but one has to be careful.'

'I understand.'

The motorcyle policeman glanced at his colleagues. 'BKA. *Oberkommissar* Fieseler.'

They relaxed.

'Where's the boat?' Heurath asked.

'What's left of it is over there.' The motor-cycle cop jerked a thumb in the general direction of the glow of lights. 'About a kilometre down the access road.'

Heurath nodded. 'Right. If your friends will move one of their cars, I'll be going through.'

'Of course, sir.' The officer waved to his colleagues, and one got into a patrol car to move it out of the way. '*Oberkommissar* Alsterhoven of the water police is in charge. But I'd better alert the special armed team who are out there somewhere. Don't want them to shoot you by mistake, do we, sir?'

Heurath gave one of his dead smiles. 'I would not like that one bit. Thank you,' he added as he returned to his car.

By the time he was driving off, the motor-cycle policeman was on his radio to the special armed team.

'An *Oberkommissar* Fieseler, BKA, coming through. Don't shoot him.'

The person at the other end laughed softly. 'BKA. Wondered how long it would be before one turned up. OK. We promise not to shoot him.'

The scene in the glare of the floodlights was a hive of activity. Beneath the surface, divers' lights shape-shifted among the wreckage, luminously strange aquatic creatures.

Alsterhoven was down at the water's edge, looking on as his divers and the clean-up teams brought up pieces of wreckage for the investigators. He turned and glanced up-wards, in time to see Heurath walking down the set of steps nearest to him.

He did not move, but kept his gaze on Heu-rath.

Heurath came up, hand outstretched. 'Fie-seler, *Oberkommissar*, BKA.'

Alsterhoven shook the hand briefly. 'Alster-hoven. The guys at the roadblock and the armed team warned you were on your way. But no one got in touch before to say you were coming.'

'Something like this is BKA business,' Heu-rath commented smoothly.

'Of course, but...'

'Any survivors?' Heurath cut in.

Alserhoven did not like the interruption, and frowned. 'They all did,' he replied carefully. 'We got them off in time.'

Heurath was very good at hiding the angry frustration he felt. 'Thank God for that!' he said fervently. 'You did good work there.'

'My job.'

'Of course. It's all our job ... to serve the public.'

Alsterhoven said nothing, but turned once more to survey the scene of the wreckage.

'You're angry because no one warned you in advance about my coming here,' Heurath said reasonably. 'I can understand that. First Müller dumps on you, then me,' Heurath went on casually. 'Very annoying for a hard-working river copper. I do sympathize.'

'Müller's OK,' Alsterhoven said, unwittingly confirming to Heurath that Müller had preceded him.

'I know. Pappenheim thinks the world of him.'

Alsterhoven relaxed slightly. 'You've met Müller?'

'We've met,' Heurath said. 'Good man.'

'From what I've heard, he's one of the best.'

Heurath smiled secretly. 'A challenge for those who come up against him.'

'It would seem so.'

Again, Heurath allowed a secret smile to briefly escape. 'What happened to the people from the boat?'

'We've taken them to a Schlosshotel not far from here.' Alsterhoven kept his attention on

258

the work going on. 'I would suggest not bothering them tonight. Plenty of time in the morning.'

'I wasn't thinking of seeing them tonight,' Heurath said. 'Do you mind if I just … walk around the basin for a bit? Then I'll get out of your hair.'

'Be my guest.'

The Schlosshotel gave an unprecedented and almost precipitous view of the Rhine valley. In the encroaching dark it was at once breathtaking and mysterious.

Carey Bloomfield's room had a balcony which overlooked the spectacular view. She closed the door to it, drew the curtains, then made a call to Toby Adams.

'Carey!' he began. 'Where are you?'

'Not on the boat.'

'Not on…' He paused. 'Your voice sounds strange.'

'That could be because I've just found out I've been sailing on a floating bomb. Toby … you put me on a boat with a damned bomb up its backside!'

'*Bomb?* What are you talking about? What…'

'Do you remember the *Isabella Lütz*, Toby? Do you remember a boatload of antique furniture – paid for by the tax-payer – so that we could make Hellmann believe he had a genuine cargo contract? And do you remember a certain Carey Bloomfield who was put on that boat to cover Hellmann and trap his potential killer – whom *we* want alive … *Hah!*

And do you remember—'

'Carey ... you're getting angry...'

'*Getting* angry? *I'm already there!* I'm—'

'Carey ... wait, wait! Where's the *Isabella Lütz* now?'

'Where? I'll tell you where! In *pieces*, Toby. Enough pieces to build several houses...'

'*What?* Do you mean...'

'It's what bombs do, Toby. They blow things to pieces.'

'Sweet Jesus!'

'That's the first right thing you've said.'

She cut transmission before he could respond, and switched off her phone.

Alsterhoven had watched from time to time as the man he knew as Fieseler strolled the area, stopping now and then to briefly talk to someone, but never actually getting in the way, or interrupting anyone's work.

By now his initial antipathy had waned sufficiently to enable him to respond civilly when Heurath joined him again.

'You're going to be here all night,' Heurath began conversationally.

'And the rest of tomorrow,' Alsterhoven said grimly. 'Anyway, I can snatch a doze on the boat if I feel one coming.'

Heurath nodded sympathetically. 'I've seen what I need to for now. See you in the morning, then.' He put out a hand. 'And thanks. Didn't mean to trample on your toes.'

Alsterhoven shook the hand. 'All forgotten.'

'Good. In the morning.'

'In the morning.'

Alsterhoven watched as Heurath went back up the steps, then vanished into the darkness beyond the rim of the lights.

About half an hour later, Stein climbed out of the water and went to where Alsterhoven was standing.

'There's so much stuff down there,' he said as he got out of his harness and lowered his tank carefully. 'This will take much longer than expected. By the way, who was that hardcase with the haircut I saw wandering around?'

'That, Dannie, was one of the BKA stars.'

'Oh? Who?'

'An *Oberkommissar* Fieseler.'

Stein had paused in what he'd been doing, and was staring at Alsterhoven. *'Who?'*

Taken aback, Alsterhoven looked at Stein uncertainly. 'I just told you. Fieseler.'

'Unless Willi Fieseler has a brother I don't know about, and who also just happens to be an *Oberkommissar* ... The man I saw is not Fieseler.'

'His ID is genuine.'

'Max, I *know* Willi Fieseler. We met years ago when I was on a diving job – one of my first after leaving the *Bundeswehr* – on a case that he was investigating. We've stayed in casual touch ever since. I don't care how genuine that man's ID is ... he is *not* Willi Fieseler.'

'Then who the hell is he? And how can he have access to an ID that is genuine BKA?'

'I'm just the diver around here. Perhaps he belongs to one of those little grey units that don't seem to have names or job descriptions.'

'Perhaps.' Alsterhoven spoke rapidly into his radio to one of the men at the roadblock. 'The BKA man ... which way did he go?'

'Back towards Mainz.'

'OK. Thanks.'

'What are you going to do?' Stein asked.

Alsterhoven looked towards where his police launch was moored. 'Ask someone.'

He hurried to the boat and contacted Pappenheim, using the same procedure as before. Within moments, Pappenheim had called him back.

'We had a visitor to the scene,' Alsterhoven began. 'BKA man...'

'Name?' Pappenheim asked immediately.

'Fieseler.'

'What's he look like?'

As Alsterhoven described Heurath, a sucking hiss sounded in his ear. 'What was that?' he said.

'I didn't say anything. What you just heard was me sucking the life out of a cigarette ... or a cigarette sucking the life out of me.'

'What?' Alsterhoven said, momentarily confused by Pappenheim's surreal remark.

'He certainly isn't Fieseler,' Pappenheim continued. 'Don't let any of your people try to take him on ... even the special team. There would be a bloodbath, and you would still not have him. You've been very lucky.'

Alsterhoven digested this. 'Who the hell is he? His ID was perfect.'

Pappenheim did not answer the question directly. 'It would be. Did you get his car's number?'

'A Berlin plate,' Alsterhoven replied, and gave the number.

'Not that it really matters,' Pappenheim said philosophically. 'The plate is either false, or the car's stolen ... or it's been hired or registered under a false name. Which way did he go?'

'Same direction as the hotel where the passengers and crew—'

'Tell any people you've got there to ... On second thoughts, tell them nothing. If he turns up and says he's BKA, best if they believe it and leave him alone...'

'*What?*'

'If you tell them the truth, they'll act differently, and that will alert him. They would lose any subsequent encounter with him. We have someone up there who is more capable,' Pappenheim added with some licence, thinking of Carey Bloomfield.

'*You* have? But who—'

'Come on, Max. You wouldn't expect me to tell you. And, just to make you feel better, he fooled Müller too.'

'He actually told me he'd met Müller. Used that as an opening gambit when he arrived. Cool customer.'

'*Very* dangerous customer,' Pappenheim corrected. 'Where's Müller now?'

'On his way back to Berlin.'

'Alright, Max. Thanks for letting us know. Watch yourselves out there.'

'Advice taken,' Alsterhoven said.

Carey Bloomfield was enjoying a quiet coffee on the hotel terrace, which gave a stunning, panoramic view of the Rhine valley. Her table was close to the terrace railing and she was able to look down upon the speckled lights of the town far below, and upon those on the opposite bank of the river. On the dark ribbon of water, the navigation lights of passing ships winked like multicoloured fireflies.

She had not made further contact with Toby Adams. She was still shaken by the fact that the *Isabella Lütz* had been bombed out of the water, and annoyed with those who had sent her aboard without at least warning her that the *boat* itself could possibly be at risk.

'Why, Miss Harris!' a voice said softly in English behind her. 'We do seem to be meeting unexpectedly. This is our third time within the last twenty-four hours. Coincidence, do you think?'

Though startled by this development, she did not react in panic. She turned her head round with the right amount of surprise.

'Inspector! This is a surprise.' She had not expected him to have made it to the hotel so quickly. Where were the police guards?

'*Oberkommissar*,' he corrected.

'Sorry. I can never get police ranks ... even back home. But what are you doing here? Are you off duty? This is a very beautiful hotel, with a great view. It really is quite something.'

'Alas, no break for me. Duty continues to command. There was an ... incident not far from here.'

'What incident?'

Instead of replying to her question, he chose another tack.

'Policemen,' he said, 'are by nature a very suspicious breed. I am intrigued by the manner in which we seem to cross paths, Miss Harris. First, we meet just outside an establishment I was about to investigate. Then I see you close to the port in Mainz. Now here you are, a few kilometres away from – let's continue to call it an incident – with a boat which sailed from that very port.'

'I'm on holiday, Insp– *Oberkommissar*. I travel freely. I didn't even know you were a policeman until you introduced yourself in Mainz.' She gave him the classic smile of a holidaymaker who was not very bright. 'I could even say *you're* following *me*.'

Again, Heurath ignored the remark. He glanced about him. 'I do not see your friends. You are frequently alone, Miss Harris.'

'Although I am travelling with friends, I sometimes enjoy my solitude. I go off on my own from time to time. The others are either stooging around somewhere, or up in their rooms. I just wanted to enjoy this amazing view on my own for a while.'

'Then I shall leave you to it. I have not yet quite made up my mind about you, Miss

Harris. When I do, the result could be interesting. Continue to enjoy the view ... but do be careful by the railing. The drop from here is quite precipitous.'

In the terrace lighting, his eyes were empty as he smiled coldly at her. He gave a slight nod, then went back into the hotel. He did not look round.

' "The drop from here is quite precipitous,",' she repeated slowly. 'If that isn't a warning...'

She sipped her coffee reflectively and did not glance round to check if he were surreptitiously observing her.

The view, she thought, did not now seem so benign.

A short distance from the hotel, Heurath sat in his car and fumed.

There was no doubt at all in his mind that the premature detonation of the limpet had been Müller's doing. The *Isabella Lütz* was gone because the bomb had been tamper proof; but the particular and important objective had not been achieved. 'You are beginning to anger me, Müller,' he said tightly. 'And that will not be a good thing for you.'

He had immediately spotted the policemen in plain clothes pretending to be hotel guests. The four uniformed police were also there as a clear indication that there was active protection. He did not fear the policemen, being certain they could not take him. He had not seen Hellmann, or his wife, anywhere; but the time to get Hellmann was not right. The manner and timing of Hellmann's demise had long been planned; and what had occurred with the boat had thrown the entire schedule of years of planning out of sync.

It all pointed to Müller's interference. Müller was not following the path that had been so carefully laid out for him.

'You're deviating from your programming, Müller!' Heurath snarled viciously. 'This cannot be allowed.'

And as for the apparently vacuous Amy Harris, all the finely honed instincts that had enabled him to survive his very dangerous profession over the years were screaming at him to be wary of her. But, as yet, he could not identify the reason. Nothing about her rang any warning bells. Only his continuing disquiet urged caution.

What was the real purpose of her presence? Could this vacuous airhead be truly considered a potentially dangerous foe? Or was she nothing more than she appeared to be? Time, he decided, would tell.

He started the car and put it savagely into gear.

Some time later, he stopped to make a phone call.

'Do it,' he said to the person who answered.

'When?'

'Tomorrow, at the time agreed.' He ended the call abruptly. 'Let's see just how good you are, Müller,' he added harshly.

267

He made another call.

'Yes.' There was no greeting, or expression of recognition.

'The limpet went off too soon.'

'Survivors?'

'All.'

'What happened?'

'*Müller* happened!' Heurath raged. 'Somehow, he found out enough to have the boat stopped and divers sent down to inspect the hull. The limpet went off when they tried to remove or tamper with it.'

There was a long silence.

'What do you want to do?'

'I've already done it,' Heurath answered flatly.

'The other options?'

'One of them. I want the passenger list,' Heurath added.

'That could be risky. Given what has happened, the police, and just about everyone else, will be over this like flies on a dung heap. It could take some time.'

'Just get it!'

'It will take some time,' the other person repeated firmly.

'There you are, Amy!'

Carey Bloomfield looked to her right at the sound of the familiar voice. 'Hi, Jack.'

'Mind if I join you?' Grogan asked.

'Not at all.'

'Some view, huh?' Grogan said as he took a chair that enabled him to look directly across the Rhine valley. 'Even at night.'

'It is something special, especially on a clear night like this.'

'I guess if the *Isabella* hadn't gone up, we wouldn't have gotten to see this place.'

'I think I would have preferred to have seen it under different circumstances, Jack.'

'Yeah,' Grogan agreed, staring out over the valley. 'Nasty business. One to tell the neighbours. Strange,' he went on. 'I served in this country, waiting for the whole shebang to blow. The only explosion I ever saw was some commie soldier losing his rag when we made signs at them. We used to do that when I had duty by the Wall. Now I'm getting on, I take a boat ride when the Cold War is history, and *boom*. Life ... is full of surprises...'

She nodded her agreement, but said nothing.

'You OK, Amy?'

'I'm fine. It just gives me the shivers to think how lucky we've been.'

'We've got a guardian angel somewhere out there. That's for sure.'

She glanced at him to check his expression for a hidden meaning; but he was still looking out over the valley, apparently deep in thought.

'The police have got Captain Hellmann,' he said after a while, 'and his wife and the crew, under close guard. Those two haven't done anything. It was *their* boat that got bombed.'

'I think it's more for their protection,' she said. 'Whoever did the bombing must have some kind of grudge.'

'I suppose.' Grogan paused, then continued, 'Real reason I'm here is to tell you that the captain has decided to have that dinner. He got the manager to give us the news. Now I'm passing it on to you. He wants us to join him and his wife in a private room in the hotel. The manager's even agreed to allow the *Isabella*'s chef to do the cooking. I think that's kind of a good thing for the captain to do under the circumstances ... which for him must be hell.'

She nodded. 'I can imagine.'

'So? You'll be there?'

'I'll be there. When?'

Grogan glanced at his watch. 'About half an hour to go.'

'I'll be there,' she repeated.

'OK.'

'But I'll come as I am. All my stuff, as you know, is saying hello to the river fish.'

'I don't think anyone's going to worry about dress code tonight.'

She smiled tiredly. 'I wouldn't think so.'

Grogan fell silent once more, staring out across the river.

'I reckon we'll call a halt here,' he went on. 'When the police are finished with us we'll stay a few days, then go on back home. There'll be another time for Budapest. The Kohlers are going back to the north. The bombing of the *Isabella* has done it for them. What are you going to do?'

'Truth is, I don't know. Probably the same

270

as you ... stay a few days, get some new clothes somewhere, then I'll see. Right now, I'm like a ship without a rudder...'

Grogan was looking at her. 'I think I understand. What about that young guy we saw you with in the café? Perhaps you should get in touch with him. He looked OK to me. Betty thinks you two should get together.'

'Does she?'

'You know my Betty. She told me so. Perhaps he can show you around ... being German and all.'

'Oh, I don't know.'

Grogan got to his feet. 'Whatever you decide, you take care, Amy. You hear?'

'I will, Jack.'

'OK. See you at dinner.'

'You will.'

He gave her shoulder a brief pat, and left.

She waited until Grogan had entered the hotel before returning her gaze to the darkened river.

'Where are you now, Müller?' she wondered softly.

Nine

Müller was driving as fast as he was capable, given the road conditions. It was raining, but traffic on the A7 Autobahn just past Göttingen was sparse.

The Porsche's lights cut a bright swathe through the rainy dark, its fat wheels clinging with awesome surefootedness to the wet road as it hurtled him towards Berlin. On the CD, the mighty basses in the introduction to Stravinsky's *Firebird* rumbled through the ten speakers with a menace full of forboding. This section of the music perfectly matched the darkness of his own mood. He felt as if he were indeed probing his way deep into a hostile forest where the very air, invisible and malevolent, had wrapped itself about him.

The decision to eliminate the entire Romeo Six cell was producing unforeseen and unwanted consequences. Expanding in a multi-tentacled spread that was reaching deeply into the very heart of the nation, it was a destructive virus that would poison all that it touched. As with the forest of the firebird, Müller felt unseen eyes upon him, following his every move.

'I have been programmed,' he muttered to himself.

But by whom?

Seared into his mind like an acid scar was the description of Romeo Alpha, as given to him by Hellmann. If Hellmann had not been mistaken, then a nightmare was being revisited upon him, to add to the others that seemed to be mushrooming by the hour.

Müller stared out at the glistening road surface, an obsidian ribbon that reeled past beneath the wheels in the brightness of the headlights. He was at one with the car, listening to its every cadence, even as he let Stravinsky's musical tale of the mythical avian creature flow around him.

He had programmed the CD to repeat the section over and over as the car tore through the dark towards Berlin.

In their hotel room, Udo and Isabella Hellmann were getting ready.

She had not been crying, but there was still a slight redness about her eyes. 'Do they look bad?' she asked him.

'No,' he told her gently. 'Your eyes never look bad to me.'

She smiled sadly, then patted her dress, turning before the mirror. 'For once, it's true when I say I have nothing to wear. I look terrible.'

'No, you don't.'

Through the mirror, she saw him studying her with a desperate longing. She turned round, went close, and put her arms about him.

'Don't worry, Udo,' she said against his chest. 'When the police have found out, Max will let us know whoever's behind this. Now let's go out there and show our passengers the Hellmanns are not down, or out. We'll rebuild the *Isabella* even better than before.'

He stared at their image in the mirror. He stroked her hair with an almost hesitant gentleness, eyes fixed upon a far distance they did not find pleasant to look upon.

'We'll rebuild,' he said.

Carey Bloomfield had returned to her room and was freshening up before going down to dinner. Satisfied, she glanced at her watch. There were still fifteen minutes to go. She checked all windows and doors to ensure that there was no chance of being overheard, and decided to give Toby Adams a quick call.

'*Carey*!' he immediately began. 'Where the hell are you? I've been trying to make contact...'

'No time for explanations, Toby. I'm on my way to dinner...'

'*Dinner?* What the...'

'In just the clothes I'm standing in. Have you any idea what it feels like to have all your personal effects at the bottom of a river? I've had to make do with stuff from the hotel shop...'

'Carey, I—'

'And I've had the third of my meetings with

the man we want. He's not sure about me, but he's certainly put his brain cells into high gear working it out. When he's made up his mind, I'll bet your Audemars Piquet he's going to come looking. He's said as much...'

'What about Hellmann?'

'For the moment, he can't get at Hellmann, because the police are everywhere. But my gut tells me the police don't worry him too much. He'd just shoot his way through them if he wanted Hellmann now. He's been here in the hotel, for God's sake...'

'*Hotel?* What hotel?'

'You'll get it all in the report when this is all over, Toby ... whenever that happens to be. As for our man ... I think he's waiting for something. His original plan's gone sour. Everything's happened too soon, so he has to make some adjustments. He's either going to do something quite unexpected ... or he's going to a fall-back position. He has to. And talking of plans ... ours went up in the air ... literally ... and into the river...'

'Carey, we couldn't possibly have known...'

'So you say.'

'Müller,' Adams said, shifting off the uncomfortable subject. 'Where's Müller?'

'No idea...'

'But I thought you two were—'

'Müller plays his own game, Toby. He's telling me only what he wants me to know, when he wants me to know it. So far, he's managed to keep the press out of what happened today. I don't want to be around when

275

they come running.'

'Are you telling me everything?'

'Are *you*?' she countered, and broke contact.

In Berlin, Toby Adams, in a suit that would have fooled anyone into believing he was a stock-exchange predator, put down his phone slowly.

'Damn it, Carey!' he said as he went over to a large window to look out on the city nightscape. 'City of many secrets,' he went on softly. 'You have much to tell, and you hide much ... but we'll unlock some of it.'

The hotel management had prepared a room that ensured privacy, and the chef of the *Isabella Lütz* had excelled himself.

Hellman was on his feet, speaking to his passengers.

'Thank you all for coming,' he began in English. 'I am certain it will not be easy for you to forget what happened. Isabella and I decided we should have our dinner as planned. I would also like to tell you that we shall rebuild the *Isabella Lütz*, even better than before ... and, on her first voyage, to Budapest, we would like you all to be our guests.'

'Now I like the sound of that!' Grogan said. 'We'll be there, Captain.' He glanced at Carey Bloomfield. 'Amy?'

Knowing the reality of the situation, she doubted whether Hellmann's dream would be fulfilled; but she nodded.

'I'll be there.'

Grogan looked to the Kohlers.

They too, nodded.

'There you go, Captain,' Grogan said. 'You've got a full complement.'

Hellmann smiled. 'Then let us enjoy the great dinner our chef has prepared.' He sat down and raised a glass of champagne. 'The *Isabella Lütz*.'

They all raised their glasses.

'The *Isabella Lütz*,' they said together.

Müller was on the A2 Autobahn, heading away from Braunschweig and towards Magdeburg. He pulled into the Helmstedt service area for fuel and, once he had paid, drove away from the pumps towards a row of public telephones next to the toilets and stopped.

It was still raining. Huge trucks, large tyres swishing on the soaked ground, slowly hissed past, giant mechanical beasts herding together as they searched out the lorry parking area. In the soulless lighting, it gave the place an alien, hostile atmosphere.

Müller got out of the car and hurried to one of the phone cubicles. He had decided to contact Carey Bloomfield. Using the public phone meant less chance of an eavesdrop.

'Miss Amy Harris, please,' he said when the hotel receptionist answered.

'Yes, sir.' Müller heard the receptionist make the connection to Carey Bloomfield's room, but she was soon back on the line.

277

'She's not in her room, sir. I believe she may be at dinner. I could send someone...'

'Yes, please.'

'One moment, sir.'

There was a wait of about a minute, then Carey Bloomfield's cautious voice came on.

'Amy Harris...'

'Is there a stand-alone telephone close by?'

Müller heard her soft intake of breath, but she recovered quickly. 'Yes,' she said after a short pause.

'Check its number. I'll call you there.' There was another pause as she went to check, then she was back. 'It's in an enclosed cubicle,' she informed him, then gave the number.

'I'll call you in one minute,' he said, and hung up.

Exactly one minute later, he called the number. She picked up the phone immediately.

'You're a man of constant surprises, Müller,' she said. 'I was enjoying a quite fabulous dinner.'

'You can continue to enjoy it ... Which reminds me, I'm hungry. Good hotel cooking?'

'Good *Isabella Lütz* cooking. The Hellmanns decided to give the passengers a special dinner. Good psychology, but Hellmann talked about rebuilding the boat better than ever. A triumph of hope over reality, I think ... But give him full marks for hanging tough. So, Müller, to what do I owe this pleasure ... and where are you calling from?'

278

'Not too far from Berlin ... which is where you should be by tomorrow.'

There was a longish pause. 'Giving me orders again?'

'Humour me.'

'And that phrase again...'

'It's not going to be long before the hair-brush realizes you're more than Amy Harris...'

'You must be psychic, Müller.'

'Just a policeman reasonably good at his job, I hope.'

'He's paid me a visit ... here at the hotel.'

'As you're still alive, he's not yet certain...'

'Such nice things you say, Müller. But you're right on the button. He came to check me out, itemizing the times we ran into each other. He certainly remembered that first time by Diefenhausen's café.'

'All the more reason for you to be out of there before he returns. And return he will. He hates loose ends; and he will be in a foul mood.'

'Worried about me, Müller?'

'I'm certain you can take care of yourself...'

'It's OK to say you are,' she commented drily. 'And what about Hellmann?'

'We want him alive as much as you do. By the time you leave for Berlin, Pappi will have arranged extra cover.'

'Swamping the hairbrush with extra man-power?'

'Something like that.'

'Why should I come to Berlin?'

'It's in your interest. Firstly, among other things, you'll be away from the hairbrush...'

'And secondly?'

'Humour me.'

'You're an infuriating man at times, Müller.'

'I never said I was perfect. Enjoy the dinner, and see you in Berlin tomorrow...'

She was reluctant to give in. 'I'll see if I can make it.'

'You'll make it. You know where we are.'

He hung up before she could say more.

Müller left the cubicle feeling better. He knew from experience that she was good, but Heurath was far more dangerous than anyone else she had come up against. There were times when discretion was by far the better part of valour; and this, certainly, was one of those.

He got back into the Porsche, and continued his journey to Berlin.

Carey Bloomfield returned to her dinner. They all looked at her as she entered the room.

'Good news?' Grogan asked as she sat down.

She nodded. 'Yes.'

'I'll bet it's from that young man,' his wife said.

'If it is,' Grogan said, eyes twinkling behind his glasses, 'I hope you'll meet up with him. Comes from Berlin, doesn't he?'

She nodded once more. 'Yes.'

'There you go. Couldn't be better. Go on

up to Berlin with him. Have some fun up there.'

She glanced at Grogan and, just as before on the terrace, checked for hidden meanings; but he was smiling guilelessly back at her.

Hellmann was looking at her curiously. 'A young man?'

'Why yes,' Betty Grogan said. 'Jack and I met them in a café in Mainz. Very, very nice young man.'

'I see,' Hellmann remarked thoughtfully. 'From Berlin.'

'That's what he told us,' Betty Grogan said.

'It's good advice, Miss Harris,' Hellmann said to Carey Bloomfield. 'Nothing better than having a native of Berlin to show you around.'

'Come on, people!' Grogan put in. 'Enough of the Miss this and Mr that. There are no strangers here any more. We've just been through a traumatic experience, we're having a fine dinner and we're all going to meet up again sometime soon. I'm Jack, this is Betty, and here's Amy...'

'Sigrid and Hans...' Kohler added.

Hellmann smiled. 'Thank you, Jack,' he said to Grogan. 'Thank you all. Isabella, and Udo.'

'There you go. Let me pour you some more of that fine wine, Isabella, and you too, Udo.'

As Hellmann put his glass forward for a refill, his eyes, full of questions, held Carey Bloomfield's briefly.

★ ★ ★

Müller continued to be lucky with the traffic on his fast dash to Berlin from Helmstedt and by 01.30 was parking in the underground garage of the police unit's building.

He had taken the incomplete Esske statement from its hiding place in the magazine pouch and put it into the envelope containing Diefenhausen's comprehensive whistle-blowing document. The minidisc Alsterhoven had confiscated from Grogan was also in there. Taking the envelope with him, and the unmarked Makarov belonging to the mystery man in Esske's house in Bonn, he made his way to Pappenheim's office.

'Ah!' Pappenheim said, looking up from his desk as Müller entered. 'There you are.' He pointed to a corner of the crowded desk, where a package waited. 'Hot pizza, and very good coffee.'

Müller shook his head slowly. 'How did you know?'

Pappenheim grinned. 'Max Alsterhoven told me you were on your way. Knowing how you sometimes drive, I made a rough calculation about your time of arrival. Berger went out to get this. Just about all the toppings you like, and no anchovies or pepperoni. Not lobster, you understand, but the best under the circumstances.'

'I'm so hungry, this *is* lobster.' Müller put the envelope and the gun down on a chair already loaded with files and began to open the package. 'Thanks, Pappi.'

Pappenheim glanced at the weapon. 'Nice

gun. Nice, shaped wooden handgrip. Going for Makarovs now, are we?'

'Our unknown man in Esske's house pointed it at me,' Müller explained. 'Unfortunately for him, he was Heurath's colleague and he now has no further use for it.'

'Cobras make nicer bedfellows.'

'For him, that might have been a better choice,' Müller said drily. He paused, sniffing.

'What?'

'Smoke. There doesn't seem to be as much smoke in here. I can actually breathe.'

'Funny man. I was just taking a break.' Just to prove the point, Pappenheim immediately lit up.

Müller looked at him. 'When you stop smoking, it's a sure sign you're worried. Worried about me, Pappi?'

Pappenheim blew a smoke ring at him. 'Of course not.'

'If you say so,' Müller said with a tiny smile, and continued working at the package. 'Have you been home at all?'

'I took a shower here, and I have a clean shirt on.'

'Sleep?'

'I'm fine. You probably need it more than I do.'

'I'm fine,' Müller said.

He took a slice of pizza, placed it on one of the paper napkins that had been supplied and drew the single free chair close to the desk. He sat down and began to eat, while Pappenheim smoked contentedly.

'You will note,' Pappenheim began between puffs and glancing at the laden chair, 'that I have not asked about that envelope.'

Müller finished the slice of pizza. 'You just did.'

'So I did.'

'In a moment, Pappi. One more slice, some coffee, then I'm ready.'

Pappenheim blew three of his better smoke rings towards the ceiling lights. 'OK.'

'So who starts first?' Müller asked, after he had finished off a second slice of the pizza.

'Rank before beauty,' Pappenheim replied. 'You first.'

Müller leaned over to get the envelope. 'In that case, you might as well go through this while I finish the coffee.' He placed the envelope on the desk.

Pappenheim picked it up and turned it over to study the address. '*To* Hellmann?'

'To Hellmann. You'll need a full pack of cigarettes after you have read what's in there,' Müller continued. 'I think I'll have another slice of that pizza while you walk into a nightmare.' He reached into the package for a third slice.

Pappenheim glanced at him. 'Bad, is it?'

'Worse.'

Pappenheim opened the envelope gingerly, as if expecting a scorpion to scramble on to his hand. He peered in, then turned it slightly over to allow the minidisc to slide out. He then removed the sheets of paper. He briefly stared at the contents of the envelope, and picked up the minidisc, turning it over as he studied it.

'Never seen one of these before, but our electronics genius should be able to make it work.'

Müller paused in his eating. 'Herman Spyros is still on duty?'

'Plus his team of two ... and Berger ... and Reimer. They're all on this for the duration. I think Herman has sent one of his people off to catch up on some sleep ... but let's see.' Pappenheim picked up a phone. 'Herman, I've got something here to exercise your brain cells. Care to check it out? OK.' He ended the call, adding to Müller, 'One of them's coming to get it. So what's on it?'

'A passenger on the *Isabella Lütz*, Grogan, took a video of the explosion as it was happening. Max Alsterhoven took this off him. If Spyros can make it work, there may be something on there that might be of use to us.'

Pappenheim nodded slowly. 'Well, let's see.'

A knock sounded on the door as he finished speaking.

'In!'

A tall young woman entered, ethereally pale and dressed all in black, with gleaming black hair and blue eye shadow. 'You're back, Chief,' she greeted with a smile when she saw Müller.

'I'm back.'

'And hungry,' she said, glancing at the

remains of the pizza on her way to pick up the minidisc that Pappenheim was holding towards her.

'And very hungry.'

'Tell Herman we need it as quickly as possible,' Pappenheim told her as she took it.

'Yes, sir.'

'Thanks, Hedi.'

She smiled at them both and left.

'That frail-looking Goth is Herman's secret weapon,' Pappenheim said as the door closed behind her. 'What that kid does not know about computers and electronics would also be lost on a pinhead. She's almost as good as Herman himself. I once watched her put a computer together. Unbelievable. God knows why she's with us. Definitely not because of the pay. She could make a fortune if she left the police. She's even a better shot than Berger. And Berger – as we both know – is good.'

'But Berger's been under fire. We also both know that being a good shot is not enough.'

'We do indeed.' Pappenheim turned to the statements from Diefenhausen's envelope. 'Who sent this to Hellmann?'

'Someone called Diefenhausen. I met him in Mainz...'

'Diefenhausen?' Pappenheim was rapidly sifting through the other papers on his desk. 'Ah. Here it is. Diefenhausen's dead.'

Müller stopped eating. 'What!'

'This came in while you were on your way back. Young woman called Anne Sattler...'

'I know her. She works there...'

'Well, she's out of a job now. According to her statement, she returned to the café after she'd been given the rest of the day off, to get something she had forgotten. Her boss, she remembered, had been quite agitated about something...'

'With very good reason,' Müller said.

'As it turned out,' Pappenheim continued, 'she found more than she was looking for. There was her former boss, covered by his crockery and neatly punctured by two bullet holes...'

'Heurath!' Müller commented grimly. 'It has to be. He was going into the café when Carey Bloomfield smartly ran that interference for me. It gave me time to warn Diefenhausen. Heurath must have returned later.'

'From what you've told me during our chats on the phone ... and from what I've been able to find out about that psychotic bastard, it certainly looks like it. I've got some bone-chilling things for you about that character.'

'So have I,' Müller said. 'Better read those documents. You have a few surprises in store. It's all there. Names, dates and the concept behind the operation. Many puzzling things, even outside the scope of this case, will fall into place. You are looking at the blueprint of a nightmare vision.'

Pappenheim studied Müller for some moments, then began to read. A minute or so later he paused, the half-smoked cigarette held just beyond his lips. He brought it back down to the ashtray and stubbed it out. He put down Esske's unfinished document slowly, then started on Diefenhausen's unburdening.

Barely a page through, he uttered softly, '*Shit!*'

Then he went completely silent as he read through the entire document.

Müller watched him, noting the changes in his expression as he came to particular sections of Diefenhausen's outpourings. Sometimes he would read particular passages twice as if to confirm to himself what he had read the first time.

At last he finished. He carefully put the papers together, then back into the envelope. He leaned forward to place it before Müller, then leaned back in his chair, hands gripping the edge of the desk.

'There are a lot of people,' he began at last, 'who would kill for this ... and not only Heurath. This puts you directly in the firing line from a lot of guns ... both literally and metaphorically.' He pointed to the envelope. 'This thing is a virus, with a potentially wide spread of infection. I don't want to believe the names in there. I don't want to believe what these people, who seem to have managed to infiltrate all sorts of hidden corners of our society ... actually planned to do to this country.'

'I didn't either. But we have the deaths, the *Isabella Lütz* turning into shrapnel ... and Heurath, to awaken us to reality...'

to Mrs Miranda Keene, your housekeeper, last Friday evening, when you learned that she would be alone in the house for the weekend, you decided to seize the opportunity of a few hours with her in the hope and belief that your visit would pass unnoticed.'

'That's right.' Kirtling stared defiantly back at DI Castle and DC Page across the table in the interview room.

'You were aware, of course, that such a visit was a breach of the terms under which you were granted bail after being charged with the murder of one of your employees, Una May, and that if the breach should be discovered it would almost inevitably result in your return to custody.'

'Of course.'

'And what decided you to take that risk?'

'You're a man of the world, Inspector. I would have thought that was obvious.'

'You mean Mrs Keene is your mistress and being separated from her was causing you a certain degree of, shall we say, frustration?'

'Exactly.'

'Sir Digby,' Castle made a show of referring to the file that lay open in front of him, 'it is true, is it not, that you also have a regular sexual relationship with another of your employees, Ms Fiona Slade?'

Kirtling turned a dull red and sat bolt upright in his chair. 'What the hell—' he began, but his solicitor, a middle-aged man called Whitlock who was sitting beside him, put a hand on his arm and he sat back, glowering.

Whitlock cleared his throat and said in a firm, authoritative voice, 'I cannot see that my client's sexual relationships are of any relevance to this enquiry, Inspector.'

'On the contrary, I believe in this particular case they are of considerable relevance,' Castle retorted. 'It is clear from previous evidence that there was no need for Sir Digby to travel to Muckleton merely to satisfy his sexual appetites and we believe he is not telling us the truth when he claims that was the sole reason for his visit last Friday.' He turned back to Kirtling. 'Sir Digby, during your telephone conversation with Mrs Keene on Friday, did she tell you where her niece was going that evening?'

'Only that she was going clubbing with some friends.'

'Did she tell you the name of the club where they planned to go?'

'How could she? I don't suppose she knew.'

'All right, I'll come back to that in a moment. You have no doubt read or heard reports of a number of recent thefts of art treasures in Gloucestershire and the neighbouring counties?'

'Naturally, but I don't see what this has to do with me.'

'And that there has also been at least one case where a fraudulent dealer attempted to pass off a fake painting as a genuine work by a well-known artist?' Castle continued as if he had not heard the interruption.

'I may have done.'

'Did Mrs Keene also mention during your telephone conversation that her niece had told her she thought she had identified one of the people behind the robberies?'

'No, why should she? It's of no interest to me.'

'You're sure about that?'

Kirtland thumped the table with his fist. 'Of course I'm sure,' he said angrily. How many times—'

'So it would surprise you,' this time it was DC Page who took up the questioning, 'to know that Mrs Keene has made a statement to the effect that she not only told you about her niece's discovery, but also mentioned the name of the night club where Anne-Marie would be that evening?'

Kirtling's jaw dropped and his colour faded. 'The stupid bitch!' he muttered.

'Did she?' Page persisted.

Kirtling cast a despairing look at his solicitor, who compressed his lips and shook his head before turning to Castle and saying, 'Inspector, I should like an opportunity to confer with my client.'

'Very well. Interview suspended at 9.30

291

am,' Castle said and switched off the tape recorder.

Half an hour later Whitlock informed the detectives that his client was prepared to give a full account of his movements from the time he left London on Friday evening until the time of his arrest, but that he wished to make it clear at the outset that he denied all knowledge of or responsibility for the murder of Anne-Marie Gordon.

Twenty-Seven

'Kirtling's a broken man, Sook. I'm beginning to feel almost sorry for him.'

It was Wednesday evening. Drained and frustrated after hours in the interview room with the prisoner, DI Castle sank down on the couch in Sukey's sitting room and closed his eyes. 'You have to hand it to him,' he said wearily, 'he's a tough nut to crack. He's had to face questioning from one member of the team after another throughout the day, but we've made hardly any progress.'

'He's still denying everything, then?' she asked.

'Not quite everything. He's finally admitted being at Muckleton on Friday evening, but insists his sole reason for going was to spend a few hours in the arms of his lady-love. He categorically denies having seen Anne-Marie while he was there, or knowing anything about her disappearance. He says he left Muckleton in a hurry on Saturday night when Miranda Keene said she was going to contact the police to inform them the girl was missing. He knew that if it came out he'd broken his bail conditions he'd be back in the nick in no time.'

'What made him choose Coventry?'

'There doesn't seem to be a logical explanation other than the one he gave us – he simply panicked. He's already awaiting trial for murdering the woman who was carrying his child; next thing, another woman staying in his house goes missing while he's there himself.'

'It must have seemed a frightening combination of circumstances,' Sukey remarked. 'Lots of people have been known to behave irrationally in that kind of situation.'

'That's exactly what he's saying. He claims he simply went to pieces and his one thought was to hide away in a place where no one knew him.'

'Presumably he'd sworn Miranda to secrecy about his visit?'

'Naturally, but he must have been afraid she'd blurt it out under questioning. He says he realizes now that his best bet would have been to go home, hope that no one had missed him and that Miranda would keep quiet about his visit. As it turned out, of course, it wouldn't have made much difference in the long run. When the girl's body was found on his land he'd have been a suspect from the word go, especially as we already had a shrewd idea that he'd been at the manor.'

'But if he still maintains his innocence, why do you describe him as a broken man?'

'He believes Miranda has betrayed him and that seems to have affected him more than being suspected of a second murder.'

'Because she broke her promise and admitted he'd been at Muckleton Manor the night her niece disappeared?'

'Partly that, but mainly because she said in her statement that she told him about the girl's researches and where she was going on Friday night. At first he denied that she did any such thing and insisted he knew nothing about the girl's movements, but when we confronted him with her evidence all the bluster went out of him. Until then he believed – with good reason as you well know – that she was so besotted with him that he could get away with, if not literally murder—' Jim broke off and ran his long fingers through his hair in mute frustration; for the first time, Sukey noticed flecks of grey among the brown. 'He feels he's lost his sheet anchor,' he went on. 'It's almost as if he doesn't care what happens to him any more.'

'But he still maintains he knows nothing about Anne-Marie's murder?'

'Oh yes. We haven't been able to shake him on that.'

'What about Miranda? Does she believe he's guilty?'

'The poor woman doesn't seem to know what to believe. You don't need me to tell you that she's always refused to hear a word against him, even when the evidence that he killed Una May was stacking up. The first time we interviewed her after she reported Anne-Marie missing she stoutly denied he'd been to Muckleton since being granted bail. After the girl's body was found she broke down and admitted he'd been there, but said she believed him when he said it was because he was missing her so badly and simply wanted to see her. The fact that he took off late on Saturday leaving her to cope with her niece's disappearance on her own must have hurt, although she says she accepted his reason for it at the time and assumed he was going back to his London flat. It came as a shock to hear he'd done a runner.'

'Didn't it strike her as odd that he hadn't been in touch since he left?'

'You'd have thought so, wouldn't you, knowing how worried she was – but they seem to have had the sort of relationship where he came and went as he pleased. I suppose from one point of view it figures – after all, he is her employer. In any case, she claims she was so distraught at her niece's disappearance that she could think of nothing else.'

'How is she now?'

'Devastated. It must have been bad enough to know he'd gone missing, but learning he'd denied knowing anything about Anne-Marie's movements, when she knew jolly well she'd told him, must have raised serious doubts in her mind about his motives. The FLO says she's on the verge of a breakdown, although she's doing her best to be strong for her sister's sake.'

'Poor Miranda, what a reward for all that loyalty,' Sukey said sadly. 'So Kirtling's story is that he left London late on Friday night, drove to Muckleton, hid his car in the shed where Anne-Marie's body was found and sneaked up to the house via the field behind it the way I did?'

'That's right.'

'And left twenty-four hours later, having spent the whole time at the manor with Miranda?'

'That's what he claims, and Miranda confirms that part of his story.'

'But if it's true, Anne-Marie's body must have been there when he left. How come he didn't see it?'

'We put that to him, of course, but he claims he drove in and out without lights to avoid being spotted until he got to the road. It's feasible, I suppose; there was bright moonlight on both nights and it's his land so he knew the layout. In any case, the body was half concealed under the trailer and covered with sacking. It could have lain there for ages without being discovered if that drunk hadn't blundered in.'

'Did you question him about the cause of death?'

'Naturally. He swears he's never possessed a gun and so far we haven't been able to prove otherwise. He admits he was a fool to go to Muckleton in the first place and then go to ground as if he was guilty, but that's all. The hard truth is, we simply haven't got any evidence against him.'

'So you've had to let him go?'

'No, he's still in custody for breaking his bail conditions. He's asked to see Miranda, but so far she's refused. I'd say that as far as he's capable of loving any woman, as distinct from a purely sexual relationship, she's the one. Dalia maintains he puts down her refusal to see him as proof that she believes he killed her niece and Una May as well. I've no doubt she's right,' Jim added, with what Sukey considered unnecessary warmth. 'That young woman shows a remarkable insight into the way people's minds work.'

With difficulty, Sukey bit back the sarcastic comment that almost escaped her. 'What about the art scam?' she said. 'You said you suspected he might be involved in that.'

'We put that to him in an attempt to put him off his guard by a sudden change of tack, but that didn't work either; all we got was a flat denial. In any case, we've got no firm evidence, only hearsay.'

'Have you questioned the other suspects? Could any of them be the killer?'

'You think we haven't thought of that? One's been in New York for the past week and the other is in hospital recovering from a hip replacement. You know something,' Jim went on in a flat, weary voice, 'I'm beginning to ask myself if we've missed something.'

It was on the tip of Sukey's tongue to mention that she had her doubts all along and had said so to Fergus the previous evening, but she merely remarked, 'It would be interesting to know what Anne-Marie found out. I don't suppose her handbag has turned up yet? She might have made some notes in her diary that could have helped.'

'I daresay that's what her killer – whoever he was – had in mind,' Jim said grimly.

'Probably.' Sukey glanced at her watch. 'Tell you what; it's time for a drink. Dinner will soon be ready and the wine should be nicely *chambré'd* by now. And I vote we think about something else for the rest of the evening.'

'Such as?' he asked with a sidelong glance at her.

She stood up, grabbed his hand, pulled him to his feet and gave him a fleeting kiss on the cheek. 'I'll tell you later,' she said in a throbbing contralto.

Despite some blissful moments with Jim the previous evening, Sukey's first thoughts when she awoke on Thursday morning were of Anne-Marie and her grieving family. She had not so far made any attempt to contact Miranda for fear of incurring Jim's disapproval and she resolved to have a word with him later to ask if he had any objection to her going to Muckleton to offer her sympathy.

In the meantime there was work to be done. Her first three assignments were in and around Gloucester city centre, but the next was to a break-in at the office of a firm of solicitors on Cheltenham's Imperial Square. As she reached the outskirts of the town she found herself thinking with compassion about Philip Montwell and what she had recently learned about the tragedy of his sister's death. She recalled Anne-Marie's description of his reaction when she had innocently enquired if the picture on his desk was of his wife or girlfriend. She suspected that his distant and at times arrogant manner was due, at any rate in part, to a need to avoid betraying his private feelings and she wondered how Anne-Marie's murder had affected him. It must surely have come as a shock to learn that someone who had worked for him, and whose talent he seemed to have been nurturing, had met with such a violent end.

The weather did nothing to lift her spirits. The day was dull and cheerless with a hint of autumn in the air. As she got out of her van a chill wind blew dust in her face and sent flurries of dead leaves from the chestnuts in the Promenade swirling above her head. By the time she had finished checking the crime scene and labelling her samples it was nearly one o'clock and she set off to find a quiet place to park her van and eat her sandwiches. Almost without realizing what she was doing she found herself driving past the Phimont Gallery. Spotting a notice in the window, she pulled up a short distance away and walked back to read it. It was short and to the point: 'Closing-Down Sale of Paintings and Objets d'Art. All reasonable offers considered'. Without thinking, she pushed open the door and stepped inside.

The walls in the showroom were crowded with canvases; even to Sukey's untutored eye they seemed to have been hung without any apparent attempt to classify them in terms of style or content. In the middle of the floor was a trestle table on which a few artefacts of metal, pottery and glass had been placed in a similar haphazard arrangement.

'Are you interested in buying or are you simply here to fill in some time?' Montwell had entered silently through the door in the far corner. Sukey jumped and turned round.

'I ... well ... neither, I suppose,' she said awkwardly. 'I happened to be passing and I saw the notice. I don't suppose you remember me, I—'

'I do, as it happens,' he interrupted. 'You're from the police, but you haven't come to tell me you've recovered the stolen painting.' His mouth twisted in a bitter smile. His features were as handsome as she remembered them, but the supercilious manner had gone and in its place was a kind of world-weariness. 'Anyway, now you're here, feel free to look round.' He went over to the table, picked up a pottery vase decorated in the Greek style and caressed it with his slender, artist's fingers. 'I picked this up in Thessalonika,' he said. 'It's modern, of course, but it's a nice piece.' He held it out to her and she felt obliged to take it.

'It's lovely,' she agreed, 'but I'm afraid I couldn't afford it.'

'There are more things in the back room,' he said. 'I don't charge for looking.'

Feeling vaguely uncomfortable, Sukey was tempted to make her excuses and leave, but he seemed almost pathetically anxious not to let her go so she went through the door he held open for her. The room was very much as she remembered it, except that the photograph on the desk was missing. There were a few pictures on the walls and a pile of expensive-looking art books on the table. Montwell picked one up and offered it to her.

'If you can't afford a picture, perhaps you could run to one of these?' he suggested.

'I really don't think—' she began, broke off and then stumbled on, 'I mean to say ... that is, I didn't plan to come here today, but as I'm here I just want to say that the police are doing everything humanly possibly to find Anne-Marie's killer. I'm sure you must have been particularly upset when you—'

'Be quiet!' Sukey jumped at the harsh, almost despairing note in his voice. 'Don't say another word.'

'I'm sorry, I didn't mean to—'

She got no further before a voice behind her said, 'Philip, what are these doing stuffed at the back of your wardrobe? Oh, sorry, I didn't realize—'

Sukey turned round. Athena Letchworth, the woman she had last seen in the restaurant having lunch with Philip Montwell, had just entered through a door that appeared, from a glimpse it afforded of a staircase, to lead to the next floor of the building. In one bejewelled hand she held a pair of a man's brown leather loafers. Her voice trailed away as she looked first at Sukey and then at Montwell. Turning back, Sukey felt a cold sensation on seeing the expression on his face. His gaze was fixed on the shoes as if they were a snake about to strike; in that moment, the nagging doubt that had been troubling her for days, the vague but persistent feeling that something vital had been overlooked throughout the recent investigations, suddenly crystallized into a terrifying certainty.

Twenty-Eight

The realization caught Sukey unawares; she gave an involuntary gasp and put a hand to her mouth. 'Of course!' she breathed before she could stop herself. Too late, she knew that she had blundered; the sour taste of fear rose in the back of her throat and her one thought was to get away. The door leading to the outer showroom was still open. She glanced through it, hoping to see a passer-by who had dropped in while they were talking to look at the items on sale. The presence of such a person would have increased her chances of escape, but there was no one there. Praying that Montwell had not realized the significance of her startled reaction at the sight of the shoes, she murmured a conventional excuse and moved towards the door, but he was too quick for her. He grabbed her, clapped a hand over her mouth, dragged her to one side and shouted over his shoulder, 'The front door – lock it ... now!'

Athena rushed to obey while Sukey tried desperately to free herself. She used every trick she could remember from her self-defence classes, but to her dismay he anticipated and countered them all. His strength was prodigious; he stifled her screams with one hand while his free arm pinioned her against his body so tightly she could hardly draw breath. When Athena returned he said tersely, 'Go and get some of your scarves – lots of them. We have to gag her and tie her up while we decide what to do with her. Don't argue!' he snarled as she appeared about to speak. 'You've caused enough trouble already, nosing around where you've no business to be.'

Athena scuttled upstairs and returned carrying an assortment of silk scarves, one of which she tied round Sukey's mouth before she and Montwell bound her wrists and ankles. They worked in silence; when they had finished he slung her over his shoulder, carried her upstairs and dumped her on a couch in what was obviously his studio. Still breathing a little heavily from their exertions, her captors stood looking first at her and then at each other, as if in some doubt as to what their next move should be. After a moment Athena broke the silence by saying, 'Well, Philip, perhaps you'll tell me what this is about. What is it about those shoes that you know, and she appears to know, but I don't?'

Lying there staring up at them, Sukey saw his attitude change. His shoulders sagged; his initial anger seemed to have given way to despair. His eyes had a haunted, almost defeated expression and he passed one hand over his forehead. 'I should have got rid of them,' he said, half to himself. 'I was afraid they might somehow be traced – that's why I hid them instead of throwing them out.'

'You mean they're the ones you were wearing that day at Muckleton?' Athena's glittering black eyes narrowed. 'Now I understand. We were asked to hand over our shoes for examination because the police had found fresh evidence. You'd already left; you must have given them a different pair when they called to ask for yours.'

'I didn't have to give them anything, of course – they made that clear – but I thought it would look bad if I refused. I was pretty sure the fresh evidence they were talking about was broken glass.'

'From the one Una May broke when you ... when she ... ah, now I understand. And so, I think, does she.' Athena jabbed a scarlet fingernail in Sukey's direction. 'Who is she anyway?' She spoke with a trace of a foreign accent and her voice had a soft, sibilant quality that sent a shiver down Sukey's spine. 'Didn't I see her in the restaurant with Kirtling's housekeeper? They walked out when they recognized you.'

'That's right,' he replied. 'I don't know what she was doing there with Mrs Keene, but I do know she works for the police. I think she was probably the one who found the pieces of glass.'

'Indeed?' Athena's eyebrows lifted and a faintly mocking smile lifted the corners of her mouth. 'Don't tell me she came to arrest us!'

'Hardly. She came to offer her sympathy over the death of—' Montwell's voice wavered and died. As before, reference to the death of his protégée appeared to cause him pain.

His partner had no such reservations. 'How touching!' she sneered. 'Well, Miss Police Lady,' she went on, gazing down at Sukey, 'like you, little Anne-Marie was too clever by half. You know what happened to her, so you know what to expect, don't you?'

'Oh, my God,' Montwell moaned. 'Do we

have to? Hasn't there been enough killing already?'

'You want to spend the rest of your life in gaol while Kirtling goes free?'

'You know I don't, but—'

'Then stop arguing and let's decide when to do it.'

Sick with terror, Sukey turned away and closed her eyes. She was going to suffer the same fate as Anne-Marie and Sir Digby Kirtling would be tried, and probably convicted, for a murder that it now appeared Montwell had committed. Anything further that she might learn between now and what seemed her inevitable death could never be passed on to the police. All there was to hope for was that he and his accomplice would make some mistake, perhaps by leaving some forensic evidence, that would eventually lead to their arrest. It seemed a safe bet that they were involved in the art scam as well and that somehow they not only knew that Anne-Marie had uncovered incriminating evidence against them, but had also managed to spirit her away and silence her without anyone noticing. Whatever the final outcome, one thing seemed certain: she, Sukey Reynolds, would not live to see it.

Following these few moments of despair, her fighting spirit returned with a rush. She wasn't dead yet and she gathered from their muttered exchanges, of which she could make out only the odd word, that they were having a problem in deciding how to deal with her. While there was life, there was hope. She opened her eyes and glanced cautiously round the room. Against the wall, just a couple of feet from where she was lying, was a table on which tubes of paint, jars of brushes and other items of artist's equipment were spread out. Among them was a thin-bladed knife that looked wickedly sharp. In their haste, her captors had made the mistake of tying her wrists in front of her. Even more obligingly, they had retreated into a corner with their backs towards her and their heads close together, absorbed for the moment in their deliberations.

As a result of regular workouts, Sukey's abdominal muscles were strong. With her stomach churning and her heart pounding madly against her ribs, she managed to sit upright without attracting attention. Inch by inch, she swung her bound legs over the side of the couch and stood up. There was still no indication that the conspirators, who were now behind her, were aware of her movements. She reached out for the knife; it was just beyond her reach and her feet and legs were tightly bound in several places with Athena's scarves, making it impossible for her to take a single step. There was only one thing to do, and that was to crawl. She sank to the floor, dragged herself on hands and knees to the table and struggled to her feet. The knife was within reach; she grasped it and turned towards her would-be killers.

They must have become aware of the movement. Now they were facing her across the couch and even in her desperate situation she noticed a difference in their expressions. Montwell's registered astonishment and alarm, but it was the look in Athena Letchworth's eyes that made her shiver. They seemed blacker than ever and there was a hatred akin to madness in them that reminded her of the actress who played the sorceress Medea in a performance of the Greek tragedy she had seen while still at school. It had given her nightmares at the time; now the horror had become a reality. Her situation appeared hopeless, yet she held the knife in front of her, pointed towards them, defiantly determined to do as much damage as possible to the one who reached her first.

The events of the next few seconds seemed to fuse into a blur. Later, when giving her account to the police, she remembered Athena saying, 'Oh, the hell with it! If we wait for you to make up your mind we'll wait for ever!' and seeing her reach into the pocket of her jacket. She heard Montwell's shout of, 'Not now, not here!' before she had instinctively thrown herself to the floor. She vaguely recalled sawing awkwardly with her bound hands at the scarves securing her legs and praying the argument would continue long enough to free them and give her a chance, however remote, of escape. She heard sounds of a struggle, then a pistol shot, a woman's scream and a thud as if someone had fallen to the floor. There was a gasp from Montwell that was almost a sob. 'Athena,' he groaned. 'Oh my God, I've killed you!'

Sukey sat up and peered over the couch. Philip Montwell was crouching over Athena's recumbent body. Her eyes were closed and there was blood on her blouse; he was holding her deathly white face between his hands and repeating, 'I've killed you!' over and over again in a broken whisper. Knowing intuitively that she was no longer in danger, Sukey levered herself to her feet.

At that moment Athena stirred and gave a feeble moan. Montwell swung round and said, 'She's bleeding, but she's still alive. Oh, dear God, what am I to do?'

Sukey made an inarticulate sound and with her bound hands indicated the scarf round her mouth. He seemed bemused with shock; an eternity seemed to pass before he understood and untied it with trembling fingers.

'I've done first-aid training; if you want me to help you'll have to untie me ... and be quick about it before she bleeds to death,' she gasped as the gag fell away. She was in the driving seat now; without a word he took the knife, cut her hands free and then did the same for her legs. 'Get me some clean towels,' she commanded, 'and give me back the knife. Now!' she insisted as he hesitated. 'I'll have to cut off her sleeve to get at the wound.'

It was only a matter of seconds before the bright red blood pumping from Athena's left arm told Sukey that the bullet had torn through an artery. 'We must get her to hospital,' she said. 'Call an ambulance.' Montwell, who had returned with an assortment of tea towels, appeared once again to hesitate and she guessed what was going through his mind. 'If you don't want her to die, call an ambulance – now!' she screamed as she snatched the towels from his hands. At last he responded; while she worked on the patient she heard him giving directions on his mobile. She did what she could by applying pressure, first to the wound itself using a towel as a dressing and then to the pressure point in the wrist. When that failed she gently raised the injured arm in a further attempt to check the flow of blood, but it was clear she was fighting a losing battle.

She had almost given up hope when they heard the sound of a siren. Montwell rushed downstairs to admit the paramedics and within a very short time they were carrying

Athena downstairs to the waiting ambulance. Montwell followed, informing Sukey over his shoulder that he was going to the hospital and what she did from now on was up to her. Then she was alone with the heap of blood-soaked towels and the shredded remnants of Athena's scarves scattered on the floor at her feet.

It was several minutes before she was sufficiently recovered from her state of shock to call the station and inform CID of the events of the past half hour.

Twenty-Nine

'When you come to think of it, it's a pretty ironic result,' Jim remarked as he handed Sukey a glass of wine before settling down on the couch beside her.

It was Saturday evening and the first time since the dramatic events of Thursday afternoon that Sukey had felt able to relax. She leaned against his shoulder, took a long, slow mouthful from her glass and gave an appreciative nod. 'Mmm, that's good,' she said. She thought for a few moments while savouring the wine before adding, 'How d'you mean, ironic?'

'If Athena Letchworth hadn't shot Anne-Marie, Montwell might well have achieved his objective in killing Una May.'

'You mean by seeing Kirtling convicted of a crime he didn't commit?'

'Right.'

'But if Anne-Marie really had come up with evidence about the art scam that would have incriminated him and the rest of the gang, I suppose the pair of them felt they had no choice.'

'Ah, but another ironic twist to that part of the story is that Montwell has never been involved in the scam and had no idea Athena was part of it.'

'He didn't know she was behind the theft of his copy of the Matisse?'

'He didn't have a clue.'

'So the reason he was so upset about it was purely the financial loss?'

'No, it was because it had a sentimental attachment for him. In fact, it wasn't a commission, although that's what he led Anne-Marie to believe. He painted it in memory of his sister; the two of them saw the original together on a trip to St Petersburg some time ago and it was always one of their favourite pictures. He actually made an earlier copy of it and gave it to her, but she sold it for a pittance to buy the drugs that eventually killed her.'

'After Digby Kirtling dumped her, you

mean?'

'That's right.'

'What a sad story. No wonder he was in such a state when the second one was nicked.'

'Yes, it's quite understandable,' Jim agreed. 'Going back to Athena and the art scam,' he went on, 'Montwell swears he knew nothing of her part in it until Anne-Marie started telling them about her discovery.'

'I've been wondering about that. Have you found out exactly what it was?'

'Oh yes, Montwell's told us the whole story. It seems she'd been doing some research on the Internet for her course when she stumbled across an article in an American magazine about an artist who specialized in faking copies of well-known paintings. One or two were so good they'd been sold at auction as original works. She went and looked up the *Gazette* reports about the art thefts in our area to see if there was any mention of copies being nicked, apart from Montwell's Matisse, but of course there wasn't. Just the same she thought she was on to something, especially as she remembered Montwell telling her that his copies had been known to fool the experts. In fact,' Jim added reflectively after breaking off to give some attention to his wine glass, 'I remember him boasting about it to me when I interviewed him over the Una May killing.'

'So she told young Picasso what she suspected and he panicked and nipped out of the Oasis to alert his father,' Sukey said sombrely.

'Right. He denied it at first, but admitted it when we told him he'd been picked up on one of the security cameras using his mobile. Andy Radcliffe has had his suspicions of Professor Dawden for quite a while, but he'd been covering his tracks so cleverly he could not get the evidence he needed to nail him.'

'They must have been in a real froth when they realized what would happen if Anne-Marie went to the police. I suppose they alerted Athena and suggested she try and intercept the girl when she left the night club?'

'No, that was just an appallingly unlucky coincidence. She and Montwell had been out for the evening and they happened to be driving past the Oasis just at the time when Anne-Marie was hanging about waiting for her friend's car to be fixed. Their offer of a lift was perfectly genuine; it wasn't until she got into the car and started telling them about her discovery that Athena realized the whole scam was in danger of being blown out of the water. The girl was so excited, Montwell says, especially as she thought it might mean we'd get his precious Matisse back for him.'

'Poor kid.' Sukey brushed away an unexpected gush of tears. 'If only she'd gone straight to the police instead of blurting it all out to them—'

'If Montwell had been on his own he wouldn't have killed her – as far as he was concerned there'd have been no need.'

'He would probably have told Athena,' Sukey said. 'They were pretty close; she knew he'd killed Una May.'

'That's true, but he swears he couldn't have been more shocked when she pulled the gun.'

'He was quick enough to grab me and tie me up when he realized I'd twigged the significance of the shoes,' Sukey pointed out. 'I wonder what made him change his mind about letting her kill me.'

'He probably knew the game was up. He admits he's sickened by Anne-Marie's death and Athena's betrayal, which is why he was closing down the gallery. Grabbing you was a panic reaction that he regretted almost immediately.'

Sukey gave an involuntary shudder at the thought of what might have happened. Jim put an arm round her and held her close. 'I keep picturing the scene outside the night club,' she whispered. 'Anne-Marie must have been over the moon when Montwell came by and offered her a lift. She hero-worshipped him; having the chance to tell him what she'd found out must have given her a terrific kick. Has he told you exactly what happened that night?'

'Oh yes, and to give him his due, it seems he was horrified at what Athena did, but it all happened so quickly and there was nothing he could do to stop it. He was driving and at one point – when presumably she saw that Anne-Marie was a threat – she told him to turn the car round and drive into Muckleton Woods. He wanted to know why and she told him not to ask questions. Next thing, she pulled out a gun; the girl took fright and tried to jump out of the car, but she wasn't quick enough.'

'That woman seems to carry a gun with her like other women carry a lipstick,' Sukey remarked.

'It seems her grandfather was a crack shot with a pistol and joined the Greek resistance during the war. He taught all his children and grandchildren to shoot and filled their heads with horror stories about what happened under the occupation. Just before he died he gave each of them a gun and made them swear to carry it with them at all times.'

'He must have been a nutcase.'

'Disturbed, certainly. I suppose his experiences under the Nazis had something to do with it. Montwell seems to think Athena is the only one who kept the promise; she idolized her grandfather.'

'I'll bet he never intended his gift to be used that way.' Sukey covered her eyes at the thought of Anne-Marie's final moments of terror. 'That poor girl,' she whispered.

'It was touch and go for you as well, wasn't it, Sook?' said Jim. 'I know you've been having nightmares about it – and believe it or not, so have I.'

'It was a bit hairy,' she admitted. She took another deep draught of wine before saying, 'Montwell may be singing like the proverbial canary now, but he's hardly the gallant hero, is he? He helped his lover dispose of the body of an innocent girl after killing a woman he'd never seen before in his life with the sole intention of getting a man he hated convicted of murder. I assume that was a perverted form of revenge for what Kirtling had done to his sister?'

'Right. He'd harboured a grudge against the man ever since she OD'd after he dumped her.'

'The same sort of treatment he handed out to Una May?'

'More or less. When Montwell overheard him rowing with Una in the shrubbery that afternoon he realized that here was a situation where a man might be driven to murder a troublesome mistress in a fit of rage. He knew Una's pregnancy would come out at a post-mortem; Kirtling would have to admit the child was his and with any luck – as he saw it – he'd be charged with killing her. All his pent-up hatred for the man simply boiled over and the minute Kirtling was out of the way he grabbed the poor woman from behind and strangled her. He's claiming he acted in a moment of uncontrollable rage and I imagine his counsel will plead temporary insanity.'

'D'you think he'll get away with it?'

Jim shrugged. 'Who can tell? To be honest, I think he's past caring.'

'That was my impression when he left me in the gallery to go to the hospital with Athena. What I don't understand,' Sukey went on after some further thought, 'is, if he hated Kirtling so much, why did he agree to copy *The Luncheon of the Boating Party* for him in the first place? He couldn't possibly have foreseen what was going to happen.'

'No, of course not, and he claims his initial reaction was to turn down the commission. Athena told him a refusal wouldn't do her business any good so in the end he agreed by way of a favour to her, but he says he never hated a job so much.'

'In a way that bears out something Miranda Keene told me.'

'What was that?'

'She says Montwell charged an extortionate fee for what she suspects is an inferior piece of work. She hasn't got a good word to say for him, by the way, because of the supercilious attitude he adopted towards her beloved Digby.'

'I wonder if she'll have Digby back, now all charges against him have been dropped?'

Sukey shook her head. 'After all the other revelations about him, I very much doubt it. If only I'd thought about the shoes earlier, when Anne-Marie told me the police had asked for them,' she went on sadly. 'It never entered my head at the time that Montwell might have handed over a different pair because everyone thought he was the one person who couldn't possibly have had a motive for killing Una May. I had a feeling for some time there was something I'd missed, but it just wouldn't come to me.'

'You mustn't blame yourself,' Jim said firmly. 'Even if it had occurred to you, I doubt if we'd have given it any serious consideration. As you say, Montwell was the one person we felt able to eliminate from the outset; we did follow up his claim never to have seen Una May before the party, of course, and it all checked out.' He held out a hand. 'Come on, love, let me give you a refill while you see how our dinner's getting on.'

'Right.' She surrendered her wine glass, stood up and led the way to the kitchen. 'You know something?' she said as she tested the potatoes. 'I'm still waiting for you and DCI Lord to give me a rocket for overstepping my function as a Crime Scene Investigator.'

'You know you deserve one, don't you?'

'On the contrary, I deserve a bouquet.'

320

police ID. 'Margit Neuss, *Kommissar*in. *Direktor* Kaltendorf is my boss.'

'Oh!' the startled Solange said. 'You've just missed him.' She did not invite her into the house.

'I know. In fact, knowing we were in the area, he radioed us on his way to the office. I'm here with a message for you.'

'Oh?' Solange said again.

The woman tilted her head slightly and asked, 'You *are* Solange, aren't you?

'Yes,' Solange replied, frowning briefly.

The woman sighed with relief. 'For a moment, I thought I might have made a mistake. Your father is a lucky man to have such a beautiful daughter.'

'My ... father?'

Again, the woman looked uncertain. 'Yes. *Direktor* Kaltendorf...'

'Oh,' Solange said for the third time, opening the door wider. 'Please come in while I switch something off.' She put the backpack down.

'Thank you.'

The woman began to enter. Solange moved. Her right foot swept up with astonishing speed, instep slamming with crippling force against the woman's crotch.

The woman screamed *'Shit!'* in German as the force of the blow sent her tumbling out the door.

Solange slammed it shut. 'It hurts differently for a man, but it still hurts!' she shouted. 'And no one who works for my father knows I'm his daughter!' She turned to run for the phone in the hall.

'No, no, *no*, my sweet Solange!' the soft voice said in English. 'You won't kick *me* in the crotch, will you?'

She froze to the spot, staring wide-eyed at the man standing by the phone, and pointing a gun at her. He ripped the phone from its moorings.

'The kitchen,' he explained. 'I know how to open locked doors.' He smiled at her.

Müller and Pappenheim would have recognized Enteling.

'That was a neat little trick,' Enteling continued conversationally. 'Where did you learn that?'

Solange forced herself to remain calm. Eyes riveted on the gun, she said, 'My ... my grandfather. He was a policeman. He taught me. He ... he said I was to use it on men who...'

Enteling nodded slowly. 'I think I understand. Painful ... but better my colleague on the receiving end, than I.' He did not sound particularly worried for the blonde woman's plight. 'And now that we understand each other,' Enteling went on in the same conversational tones, motioning with the gun to emphasize the point, 'let's go outside, shall we? She must be in a foul mood by now.'

Staying calm but eyes still riveted on the gun, she said, 'Who ... who are you? What do you want?'

'Who I am matters little to you. What do I

want? Why ... sweet Solange ... you, of course. Now please ... open the door like a good girl.'

'My ... my father will find out and...'

'Of course he'll find out. We want him to. We'll tell him ourselves. Now no more stalling, Solange. Out the door!'

She obeyed, and opened the door.

The blonde woman, face screwed up in pain and anger, was getting unsteadily to her feet.

'You little bitch!' she snarled at Solange, and began to draw her weapon.

'Ah-ah!' Enteling warned, casually pointing his own gun at her. 'We keep our heads ... unless you want to argue it out with the man who sent you here.'

The dark brown eyes glared at him with barely restrained fury. 'Point a gun at me again,' she snapped, 'and you won't live to regret it.'

'The next time you give me reason to point a gun at you,' Enteling said calmly, 'I won't waste time talking. You have only yourself to blame for what happened. Your information was incomplete, or you would have known that none of Kaltendorf's colleagues are aware of sweet Solange's existence.'

'If you knew, why the hell didn't you tell me?'

'You didn't ask.' He took Solange by the arm. 'Come on, my dear. We're going on a little drive. Hell hath no fury like a woman kicked in the crotch by another woman.' He glanced at the blonde woman. 'Coming?'

Her eyes glared poisonously at him as she followed.

At one minute after nine, Noni Erlenhausen's blue Volkswagen Polo pulled up before the Kaltendorf home. She climbed out, frowning at the slightly open door as she went up to it.

She pushed at it cautiously. 'Solange?' When she received no reply, she hesitated on the doorstep, then entered. 'Hello! *Solange?*' Then she saw the backpack, and the ripped-out phone. 'Oh my God,' she whispered to herself in German. *'Solange! Solange!'* She picked up the backpack.

She ran through the house, checking everywhere, and calling out Solange's name.

When she had checked every room, she ran out of the house, slamming the door shut behind her, got into the Polo and drove off at speed.

Berger and Reimer were parked in a side street that gave them a clear view of the corner of the leafy road where Gauer's building stood. Berger was behind the wheel, leaving Reimer in the passenger seat to make regular sweeps of the immediate area with a small but powerful pair of electronic binoculars.

'Where are those bodyguards?' he muttered. 'They should have been here by now to pick him up.'

'Perhaps he's sleeping late.'

'Perhaps they've killed him,' Reimer joked

morbidly. 'Ah! Here they come. Better late than never, I suppose.'

He watched as the big car drew up to park outside the building. He watched as the two men got out. He watched, and suddenly stiffened.

'Those are not the two guys from the other night.'

'Give me!' Berger took the binoculars from Reimer and had a quick look. 'You're right!' She handed them back to him, then drew her gun. 'Let's just wait and see what they're up to.'

Reimer got his own pistol out, then one-handedly held the binoculars to his eyes.

He began a running commentary. 'They're standing around, as if waiting for something. Now one of them is going up to the door. He's looking for the name plate. Wouldn't the real bodyguards have known where to look?'

'Yes.'

'Well, it's the same car ... so what happened to the other guys?'

'You're asking me?'

'Rhetorical.'

' "Rhetorical",' she said. 'Mmm. That's a word for the morning...'

'Now he's found it!' Reimer interrupted tensely, ignoring her quip. 'He's pressing the buzzer ... now standing back to look up ... presses again ... hand moving into his jacket ... door opening...'

'*Go, go!*' Berger said sharply. 'And close your door quietly!'

325

She was already opening her door. Reimer dropped the binoculars and began to get out.

They left the car quickly, pushed the doors shut, and spread to separate sides of the street on silent feet. The men had still not spotted them. They drew rapidly closer as the second man began to follow the first.

Then, as he turned to make a last check of his surroundings, he saw them. He shouted something to his colleague, who stopped in the act of entering and whirled to meet the threat. Both men now had silenced guns in their hands.

'*Shit, shit!*' Berger hissed to herself, glancing rapidly to where Reimer was positioning himself.

The men fired first.

Berger dropped flat behind a parked car, beneath which she could see a pair of legs on the other side of the road. One of the men.

Then she heard the roar of Reimer's gun. Two shots. The tyres on the big car hissed out their air.

'Good thinking, Reimer,' she said quietly. 'Now they're going nowhere. Should have had self-sealing tyres.'

She held her gun two-handedly and, bracing her elbows against the pavement, fired three rapid shots at the legs she could see.

Screaming curses told her she had scored. The person fell heavily and rolled away out of sight.

Something slammed against the car behind which she lay. Her target had either found her, or it was his colleague.

Reimer's gun roared again.

There was a sudden silence.

She remained where she was, looking urgently about her. She did not call out to Reimer. She hoped he would be smart enough to also remain quiet, so as not to give away his position.

Then she felt a presence behind her. She rolled swiftly, gun pointing. Then let out a breath of relief. A little girl was staring at her.

She grabbed the child, pulling her down. *'What are you doing? Stay down!'*

'A man,' the child said. 'A man is lying by the street. He is not well.'

'What are you doing here?' she asked the child urgently. 'Where's your home?'

'There.' The child pointed to a house a mere two metres or so away. 'This is our car.' She touched the car that they were hiding behind.

Berger closed her eyes briefly. 'Where are your parents?'

'I don't have a daddy. My mummy's in the bathroom.'

Just then, Berger heard a shout. *'Eva? Eva!'*

'I think that's your mum looking for you. *Stay* here. I'll talk to her. *Police!'* Berger shouted. *'Stay in the house!'*

Great, she thought. Now I've told those men where I am.

A gasp followed this, then a scream. *'Eva!'*

'Stay in the house!' Berger repeated. 'Eva is safe. She's with me!'

Then Reimer was calling. 'It's alright, Berger. One is dead, and the one you hit in the legs has given up.'

Berger breathed another huge sigh of relief. 'Alright, Eva. You can go to your mummy now.'

The child ran to the house.

'Oh Eva, Eva!' came a weepy voice. 'How many times have I told you *not* to go out into the street without me? How many times?'

The door to the house closed shut as Berger stood up.

'You should have heard *my* mother when I was that age,' she said in a low, dry voice as she went to join Reimer.

People had begun to gather round, to stare ghoulishly.

'Stand back!' Reimer said to them sharply. 'Go back to your homes!' To Berger, he said, 'The dead one's on the steps, there.'

She looked and saw the sprawled body, head on the pavement. Its chest was a large bloom of red.

'You hit the other right in the kneecaps,' Reimer went on. 'Nasty. He's leaning against his car. I've got his gun.'

She went over and looked down at the man. His knees were a mess, blood soaking his trousers.

'You don't look so good,' she said.

'*Bitch!*' he snarled weakly.

'That's me.'

'I need a doctor!'

'You need something.' She turned from him

to look at Reimer. 'Where's the sunshine boy?'

'Afraid to come out, I think.'

She glanced up the building. 'The asshole. So who goes to get him?'

'I'll do it,' Reimer sighed. 'But I won't be gentle. Oh, and I've already told the boss...'

'Müller? Or Pappenheim?'

'Pappenheim. Some people should be here soon to collect those two. He also said we should grab Gauer and get out of here as soon as they arrive ... and before any uniforms come on the scene.'

She nodded. 'OK. And watch it with those prophetic jokes.'

Reimer grinned, stepped over the body and hurried inside.

Carey Bloomfield was in the air, on her way to Berlin. At that same moment in time, Kaltendorf gave a sharp knock on Müller's door and entered without waiting for a response.

Müller rose to his feet as his superior officer approached purposefully.

'Ah ... Müller!' Kaltendorf began. 'Glad to see you're back.' He paused, staring at Müller expressively. 'Good God, man! Your clothes!'

'A slight argument with a wet pavement last night, sir.'

Kaltendorf's eyes raked him, dancing with what looked suspiciously like triumph. At last! they seemed to say.

'Did you sleep in them?'

'No, sir. But I slept here.'

'*Here?*' Kaltendorf made a point of looking around the room. 'Where?'

'I've got a collapsible bed, sir.'

Kaltendorf stared at him. 'Do you do this often?'

'Only when a case demands, sir. This one does.'

'Ah! Glad you brought that up. I came here to ask you about it. Have you got a report for me?'

'I soon will have. I need just a little more time. Not much longer. There are some major developments. You gave me the case on Monday, sir. It's Wednesday morning today. We have made some good progress ... but I want to be very sure of my facts before I present them to you.'

Kaltendorf looked at Müller as if he were certain Müller was lying to him. But he was stuck. Müller could not be faulted for wanting to report hard facts instead of conjecture.

Kaltendorf's eyes raked Müller's clothes once more. 'Pappenheim must be rubbing off on you.' He turned to leave. 'Keep me informed, Müller,' he added, not looking back as he went out.

'Yes, sir,' Müller said to the closed door.

It was 10.15.

Noni Erlenhausen was parked about fifty metres from the police building. She sat behind the wheel of her Polo, gnawing with extreme nervousness at her lower lip as she tried to decide what to do.

Unwilling to raise an alarm unnecessarily, and even though the ripped-out telephone continued to disturb her, she had driven back to the house to check if perhaps Solange had been somewhere outside, and had not heard when she had called. She would have felt foolish to find Solange desperately looking for her missing backpack.

But the house had been spookily silent. No one had come in answer to her loud banging on the closed door.

She had looked briefly into Solange's backpack, and had seen the mobile in there. Solange would never have left the phone. Something *must* have happened to her.

Pale and thin with dark, cropped hair, Noni's sole homage to rebelliousness was a single stud in her left nostril. Apart from that, she was as conventional as could be expected of someone born into a comfortable family. At just eighteen, she already knew the route map of her life, which, until today, had been followed with frightening certainty. Not knowing what had happened to Solange was a major aberration in that certainty.

So preoccupied was she with her own thoughts, she did not even notice the car that went past and stopped a short distance in front of the Polo.

Berger, now in the passenger seat, glanced back.

'Did you see that girl in the blue Polo?' she asked Reimer.

'What blue Polo?'

'Sometimes, Reimer ... Are you a police-man, or what? That bright-blue car parked behind us. She looked very worried about something.'

'Probably boyfriend trouble,' Reimer said indifferently as he turned off the engine.

'I'm going to check.' She glanced at Gauer, who sat scowling in the back. 'For a man whose life we just saved, you look very un-grateful.'

'What do you want?' Gauer snapped. 'A written document?'

'From you? No thanks. I don't know where your hand has been. Who would want to kill you, Gauer? Someone from your past in the bad old days of the DDR?'

Gauer paled as, unknowingly, Berger hit the bullseye. Then he turned pink with outrage. 'I will report you to your superiors. *Both* of you! You have treated me with great disrespect.'

Reimer, who had been listening to the exchange with growing impatience, turned round to glare at Gauer.

'Listen, asshole,' he said. 'My gut instinct was to let those two make a colander out of you. But duty says I have to protect you. You want to report us? Please do so. Our boss just loves crapheads like you. Now shut up!'

Gauer gave Reimer a furious stare in return, but he said nothing.

'Take the sunshine boy to our guest room,' Berger said to Reimer wearily. 'I'm going to check on that girl. Won't be long.'

332

'OK,' Reimer acknowledged. 'Come on, Herr Respectable,' he said to Gauer with biting contempt.

Berger walked quickly towards the Polo.

'Hello,' she greeted in a friendly voice to Noni, who looked up at her nervously. 'Can I help?'

'Do you ... Do you know Herr Kaltendorf?' Noni began hesitantly.

'Yes,' a surprised Berger answered. 'He's our *direktor*. Who are you? And what's the problem?'

'I'm Noni Erlenhausen. His ... His ... daughter...'

'His *daughter*?' Berger said, startled.

'No ... No. Not me. Solange.'

Faced with a stunning revelation she had not even in her wildest imaginings suspected, Berger instinctively decided not to push the questioning further.

'Look,' she said. 'Why don't you come with me? I'll take you to someone who can help.'

As if in a dream, Noni nodded.

'Lock your car,' Berger said kindly, 'and let's go.'

Again, Noni gave a slow nod and got out, taking Solange's backpack and her own soft bag with her.

Berger looked at them as Noni locked the Polo. 'Both of these yours?'

'No. The backpack is hers. I found it at the house.'

'At the...' Berger stopped. 'Alright. We'd better hurry.'

'Wait here for a moment, Noni,' Berger said quietly in the corridor outside Pappenheim's office. 'I won't be long.'

Noni gave one of her hesitant nods.

'Can I take the backpack?' Berger asked, holding out a hand.

Noni gave it to her.

'Thanks,' Berger said. 'Say nothing to anyone you see. OK?'

Again the nod.

After giving Noni a reassuring look, Berger knocked on Pappenheim's door.

'Come!'

Berger went in, closed the door softly behind her and approached the desk.

'Berger!' Pappenheim said enthusiastically. 'Nice work with Gauer. Very nice indeed. Glad you and Reimer are in one piece. I'm looking forward to talking with Herr Gauer.'

'He's going to complain about us. We didn't show him the proper respect.'

'Oh didn't you? What a shame...' Pappenheim paused in the act of lighting a cigarette and stared at the backpack dangling from her hand. 'Are you using fashionable accessories now, Berger?' He studied her closely. 'And that's a strange expression you've got on your face, come to think of it.'

Wordlessly, she put the backpack on his desk.

He looked at it. 'A present for me?'

'There's a young girl in the corridor,' Berger began. 'She says this belongs to *Direktor* Kaltendorf's daughter ... who is missing.'

Pappenheim slowly put down the cigarette. 'A *daughter*?'

'A daughter. Did you know he had one, boss?'

'No,' Pappenheim lied smoothly. 'This is...' He moved a hand helplessly. 'This is...'

'I know. That's how I feel. What do we do?'

'We do our job. Ask the young lady to come in.'

'Her name is Noni Erlenhausen.' Berger went to the door and opened it. 'Come in, Noni.'

'Erlenhausen ... Erlenhausen...' Pappenheim was muttering to himself, frowning at his desk. 'I know that name from somewhere...'

He looked up as Noni hesitantly entered.

'Miss Erlenhausen,' he greeted her brightly. 'Let's see what we can do to help, shall we?'

Eleven

Müller looked up as Pappenheim pushed the door open and entered.

'Great work by Reimer and Berger, Pappi,' Müller said with satisfaction. 'Now that we've got Gauer, and the wounded hitman, we should get some interesting things out of them. Gauer will try to bluff his way out, but he'll soon shrivel when he realizes how much we do know about him...' Müller stopped as he stared at the continuingly grim expression on Pappenheim's face. 'What?'

'We've got a problem.'

'So what's new? We *always* have problems.'

'Not like this one,' Pappenheim said in a voice that was devoid of all levity.

Müller slowly got to his feet and waited for Pappenheim to continue.

'We now have the explanation for Kaltendorf's keeping out of our hair yesterday...'

'Well he's back to his usual self. He came in a short while ago to give me the usual pep talk...'

'And from now on his day is going to get darker.'

'You're talking in riddles, Pappi.'

'Kaltendorf was out of the way yesterday ...

336

because he was picking up his daughter from the airport and spent the day with her.'

Müller stared at him. '*The* daughter we're not supposed to know about?'

'The very same.'

'So his daughter's in Berlin. Why the grim face?'

'She's missing.'

Müller's mouth came open, then shut again slowly.

'Shit,' he said after Pappenheim's words had sunk in. 'Shit, shit, *shit*!'

'And the rest.'

Müller turned to face the city panorama beyond his window. 'We didn't need this.'

'Nobody needs this.'

'What happened?'

'Noni Erlenhausen.'

'And who is she?'

'The daughter of one of the GW's close pals. Gerd Erlenhausen is a major player in finance. He has the ear of many a politician...'

'Which is of benefit to our lord and master.'

'Quite. The Erlenhausens are the only people in all of Germany – supposedly – who know of the secret daughter ... apart from us, of course; and we found out ... er ... let's draw a veil on how.'

'I think we should.'

'Now Berger has discovered it by accident. She brought in the girl.'

'You said "supposedly"...'

'I'm coming to that,' Pappenheim said. 'The girl was due to pick up the daughter at the GW's house at nine. They had planned a day together, checking out the city, especially the cafés, and doing what people of that age do. Noni turned up at the house in her Polo. She found the front door open, the phone in the hall ripped from its connection and the daughter's backpack on the floor...'

'She was snatched,' Müller said tightly. 'So someone *knew* she was Kaltendorf's daughter.'

'Exactly.'

Müller glanced wearily up at the ceiling. 'Don't we have enough on our plates?'

'Praying to the ceiling won't help. *He*'s not going to interfere.'

'It makes me feel better.'

'Then pray for me too.'

Müller allowed himself a brief, grim smile as he turned to face Pappenheim once more. 'I have a thought in my head that I'm not liking at all.'

'Must be the same one I've got.'

'You first.'

'Oh no,' Pappenheim said. 'As always, rank before beauty.'

'Alright. We're getting too close and this is Heurath's way – or that of those behind him – of raising the stakes. Someone, somewhere will then pressurize Kaltendorf into ordering us to drop it ... or else.'

'Amazing how we think alike.'

In his office, Kaltendorf picked up his phone after a single ring. He smiled, expecting

Solange.

'Kaltendorf?'

Kaltendorf frowned. 'Yes?'

'Take Müller off the case.'

'*What?* Who the devil are you?'

'Take Müller off! We've got Solange.'

The line clicked dead.

A grey pallor had suddenly come to Kaltendorf's face. With a shaking hand, he tried to replace the receiver. It took him three attempts.

'Oh my God!' he said weakly. It sounded like a whimper of pain.

He sat at his desk, unmoving, for several moments; then he stood up, went to a window and spent some minutes composing himself. Satisfied, he went out into the corridor, heading for the one that led to Müller's office.

Müller and Pappenheim were still there when Kaltendorf pushed the door open.

'Ah,' he said, face stiff. 'Glad you're both here. Sorry to be so peremptory, but you're off the case. Prepare a report of what you've done so far, then pass it on to me.'

Müller and Pappenheim exchanged glances.

'Just like that, sir?'

'Are you questioning my orders, Müller?'

'No, sir, but—'

'I gave you the case, I can take it back. Do you have a problem with that?'

'No, sir,' Müller repeated. 'You have.'

339

Pappenheim looked away with expressive eyes. 'Kamikaze...' he said under his breath.

'What was that?' Kaltendorf barked.

Pappenheim looked at his superior. 'Do you mean me, sir?'

'No! Müller! What did you say, Müller? *I* have a problem with my own orders?'

'Yes, sir,' Müller replied calmly. 'We know about your daughter, sir.'

Kaltendorf's mouth opened and closed like a fish out of water. 'You ... You ... *know?*' The last word was spoken so softly, it was barely audible.

'Noni Erlenhausen is here, sir. She's in Pappenheim's office. She told us what happened. We suspected that sooner or later, you would come under pressure to take us off the case. It's because we're making more progress than expected. I think it possible that we were intended to fail.'

All pretence no longer valid, Kaltendorf's face crumpled. The painstakingly constructed cloak, years in the making to hide his secret, had abruptly vanished, leaving it bare to the world. Pappenheim looked away, not wanting to see the man so naked.

Kaltendorf went to a chair and sat down, looking suddenly aged. He stared at nothing. 'What am I going to do? She's all I've got.'

For the very first time in his life, Müller felt an emotion he had never imagined possible. He felt sorry for Kaltendorf.

'We'll find her, sir,' he promised, with more gentleness than he'd intended.

Kaltendorf stared at him, petrified. 'No! Are you mad? You must not even try! They'll ... They'll kill her!'

'Sir,' Müller said with deliberate brutality. 'They'll kill her if we do nothing. The people we're dealing with are the kind of individuals who will do so ... if only to prove their point. Your daughter is in very real danger. We *must* act.'

'You can't ask this of me, Müller! You are off the case! *Leave it!*' Kaltendorf looked to Pappenheim for help. 'Pappenheim! Talk sense to him!'

'I'm sorry, sir,' Pappenheim said, 'but he is right. What we have discovered about these people makes it very important that we take his advice. You may not like his methods, sir ... but he is good at his job. I would suggest you listen to him.'

But the distraught Kaltendorf, perhaps weighed down by the years of guilt for the lonely suicide of Solange's mother, was not thinking like a policeman. For the moment, he was a panicked father, scared to lose the one person he truly valued: the daughter who looked up to him and who made him feel clean again.

He stood up abruptly, shaking his head. 'I can't sanction this. I can't!'

He stumbled out, without another look at them.

Pappenheim looked at Müller. 'Now what?'

'You're still here?'

'Ah. I get it. I might as well join the kamikaze club.' Pappenheim pointed at Müller's suit. 'And now you don't even have the time to change.'

'You leave my suit out of this.'

Müller permitted himself the most fleeting of smiles as Pappenheim went out.

Carey Bloomfield's plane had landed. She went through passport control without any problems and made her way to the arrivals exit. She had not spoken to Toby Adams, who thus had no idea she was in Berlin. She entered the arrivals lounge and was astonished to see Müller waiting.

'Wow!' she said as she came up to him. 'That's what I call service. How did you know I'd be here?'

'I'm a policeman. I know many things. Good flight?'

'Good flight.' She gave him a sideways look. 'What's wrong? There's an edginess about you, and...' She glanced at his suit. 'Been sleeping in your clothes?'

'Ha, ha,' he said. 'So ... shall we go?'

She hurried after him, and they did not speak further until they were free of airport traffic. Surreptitiously, she kept glancing at him.

'I have a message for you,' she said.

'Mmm.' Müller concentrated on his driving and waited.

'Vladimir sends his regards...'

'*Vladimir?*'

'He also said to tell you ... now let me

342

get this right ... "Computer programs can't change their programming unilaterally – at least, not yet – but humans still can." That's it word for word. I take it you understand?'

'Perfectly.' Müller shook his head wonderingly. 'Grogan. The good old homeboy is a Russian. Makes sense, given what I've seen.'

'He knew all about me,' Carey Bloomfield confessed ruefully. 'I was sitting at breakfast and he addressed me by my real name.'

Despite the situation with Solange, Müller found he had to smile. 'He *knew* about you?'

'Yep, damn it. That's not so funny, Müller. He could have been an enemy.'

'You can handle yourself. He may not be an enemy ... but I'm not certain he's exactly a friend. If you think about it, he's been doing some programming of his own. He's getting the result he wanted.'

'Will you show me what he sent you?'

'He told you about that?'

'He did.'

'Programming,' Müller said drily. 'We are doing exactly as he wanted. But given what he's done for my investigations, I can't complain. It makes sense that he's a Russian. Only someone with easy access at the time could have got the information he passed on to me. So I'm grateful. He has unlocked many puzzles. It could have taken a very long time to get where we currently are.'

'He actually said he had duty by the Wall...'

'And Checkpoint Charlie...'

'He just told us the wrong side...'

343

'Or we assumed...' Müller said.

Carey Bloomfield flinched as a taxi cut across their path. 'Jesus! Did you see that? He jumped a red light!'

'Never a policeman there when you want one,' Müller remarked as they turned a corner.

She looked at him as if he were not all there. 'You OK, Müller? And are you going to tell me what's biting you?'

'I'm going to need your help.'

'Well ... waddaya know?' she mimicked a famous screen actress. 'The guy wants ma services.'

'This is very, very serious.'

'OK. Joke over. I'm all ears.'

'Kaltendorf's daughter.'

'That sweet kid we saw in the south of France last time we ... er, worked together?'

Müller nodded. 'Solange. Yes.'

'Solange? You know her name?'

'I do now. She's in Berlin...'

'Kaltendorf brave enough to let people know?'

'Perhaps if he had been, this would not have happened.'

She stared at him. 'What's happened, Müller?'

'She's missing. Kidnapped.'

'Sweet ... Jesus. When?'

'Today. They took her out of his house when she was alone.' Müller told her about Noni Erlenhausen, then went on, 'Someone called Kaltendorf, warning him to take me off the case ... or else.'

'Oh my God!' Carey Bloomfield said quietly. 'The brush-haired man?'

'All my instincts tell me it's people associated with him. He has no intention of returning her alive, whatever Kaltendorf hopes. That man will kill her just for the effect it will have ... on Kaltendorf ... on me. Kaltendorf has persuaded himself that if he obeys the warning, she'll be left unharmed. I happen to know better.'

'So you're going after her?'

'Do I have a choice?'

'I guess not. But how will you know where to look?'

'I have a feeling I'll be led there.' They had reached the police building. 'And here we are ... home sweet home base. We'll go down into the garage, then I'll take you to see what our friend Grogan sent me.'

'Which reminds me,' she said. 'He also gave me this.' She got out the envelope and handed it to Müller.

Curiously, he stared at the form of address. 'Sense of humour,' he said, turning it over. 'Blue seal. Interesting.'

'You recognize that seal?'

'No. But it's a small one. A ring, perhaps.'

'Grogan does not wear a ring ... not even a wedding ring. There are no tell-tale marks on his fingers.'

'Not wearing one does not mean he hasn't got one.' Müller put the envelope into a pocket. 'I'll read it later.'

'Still not trusting me?'

'I'm already trusting you with plenty.'

'That's a matter of opinion.'

He smiled at her and got out. 'Coming?'

Müller knocked on Pappenheim's door.

'Come in, come in, whoever you are!' Pappenheim sang out in English.

Carey Bloomfield entered first.

Pappenheim rose from his desk and brushed the specks of ash off his clothes hurriedly.

'Miss Bloomfield!' he greeted. 'So good to see you again.' He went towards her, hand extended.

'You were expecting me, Pappi,' she accused mildly as they shook hands.

He glanced at Müller, who followed her into the room and closed the door. 'I cannot tell a lie. I knew he was picking you up at the airport.'

'And still smoking yourself to death.'

'Ah well ... as the sage once said, once the halfway mark is passed, it is easier to continue than to return. At least, that's my excuse.' He grinned at her.

'Müller has told me about the boss's daughter.'

Pappenheim's face clouded over. 'Yes. It's a very bad situation. We are going against his orders ... but we have little choice.'

She turned to Müller. 'I'll help all I can.'

'What about your people?' he asked.

'This is still the mission and ... they don't

know I'm here.'

Pappenheim grinned once more. 'We're a bad influence. It happens if you hang around here long enough.'

'Why don't we show her our rogues' gallery, Pappi?' Müller suggested. 'I think she will find it ... informative.'

'I think so too,' Pappenheim said. 'Please come with me, Miss Bloomfield.'

'I'll join you in a minute,' Müller said.

Pappenheim gave him a neutral glance. 'Fine.'

Carey Bloomfield's own glance was more pointed, but she made no comment as she went out.

Müller waited until the door was closed before he took out Grogan's envelope. He opened it carefully, working round the seal so that it remained intact as he tore at the paper. He removed the single, notepad-sized sheet.

'The ultimate objective,' he read

is to infiltrate the nation at all possible levels over a long-term period, so that the continuing shift of the country will be almost imperceptible. This is the slow drip of water on a stone. No one notices ... until it is too late to reverse it. You have allies in the unlikeliest of places.

There was no signature.

Müller folded the note slowly and put it back into the envelope, which he returned to his pocket.

Then he went out to catch up with Pappenheim and Carey Bloomfield.

After leaving Pappenheim's office, they had
turned left down the corridor. They passed
two doors, each with a dark brown finish.
They stopped at a third. This one was finished in gleaming black. It had a keypad where
a knob would normally be. Pappenheim
tapped rapidly at it. A red pinprick of light
flashed once, turned green, then the lock
snapped open. He pushed at the door. Bright
lights came on automatically.

'After you,' he said to Carey Bloomfield.

Müller caught up as she entered, followed
by Müller and Pappenheim, who shut the
door. It clicked home solidly.

There were no windows in the large room.
Every wall except one, from floor to ceiling,
was lined with wide steel cabinets, each with
its own keypad. The exception had a cabinet
missing and in its place was a desk with a
powerful computer on it. The computer's
monitor was a large plasma screen. Connected to the machine was a top-range sound
system. A high-backed leather chair had been
pushed close to the desk. A wide table, with a
white top reminiscent of a vast photographic
light box, formed the centrepiece of the
room.

'Our storage and special viewing chamber,'
Pappenheim explained. 'It is fully air-con-
ditioned.'

He went to one of the cabinets and tapped at the keypad. The entire front moved outwards to reveal serried banks of plain brown envelopes, each with a group of letters and numbers at the top left-hand corner as identification. He removed five and took them to the table.

'Please, help yourself,' he said to Carey Bloomfield.

Pappenheim and Müller stood back while she began to open the first envelope. Müller looked on interestedly as she took out the photographs and spread them fan-like on the table. As he watched her, he remembered his impressions of her the first time they had met. He hid a smile as he also remembered Pappenheim telling him she had a sexy walk. She did, he now thought, especially because she walked with her feet slightly turned in.

Not pretty in the obvious, in-your-face sense, she was nonetheless an extremely good-looking woman whose beauty lay hidden, as if deliberately so; like a quality to be revealed only when she desired it. Her deep brown eyes were perfectly suited to her gleaming dark hair, which she wore in a cut that reached just past her ears. He liked the way every time she turned her head, her hair appeared to briefly float upwards. He also liked the natural, dark crescent shape of her strong eyebrows, which seemed etched upon her skin. The way she now stood at the table accentuated the shape of her slim, yet fully curved body.

Pappenheim glanced at him, noting his gaze, and raised an amused eyebrow.

Müller gave him a stony look; but Pappenheim smiled.

Carey Bloomfield studied the photographs from the first envelope in complete silence. When satisfied, she returned them to the envelope, then opened the second. In this manner, she went through each, again in complete silence. Her face was very still as she closed the last envelope.

She took a deep breath, then turned round. 'Were these made from the disc Grogan gave you?' she asked Müller.

He nodded slowly, eyes looking at her steadily.

'I saw the water moccasin,' she said.

'Dahlberg,' Müller explained to Pappenheim.

'Ah.'

'We have nothing like this,' Carey Bloomfield continued in some awe. 'You were given a goldmine.'

'There's more,' Müller said. 'The last one, please, Pappi.'

Pappenheim moved to the cabinet to take out a sixth envelope and handed it to Carey Bloomfield.

She looked at each man in turn, before repeating the routine with this new envelope. One particular picture made her give an involuntary gasp.

'Grogan!' she exclaimed.

'Or Vladimir,' Müller said.

Pappenheim looked at him. '*Vladimir?*'

'Our benefactor may be Russian,' Müller told him.

'It would explain a lot,' Pappenheim said.

'I thought so too...'

'My God!' said Carey Bloomfield, almost shouting. 'We thought he was dead!'

They crowded round to look. Her finger jabbed at a face, not far from Grogan's.

'Who is it?' Müller asked.

'He is one of ours,' she began. 'Fifteen years ago, when I was still a kid – just entering my teens – this guy was supposed to have died on a mission. When I was being trained, he was held up to us as a hero. But ... But here he is ... *alive*...' Her voice faded as she tried to assimilate this totally unexpected possibility. 'Grogan wanted me to know,' she added softly. 'He *knew*...'

'And now he's given you something too,' Müller said.

'Even before you asked me to come to Berlin,' she went on thoughtfully, 'he kept suggesting that I link up with you. Perhaps you would show me his little present, he said.'

'A clever programmer, is our Vladimir.'

'Can I have a picture of that man?'

Müller nodded. 'But without Grogan/Vladimir.'

'That ... is understood.'

Müller looked at Pappenheim.

'Hedi Meyer can make a copy in no time,' Pappenheim said. 'I'll see to it. We'll leave everything in here,' he went on to Carey

Bloomfield. 'But you'll have your photo before you leave Germany. I shall ensure it.'

'Thanks, Pappi.'

Pappenheim gave a little nod of acknowledgement.

'Will your people be interested in knowing he's still alive?' Müller asked her. 'Or was ... when that picture was taken?'

'And how!' she replied.

'Then this is good for you.'

'This is very good for me.'

'Good old Vlad the Impaler,' Müller said.

Pappenheim looked at Carey Bloomfield. 'That's what an Oxford education does for you,' he said conspiratorially. 'Gives you that dry, British sense of humour.'

'So that's what it is.'

Müller looked at them both. 'When we're quite finished having fun...'

'Yes, sir,' they said together.

'Time for our little film, Pappi,' Müller said, straight faced.

Pappenheim nodded, went to the open cabinet and took out the CD that Hedi Meyer had recorded. He moved to the computer desk, pulled out the chair and sat down. He switched on the machine and, when it was ready, inserted the disc.

After a few seconds, the film began to run.

'This,' Müller said to Carey Bloomfield as they went closer to the computer, 'is a copy of the film on the minidisc that Grogan sent. It's an eye-opener.'

They watched the entire film in silence. There was continuing silence as Pappenheim removed the disc and switched off the machine. The silence lasted until both disc and all envelopes were back in the cabinet, and the cabinet itself locked.

'Woo!' she said at last. 'That ... That was something. I take back what I said about a goldmine. What you've got is worth many goldmines. This was put together by someone who was on the spot and was able to film it either clandestinely ... or openly because he was part of what we've been looking at.'

'Or a sufficiently high-ranking observer from the commanding nation.'

'It has to be Grogan/Vlad. The Spetsnaz footage was not media archive material ... especially the section where Heurath shot that man.'

'Got around, didn't he?' Müller said drily. 'But we should be thankful to him.'

'You've also got a hot potato,' she said, glancing about the room. 'Looks solid enough.'

'If you're thinking about someone trying to break in,' Pappenheim said, 'forget it. As soon as we're out of here and the door is shut and locked, the security systems immediately go active. The floor itself has sensors that detect footfalls, which it then maps and passes on to our duty desk.'

'A regular Fort Knox.'

'Not quite, but it does the job.'

As they were about to leave, Müller paused,

looking at Carey Bloomfield. 'Miss Bloom-field...'

'Carey...'

'Miss Bloomfield, did you bring your cannon?'

She shook her head. 'No. As I was travelling to Berlin without official cover, so to speak, I didn't want complications at the airport. The gun is back at my hotel. There's a safe in my room with a combination. It's in there. Grogan thought I was checking out, but I was just extending my stay.'

'So the room is in your name for—'

'Amy Harris's...'

'For how long?'

'A week. We should be done by then, shouldn't we?'

'If we're not,' Müller said evenly, 'everything's gone wrong. Meanwhile, you need a weapon.'

'I got a Makarov to spare,' Pappenheim said, looking at Carey Bloomfield. 'One known owner ... deceased.'

'Er ... no thanks. Good gun, but I prefer the Beretta, I'm sort of at home with it.'

Müller took out his own Beretta. 'Here. You can have this. Pappi will find a harness that will fit you.'

She took the automatic, stared at it, then at Müller. 'Your gun? But what will—?'

'I've got another.'

'He's got three in all,' Pappenheim said.

She gave Müller a searching look. 'You've got *three* Berettas?'

354

'Better too many than too few.'

'That's an answer,' she said.

The powerful black BMW was rushing at high speed westwards from Berlin. It was not the same car that had been to Kaltendorf's house.

Solange was alone in the back. The woman she had kicked was at the wheel, while Enteling sat next to her in the passenger seat. Not for the first time, Solange looked about her, checking out the door locks.

Enteling spotted her. 'It is no use looking at them,' he said easily in English, turning round as he spoke. 'I have seen you do that a few times. They are locked, and can only be opened from the front. And do not try to kick out a window. They are of armoured glass. Even if you did the impossible and succeeded, we are at high speed on the Autobahn ... and even if a truck, a car, or the centre barrier did not get you, you would still not survive the fall. So sit back and enjoy the ride. Behave, and nothing will happen to you.'

'Where are you taking me?'

'To meet someone who is looking forward to meeting you.'

'He does not know me.'

'Oh, but he does. He has known about you for some time.'

'Why don't you just *shut up*, you little bitch?' the woman snarled. 'I don't want to listen to your stupid French voice for the rest of this trip.'

Enteling turned to her. 'Don't overstep your authority,' he warned mildly in German.

'Are you giving me orders?' she asked tightly.

'*He* is. Remember that. And leave her alone, or I'll be forced to report every detail of this journey.'

'Don't push your luck with me,' she snarled. 'That little Polynesian bitch hurt me. I hurt people who hurt me.'

'Your fault. And she's not Polynesian. She doesn't even look it. She's rather ... exotic.'

'I *knew* it. You're thinking with your balls. You're disgusting!'

Enteling did not take offence. 'I'll accept that as a compliment, coming from a frigid, man-hating, cold-blooded killer like you. And besides, no one's going to touch her ... unless *he* decides to.'

In the back, Solange tried to eavesdrop; but her German was not good enough for her to determine what was being said.

'Where are we going?' Carey Bloomfield asked.

The Porsche was at a set of traffic lights, waiting for them to change. A fine drizzle had started to fall. The wipers sighed on intermittent.

'To a little shop I know in Wilmersdorf. You need some emergency replacements for the things lying at the bottom of the Rhine.'

'Hey ... anywhere you shop, I can't afford.' She sniffed at herself. 'Do I stink?'

The lights changed.

He smiled secretly as he looked away from her to take the left turn. 'You don't stink. In fact, you have a very pleasant scent.'

'I do?' She sounded very pleased, then, as if catching herself, went on, 'Hey! You don't know me well enough to say things like that.'

'That's true.'

He'd completed the turn and was looking straight ahead once more, so he wiped the smile off his face.

After a moment's silence, she said, 'That was a very nice thing to say.'

'You're welcome. And here we are.' He pulled into a parking bay directly in front of the shop. 'You go in and have a look while I get a permit from the machine. We have people called *Politesse*. They are anything but. Ravening creatures when it comes to giving parking tickets or having your car towed away. A car like this attracts them like flies.'

'You bought it.'

'Yes, and I don't intend that any tow truck merchant gets the chance to damage it. Now go and look for your things. That's the shop. Celts.'

'*Celts*?' She peered doubtfully at the shop-front. The drizzle had stopped and she could see clearly through the windscreen. 'As in Celtic?'

'The very same.'

'I'm not into New Age gear, Müller.'

He chuckled. 'Sinead doesn't sell New Age clothes. She designs her own. She calls the

357

shop Celts because she is Irish. She is married to a German. A great lady. I have known her for years. Now go on. She'll look after you. Look. There she is. She knows the car.'

She saw someone waving from inside. 'If the stuff in there costs six arms and legs, your butt is mine, Müller.'

She got out, and went into the shop.

Müller was about to go to the ticket machine, when his mobile chirped. He frowned. There was no caller's number on the display.

'Müller,' he answered.

'Are you off the case?'

Müller felt his body tighten. *Heurath*! He recognized the voice from Bonn.

'How did you get my number?' Müller snapped. 'It is embargoed to all but those I wish to know it.'

'Come, come, Jens,' Heurath said easily. 'You are not talking to a simple hacker. I can do many things.'

'I am sure you think you can.'

'Don't ... patronize me!' Heurath was suddenly angry. Then, just as abruptly, he was again calm. 'So? Are you off the case?'

'I am.'

'I thought as much. I called your office. All I got was your message machine. I left a message, but as we're chatting, that's irrelevant. But are you *really* off the case?'

'I just told you...'

'I am sure you think you're off the case.' Heurath gave a sudden, barking laugh. 'See?

358

I turn your own words upon you. I know policemen like you, Müller. You hate giving up...'

'I've told you. I'm off it. You have put the fear of God into Kaltendorf. He personally ordered me off.'

'Ah yes, Kaltendorf. My old superior, your cousin – whom you *killed* – turned him into jelly once before. I am only carrying on the good work...'

'You obviously like to hear yourself talk.'

There was a long silence.

'Alright,' Müller said. 'I'm ending this conversation...'

'You're not going to make me lose control, Müller. Better people than you could ever be have tried. Most are dead.'

'Is that supposed to make me nervous?'

'Oh, you are the proud one. Pride comes before the fall...'

'Goodbye.' Müller ended the call and switched off his phone.

He hoped he had judged Heurath correctly. Solange was in mortal danger, but he had to play games with Heurath's mind. It was the only way he could hope to gain an edge in a situation where all the cards were held by Heurath. He knew that Heurath would now be furiously attempting to re-establish contact, and would become increasingly enraged by the second. He knew he was taking a risk; but he knew also that Heurath wanted an audience; specifically...

'Me,' Müller said to himself. 'He needs to

show me how good he is ... for reasons I still don't quite understand. But, as long as he does, Solange will remain alive.'

It was a question of discovering where that boundary existed, and reaching it before Heurath.

Müller went to the machine to get the parking permit and had just returned to the Porsche, when a voice demanded, 'Is that your car?'

He turned to see a large, truculent woman staring hard at him. 'I'm certainly not here to steal it.'

Her manner had immediately annoyed him. After the conversation with Heurath, he had no patience for this. So much for politesse.

'Don't get smart with me!' the woman snapped. 'You're supposed to have a timed permit. You can get one from that machine over there.' She had her notebook ready, eager to put down his number.

Any minute now, he thought, she'd be getting out her little digital camera to take a picture of the car. Evidence.

'Are you blind as well as stupid?' Müller said, brandishing the permit he had just bought. 'I have my permit, and I'm going to put it in my car. Now please go and annoy someone else.'

But the woman refused to let it go. 'You can't talk to me like that!'

'If you behave without manners, expect it.' Müller put the permit beneath the wind-screen on the driver's side, locked the car and began to move away.

The woman began to write in her notebook.

'What are you doing?' Müller asked.

'Reporting you to the traffic authorities.'

'Good. Have fun. Report me to the police as well.'

She stopped and stared at him. 'What did you say?'

'Report me to the police, then I can interview myself.' He showed her his ID. 'Müller, *Hauptkommissar*. Now push off!'

She looked stunned, clamped her mouth tightly shut, put her notebook away and stomped off.

'I enjoyed that,' Müller said as he went into the shop.

Sinead Bromme was an elegant woman in her fifties. Her jet black hair, cut in a fashion reminiscent of the 1920s, was set off by startlingly, clear blue eyes. Having seen Carey Broomfield arrive with Müller, she had greeted her effusively.

'Hello, my dear!' she had welcomed her in German.

'Hi.'

'American!' In reply had come the cheerful Galway accent in English. 'It gives me a good excuse to use English. Welcome to my humble establishment.'

Carey Bloomfield had glanced around. Two young women were in different parts of the tastefully decorated shop, arranging the elegantly cut attire.

'I would not call it humble. You've got beautiful stuff in here.'

'Thank you. All my own designs.'

'Müller said.'

'*Müller*? You call him *Müller*?'

'It's our way.'

'Ah ... I see,' Sinead had said, completely misunderstanding. She had then spotted Müller arguing with the traffic warden. 'I see this every day. These people are so annoying. You've no idea how many tickets they've given me. In front of my own shop! Let's see what Jens does.' Then she had burst out laughing. 'I think she got a flea in her ear. Hallo, Jens,' she greeted Müller in English as he entered. 'Trouble again with the traffic angels?' She gave him a quick hug and a kiss on the cheek.

'Aaargh!' he said. 'These people are manic. So? Are you looking after my friend? Don't fleece her, Sinead. I'll be in trouble if you do.'

Sinead gave him a playful pinch on the cheek. 'Shame on you! Of course I won't fleece her. Just keep out of the way. Come on, dear,' she went on to Carey Bloomfield. 'Men understand nothing. Marie ... could you please get the *Hauptkommissar* a coffee?' she called to one of the young women in German.

Carey Bloomfield glanced back at Müller as she was led away. She raised an eyebrow at him.

'Have fun,' he said.

As they went off, he decided to switch his

phone back on. It immediately rang.

'Müller.'

But it was not Heurath.

'There you are,' Pappenheim said. 'I've been trying to reach you.'

'I hung up on Heurath.'

'That explains it. He called me...'

'So he's got your number too.'

'I think it safe to assume he can tap into all our numbers. What did you say to him? He sounds as if he has a hot poker up his backside.'

'I'm puncturing his hubris.'

'Is that wise ... under the circumstances?'

'It's a risk ... but our best chance of unsettling him enough so that he makes a mistake.'

'Well he's left you a message. If you want the girl alive and well, you're to meet him somewhere in Altenahr. And he'll be in touch...'

'*Altenahr*? But that's...'

'Indeed. Back out there in the west. You've got another long trip ahead of you. But in that car of yours ... I think he stayed there,' Pappenheim went on quickly before Müller could intervene. 'And one or two of his people made the snatch. They must be taking her to him...'

'What have Berger and Reimer found at the scene?'

'Nothing much. They escorted Noni Erlenhausen back and stopped by the house. Nothing was disturbed in there, so there was

363

apparently no rough stuff ... except for the ripped-out phone. Solange must have tried to reach it. But interestingly, Berger found someone who saw a man and a woman in an ordinary saloon, not far from the house at about the time it happened. Of course, they will have changed cars by now.'

'Just as there's always someone with a video camera...'

'Which is a mixed blessing...'

'Even so. There's always a witness some-where, thank God. Descriptions?'

'Are you ready for this?'

'Try me.'

'The description of the woman rings no bells. Could be the way she made herself look for the job. But the man was unmistakable...'

'Keep up the suspense, Pappi. I'm enjoying it.'

Pappenheim ignored the mild sarcasm. 'The duckling,' he said.

'*What? Enteling?* That's...'

'Impossible?'

'Well...'

'The dirt is everywhere, it seems. Even among the blue folders.'

'But why send this to us in the first place?'

'In my humble opinion, someone deep in there got worried and couldn't trust his own people. He sent the files, then Enteling, to force things out into the open. It worked. Enteling could hardly have refused an order at that stage of things.'

'Your contact?'

'Could be.'

'Perhaps Romeo Six is hiding deep in there.'

'That would certainly be something.'

'Catastrophic for them. What did you get out of Gauer?'

'Hah! That one. As you thought, he shrivelled like a prune when I gave him a hint of what we knew about him. Now he's so scared, he won't leave the building. We've got to feed the bastard. Left to me, I'd let him starve to death. So much for his new, greater Germany. Asshole.'

'Is he blabbing?'

'Couldn't stop him if I wanted to. We'll get plenty out of him to add to the stuff we've already got.'

'And Kaltendorf?'

'Locked in his office. Doesn't answer his phone, nor respond to knocks on his door. He seems to have forgotten he's a policeman. He's a father, and that's it. I think he'll go right off the edge if she dies, Jens.'

'I'll do my best to make sure she doesn't.'

'If you succeed, you know he won't thank you for it.'

'Where have I heard that before?' Müller remarked drily. 'I'm not doing it for him.'

'Thought not ... but where have *I* heard that before? Shall I set up a search for the car?'

'No. They would shoot the girl before anyone got close enough, or if they suspected they were being followed. We're not dealing with your average hostage taker. Heurath wants to lead me somewhere...'

'The killing ground. *You* were supposed to be leading *him* to one.'

'Don't remind me,' Müller said grimly.

'Then I won't. Better let you go, then. Heurath must be getting impatient.'

'He can wait. And call Segelmann, will you? Ask him to meet me in Bonn this evening, and to bring his artillery piece...'

'Artillery?'

'He'll know. Tell him he's also got the chance he wanted. He'll understand that too. I'll call him when I'm nearing Bonn. Give me his number.'

Pappenheim did so.

'OK, Pappi. Set things in motion for pulling those "greater" Germans in; but keep it tight. We don't want to give them warning. Once we've got Solange safe and sound, go for it.'

'Any exceptions?'

'None. I don't care how high it goes.'

'You're talking my language,' Pappenheim said. 'You know, of course, they'll hire a regiment of lawyers and use the constitution in their defence.'

'I know they will. The irony of people actively planning to subvert the state, then misusing its democratic, constitutional laws in order to escape their deserved fate, is not lost upon me. But even if they all escape, the slime on their faces will be public, and they'll know we know all about them. They can't hide any more.'

'You're still talking my language.'

366

They ended their conversation just as the young woman arrived with the coffee.

'Thank you,' Müller said to her.

'My pleasure.'

' "My pleasure",' another voice mimicked behind him as Sinead's assistant went away.

Müller turned to see Carey Bloomfield in a calf-length red dress that seemed to float on her body, yet close enough to define her shape. She looked stunning. Sinead Bromme stood to one side expectantly.

'Well?' Carey Bloomfield asked challengingly.

'It's ... beautiful on you.'

She beamed, and turned to Sinead. 'I'll take it. Let's look at some other things. See you later, Müller.'

'Don't take too long,' he said as she turned to go. 'We've got some travelling to do.'

She looked directly into his eyes, understanding. 'OK.'

The black BMW was racing along towards Hannover.

The woman glanced up at the sky, which had brightened considerably. 'No helicopter following. Perhaps they don't know as yet.'

'They know,' Enteling said. 'He will have called them.'

'So Müller is off the case?'

'Who knows? From what I know of him, he's not very good at obeying orders.'

'Bad news for that bitch in the back if he doesn't.'

Enteling glanced round. Solange was looking back at him stonily. He smiled at her. She just kept staring at him.

'We'll stop soon to get you something to eat,' he told her in English. 'And a fruit juice or something ... if you want one. You won't try anything stupid, will you?'

She kept looking at him, and did not respond.

'Let her starve,' the woman said harshly as Enteling turned round again.

'The decision is not yours,' Enteling said.

Solange had listened to their conversation, not understanding what was being said. But she had recognized one word.

Müller.

She remembered her father's mention of him. Who was Müller? Had he ordered her kidnapping? Was that why her father had said he hoped she would never meet him? Was Müller one of the people her father believed would do harm to her?

She dozed off, the name imprinting itself upon her mind.

Carey Bloomfield came towards Müller with three bags full of new clothing.

He stared pointedly at them.

'Well,' she said. 'I've nothing to wear.'

Müller looked at Sinead.

'She made some very good choices,' Sinead said.

Müller gave her a quick kiss on the cheek. 'Thanks, Sinead. And thanks for the coffee.

I'm afraid we must hurry.'

Her eyes twinkled at them. 'Enjoy yourselves, darlings.'

'We will,' Carey Bloomfield said.

As she turned to follow Müller, Sinead gave her a quick kiss on the cheek as well. 'And don't let him bully you.'

'I won't. Don't you worry.' She smiled sweetly at Müller, who had glanced round to look.

They went out to a goodbye wave from Sinead.

Müller took the bags from her to put into the luggage compartment in the front.

She watched as he opened the nose of the car. 'This is where the engine should be,' she said. 'You guys put the trunk there instead. It always gets me.'

'It's a boot,' he said, shutting it.

'Me, American. We say trunk. You, German with a German and Brit education, you say boot. Let's leave it at that.'

'Please get into the car,' he said. 'Sinead's watching.'

She turned to wave at Sinead before getting in. 'She thinks we've got something going,' she said as Müller got in behind the wheel.

He started the engine. 'Thoughts are free. But I did mean it when I said you looked good in that dress.'

'Why, thank you, kind sir.'

With a last wave at Sinead, he drove away. 'So? Did it cost much?'

'Considering what I've bought ... no. You

369

were right. She makes great clothes.'

'They're unique, and exclusive.'

She gave him an inquisitorial look. 'Did she drop her prices for me?'

'No.'

'There's one thing worse than not being able to afford something you want ... and that's having the prices dropped for you. You can't afford it? Here, you poor thing. We'll lower the price for you.'

'I always grab a bargain when I find it.'

'You're rich. You don't understand.'

He shook his head slowly.

They travelled in silence for a while, then she asked, 'Where are we off to?'

'I had planned to go to my place first for a quick change, and to give you a chance to freshen up if you wanted to.'

'But?'

'New plans. We're heading back west. First destination, Bonn.'

'You've got to be kidding me.' She stared at him. 'I just flew all the way to Berlin today, just to take a car ride almost back to where I came from?'

'Look at it this way ... you've got some very valuable information you would never have got otherwise ... information which will con-siderably raise your profile with your people.'

'True...'

'And you've got some new *and* exclusive clothes ... for a bargain.' He was smiling.

'Sometimes, Müller...' But a tiny smile crossed her lips. 'Now that you've poured the oil, tell me why we're going to Bonn.'

'To meet up with someone we'll need to help us get Solange back alive...'

'And...?'

'To kill Heurath, if I have to.'

They had stopped at a traffic light. A blue sign with white lettering pointed to the left, indicating the route to the Autobahn.

'That's nice and succinct. And have you got another gun in your holster to replace the one you gave me? Or are you going to strangle him?'

'I've got one. The harness Pappi gave you ... it fits?'

'It fits OK. I've got the whole rig in my bag. He found me a silencer that fits your gun too.'

'A *silencer*. Pappi thinks of everything.' The lights changed and Müller took the route to the Autobahn. 'Before we're out of the city, I'll stop for a short while.'

'Do you need gas?' She glanced at the instruments. 'But you've got a full tank...'

'I'm expecting a phone call.'

'Pappi?'

'Heurath.'

'Now *that's* something.'

'I got the first call just as you went into the shop. I hung up on him.'

'Are you *nuts*?'

'Not the last time I checked,' Müller said calmly. 'Heurath's is a complex personality. He's a psychopath who needs to show off. He's also very, very clever. I've got to get him off balance. I need an opening.'

'If he's so smart he'll know what you're trying to do.'

Müller nodded. 'True enough. I need to eat,' he remarked suddenly. 'Do you need to eat?'

'I could eat two horses on the run, but—'

'Good. I know a little place.'

'Another little place? I thought we were going to the Autobahn.'

'We are. It's on the way.'

'And Solange...?'

'Is still a long way from Heurath. She's reasonably safe till then.'

A few minutes later, Müller turned on to the Kurfürstendamm, then turned a corner to park a short distance from a newish-looking hotel.

'They've got a New York style delicatessen in there,' he said as he cut the engine.

'I'm not from New York, Müller. There was no need to—'

'I like it. Treat's on me. Come on. We haven't much time. Please go in and wait for me. I won't be long. Order whatever you like.'

'Bribing me, Müller?'

'I wouldn't dare.'

'Alright, Müller. I'll go in and see what they've got. Don't be long,' she added deliberately as she got out of the car.

He gave her a tight smile, waited until she had entered the hotel, then called Pappenheim.

'Slight change of plan, Pappi. Have you called Segelmann?'

372

'Not yet.'

'Good. I won't be calling him, just in case we're still being piggy-backed. Use the Mondrian code to call him. Tell him to meet me where he had parked his car when we met in Bonn ... but before he does that, he has to pick someone up at Cologne/Bonn airport.'

'Oh? Who?'

'The best bomb wizard we can get.'

'That's easy. Baude. But why a bomb disposal man?'

'I don't trust Heurath any more than he trusts me. I expect him to leave a little present.'

'A booby trap.'

'Got it in one. But where would he ... oh shit ... on the girl...'

'Got that in one again. Then we need Baude...'

'Not Baude.'

'*Not* Baude? He's disarmed so many bombs, mines, hot bombs, cold bombs, phosphorus incendiaries...'

'I know his CV, Pappi. I'm thinking of someone you would not even dream of. I am thinking of Hedi Meyer...'

'*What*? She knows nothing about explosives. She's an electronics gen ... ius...'

'I can tell you're getting there.'

'And Heurath is an electronics genius. You want her to disable the electronics of the bomb.'

'That's it exactly. I can only speculate about the type of device he'll dream up. But from what Stein had to say after the *Isabella Lütz* learned to fly, I am certain he will concentrate on creating an electronic nightmare. Kill that and we kill the device. The big question is whether Meyer feels she can handle it. Don't order her to do it. Give her the option to say no, without pressure. If she's scared or shaky, it will be worse than having no one. I don't want her there just so she can commit suicide. Let her know exactly what she's in for and, if she still wants to do it, get her on a plane. She can take anything she feels she'll need.'

'Got it.'

'I didn't hear you take a single drag, Pappi.'

'It's dying in the ashtray. I've been trying to imagine the kind of mind that bastard has.'

'You saw an illustration in that film.'

'We don't want to lose those two young women, Jens. I don't want that nightmare.'

'Neither do I. And remember, Pappi ... don't order her.'

'I won't. You make certain he doesn't turn *you* into Emmentaler.'

'I love my suit, dirty and rumpled as it is.'

Pappenheim laughed. 'Break a leg.'

Müller and Carey Bloomfield took twenty minutes with their early brunch and were on their way again.

'That was good stuff back there,' she said.

'I knew you'd like it.'

'Don't be so smartass all the time, Müller.'

'I'll try my best not to be,' he said easily.

They were on the Kurfürstendamm, heading for the A10 Autobahn which would in turn feed them on to the A2 for Hannover.

'Did you enjoy your chat with Pappi?'

'You wait until now to ask me if I talked with Pappi?'

'Just giving you time to think of an excuse.'

'No excuse needed. I did talk to Pappi. I asked him to fly someone out to meet us in Bonn.'

'Extra firepower?'

'In a way ... To disarm a bomb.'

'*Another* bomb? I've had enough of bombs,' she said with feeling. 'Where this time?'

The traffic was heavy at that point so Müller waited until it had thinned out before replying.

'I believe Heurath will attach one to Solange.'

She turned her head slowly to look at him. 'Are you *serious?*'

'Very. It is exactly what I think he will do. It fits the way his mind works. You saw the film and the photographs. Nothing is too extreme for him. Even this journey we're making has been engineered by him. Why? Because he wants me to witness his masterpiece. He wants me to be there when he kills Solange.'

'The guy's sick.'

'Most certainly ... but very clever too ... and very dangerous. He will kill her if I make a mistake ... but the one I will not make is that of underestimating him. My phone is back on. I expect him to call again soon.'

'What will you do then?'

'Talk briefly, then hang up on him.'

'You *are* nuts. That will make him even madder, and he'll take it out on Solange...'

'He won't touch her until he has me for an audience ... I hope. He wants to make this very personal. From his point of view, I took it upon myself to challenge him. I have wrecked his plans. He has to do something about that. A matter of warped pride and honour...'

'And to do this he has first to humiliate you by killing Solange while you watch or listen helplessly, then kill you too...'

'Then try to kill me...'

She looked straight ahead, saying nothing.

'I just got me some nice new clothes, Müller,' she said after a while. 'If they get ruined, *I'll* kill you.'

He glanced at her. '*What?*'

'My way of saying be careful.' She did not look at him.

The mobile made its urgent sound.

Müller had been cruising on the inside. He set the hazard lights flashing, pulled in to the side of the road and stopped. Finger briefly held to his lips to warn her to remain silent, he picked up the mobile.

'Müller...'

'That was *not* polite!' remonstrated Heurath's voice, full of anger. 'You are in no position to hang up on me! Don't do it again. You are endangering the girl's life.'

'Let's get this straight,' Müller said coldly.

'*You* are endangering her life. *You* had her kidnapped. And in any case, as I am no longer in charge of this, why are you calling me?'

There was a pause. Müller waited.

'You are still on it,' Heurath said.

'Your hearing is not working properly. I've told you...'

'You are back on it, because I say so.'

'I don't take orders from you.'

'You'll have to. You must.'

'Or...?'

'The girl dies.'

Heurath cut transmission.

Muller stared at the phone. 'Very original. This time,' he added to Carey Bloomfield, '*he* hung up.'

'What now?'

'We wait here for a while.' He glanced back. 'We have a visitor.'

She turned to look, and saw the green leathers of a motorcycle policeman on his green and white bike.

The bike stopped behind the car. The policeman climbed off, approached cautiously, hand on sidearm. He indicated that Müller should lower his window. Müller did so.

The sound of the policeman's radio stuttered in.

'You can't stop here,' the policeman said, peering in. His eyes raked Carey Bloomfield.

'Müller, *Hauptkommissar*.'

The policeman glanced at Müller's hair and was not impressed. 'ID?'

377

Carefully, Müller got it out to show him.

'Oh. Er … sorry, sir. I thought…'

'That's alright. Just doing your job.'

'Yes, sir. Thank you, sir.'

The motorcycle cop hurriedly returned to his bike, climbed on and roared away, giving Müller a brief salute as he passed.

Carey Bloomfield was laughing silently. 'Bet he said shit to himself when you showed him the ID.'

'I am certain he did.'

'You enjoyed that.'

'One has to take small enjoyments when-ever, and wherever, one can.' The mobile came alive again. 'Guess who?' Müller added as he picked it up. 'Müller.'

'Did you consider what I said?'

'I always consider what you say. What I choose to do about it is a different matter altogether.'

Heurath seemed to think about that. 'You're back on the case,' he said.

'You're repeating yourself.'

'I don't like doing that,' Heurath warned. 'So don't make me! We are policemen, Müller,' he continued, as if to a colleague. 'When the going gets tough, we get tougher. But those who give us orders are only interested in power. When things get hot, *they* turn to jelly. Are you with me?'

'Very much so.'

'I knew you would understand. You're given a mission. You are told it is a matter of honour to do the things you must, for your country.

Then the people in whom you have put your trust and loyalty bend before political expediency. They lose their way. They think only of covering their backsides. Suddenly, you are too extreme for them. They give counter orders ... but you are already deep in your mission. The world has changed, they say. But who changed it? *They* did. The world did not change by itself. *They* got scared, so they compromise. They still want the power, of course ... but they no longer have a use for you...'

Heurath's voice was full of hate, contempt, and a sense of betrayal.

'Are you still there?' he asked.

'I'm here.'

'But I refuse to end my mission. I have loyal people ... just as you have. The mission continues...'

'Then why are you killing the Romeos?'

'They are worthless. They, too, turned to jelly and fattened themselves in the West. I long realized you knew about them. You also took something in Bonn that belongs to me. But we'll leave that for now. It will all be resolved very soon. There are betrayers among us,' Heurath continued. 'They must be eliminated.'

'You may have made some mistakes in your choice of targets.'

'Every war has collateral damage.'

'I see. Does that include the girl?'

'She serves another purpose...'

'To get me.'

379

'We stand out, you and I ... but I am better. I am better than my late commander, whom you defeated. I was better than he could ever have been ... and he *was* good. It interests me greatly that you were even better. I have known about you for some time, Müller. Your dead cousin used to talk about you. I think he secretly envied you. I do not.'

'I'm glad to hear it...'

'Careful! Don't try to patronize me again.'

'I won't.'

'Very well. I gave your loyal Pappenheim a message for you.'

'He told me.'

'Then we meet in Altenahr ... in the ruined castle. Burg Are. You know it?'

'I know it.'

'There's a legend about it...'

'One of the Ruland chronicles of the legends of the Rhine ... "The Last Knight of Altenahr"...'

'You are widely read...'

'I was given many of the legends to read as a boy,' Müller said conversationally. 'I still have them.'

'Then remember this one when you come. But, unlike the last knight, I'm not going to kill myself on a milk-white charger. If you beat me – which I very much doubt – the girl's life is yours. But you'll lose, of course, and she'll die. Too bad. She's a pretty thing. Collateral damage. *C'est la guerre...*'

'So you speak French...'

'Don't patronize me!'

At that moment, Müller ended the call and switched off the mobile.

He looked at Carey Bloomfield, who was staring at him. He raised enquiring eyebrows at her.

'Even I could hear that scream of rage,' she said. 'I hope you know what you're doing.'

'So do I. So do I.'

Müller switched off the flashing indicators and eased back into the traffic.

'Heurath has gone rogue on his masters,' he said to her. 'He is strung out on a burning sense of betrayal, matched only by his contempt for those he considers have betrayed him. He will continue his mission, no matter what. He believes he is right to do so. He wants me out of the way so that he can continue unhindered.'

'You should be flattered he sees you as so important.'

He glanced at her. 'Is there a bite of something in there?'

'No. I'm making a valid point.'

'Because he sees me as so important ... *I* am his weak link.'

'Exactly. Because he is so focused on you, it should make it a little easier for you to manipulate him.'

'Miss Bloomfield...'

'Carey...'

'Miss Bloomfield, you have a point.'

On the B267, just past Mayschoss in the valley of the River Ahr, Heurath fought to control the rage he felt. Parked at the side of the road, he looked at his mobile as if he wanted to strangle it. Finally, he gave in to the powerful emotions that were consuming him.

'*Müller!*' he screamed.

Twelve

'Who do you think Romeo Six is?' Carey Bloomfield asked.

Müller was driving at very high speed. The question was as much to put her mind on something other than the road, which appeared to be going into warp before her eyes, as the result of genuine interest in the mystery of this man of the shadows.

'Is my driving causing you anxiety?'

'I've driven at high speed with you before.'

'That is question avoidance ... not an answer.'

'I have no problem with your driving.'

'But?'

'It's the others I'm worried about. I remember a white van last year, in the rain. He pulled out without looking, or indicating...'

Müller did not slow down. 'But we stopped well in time. These brakes are phenomenal...'

'You don't have to sell the car to me.'

He eased off.

'Hey,' she said as she felt the Porsche slowing down. 'You don't have to...'

'If you're scared, I should not drive so fast.' He did not sound annoyed.

'Compromise,' she said, feeling foolish.

'I'm open to one.'

'Music. Something that will work well with the sound of the engine. I'll listen, drift away, and you can look after the road.'

'And your choice?'

'You won't have it.'

'Try me.'

'It's a 1998 CD, so I'm sure you won't have it ... and you probably hate them. I usually play it when I'm on the open road, but because I'm driving I can never sort of drift ... Look. Forget it. You can't possibly have it.'

'Are you quite finished? Just tell me what it is.'

'Air,' she said, almost guiltily.

'Air, 1998. Let's see...' He turned on the system. Air's 'Moon Safari' came sibilantly through the speakers. 'More volume?' He turned it up.

She was staring at him. 'This is weird, Müller. You like music *I* like?'

'I've told you before, I have eclectic musical tastes. Now drift away to your heart's content. We have a killer to stop.'

The Porsche surged perceptibly as they hurtled towards Hannover.

At the same time, the black BMW had already passed Hannover and was on the A2 Autobahn, racing past Bielefeld.

The woman was still driving. Enteling craned his head round to check on Solange. She was fast asleep. They had stopped to allow her to go to the toilet and to get some

384

food. Enteling had got the food, while the woman had stayed with her, even following her into the toilets.

'She's out,' Enteling said as he settled back once more in his seat. 'She's either very scared, or the car's made her drowsy.'

'Whatever it is, I don't give a fuck. The sooner we get rid of her, the better.'

'He won't let you kill her, you know. He's reserved that pleasure for himself. I'd advise you not to get in his way.'

'When I need your advice,' she snapped, 'I'll ask for it. Now shut up and let me drive!'

Carey Bloomfield came awake to the sound of Müller's mobile.

'Where are we?' she enquired sleepily.

'Not far from Dortmund. You succeeded in drifting off so completely, the record played twice over and, as you can tell, Bach's *Italian Concerto* has taken over.'

'Did you drive fast?'

'Very. You've been asleep for two hours.'

'God! I'm sorry...'

'Why? It's perfectly alright.'

The mobile did not stop.

'Are you going to answer that?'

'Not while I'm driving.'

'What if it's Pappenheim?'

'He would have assumed I'm at the wheel and sent a message on the system instead ... which he has already done. I'll be stopping at the next service area to fill the tank. I'll talk to Pappi then.'

'So it's Heurath?'

'I'm certain of it.'

'He'll be getting mad.'

'Let him.'

The phone stopped.

'There you are. He's got the message.'

The mobile was still silent when they stopped a few kilometres later.

'If you need the toilets,' Müller said, 'now's the time. We won't be stopping again till Bonn.'

'I'll take the opportunity.' She grabbed her bag.

'I'll be getting some snacks to take with us. Any preferences?'

'You know me by now. I'll eat anything. I'll leave it to you.'

'Alright.'

Müller filled up, went to the toilet, got the snacks, then parked in a bay where there were no cars close by.

He called Pappenheim.

'She's taken it,' he told Müller. 'She said yes before I had even finished telling her what it was about. Only then did she listen to all I had to say. She was so calm, it was unnerving.'

'I hope we don't live to regret it. Thank her for me.'

'Already done so. She'll have a companion.'

'A companion? Who?'

'Engels.'

'*Engels*? Pappi, what has Engels to do with disarming bombs? She's a trainee helicopter pilot...'

'And a fully qualified observer. I've arranged a chopper as back-up in case you need it.
It will have infrared cameras. Handy if you
have to find someone in the dark. Engels, as
we know, is very good with these things. The
chopper will not arrive on the scene until you
call for it. It will be close enough, but sufficiently far away so as not to spook Heurath
or his minions. It will be waiting on the
ground, at Adenau ... which is mere minutes
away by air.'

Müller considered what Pappenheim had
said. 'You may be right. A back-up is good.
Engels must ensure that the pilot does not get
too eager for action and does *not*, under any
circumstances, turn up unless first requested.
In April 1997, a helicopter crashed near the
castle. I don't want any mistakes tonight.
Give her the authority to sit on whoever it
happens to be, regardless of rank.'

'Your responsibility?'

'My responsibility.'

'I love it when you say that. Consider it
done. One new thing has come in,' Pappenheim went on. 'We have identification for the
woman.'

'That is good news ... but how?'

'We made an electronic photofit from the
basics we got. Hedi Meyer did some of her
magic and constructed a likely resemblance. I
... er, e-mailed it to someone I know who lives
on the, er ... edge of the law. The reply came
back rocket-assisted. Her name is Helga

387

Bramberg. An irredeemable believer in the principles of the old DDR. A cold-blooded killer, she is also a highly skilled sniper. I would not be surprised if it later turns out she did some of the killings we've had so far. Something in on Enteling too. Ex-*Bundeswehr*, special duties training. Did a spell with the American SEALS...'

'Oh marvellous. One headcase with Spetsnaz experience, and another with the SEALS. I really needed that.'

'Life, as the man once said, reeks.'

'I think he put it differently, but I get the message...'

'Talking of smells ... heard from Heurath?'

'He's turning into a phone pest.'

'Aren't you the lucky one. Watch your back, Jens.'

'Always.'

They had barely ended their conversation when the mobile rang.

'Müller.'

'You should not test my patience, Müller,' Heurath said tightly. 'Why did you not answer your phone?'

'I was driving, and I never use the phone when I'm driving. I'm on my way to our meeting. You're lucky. I've just stopped to fill up.'

Heurath digested this. Müller knew he could not fault this reasoning.

'OK,' Heurath said. 'I won't be calling again. I expect you in Altenahr no later than 19.30 hours. Go to the big car park by the river. One minute later and the girl's dead.'

'You must give me some leeway.'

'You've got a fast car,' Heurath said. 'You can make it.' He sounded amused.

Then he ended the call.

'I really needed that too,' Müller said as he made a new call to Pappenheim. 'Pappi,' he went on when Pappenheim had answered. 'Another change.'

'What happened?'

'Heurath. He called just after we finished. He has set a deadline ... 19.30 hours in Altenahr. A minute later, and the girl's dead. We've been making good time, but I want a margin of safety ... just in case we meet traffic jams. So I'm giving Bonn a miss and going directly on to Altenahr.'

'Could he be bluffing?'

'A possibility. He wants me there to see him do it. But I don't want to take the risk with the girl's life. So tell Segelmann to first take Engels to the chopper at Adenau, then come on to Altenahr with Hedi Meyer. He is to approach Altenahr via the B257 then, once there, park opposite a half-timbered building to his left ... he can't miss it. He must *not* get out before I arrive. Hedi Meyer can, if she wants to. They don't know her.'

'You expect them to be watching the traffic with binoculars?'

'It's what I would do. Heurath will have his people positioned at the ruin, to check who arrives. If they see a back-up – *and* Segelmann, whom Heurath of course knows –

389

there's no telling how he'll react. I'm gambling enough as it is. I don't want to tip the balance further. Where I've asked Segelmann to park is out of his line of vision from the ruins ... but you never know.'

'What about tourists who want to visit the old castle?'

'All he has to do is put "closed" on the information board. They'll believe it. If he has trouble with some official, he shows one of his IDs.'

'Then I'd better see to everything.'

'Thanks, Pappi.'

They ended the call just as Carey Bloomfield came into view. She studied Müller's expression.

'Trouble?'

'Your visit to the toilet will have to last a while,' he said. 'We're not stopping in Bonn, but going straight on. Heurath gave me another call. I am to be there by 19.30 hours. One minute later, and he kills Solange.'

'What a sweetheart. Can we make it?'

'I'll do my very best. I am afraid this means more fast driving. More music?' he added as they got back into the car.

She shook her head. 'I'm OK.'

He gave her a quick glance. 'Are you certain? I will be driving very fast.'

'I'm sure.'

'Alright.'

He started the engine and drove slowly until they reached the Autobahn access. Once back in the traffic, Müller pulled away and into the fast lane, to rocket the car towards his destination.

Carey Bloomfield fought not to close her eyes.

'The music is there if you want it,' he said. 'I'm OK. I'm OK.'

The black BMW arrived in Altenahr an hour and a half before Müller was due.

Helga Bramberg parked where it was most convenient: the same area where Heurath had instructed Müller to park.

As they got out, Enteling said to Helga Bramberg, 'We won't be needing that again.' He went to the back and took Solange firmly by an arm. 'Come on, Solange,' he went on in English, with a gentleness that was menacing. 'There's someone who is eager to meet you.'

Helga Bramberg said nothing. She opened the boot and took out two long sports bags.

She looked at Enteling. 'I'm not carrying your stuff.' She dropped one bag to the ground.

'Be careful with that!' Enteling told her sharply.

She ignored him, slammed the boot shut and walked on.

Enteling shook his head slowly and stooped to pick up his bag, keeping Solange firmly in his grip. She had to lower herself slightly as he did so.

'Totally without humour,' he said conversationally as he straightened, 'and the milk of human kindness. In fact, she has no milk at all. I would be very careful of her. She has not forgotten that kick you gave her.' He glanced at Solange. 'You look disgustingly fit and healthy. We've got a climb ahead of us, but I am certain you can handle it easily.'

'Are you taking me to Müller?' Solange said, as she allowed him to guide her forward.

Enteling was startled. '*Müller*? Whatever gave you that idea?'

'My father said he hoped I would never meet Müller.'

Enteling looked her up and down. 'I can understand why.'

Helga Bramberg had stopped to look back. 'Stop leering, Enteling. Always thinking with your balls. We're supposed to be a family group, so let's look like one.'

'As I said,' Enteling continued to Solange. 'Totally without milk.'

From the car park, they walked along the road past several restaurants and cafés that catered for the tourist trade, up to the T-junction. They turned right and came to the access point for the ruined castle. The paved way took them first behind some houses, before turning into a track that led upwards into woodland.

They saw no one as they climbed and nearly twenty minutes later came to the first sections of the castle walls. Heurath was waiting for them, standing within a deep, arched doorway that looked out on to a rough earthen area dotted with tufts of scrub. He came forward as they approached, smiling at

Solange.

'Miss du Bois!' he began effusively in English, as if she were a willing visitor to his stronghold. 'How very nice of you to come. If you prefer that we speak French, that is no problem. I can speak several languages.'

She looked at him with unwavering directness, and did not respond.

'You do not look at all happy to see me,' he went on, remarkably cheerful. 'I am sorry about that...'

'What do you want with me?'

'Ah! You do speak! What do I want with you? That, Miss du Bois, is a very complex question ... but the simple answer is ... I need you.'

'Why?'

'Ah ... the directness of the young. I need to get rid of an itch ... and he's coming soon, to be eradicated. It really is as simple as that when you get down to it.'

'Then you'll let me go?'

Heurath's smile was cold. 'I told you it was a complex question.' He turned to Bramberg and Enteling. 'You two know what to do. Miss du Bois and I will get on with things.'

They nodded and began to leave.

Bramberg looked at Enteling's bag as they moved away from each other to take up their positions.

'I suppose you brought an infrared scope for that toy you've got in there,' she began disparagingly. 'I need just an ordinary scope with my rifle. I've never missed.'

'There's always a first time,' Enteling retorted sourly.

Heurath heard the exchange. 'You two!' he barked. 'Enough!'

Just under an hour later, Segelmann pulled into the parking place that Müller had told him about. He positioned his car in such a way that the building completely hid it from anyone traffic-spotting from the castle.

'Now we wait,' he said to Hedi Meyer.

She nodded hesitantly.

'Don't worry,' he said. 'You'll be alright.'

Over the millennia, the River Ahr had cut deeply into the Eifel landscape, leaving in places a valley with sheer slopes of natural battlements of rock, with clinging vineyard terraces that sometimes appeared to defy the laws of gravity.

Müller had made good time. Despite being baulked by some traffic on the approach to Cologne, he had made up for it with an extremely fast burst along the A555 Autobahn between Cologne and Bonn. From the Bonn bypass, he took the A565 to the Meckenheim junction, continuing until it fed him on to the B257.

He was approaching Altenahr from the opposite direction to the one Segelmann had taken, and was well ahead of schedule. He drove relatively slowly as the road wound its way downwards.

'You can open your eyes now,' he said to

Carey Bloomfield.

'I'm ignoring that. Are we there?'

'Practically. Just before we get to the centre,' he went on, 'I'll stop for you to get out. The climb to the ruins can be fifteen, twenty, or thirty minutes, depending on your fitness. I think you can make it in fifteen.'

'Glad you think so.'

Müller looked amused as he continued, 'The track to the castle goes up in a series of long hairpins then curves towards the first level. In places, steps have been cut into the rock, or into the earth with short logs as braces...'

'I could cut through the hairpins to save time.'

'You could, but you will have to make your way through thick vegetation in places ... and do it quietly. Your climb will also be steeper ... and Heurath's people could be positioned anywhere...'

'Then taking the direct route should give me some element of surprise...'

'If you don't make a noise. I'll stop where there's little chance of your being spotted when you get out,' he went on. 'Do you know of the legend of the "Last Knight of Altenahr"? Heurath made a point of mentioning it.'

'No.'

'It's one of the Rhine legends. The knight was besieged in the castle by the archbishop of Cologne and his army. The knight never gave up. After starvation had killed his people, the knight rode out on his white charger...'

'His *white* charger?'

'In legends, all good knights have white chargers.'

'Of course. I should have known.'

'So,' Müller continued, 'the knight charged out, shouted he would never surrender, and rode off the cliff to his death. As with all legends, there are minimal elements of truth in the background. The castle was built in 1150. It was indeed besieged by the arch-bishop in a power struggle – for nine months – but the chronology of legend and fact do not match. And as far as I know, the last knight never existed. The besieged, incident-ally, were people who had themselves illegally taken the castle. I suppose one could call them armed squatters ... like Heurath, in fact.'

'So Heurath is saying he will never be taken.'

'He also said he would not kill himself.'

'But what if he can't get off his mountain?'

'Then he might be forced to, taking Solange with him.'

'What a surprise.'

'At the highest point of the ruins,' Müller continued, 'a viewing platform has been con-structed. It is open to the elements, but has a perimeter railing and a rudimentary roof. I believe that is where he will take Solange. He wants to survey his kingdom while I make my way through his lines of defence – Enteling

396

and Bramberg, and perhaps even more –
before I get to him ... at the very top.'

'You make it sound as if he's testing you.'

'He is. He wants to see whether I am good
enough to reach him.'

'And take him?'

'He does not believe I will.'

'So he's taking this legend stuff seriously.'

'For a man who has spent his life defending
and believing in the propaganda of the DDR,
this is not so unusual. After all, whole armies
have been known to believe in myths, runic
symbols, and legends. Heurath is just another
example. He probably does think he is the
last knight.'

Müller slowed to a stop near some bushes.
The sloping road continued into the small
valley town, and a T-junction could just be
seen beyond a shallow curve. A little ahead of
the car and on the right-hand side of the road
was a petrol station.

'Convenient place to fill up,' Müller said. 'If
anyone is watching up there in the woods, the
car will grab attention, leaving you clear to
make your way up.'

She quickly dug into her bag and took out
the shoulder harness Pappenheim had given
her. It had spare magazines in pouches, plus
a belt with a pouch for the silencer attached.

Müller glanced at it. 'Pappi has done you
proud. We'll just wait till the road's clear and
there's no one looking to see you carry that
stuff.'

'OK. Müller?'

'Yes.'

'I'd better see you again. I want my nice new clothes. Better not let anything happen to them.'

'You too, Miss Bloomfield,' he said, knowing what she really meant.

'Carey...'

'And watch out for Enteling and Bramberg. They are not pushovers.'

'Neither am I.'

The moment came and she quickly got out of the car, crossed the road to an opening she had seen through the trees, and began to make her way upwards. She did not look back as Müller drove on to the petrol station.

Once within cover, she paused to rapidly put on the harness and the belt. Then she continued making her way straight up, using the trunks of mature saplings to lever herself up the incline.

She reached the first part of the track and paused for long moments, listening for anything that might warn of danger. Satisfied that she was still clear, she crossed the track and began the next climb.

As Müller had predicted, Heurath had taken Solange up precarious steps to the highest point. She was now sitting on the ground, handcuffed to the railing. Heurath was crouched before her, putting the final touches to something about her waist. It was a plain leather belt, seemingly fastened by a large buckle.

It was not a buckle. He clicked something on it, and two pinpoints of red came on alternately.

He stood up to admire his work. 'Perfect,' he said, continuing to speak to her in English. 'You could almost call this the modern version of the chastity belt. Small as this looks, it is quite powerful. I recently blew an eighty-metre boat to smithereens with something little bigger than a man's hand. Anyone tries to tamper with your new fashion accessory and ... *boom* ! Half of you goes flying in one direction, the second in another. So pray no one does try.'

She was staring at him as if at someone from another planet. She was scared, but determined not to give him the satisfaction of seeing it in her face.

But he was not fooled. 'I know you're frightened. You have every right to be. I would be in your place.'

'My father will come for me.'

Heurath looked out over the deep-green Eifel peaks and laughed loudly. 'Your father! Your father is cringing helplessly somewhere.'

'That's not true!'

'I'm afraid it is. I told your father to take Müller off the case ... and like a good boy, he did.'

'*Müller*? Müller is a policeman?'

'And the bane of my life for the moment. *Hauptkommissar* Müller gives policing a bad name. He does not know how to obey orders. In my part of the world he would long ago have been disciplined, and re-educated to properly understand the requirements of the state. But Müller seems unable to appreciate the wisdom of discretion over valour ... like your father, for example...'

'Don't say such things about my father! You don't know him.'

'Oh yes, I do. We had a huge file on him. Years of work. I know him much better than you possibly could.' Heurath stopped abruptly to speak into his radio, deliberately continuing to use English so that Solange could understand. 'Bramberg. Any sign of Müller?'

'Nothing.'

'Enteling...'

'Nothing here so far.'

Heurath turned to Solange. 'Pray, for your sake, that he does come.'

Müller had filled the tank and the Porsche was now parked next to Segelmann's car. He had entered the North-Rhine Westphalia policeman's car, and was sitting in the back.

'Are you certain you can go through with it, Hedi?' he asked.

Both men were looking at her.

'Yes, sir. The things I've brought should do the job.'

'I know Pappi will have given you full details, but you're no use to me or yourself if you feel the slightest doubt.'

'I am fine. Really.'

'Alright. So what have we got?'

'I did some reading on Heurath, until I

could begin to understand how his mind works. *Oberkommissar* Pappenheim was able to get me a file that gives great details about his electronics training. I even saw some papers that he wrote on the subject. One of his favourite methods is remote detonation *coupled* with direct detonation. He builds a timed device that will detonate if tampered with before countdown is complete; but he also has a remote that can trigger the device if he is in danger of being caught, or has been killed...'

'If he's dead, he can't use the remote.'

'He can, sir. The remote is pulse-triggered. He attaches it to a pulse centre on his body ... wrist, neck, above his heart. It is so sensitive, it will pick up the lack of a pulse, then trigger itself...'

Segelmann stared at her aghast. 'Can that really be done?'

'Yes, sir. It's not so hard to do.'

'That puts me in my place.'

'Oh ... I didn't...'

'Relax, I was only joking.'

'Oh. I see.'

Müller was smiling at them. 'Tell me, Hedi,' he said to her. 'Can you do anything about that remote ... if he has one?'

'He'll have one,' she said with certainty. 'I've brought something with me that will search it from a distance of at up to a hundred metres, and disable it.'

'Can you really *do* that?'

'Of course. He's a computer freak. So am I

'... but I'm better.'

'Of course,' Müller said. He glanced at Segelmann. 'Do you get the feeling we're out of our depth here?'

'All the time,' Segelmann replied drily.

'Now,' Müller continued to Hedi Meyer. 'What about the device he'll have attached to Solange?'

'I'll have to see what it is first ... but if he's not there to disturb me, I am certain I can handle that.'

'I must tell you that Stein, who is a highly skilled combat diver with a grounding in electronically controlled anti-shipping mines, nearly lost his life when he tried to disable one of Heurath's little jewels. The ship went up.'

'The *Oberkommissar* told me. But sir ... Heurath knew of the kind of people who would try to disarm his mine. He doesn't know about me and what I can do. I don't always follow the textbooks.'

Müller grinned at her. 'Alright, Hedi. We're in your hands.' He looked at each in turn. 'Now I'd better go and see what Heurath has planned for me. Stefan, you stick to her like glue. Nothing happens to her.'

'Don't worry. I have artillery, if anyone comes too close.'

'And you, Hedi Meyer, I know you can shoot ... but you're not here for that. *No* heroics. I want you alive *and* well, back in Berlin.'

'Yes, sir.'

'Good. Give me five minutes, then make your way to the castle on foot from here. See you two later.'

He climbed out and went back to the Porsche. He started the car and went back the way he had come until he again came to the T-junction. He turned right in the direction of Mayschoss, and drove to the large parking area near the river, just before the rail bridge. He parked the car nose towards the river, and in full view of anyone looking from above.

'I have him!' Bramberg said into her radio. 'He's in the car park.'

'Excellent! Now take up your positions.' Heurath looked down at Solange, smiling coldly, dead eyes boring into her. 'He's come for you ... and he's in good time. I knew he could make it if he tried. Now the fun begins.'

Carey Bloomfield had reached the first level. Her clothes were dirty, for she had also crawled upwards the closer she came to the ruins. She was lying flat on a shallow incline. She peered over the top and saw next to a cluster of five trees a picnic table that seemed to have been made out of material from the surrounding woodland, with a rough-hewn circular bench seat around it. From her position, she could see the remnants of adjacent walls a short distance beyond the table.

She inched forward until she lay in a hollow, hidden by a screen of low bushes. She drew the gun and fitted the silencer. She looked about her. Clear. Over to her right, the sky seemed darker, promising rain.

'Not before we're done here,' she muttered in prayer.

She settled down in her hiding place to wait.

Müller was about to get out of the car, when the mobile rang.

'Müller.'

'There you are!' came Heurath's unnaturally cheerful voice.

'You sound happy.'

'Oh I am. You're here, and Solange is here. What more could I ask for? Come on up. And do bring your gun. Not much fun without it.'

'On my way.'

Heurath again turned to Solange. 'What I like about that man ... even though I hate him, is the way he is not deflected from his purpose. We could have used someone like him...'

'But you said he was a bad policeman...'

'I can contradict myself if I want to. Now shut up! I have some thinking to do.'

Segelmann and Hedi Meyer saw Müller make his way round the corner to the access point, then disappear up the path behind the houses.

Segelmann motioned to her to pause.

Hedi Meyer was dressed all in black, with a black backpack slung behind. Instead of the customary long dress, she wore black jeans and a long-sleeved T-shirt, and paratroop-style black boots. She had a gun in the backpack.

Segelmann carried his own pump-action gun in a bag that looked very similar to the ones Bramberg and Enteling had carried. He also had a pistol in a shoulder holster beneath his summer-weight jacket.

'OK,' he now said to her. 'Let's go on.'

Müller was a short distance from where Carey Bloomfield lay, when he heard a noise behind him. He kept walking.

'Stop!' a voice commanded. *Enteling.*

He stopped.

Enteling approached, but not too close. 'Turn round, Müller.'

Müller turned, and glanced at the automatic rifle Enteling was pointing at him. 'Haven't I seen you somewhere before?' he asked quietly.

'Very funny. You must be stupid, coming up here. Drop the gun I know you're carrying.'

'Sorry. Heurath said I should bring it. No fun otherwise, he said.'

'Do you think *I'm* stupid? Why would he say that? He intends to kill you.'

'Why don't you argue the point with him? Where's Bramberg hiding?'

The question took Enteling by complete surprise. He had not expected that Müller would know of Bramberg, and could not prevent himself from fleetingly glancing in her direction.

Müller hoped that Carey Bloomfield was close enough to have spotted it.

Carey Bloomfield had heard the voices, and had manoeuvred herself into position.

'Hi,' she said.

This second and totally unexpected development so disrupted Enteling, he could not help freezing for a fraction of a second. Even so, he was fast ... but not fast enough.

He whirled to face the new threat, rifle tracking. But Carey Bloomfield had already zeroed on her target.

She fired twice. The Beretta seemed to gasp with a rising wheeze that blended with Enteling's. His eyes widened in horror and surprise that this was happening to him. His mouth moved frantically, but no sound came out. Then he began to topple. Müller grabbed the rifle as the body fell.

'Into the bushes over there,' he said quickly to her.

Rapidly, they dragged Enteling's still-quivering body into cover.

'Good work, Miss Bloomfield. Did you spot where Enteling glanced?'

She nodded. 'My next port of call?'

'If you don't mind. I must go on, before Heurath becomes suspicious and calls one of them to check. You didn't tell me to use Carey,' he added.

'At least that got you to say my name.'

She hurried away before he could respond.

He shook his head slowly as he watched her go. 'Be careful, Carey,' he said softly as he removed the magazine from the rifle.

He shoved the weapon deep into rotting vegetation. He then quickly emptied the magazine, buried the rounds at a spot he would remember, then scooped dirt into the magazine and buried that at another location. It did not take him long, and he was soon continuing his journey.

He made his way towards the steps that would take him into another area where once was perhaps a baronial hall. He wondered whether Bramberg had him in her sights. Though the brief conversation had not been loud, had their voices still carried sufficiently for her to hear? In a place like this, it probably had. She was more disciplined than the duckling had proved. He didn't think she would shoot. And what about Heurath?

He walked on.

Segelmann and Hedi Meyer were not far behind. They had heard voices, but not loud enough to be distinguishable.

They moved on cautiously.

Müller would have been astonished to see Bramberg. She was not in her expected position. *She was in fact going down the mountain* .

She had indeed heard Enteling and, when she had heard nothing further, reasoned accurately that Enteling would not be going back alive. That meant Müller had somehow

407

got more people in place than Heurath had thought.

She had no idea how many people she would be facing. Again, she had reasoned that Heurath had perhaps this time bitten off more than he could chew. Her brief was not total loyalty to Heurath. He was not her overall commander.

So, rifle packed away, Bramberg hurried back down to the BMW.

Müller had got to the last level before the very top itself. As he approached, he looked up and saw Heurath looking down at him.

'At last!' Heurath called. He had a gun in his hand, pointing down.

'*Oberkommissar* Segelmann? Or is it Renner? Or perhaps Lörrandt?'

Heurath grinned down at him. 'What can I say?'

'And now what?' Müller asked.

'First, you drop your gun.'

'But I thought you were the last knight...'

'Jens, Jens, *Jens*. I told you I did not intend to commit suicide like that poor, noble fool. One of the reasons I've survived in this business is that I *never* gave *anyone* a chance. Now drop the Beretta! Oh yes. I know you carry a Beretta. Now there's a good boy.'

Müller put a chagrined expression on his face, took out the gun and dropped it to the ground.

'Excellent. Now come up to my eyrie and see who's been waiting anxiously for you.'

Carey Bloomfield was baffled to find that Bramberg was nowhere to be seen. However, she did spot the impression in the low grass, where someone had been lying. The position allowed a clear field of fire.

So where had Bramberg disappeared to?

Though she used up valuable minutes looking, there was no sign of Bramberg.

'She's bugged out,' she said to herself in amazement. 'I'll be damned. That must be it. She's bugged out on Heurath.'

Segelmann and Hedi Meyer were now in cover close enough to see Müller climbing the steps towards Heurath.

While Segelmann kept watch, she removed her backpack and began to unpack the gadgets she had brought. She took one that looked as if it had been put together by a child and pointed it in Heurath's direction.

Segelmann stared at it. '*That* thing will work?' he whispered, clearly not believing it would. 'It looks like a woman's shaver. There are not even lights on it. Electronic things have lights.'

'The light will come on when I've killed that thing he's carrying somewhere on his body ... as long as the *Hauptkommissar* doesn't get in the way. Now *shhh*!' she hissed. 'Let me work!'

Müller looked down at Solange. 'We'll get you out.'

409

'I don't believe it,' Heurath said in wonder. 'Even now, you hang on to your belief that you can win.' He turned to Solange. 'Do you see what I've been saying? He doesn't seem to know when he has lost.'

She looked fearfully at Heurath, then hopefully at Müller.

'Forget it, Solange,' Heurath said. 'He was never going to win. I wanted him here ... and he is here. I'm sorry you have to be sacrificed, but that's—'

'*La guerre*?' Müller suggested slyly.

For the briefest of moments, Heurath looked as if he were going to lose it. Then he smiled thinly. 'Oh no. You are in no position to annoy me, and I won't bite.'

'If you say so. Do you still see any of your Spetsnaz comrades?'

Heurath's eyes narrowed dangerously. 'How do you know that?'

'I know quite a lot about you, Heurath.'

Heurath stared at him. 'My name! You know my name!'

'I know a lot more. I know you've got Helga Bramberg out there somewhere ... and Enteling...'

There was clear shock in Heurath's eyes. He'd expected that Müller would know something about the Romeo Six mission ... though only what had been fed to him. But Müller was now entering territory he was not supposed to.

'I've seen a picture of you, for example,' Müller went on. 'Shooting that man in the

410

head...'

'*Where* ... Where did you get that?'

'People are betraying you more than you realize, Heurath. Call Enteling. See if he's still around.'

Heurath glared at him, not certain whether to believe it. Then he barked into the radio, 'Enteling! *Enteling*! *Report*!'

Silence greeted him.

'Bramberg!' he tried next. 'Bramberg!'

Bramberg was just getting into the BMW. She did not respond.

'Fuck you!' she snarled as she started the engine.

Heurath stared at Müller. 'How do you know these things? You have countered every move I have made. You are destroying my mission...'

'Not I ... *you*! You told me yourself that your people found you too extreme...'

'*Weaklings*!'

'Now, your own followers are deserting you...'

'I'll get them all! They will pay for their betrayal, just as you will for interfering!'

Segelmann was watching Heurath and Müller.

'If that thing is going to work,' he said sharply to Hedi Meyer, 'it had better be now. He's working himself up to shoot Müller!'

Hedi Meyer tensed then gave a huge sigh of

411

relief as the light came on. 'It's dead!'

'That's all I want to know!'

Segelmann ran from cover until he was close enough not to miss. '*Heurath*!' he shouted.

Heurath's eyes widened and he turned swiftly to see who had called his name.

Segelmann did not hesitate. Heurath was squarely in his sights. The pump-action shotgun roared three times. The shots slammed Heurath against the railing. Solange screamed as blood and shredded flesh spattered her.

Then Segelmann was hurrying up the precarious steps to the platform as fast as he could. When he got there, Müller was stooped low, listening to something that the dying Heurath was trying to say.

'You ... you still ... haven't won. My bomb will go off. I have a remote...'

'It's dead.'

'Not ... not possible. As soon as my pulse...'

'We knew about that too ... and knew how to kill it.'

Heurath's failing eyes were becoming opaque, but the sense of betrayal was strong in them. 'Not ... not ... fair...'

'I don't give chances either,' Müller said.

'The girl ... will ... still die...'

'Not if I can help it.'

'And ... you still ... have ... to ... meet ... your ... destiny...'

Just then, Carey Bloomfield arrived, followed by Hedi Meyer, who turned her head away from the bloodied mess.

412

Carey Bloomfield looked down at Heurath. 'Bramberg's gone, Heurath ... and Enteling's dead.'

There was still enough in him left to recognize her.

'Miss ... Harris...' he whispered. *'Et tu...'* The whisper faded.

'The last knight's gone,' Müller said, then he moved to Solange. 'We'll get you out of this, Solange.' From an inside jacket pocket, he took out a handkerchief and began to wipe Heurath's blood away from her face.

Her eyes were fixed upon him.

Hedi Meyer came up and, trying not to look at Heurath, squatted on her heels and began to take another of her gadgets out of the backpack.

Segelmann peered at it. 'This one looks like a hair clipper.'

'Alright!' Hedi Meyer began in a firm voice. 'Everyone out.'

'Are you sure...' Müller began.

'Out, sir. All of you. If I screw up, then only two people go. With all of you here looking over my shoulder I'll just get nervous. So please...'

Müller looked at the others. 'You heard the lady...'

As they went back down, Solange's eyes followed Müller.

Hedi Meyer looked at her. 'OK, Solange,' she said in careful English. 'We are going to get this off you. Do not doubt it. I can do it. OK?'

'OK,' Solange confirmed uncertainly, face tense.

'Now just relax. Whatever happens, do not lose your nerve. We are in the same boat. You will have company if I make a mistake.' She smiled wanly, and tried not to look at Heurath's body. 'Just remain still. We have to assume he has put many little traps in there. I have to beat each one. He had a remote detonator, and I killed that. I can kill this one. Ready?'

Eyes wide with fear, Solange gave a barely perceptible nod.

Hedi Meyer held the instrument Segelmann had disparagingly called a hair clipper within a few centimetres of the electronic buckle. She switched it on. Immediately, pinpricks of light began racing beneath its misted surface.

'Ooops,' she said. 'Wrong sequence. Do not worry. I will try another.'

She adjusted a small circular wheel with a serated edge by one click, and tried again. The lights did not come on.

'OK,' she breathed. 'I think we were lucky. Now all we must do is wait for this to do the job.'

'My nose!' Solange squeaked suddenly.

'What?'

'Something's walking into my nose!' She was desperately trying to remain still.

Hedi Meyer peered at the nose. 'Nothing there. The situation's making you imagine it. Don't move, Solange! We don't want those

414

lights to start again.'

'Oh God!' Solange said in faint, high whisper. 'It really is there! I want to sneeze!'

'Try not to!' Hedi Meyer hissed. 'Just hang on. My gadget is doing its work. There are no lights. We're OK ... We're OK...' She stopped suddenly, listening. 'What the hell's that?'

Faintly, a low thrumming sounded, growing louder. She recognized the noise. Helicopter. A sudden glow made her look down. The lights on the belt had started once more.

'Shit!' she said softly. 'The helicopter! The damned helicopter! The belt is reacting to its sound! What did that madman put in there? Every time I catch it, it shifts.'

'What ... What does that mean?' Solange asked.

'It means,' Hedi Meyer answered calmly, 'he's laid many traps. Each one I beat leads to another. But he can't beat me ... and the more I eliminate, the closer we get to killing his little monster. He was very clever, but we're going to make it. OK?'

'OK.'

On the ground beneath the platform, they were all looking up.

'She's got guts,' Segelmann said. 'In the car she was nervous ... but to do what she's doing...'

'I think she's switched off her fears,' Müller said. 'Right at this moment it's a challenge to beat Heurath. She's concentrating on that.' He paused, listening. 'What's that helicopter

415

doing? It's not supposed to be here yet.'

The others glanced vaguely in the direction of the sound, but said nothing.

Fifteen long minutes went by as the day got increasingly darker.

'Let's look at it this way,' Carey Bloomfield said. 'The platform is still there, so that's good news.'

Müller and Segelmann remained silent.

The waiting continued. Another fifteen minutes went by.

'I'm going to sneeze!' Solange cried softly with desperate need. 'I thought it had gone, but it's still there ... moving...'

'Just ... don't ... sneeze ... Let me adjust this...'

With rapid but very steady fingers, Hedi Meyer readjusted the knurled wheel.

Then Solange sneezed. Her entire body shook.

Hedi Meyer shut her eyes tightly and waited for the inevitable. 'What a way to go,' she whispered to herself.

She felt Solange's ripped flesh and sprayed blood. Solange hitting her...

But she could still hear the sound of the helicopter, faintly again now. Then she opened her eyes.

'Are we still alive?' she heard Solange ask diffidently.

Hedi Meyer stared at the belt. The lights were out.

'Oh my God!' she uttered softly. 'We're

416

alive,' she added to Solange, continuing to stare at the belt. 'And the little monster is dead.'

'Did I just hear a sneeze?' Carey Bloomfield asked disbelievingly.

'I heard it too,' Müller replied. 'So you're not dreaming. If Pappenheim were here,' he continued, 'he would have smoked two packets by now.'

'As I don't smoke,' Carey Bloomfield said, 'I'd be chewing them.'

Then Hedi Meyer was looking down at them. 'Could someone please come up to get the handcuff keys from the body? I ... don't want to touch it.'

Müller called Pappenheim. 'Start the ball rolling, Pappi.'

'I thought I heard the helicopter,' Hedi Meyer called down as Segelmann went up to the platform.

'You did,' Müller replied. 'The pilot's circling over to the west. He was earlier than he should have been. I'll chew him out.'

'Don't! Er ... sir. The sound gave me an idea.'

The helicopter took Solange back to the airport. Accompanied by Engels, she was flown back to Berlin.

Kaltendorf, face composed and once more looking like a senior policeman, was waiting in the arrivals lounge. If Engels thought it strange that he had come in person to meet a kidnap victim, she gave no indication.

'Well done, Engels,' Kaltendorf greeted her, completely ignoring the fact that he had originally opposed Müller's recommendation to add her to the unit..

'I only sat in the helicopter, Herr *Direktor* . *Hauptkommissar* Müller—'

'Yes, yes ... but you were part of the team.' Kaltendorf glanced in the direction of a man waiting a short distance away. 'That's my driver. He'll take you to the car. I want a few words with Miss du Bois...'

'Yes, sir.'

Kaltendorf waited until Engels and the driver had gone out of sight. Then he opened his arms to Solange.

'Thank God ... Thank God!' he said, voice shaking as he hugged her tightly.

'Papa...' she said, very softly. '*Hauptkommissar* Müller was brilliant,' she added, voice brimming with admiration. 'And Hedi Meyer too...'

But Kaltendorf heard only one name.

'Müller...' he said in tones that could have meant anything.

Berlin, two days later. 08.00 hours.
Müller entered his office to find Pappenheim waiting.

'Nice suit,' Pappenheim greeted. 'So you're really going to drive down to France.'

'What better way to spend a Friday? I'm really going to drive down to France. I prom- ised a lady I'd take her to the opera.'

'Miss Carey Bloomfield.'

'To tell you the truth, I'm not sure whether she'll turn up. After we returned from Altenahr she went off somewhere, presumably to report to her people. I haven't heard since.'

'She'll be there,' Pappenheim said. 'And, as you're going to France, someone wants a lift.'

'You mean Solange. After what had happened, Kaltendorf doesn't want her to travel alone.'

'That's his job ... not yours. What was that he said? Important conference. What he means is new contacts to make, since many of those he knew are falling into the net. He's back to his old self.'

'So how's the round-up going?'

'The lawyers are gathering in regiments.'

Müller took out the envelope that Grogan had sent. 'Then you should see this. Grogan gave it to Miss Bloomfield to pass on to me.'

Pappenheim took it gingerly. 'A blue seal?'

'It could mean anything.'

Müller watched as Pappenheim silently read Grogan's note. No emotion showed on the *Oberkommissar*'s face.

'Sweet people,' Pappenheim finally muttered in contempt as he returned the note to the envelope.

'You keep it,' Müller said. 'Put it into our Fort Knox with the other material. How many,' he went on, 'do you think will escape what we laughably call justice?'

'Most.'

'That's what I thought you'd say,' Müller commented drily. 'That's why I need this break. I can't see any more of these brazen people going on television to bleat that their rights are being violated, while they plotted to take ours away. You should grab a break too, Pappi. Take Berger somewhere. Have fun.'

'I'll think about it.' Pappenheim was looking intensely at Müller. 'We did damned good work.'

'We did damned, damned good work ... but it continues. Those bastards out there don't realize how much we do know, and that we've also got Grogan's treasure trove.'

'But we still don't know who Romeo Six was.'

'I intend to keep trying to find out,' Müller promised. 'I won't leave this one alone. Grogan used that blue seal deliberately. It belongs to some organization ... or to someone. He wanted me to know that.'

'Romeo Six?'

'Perhaps.'

Pappenheim considered the possibility, then said, 'Has the Great White thanked you yet?'

'What do you think?'

'He won't,' Pappenheim said with a certainty born of experience. 'Or we'd have to start liking him. Right then. I'm off for a smoke, and you're off to France.'

'Back in a week.'

Pappenheim nodded and began moving

towards the door.

'And think over what I said about Berger,' Müller added.

'I will.'

The Rhine Schlosshotel. 15.00 hours.
Udo Hellmann was standing on the terrace, looking down upon the river that had been his life for so many years.

'Captain Hellmann! Udo!'

Hellmann turned to see Grogan approaching.

'Mr Grogan...' he greeted.

'Jack,' Grogan corrected. 'No more formalities ... remember?'

Hellmann smiled tiredly. 'Of course, Jack.'

Grogan glanced around. 'The lovely Isabella not with you?'

'In our room. We're getting ready to leave. The police don't think it necessary that we should remain here. They can reach us at any time.'

'For sure.'

A silence fell between them as they both turned to look down on the river.

'You've got to get back on the water,' Grogan said after a while. 'You'll miss it otherwise.'

'I'm missing it already.'

'There you go.'

Another silence fell.

'You're going to have to tell her, Udo,' Grogan said, still looking at the river. 'You know that, don't you?'

421

'What … What do you mean?' Hellmann had turned to stare at Grogan warily, face pale, an animal suddenly caged.

Grogan still did not look round. 'You know what I mean, Udo. You've got to tell her … if she means anything to you. She's a good woman. At first, she will want to tear your guts out. She'll cry, and she'll curse you. She might even hate you for a while … but you'll have to take it and let her know how important she is to you. If you've got the balls, you'll make it. In time, she'll understand what it cost you to tell her. If you don't have the balls … you can always keep running…'

Grogan moved from the railing and began to leave.

Hellmann was still staring at him, almost fearfully. 'Who … Who are you?'

'A friend, Udo. That's who I am.'

Grogan kept walking.

Hellmann entered the hotel room and found his wife sitting on the edge of the bed.

She smiled up at him. 'I'm ready. We've got a boat to rebuild.'

He sat down next to her, and took both her hands in his.

'We have plenty to rebuild,' he began. 'Isa … I've got something to tell you…'

France, the N202, not far from St André-les-Alpes. 23.00 hours.
Müller was savouring driving the Porsche along the empty back road, lights turning the night almost into day. Solange had reclined

422

the seat and was fast asleep.

He smiled to himself. She hadn't talked much during the journey. But that was only to be expected after her ordeal.

He glanced in the mirrors. A single bright light was fast approaching. He felt a slight annoyance, wanting the solitude of the road to himself.

'Fix your second light,' he muttered. 'I'll let you pass, then you'll be gone.'

He slowed down. The light caught up rapidly. As he entered a sweeping left-hand bend that skirted a deep gorge, he realized the light was not a car with one light, but a motorcycle.

The motorcycle roared forward, leaning into the bend, coming abreast and matching speeds. What was the idiot doing? Müller glanced to his left and, in the backglow of the lights, saw the pointing hand.

Gun!

He braked hard. The Porsche halted in its tracks.

The motorcyclist shot forward, lost balance, and tried to correct one-handedly, hanging on to the gun. The motorcycle veered to the right. It hit a low barrier and flew over it. Motorcycle and rider plunged into the gorge.

Müller thought he heard a rising scream that sounded female. He could not know that Helga Bramberg's shattered body was now lying at the bottom of the gorge.

He glanced at Solange as he drove on. She was still fast asleep.

The Villa Ephrussi, St Jean Cap Ferrat. Tuesday. 18.45 hours.

Müller stood on the terrace and looked out on the lights of Villefranche.

'Saved civilization again,' Carey Bloomfield said from behind him.

He whirled. 'Well ... you made it.'

'I made it. Thought I wouldn't get here, Müller?'

He looked at her appreciatively. She was wearing the red dress she had bought at Sinead Bromme's.

'You look ... enchanting.'

'Thank you, Müller.'

She stood close to him as they looked out over the bay.

'What I said about civilization was a joke, Müller. You can't save something that isn't there yet. I watched a TV documentary once. It was about the attacks on foreigners in the East in 1992, in places like Dessau, Hoyerswerda and the rest. A flaming building was like a bonfire in the night, and people were moving around looking like they were having a witch-burning festival. Some had faces shining with excitement ... others were just hanging around hoping for some blood. A line of riot police in robocop gear barred the street. I watched those faces.' She gave a shudder of disgust. 'What I liked about that documentary,' she went on, 'was that there was no preaching voice-over. It just let the people condemn themselves by the things

424

they said, by their behaviour, and by those terrible expressions on their faces. It was like something out of the dark ages.'

'Then, for a short moment in time,' Müller said, 'let us forget the dirty things and the dirty people we sometimes have to deal with. Let us go back into that wonderful building and be enchanted by *Les Azuriales*. Let us enjoy another fire ... the fire of *Carmen*.'

'Nicely put. Hey,' she exclaimed suddenly. 'Look who's here!'

Solange, looking stunning in a long white dress of patterned linen, was approaching, smiling hugely.

'I didn't think she'd be coming,' Carey Bloomfield said, voice low and tight. 'I'm not going to compete with a kid, Müller!'

'She wants to be curator of this place one day,' Müller said.

'Never too early to check out the territory, I guess,' she remarked ambiguously. 'Hi, Solange,' she went on brightly. 'How are you feeling?'

'I am very well, thank you.' Solange was looking at Müller with naked hero-worship in her eyes.

'Oh good!' Carey Bloomfield said. 'Anyone seen a gooseberry?'

Müller glanced at her. There was an expression of innocence upon her face.

'Well,' Müller said mildly, looking from one to the other. 'Shall we go in?'

Pappenheim was heading for his office. As he passed Müller's, he spotted a white corner peeping from beneath the door. He stopped to pull it all the way out. It was a long, slim envelope. There was no stamp and no return address. On the front was written a single word, in large capitals.

MÜLLER

Frowning, Pappenheim turned it over indecisively. He felt it carefully, checking for thin wires. He tipped it gently. Nothing shifted.

'No powder,' he said.

He held it up to the light. Large writing showed faintly.

Pappenheim took it with him to his own office, sat down at his desk and opened it. Nothing happened.

'Well,' he said to himself drily. 'It wasn't a bomb ... and you should have known better, Pappenheim. You would have yelled at a first-day recruit for doing just that.'

He took out the single sheet of paper, spread it out and stared at it, mouth agape.

You may think you have won, Müller, he read silently. *But you haven't. Your father was Romeo Six.*

Pappenheim smoked two cigarettes while he continued to stare at the note. Then he took both envelope and note, and tore at them angrily, until only tiny pieces were left.

426

'What you don't know,' he said softly, as he piled the pieces into an ashtray, 'can't hurt you.'

Then he set fire to them.